THE
BONE FLOWER
QUEEN

BOOK TWO OF THE BONE FLOWER TRILOGY

THE
BONE FLOWER

QUEEN

BOOK TWO OF THE BONE FLOWER TRILOGY

TL MORGANFIELD

FSB

THE BONE FLOWER QUEEN
BOOK TWO OF THE BONE FLOWER TRILOGY

Published by Feathered Serpent Books
Thornton, Colorado USA

Printed in the U.S.A.

ISBN 978-0-9909207-1-7

For Mom,
For always supporting my dreams.

The Basin of Mexico
10th Century CE

Tollan

Tultepec

Teotihuacan

Acolman

Lake
Meztliapan

Chapultepec

Culhuacan

Chimalhuacan

Xochimilco

Xico

Chalco

Xochicalco

PART ONE
THE YEAR SEVEN RABBIT

CHAPTER ONE

Sickness and fear knotted my stomach as I fumbled with the wash basin in my bath yard, trying to scrub away the chills with some water to my face. I didn't need to look into the obsidian mirror hanging in front of me to know I looked as if I hadn't slept at all last night; I hadn't slept well since moving into my new quarters a month ago—so I could be close to Little Reed while he recovered from his battle wounds—but now I questioned the wisdom of taking over my dead husband's private quarters. When I did sleep, I was plagued with dreams of death, and in my waking time, I felt as if I was being watched.

I flinched when someone rang the bells on my door curtain. "Who is it?" I yelled, so they could hear me from out in the yard.

"It's me, My Lady," my friend Malinalli's voice answered. I called her inside and she soon appeared at the doorway to my bath yard. She cocked her head when she saw me. "Did you just get up?"

"Am I late again?" I splashed some more water on my face then lathered up with some copal soap.

"The king asked me to fetch you." She handed me a scrap of linen to dry my face with once I rinsed. "Are you all right, Quetzalpetlatl?"

I waved her off. "It was a lot of work, handling Topiltzin's business while he was recovering, plus keeping up with my duties as high priestess—"

"I could have taken over your priestly duties while you cared for the king," Malinalli said. "I'll be doing that while you're gone anyway."

I chuckled. "And you will do a fantastic job, I know. But I'm the god's chosen high priestess—"

"That doesn't mean you can't ask for help when you need it." She picked up my brush and started working the tangles out of my long brown hair.

"You aren't my servant anymore, Malinalli," I protested. She might have been forced to act as my handmaiden while we'd been captives of my uncle, but that ordeal was thankfully over. And though I was Culhuacan's queen now, she was Quetzalcoatl's fire priestess, and having her play the part of my servant was demeaning.

But when I reached for the brush, she held it out of my reach. "No, I'm not, but that doesn't matter. My sisters and I used to brush each other's hair, and I've missed doing it."

I'd had many sisters but we'd never brushed each other's hair; that was servants' work, and while I'd brushed Little Reed's hair when he was young, I'd found it a tedious task. Even in school I'd had no female friends to share such bonding with, for most girls avoided me due to my status as the high priestess's ward.

But who was I to deny my best friend a little joy? So I let her continue.

"Besides, we'll get this done much quicker if you let me do it," she said, a smile in her voice. "All those noblewomen hairstyles are impossibly complicated, and a queen must have flair."

"Not this queen," I said with a laugh. "A simple braid right down the back will suffice."

Chuckling, Malinalli shook her head and started separating my hair for braiding. When I stifled a yawn, she said, "Maybe a sleep tonic would help keep you from waking in the middle of the night?"

Maybe, but will it stop the dreams? As a young girl, I'd suffered recurring nightmares of traveling the dangerous road into the underworld to face Lord Death, but now they happened two or three times a week; Lord Death always towering over me, the hollow eye sockets of his skull-face glowing like swamp gas, his grin pulling his thin, transparent skin painfully tight. "Welcome home, my spiny little princess," he hissed as a spider scurried out of the corner of his mouth to take refuge behind his necklace of extruded eyeballs. After dying and coming back to life, dreams of Lord Death seemed fitting.

But there were also the nightmares about Black Otter, my former husband; every night he was shot with arrows and fell into the lake, but instead of dying, he rose from the icy black depths, changed into a horrendous monster with glistening fangs and five hands—where this fifth one came from, I never could see—and he would latch onto me with his claws and drag me into the water with him, all the while shrieking, "Mine! Mine! Mine!"

"I should just move back into my old quarters," I said. "Then maybe I won't be constantly dreaming of Black Otter."

"Maybe you miss being married," Malinalli suggested.

My marriage to Black Otter had been one problem after another: having to care for and oversee his concubines, and making certain he shared his time and attention with everyone equally, something I failed miserably at. But contending with the jealousy and rivalry growing under my own roof had been the worst, and I didn't know how my mother survived so many years in such circumstances; I didn't understand how anybody could really expect us women to. Did I miss being married? "Not at all. I'm glad it's over and I can return to doing the god's important work."

She cast me a puzzled look in the mirror. "You don't miss Black Otter at all?"

That question wasn't so easily answered. Sometimes I woke in the middle of the night missing him when I found no one lying next to me, but how much of that was about Black Otter being dead rather than the cold truth that that side of my bed would always remain empty thanks to that sacrifice I made to save my brother's life? "Sometimes I do," I finally said, a hitch in my voice. "There was a time when we were good friends."

Malinalli finished my braids and pinned them up against the back of my head, then she reached out to give my hand a squeeze. "Let me cut some flowers to put in your hair and we can get on to breakfast."

"Let me pick. I want to see how the garden looks now that the servants have cleaned it up."

Every room in Culhuacan's palace had a private garden off the back, and no one had tended to Black Otter's garden after he died, nor had I bothered to ask for gardeners when I moved in. But yesterday I'd finally decided something needed to be done about the forest of gangly bushes and long grasses just off my bath yard patio.

The palace gardeners had done a wonderful job rejuvenating the foliage and flowers. Yellow marigolds, purple and white jaguar flowers, and bright orange sunflowers bloomed in the beds, shaded by a flowering dogwood. Bees buzzed among the honeysuckle bushes while blue-throated hummingbirds darted from flower to flower. There weren't any bone flowers—my favorite—and I made a mental note to ask that someone plant them for next year. I picked out a couple of newly-blossomed jaguar flowers and Malinalli cut their stems with her sacrificial blade.

Noticing a glimmer from the back corner of the garden, I leaned slightly forward for a better look as Malinalli carefully tucked the flower stems into the back of my hair. A small stone idol the size of my head sat against the back wall, and the grass was matted down in front of it, as if there had been a prayer mat there. Before the bushes had been trimmed, there would have been no clear view of it from my patio. "What is that?" I asked.

Once Malinalli inserted the last flower stalk, she followed me to the statue for a closer look. It was a small stone jaguar, sitting on its haunches with its mouth open in a grotesque grin. The glimmer that had caught my eye came from the sun reflecting off an obsidian mirror it clutched in its claws. A cold loathing welled up in my stomach.

"I think it's the Smoking Mirror," Malinalli replied. "It must have been Black Otter's."

Black Otter was going to be the Smoking Mirror's next high priest after his father—my uncle, my father's murderer, the usurper of my throne—died. He told me he had no desire for the position, but it was no secret that he gave his devotion to this demon god who sat at the core of all my life's pain; this god who despised my beloved Quetzalcoatl and tried to kill my brother, Little Reed. I'd pushed Little Reed to ban Smoking Mirror's worship here in Culhuacan, but he resisted; "We won't do the things our uncle did to Quetzalcoatl." This was something we'd never agree on.

"I'll take it out of here for you," Malinalli offered; but when she moved towards it, I caught her arm.

"Wait for me out in the hallway," I said, not taking my eyes off of the statue. "I'll be out in a moment."

After a hesitation, Malinalli left me alone.

I stared at my own reflection—so dark and grim—in the obsidian mirror as I knelt in front of the statue. The jaguar grinned, laughing at me, just as Smoking Mirror had when we faced off on the battlefield: *faith proves itself slow and dumb when pitted against fear!* it seemed to say. Smoking Mirror and my uncle had smashed my dreams, starting with my father's murder and ending with my having to sacrifice the future I so desperately wanted with Little Reed in order to save him.

Overcome with rage, I took hold of the idol with both hands and yanked on it. It was heavier than I expected, so it didn't move at first, but with a little more might, I wrenched it from its spot. Without a word, I heaved it at the wall, shattering the mirror all over the ground. The statue itself remained intact, and I had to throw it against the wall a few more times before it finally broke in half.

Breathing heavily, my stomach roiling with bile, I squeezed my eyes against the stinging threat of tears. "Someday Quetzalcoatl will make you pay for what you've done, you vile excuse for a god," I muttered. "And I hope I'm there to see it."

¤

The war council was gathered in the great hall, lounging on feathered mats in a circle around the breakfast platters, waiting for me. The smell of fried eggs, chilis, and hot tlaxcallis set my mouth watering. When both my father and then my uncle had been kings, no one took the morning meal in the great hall; Little Reed and I adopted this practice once we took the throne, for meals were times of bonding with friends and family, and we endeavored to treat our council members as if they were such.

Two months into our reign, we'd only just started exerting our personal touch over the royal palace. In my father's day, feathered banners showing the city crest decorated the walls of the great hall; in my uncle's day, it was obsidian mirrors, in honor of the Smoking Mirror, but they were now gone, and artists worked daily on murals of Quetzalcoatl the Feathered Serpent on every wall in the public parts of the palace. The one in the great hall was only partially finished, but it resembled the friezes from Quetzalcoatl's temple in Xochicalco, with paintings of noblemen and calendar dates, and giant, slithering feathered serpents; "A reminder of the home we lost," Little Reed told me, and I couldn't wait to see it finished.

When Citlallotoc saw me and Malinalli, he nudged Little Reed on the shoulder. My earlier melancholy fled with a flush of desire when Little

Reed rose to greet me, the smile I dearly loved on his face. Thanks to his divine parentage, he looked closer to forty summers old rather than twenty; white streaked his dark hair and the corners of his eyes crinkled when he smiled, but he'd regained a healthy glow now that he had fully recovered from his battle wounds.

The rest of the council rose as well but I hardly noticed anything but Little Reed as he took my hand in his. "Is everything all right?"

I breathed deep to swallow back the desire; I'd often let it guide me with Black Otter, but I couldn't do the same with Little Reed, no matter how much it howled and protested—and no matter how much my heart wanted him. *You made that sacrifice to save him and you must keep the path no matter what your heart and body feels,* I reminded myself for the thousandth time; I'd turned it into a mantra to repeat in my head every time I started losing control. The desire growled but soon retreated, letting me breathe again. "I'm fine. Just overslept."

He chuckled, ever oblivious to my internal struggles. Someday I'd tell him the truth of what I'd given up to save him, but not today. "I know you keep saying you don't want a handmaiden, but it wouldn't hurt to have someone come by each morning to make certain you rise in timely fashion. You've been working so hard, and there's no shame in asking for help."

"I know," I assured him. "But it's really not necessary. Now that you're well again, I won't have nearly as many duties keeping me up late."

In fact, one of those "late-night duties" was standing with the other men, looking annoyingly smug. For days, Flame Tongue, the king of our new ally, Xico, had been aggressively seeking to join his house with my brother's through a marriage to his youngest daughter Anacoana. A man's mother customarily listened to such requests from the father or suitors, but with our mother long dead that duty fell to me, as Little Reed's closest female relative.

And the temerity of Flame Tongue's request had struck me speechless. Anacoana was a fine young woman—bright and a highly-talented weaver—but she'd been one of my former husband's concubines. Granted, Black Otter hadn't exercised his "husbandly rights" with her— for she hadn't yet bled a full year—but to even suggest that the King of Culhuacan should take his enemy's former concubine as his legitimate wife was insulting.

Flame Tongue had come back last night promising to guarantee Anacoana's virginity and it took every shred of restraint to not have the guards throw him from my palace. Little Reed made it clear to me years earlier that he wouldn't abide arranged marriage for political reasons, and perhaps I should have dismissed the whole stupid ordeal with that reason from the beginning, but I'd worried about how his untraditional approach to traditional practices would be received by his allies, new and old alike.

Seeing Flame Tongue here left me grumpy again—no doubt he'd keep beating his drum—but Little Reed's tender grip on my hand distracted me as he escorted me to our set of reed-woven icpalli thrones. The servants decorated the top of mine with clusters of the sweet-smelling bone flowers, a practice I'd adopted from my mother. The aroma created a zone of calm that made me feel regal when I sat on my throne. Little Reed's was covered with emerald green quetzal feathers, the same ones that his father Quetzalcoatl—the Feathered Serpent—took his name from. Once seated, he motioned the servants to dish up the food.

Traditionally the royal family was served first at any meal or feast, but in our house, the poorest ate first. The servants filled the plate of the war council's single Chichimec member—a man named Ixtlilxochitl, who wore a plethora of blue and red tattoos. Little Reed had welcomed him warmly, but the rest of us showed less enthusiasm for his presence, and so he watched us with the unease of a cornered jaguar, not daring to take the first bite. The servants moved quickly around the circle, filling dishes with fried quail eggs, roasted duck stewed with spicy tomatoes, and flatbread tlaxcallis in at least a dozen different thicknesses and colors.

Our new war chief Blood Wolf shared none of Ixtlilxochitl's hesitation; he immediately dug into his eggs with his knife and chased them down with a swig of chocolate. Long ago, when my mother and I had fled Culhuacan to escape my murderous uncle, he'd personally seen us to safety in Xochicalco. He'd been my other uncle Nochuatl's best friend, and he'd been quite young and fresh-faced back then. The years in between had left him grizzled and serious. His brother Matlacxochitl— whom I'd never met before a few weeks ago—was younger by a few years and looked to have been spared the harsh military life his brother had endured. A handful of high priests and priestesses from the various orders were here as well, but no one from the cult of the Smoking Mirror, thank goodness.

My diplomatic smile slipped ever so slightly when my gaze fell upon my cousin Amoxtli. The sight of him raised my pulse most unpleasantly; he had Ihuitimal's sharp, pointed jaw and hooked nose, reminding me of a bird of prey. And though he lacked the sharpened teeth and ghastly scar on his cheek, he looked every bit as I imagined his father had looked at that age, before life turned him into a murderer. Amoxtli wasn't a member of our war council, and while he'd expressed interest in joining the priesthood of Quetzalcoatl, he still had years of training ahead before he could take the trials to become one of the god's priests. I doubted he could overcome all the years of indoctrination into Smoking Mirror's cult that his father had forced upon him. If I had my way, I'd exile him from Culhuacan before he could turn against us, as my uncle had turned on my father.

But Little Reed had stood firm against that. "We need him. He's promised to show us where he buried your father's bones, so we can start building our new city." This was all true. But still I hoped that once Amoxtli served his purpose, I might convince Little Reed to leave him behind in Culhuacan when we moved to our new seat of power. Until then I'd asked Quetzalcoatl's fire priest Mazatzin to keep an eye on him— and he was doing exactly that from across the circle, so casually that only I noticed.

Once all the guests were served, the servants filled plates for both me and Little Reed. I'd been very hungry on the way to the great hall, but now that I stared at the eggs wrapped in a hot, transparent tlaxcalli, my stomach rebelled. I started with a cup of frothy chocolate spiced with vanilla, hoping to settle it.

No one discussed city or priestly business, for we considered meals a community-building exercise rather than a political one, so it wasn't until after the servants cleared the dishes that Little Reed turned to Flame Tongue to say, "I must extend my apologies to you. My slow recovery kept us from spending much time together during your visit, but I trust that Lord Citlallotoc kept you well entertained?"

"Quite," Flame Tongue said as he took his pipe when his body servant presented it to him. "I particularly enjoyed the hunt, but it's a shame how few deer are left in the valley anymore. If we're not careful, the Chichimecs will kill every last one and we'll be left with no sport."

Ixtlilxochitl, who sat a few mats away, cast him a scathing glare but said nothing.

"We should all be mindful of how we use the gifts the gods have granted us," Little Reed answered. "You told me there was an urgent matter you needed to discuss with me before you left today."

Flame Tongue nodded. "Important matters concerning the future of your kingdom, Lord Topiltzin." He puffed to get the tobacco burning and continued, "Getting your throne back was no easy feat, and not without a scrape with the Black Dog. My own throne came to me with its share of tragedies: one of my father's concubines attempted to poison me, and her son gave me this." He tipped back his head and pulled aside his heavy gold necklaces to reveal an old scar embedded deep in the loose skin below his jowls. "I spent the first three months of my reign lying in bed, recovering. Facing one's own death makes one worry for the future, don't you agree?"

"I wouldn't argue otherwise," Little Reed said. "The future has been on my mind for a very long time, and that's why Lady Quetzalpetlatl and I are leaving for the north tomorrow."

Flame Tongue took to thumping his chest as he started coughing, his eyes watering. "Leaving? But you reclaimed your throne not even three months ago yet!"

"It's of utmost importance to the kingdom's future," Little Reed assured him.

"Forgive my boldness, but what could possibly be of interest to anyone in the barbarian north?"

"We must recover King Mixcoatl's bones, for a proper burial."

Flame Tongue stammered a moment before saying, "With all due respect, Lord Topiltzin, there is much that needs your attention here in the valley. We have a Chichimec problem."

Ixtlilxochitl's glare turned darker.

Little Reed raised an eyebrow. "Problem?"

"They're crawling all over the countryside, eating up everything and multiplying like rabbits. Your uncle brought them here—over the objections of his allies, mind you—and now is the time to send them back home, before they get restless. We have no wars to keep them occupied anymore."

"I have no intention of sending them back to the desert. Many have lived in the valley as long as I have, and have raised their families here among us, so who am I to tell them they must leave?"

As with Smoking Mirror's cult, Little Reed and I didn't see eye-to-eye when it came to the Chichimecs. He didn't remember anything of that night long ago in Teotihuacan when they'd attacked us, for he'd been so drunk he wouldn't have woken even if they'd chopped him in half. He wasn't the one who'd cut off two of his fingers to call on Quetzalcoatl to save us all. And now so many dirty, half-naked, heavily-tattooed men roamed our streets that I didn't dare to go to the market or temple without at least four guards. With nothing for these vile dog-men to do besides steal and rape, the murder rate surged and all too many of them became victims themselves when good, honest Toltecas defended their homes and their lives from them. They belonged in the harsh northern desert that spawned their barbaric ways.

"I'm not unsympathetic to your concerns, Lord Flame Tongue," Little Reed went on. "War has been the occupation of most men—Chichimec and Tolteca—for many years now, and finding purpose in a new paradigm can be challenging. We have plans for redirecting their interests; the Chichimecs will not only contribute to the shift from war to peace, but they'll also be architects of it. I ask you give it time to work, and give the Chichimecs time to prove their value and worth."

"And what if while you're gone they decide they want to be warriors, not architects?" Flame Tongue asked, looking annoyed.

Little Reed nodded towards Blood Wolf. "Our new war chief will deal with any trouble that arises while we're gone."

Flame Tongue cast a dubious glance over at Citlallotoc. "I wasn't aware you'd replaced your old war chief."

"Lord Citlallotoc is returning to Acolman to take his rightful throne." Little Reed smiled at his friend, who bowed his head. "We shall miss him tremendously, but our loss is Acolman's gain. And I'm certain he's eager to settle down and secure his own legacy."

"That is always on the mind of the wisest of us," Flame Tongue said, his mood turning hopeful again. "And certainly you're acutely aware of the issues that arise when one doesn't properly secure his legacy as soon he takes the throne. Have you yet had a chance to meet my daughter, Anacoana?"

While his temper had improved, mine immediately flared. How dare he step on my authority? "We already discussed this issue, Lord Flame

Tongue. Twice. And I rejected your proposal both times."

Little Reed glanced at me before turning back to Flame Tongue. "What proposal does she speak of?"

"He wishes you to marry Anacoana," I said, "and I informed him that she is an inappropriate candidate."

Flame Tongue's face blazed. "There is nothing wrong with my Anacoana; she is high-born, appropriately tempered, and she's still in possession of her maidenhead—our priests have verified this."

"She's twelve!" I snapped back at him.

Little Reed held up his hand for silence, looking bewildered. He turned to Flame Tongue. "Why in Mictlan would you subject a twelve-year-old girl to a virginity test?"

"Because she was one of Black Otter's concubines," I supplied. "I told him such an offer is inappropriate at this juncture." *Not to mention completely at odds with your personal standard of ethics,* I wanted to add, but already Flame Tongue was furious, and suggesting that he had no morals would only make it worse.

Flame Tongue struggled for words, but Little Reed held up his hand again. "I have no doubt that Lady Anacoana is a fine young woman, Lord Flame Tongue, and I don't hold the past against her—a past she had no say in nor control over—but there is something you should know; I've already discussed this with my other allies, many of them even before I took the throne, but due to my illness I hadn't yet had the chance to discuss it with Lady Quetzalpetlatl." He patted my hand apologetically then went on, "As Quetzalcoatl's high priest, the god has set out a specific path for me to follow, and at this point, taking a wife is not part of that plan. When the god wishes me to marry, he will tell me, not only when, but to whom. And she will know it in her heart as well; this may not be the traditional way of men, but it is the way of the god, and as one of his highest servants it is my duty to follow his example and live as he would here on earth."

I might have smirked at Flame Tongue's fluster if this whole discussion hadn't brought the nausea back. He didn't look at me when he said, "I respect your reason, My Lord. Forgive my unfortunate outburst; I am a man of great passions when I feel my family has been slighted for no fault of their own. You understand."

"I do."

Flame Tongue rose from his mat. "Thank you for your hospitality, Lord Topiltzin, but I must be getting back to Xico. I bid you a safe journey." He turned to leave, his personal guards flanking him. But he stopped and looked back when Little Reed called out to him.

"I understand your passion all too well, Lord Flame Tongue, for I feel the same way when someone slights my sister for no reason other than the body the gods gave her," Little Reed said, a careful smile fixed on his face. "In case you were unaware, she is Quetzalcoatl's high priestess, chosen by him personally, which makes her one of his highest servants as well. I say *one of* because that is a position we share, as we share the throne here in Culhuacan; we are equals, in the eyes of the god and in the eyes of our people. I realize this hasn't been the way of kings in the valley for a long time, but that is how it is here now; and when you dismiss my sister's decisions, you dismiss me. I'm quite certain this wasn't your intention, of course, but going forward, let it be known that her words are to be taken with the same respect as mine."

Flame Tongue drew in his breath as if preparing to explode, his cheeks burning bright, but instead he exhaled raggedly. He looked as if he'd swallowed a live leech. "You have my apologies, Lady Quetzalpetlatl," he said, bowing to me. "I intended no disrespect."

I bowed my head in return.

Not long after Flame Tongue left, the rest of the breakfast crowd filtered off to their duties, leaving me and Little Reed alone. "You hardly ate anything," he noted.

I shook my head. "Lord Flame Tongue left me with a sour stomach. You don't think he'll withdraw his alliance with us over this, do you?"

"I'm more worried about how disrespectfully he treated you. There's no excuse."

"It won't be the last time," I said with a laugh. "Our ways are strange to most people, men and women alike."

"They will embrace it when they see it's what the god wants. We must be patient and lead the peasants gently, for they are the ones most open to hope. But some of the nobles will see any attempts to change the status quo as an erosion of their own power, and we'll have to handle them with a firmer grip."

"We must be careful not to get bitten in the process," I warned him.

He laughed, and I melted a little inside. Gods how I adored his smile!

The desire rose again, intense and demanding thanks to my nearly empty stomach—hunger always made it worse—but I didn't feel up to fighting it off right now. "I still haven't started packing for the trip, so I should go and do that," I said, rising from my reed-woven throne. "Will there be a feast tonight, to celebrate Citlallotoc's ascension?"

Little Reed sobered and nodded. "I must admit I will miss him greatly."

"He's a good friend, and those can be very hard to come by."

"We're going to a tlachtli match this afternoon. Do you want to join us?"

"I don't care for tlachtli," I said. The last match I attended ended gruesomely, both on and off the court, and I had little desire for reminders of such things. "You two enjoy yourselves."

I started to leave but when I turned, suddenly Amoxtli stood blocking my way. I took a step back, my heart hammering. I didn't keep personal guards within the palace walls—it seemed a bit ridiculous to do so, given that most people considered Little Reed the real person of power in our duo—but at that moment I wished I did if only so he couldn't have sneaked up on me like this. I frowned, embarrassed.

He bowed his head. "I'm sorry, My Lady. I didn't mean to surprise you."

"What do you want?" I snapped before I could think better of it. I really should have made an effort to eat something.

He had started to come out of his bow, but now he winced and kept his head down. "Nothing, My Lady. I wanted to compliment you on your speech during the afternoon services yesterday, about the city moving forward into the future without clinging to the past. I found it personally moving, and I wanted both you and Lord Topiltzin to know that I stand with you completely."

Sure you do, I thought but held it back.

Little Reed clasped Amoxtli on the shoulder. "We're glad to hear that. There will be difficult times as we blaze ahead and we may feel compelled to return to the safety of the past, but our faith and resolve will see us through the conflicts, and eventually to our goal. The rewards will be great."

Amoxtli finally looked up, giving me a furtive glance before focusing on Little Reed with a relaxed smile. "I shall remember that, Your Excellency." He spared me another glance—like a whipped dog—then he hurried from the great hall.

As we watched him go, Little Reed said, "I know he reminds you of his father, but he's truly a good man, Papalotl. He could have remained silent about Mixcoatl's bones, but he didn't hesitate to tell me where they were when I mentioned needing them. He wants to do right, and I hope you can find it in your heart to judge him for the man he is, instead of by the man fate decided would be his father."

I wanted to resist, but if the years had taught me anything, it was that Little Reed was a better judge of character than I. How might things have turned out differently if I'd let him deal with Quetzalcoatl's former high priest as he thought right, rather than staying his hand? My defending Ahexotl seemed disgustingly naïve now; the man had used fear of the god's wrath to have his way with his priestesses with impunity for years, but when he survived being severely burned by the god, I'd taken it as a sign that Quetzalcoatl wanted his life spared—a grave misjudgment that almost cost me my life. I'd learned the hard way it could be dangerous to trust anyone beyond the small handful of people who'd already proven themselves to me.

Little Reed gave my hand a squeeze. "Give him a chance, Papalotl. You won't be sorry. I promise."

I sighed. "I'll think about it."

Motioning me to follow him, Little Reed said, "Come. There's something I want to show you."

I followed him out of the great hall and down the hallway, into the royal living quarters to his room. I always felt a hitch of anxiety when I went in there; it had been my uncle Ihuitimal's quarters, but even before that, it had been my father's, where Ihuitimal had murdered him in his bed and put his heart in my hands when I was only seven, to terrorize me for his own amusement. Little Reed had redecorated the entire room with frescoes of the Feathered Serpent, snakes, and butterflies, but no amount of whitewash could completely banish the shadow of the mural of Smoking Mirror that had loomed on the largest wall when my uncle ruled.

Numerous wicker baskets sat clustered in the corner near the door, waiting for the servants to move them to the staging area in the main courtyard later tonight. Little Reed picked up a large clay urn sitting hidden amongst them and brought it over to me. Deep-etched swirls and flowers decorated the outside, and judging from the fragmented swaths of yellow, white and green, it had been painted at one point. When he handed it to me, I recognized it for a funerary urn, similar to the one Mazatzin and I had put Nimilitzli's ashes in after we'd cremated her. We'd buried it under the temple's stone floor in Xochicalco. "Little Reed...you dug up Nimilitzli's urn?" I asked, uneasy.

"Omeyocan no! Xochicalco was her home, and I wouldn't think of taking her away from there," he assured me.

"Then whose is it?"

He touched my hand gently as he said, "It's Mother's."

I stared at the pottery, finally recognizing it; I'd only seen it for a moment or two before King Cuitlapanton had it committed to the earth under the shade of a copal tree in the royal gardens. Little Reed and I had visited the spot at least once a year to lay flowers, and I'd tell him about Mother, describing her as best as I could so he might know what she looked like; and because for the longest time, before I realized my memory was infallible, I feared that I would forget her face. "You dug it up?"

"Actually, I sent Amoxtli to do it and he got back with it last night," Little Reed said.

"But why?"

"With us going north to find your father's burial site and build the god's sacred city, I thought it would be a kindness to Mother to bring her with us so we can bury her with Mixcoatl; and they will both be near us always."

I clutched the urn tight. "She would like that," I managed to whisper, tears threatening behind my eyes.

"Quetzalcoatl told us to build his temple on the spot where Mixcoatl is buried, to provide a strong foundation for our reign. But it will be even stronger if Mother is a part of that foundation as well." He hugged me, pressing the urn of our mother's ashes between us. "Let us build the future on the deeds of not only great men, but great women too."

"And Amoxtli brought her home to us?"

Little Reed nodded. "And he's going to show us where our new home will be."

Maybe Little Reed was right; perhaps I wasn't giving Amoxtli the chance he deserved.

CHAPTER TWO

Amoxtli knelt in front of the Feathered Serpent's idol in the great temple, his body bent forward, arms stretched out before him, head down. Even from this angle, his resemblance to my uncle unsettled me, but I fought the impulse to turn and leave. I stayed in the doorway, watching him rise to his knees while muttering a prayer. He only saw me once he turned to leave, and it was his turn to jump, startled. "High Priestess." He bowed and swept his fingers across the ground at my feet.

Taking a deep breath, I said, "I wanted to thank you for all you're doing for me and Topiltzin...bringing my mother home, and for coming forward with the location of my father's bones. It's very important to the future that we find them."

"It was the least I could do for our family." He didn't meet my gaze as he spoke. "I know my father hurt you, in ways I can never know, and yet you granted him a proper burial with all the rites. Mixcoatl deserves the same."

I struggled to find words in the storm of emotions tearing through me, leaving me raw and exposed. But finally I found my voice again. "Please excuse my cold demeanor this morning. I don't believe the son should bear the burden of his father's crimes, and yet...I treated you as if you should, and I'm truly sorry."

Amoxtli finally met my gaze. "I understand your difficulty. My father...he was consumed by things he had no control over, things he couldn't change, and it destroyed him, long before that battle outside the city. I'm so sorry for the havoc he caused in your life."

"His obsessions didn't hurt only me—or even Topiltzin. It ended up destroying his entire family, and.... I...I'm sorry I didn't come speak to you personally about Black Otter. It was terribly thoughtless of me."

He glanced around, uncomfortable. "If I might impose upon you...what did happen to my brother? Exactly?"

Black Otter's death was a subject I didn't like to think about, let alone talk about; how could I admit to Amoxtli that his father ordered his own son's execution because he feared I'd poisoned Black Otter's mind and robbed him of his will? Even now my uncle's dying words continued to haunt me: "My son had no chance against you; no man does." I'd worried about what he meant, but with the months, I'd convinced myself that I would be better off not knowing.

My sister Jade Flower had told me Black Otter and Amoxtli had been close, and while I didn't care if the truth destroyed any remaining vestiges of love Amoxtli held for his father, I wasn't keen to tell him how mentally unstable his brother became in his final days. He deserved a better memory than that. "Black Otter feared your father would harm me and he tried to smuggle me out of Culhuacan, but Ihuitimal sent his personal guards to retrieve me, with orders to kill Black Otter as a traitor." I looked out of the door towards Lake Meztliapan, to the spot in the deep emerald waters where Black Otter had died and my nightmares began. The vision of the monster filled my mind, making my heart pulse and my stomach clench. *Mine! Mine! Mine!*

I blushed when I realized Amoxtli had spoken but I hadn't heard any of it. "I'm sorry, what did you say?" I asked, shaking the terrible image from my head.

"I said thank you for telling me the truth," Amoxtli said. "As much as I want to believe my father wasn't capable of ordering my brother's murder, I know better. He told me more than once that Black Otter wasn't strong enough to rule and that I needed to be ready to take his place." He shook his head.

"Power does strange things to people," I said.

He nodded, but before he could say more, footsteps on the temple stairs distracted me. I turned to see a man walking towards us, dressed in the black priestly robes of the Order of the Smoking Mirror. Most priests—besides Quetzalcoatl's—wore their hair matted with blood, but this man was freshly washed, with his long hair pulled back into a tidy knot on top of his head. Still, he bore the telltale scars of daily bloodletting on his arms, legs, and notched ears. He smiled when we locked gazes.

I forced myself to smile back.

He swept his fingers across the ground at my feet—the greeting befitting of a queen. "Glorious day, Lady Quetzalpetlatl."

I arched an eyebrow. "Indeed."

"I've been hoping to meet you for a while, but with the king ill and you so busy caring for city matters, I'm afraid formal introductions had to wait until now." He rose back to his full height. "I'm Ozomatli, the new high priest of Tezcatlipoca."

The day after the Smoking Mirror abandoned my uncle to die on the battlefield, Mazatzin told me some priest of the dark sorcerer god came seeking an audience with me, to discuss the future of the cult. After all I'd been through, I was in no mood to speak to anyone connected to Smoking Mirror, and so I put off the meeting. Besides, at that point I was certain Little Reed and I were going to kick Smoking Mirror's cult out of Culhuacan soon.

Or so I'd thought.

I had no interest in speaking to Ozomatli about his murderous god's cult now, but as the highest of priestesses in Culhuacan, I was obligated to do so. "It's a pleasure to finally meet you," I said, inclining my head. I looked past him before asking, "And where is your order's high priestess?"

"Oh, the Smoking Mirror has no high priestess, My Lady."

"Why not?"

"The Smoking Mirror is a god of warriors, and so women have no use for him." His smile added, *Nor does he have any use for them.*

I stood taller. "Women are warriors in their own right; I'd dare any man to endure the childbed and not beg the gods to end his suffering."

He chuckled, but guardedly. "Some gods are more useful to women than they are to men, and the other way around. It isn't a slight."

"Any god that aspires to the all-encompassing importance that Smoking Mirror did under my uncle's rule cannot afford to ignore half of the city's citizens."

Ozomatli did an admirable job of maintaining his composure; but given how he shifted from foot to foot, I could see this conversation wasn't going the way he'd intended. Good.

"If Smoking Mirror wishes to maintain a presence here in Culhuacan," I said, "he will make himself useful to everyone, and he can start by welcoming women into his cult. Ihuitimal may have granted citizen status to only men during his rule, but Topiltzin and I share the responsibility of power; the throne, as with the gods themselves, reflects the duality of the natural order: one side is incomplete and imperfect without the other— but together, working in harmony, balance and peace is achieved. A city out of balance with the gods risks falling apart; a cult out of balance with reality risks destroying itself. Certainly your Smoking Mirror acknowledges this very basic tenet of our faith in the gods?"

Ozomatli's smile twitched. "Smoking Mirror is all-knowing, My Lady, so trust he will do what is necessary to maintain the proper balance. I shall seek out a high priestess, but I beg your patience while I do so, since I haven't any experienced priestesses to choose from."

"I give you six months to train one, and choose wisely; I won't accept a simple mouthpiece, and I'd hate to see my opinion of you suffer."

He'd kept his smile throughout our discussion, but now his eyes burned. "Absolutely." His gaze flicked away to Amoxtli standing in the doorway behind me. "Good to see you again, Lord Amoxtli. My condolences on the loss of your father and brother."

Where I'd made great efforts to be at least cordial, Amoxtli took no such care. He glared at Ozomatli.

Ozomatli turned his conniving smile on me again, bade me good day, and departed down the stairs, his black robe fluttering behind him.

"You'd do well to not trust him, My Lady," Amoxtli said, watching Ozomatli weave his way through the crowd below.

"Oh?"

He nodded. "When he became the cult's fire priest, my father fell ill all the time."

"You think he was poisoning him?" When Amoxtli nodded again, I asked, "How?" I'd thought of doing the very same thing, but with all the food tasters, I'd decided that wasn't a viable option.

"His mushroom box," Amoxtli said. "My father had already been training me in the priestly arts before Ozomatli became his fire priest, and I had experience with the teonanacatl mushrooms. But six months ago, I became extremely ill while doing a vision ceremony and didn't come out of the Divine Dream for three days. Father thought I'd taken too much, but I hadn't taken any more than normal. The only difference was that I'd gotten the mushrooms from his personal box rather than the community one used by the rest of the priests."

I joined Amoxtli, gazing down at Ozomatli in the crowded precinct below. I didn't care that someone had tried to poison my uncle, but what if Ozomatli's ambitions reached higher than merely being Smoking Mirror's high priest? He required close monitoring. "Did you tell anyone your suspicions?"

"Before I left on my mission to hide Mixcoatl's bones, I mentioned to Ozomatli that I thought someone might have tampered with my father's mushrooms, but I didn't make the connection until Topiltzin told me that he'd been tipped off as to what route I was taking back from the north. Ozomatli probably thought he would execute me and he wouldn't have to worry about being found out."

A twinge of protectiveness surprised me. "Do you think he might still try, given his earlier failure?"

Amoxtli stood straighter. "I'm not afraid of him, My Lady."

"I'm going to have him watched." I glared at the crowd again, but Ozomatli was gone, no doubt to tattle on me to Little Reed. I bade Amoxtli goodbye and started down the stairs, but, suddenly struck with an idea, I stopped. "How would you feel about a ceremony on the lakeshore tonight, before we leave? To honor Black Otter?"

"That would be wonderful," Amoxtli said, his smile sober and a touch sad. "Thank you."

Smiling back, I said, "I think it will be good for both of us."

¤

There'd already been a ceremony honoring Black Otter last month, attended by his former concubines, Amoxtli, and a few close friends. Traditionally the wife of the deceased led the ritual lamentations—where the women wept in grief as loud as they could for a week—but I'd passed that honor on to my sister Jade Flower. She'd been closest to Black Otter and, besides, an uncomfortable tension fell over the room whenever all five of his women came together; I hadn't been a welcome newcomer when he was alive, and when he died, things had been said that couldn't be unsaid between me and Jade Flower. Everyone seemed happier when I stayed away, including myself.

Not that I didn't miss Black Otter; for a while, before everything turned strange and disturbing between us, I'd considered building a life with him. But with my one true love back from the dead and sharing my throne, I found it difficult to ache for him as was expected of a grieving widow. So I let the others have their peaceful ceremony without distraction.

And yet I regretted not having that final goodbye such ceremonies provided for those of us left behind. I was very glad it occurred to me to do this before we left.

I donned my high priestess robe and let Malinalli fix my hair again when she visited after dinner to help me with my last-minute packing. We passed the time chatting since I wouldn't see her tomorrow—our caravan would leave before sunrise and she had dawn temple duties.

"Are you positive you don't want me or Mazatzin to accompany you tonight?" she asked, putting the finishing touches to my hair. "I know Topiltzin has taken Amoxtli into his confidences, but...doesn't he remind you of Ihuitimal?"

"I'm hoping with time I'll learn to see him, not his father," I admitted.

"Mazatzin says he's very intelligent and will make a good priest someday. It's strange how he looks exactly like his father but is the opposite of him, while Black Otter—who looked nothing like Ihuitimal—turned out most like him."

It was on the tip of my tongue to argue with that assessment of Black Otter's character, but I stopped. Where might I be now if Ihuitimal's men hadn't stopped us? Locked up in some distant palace, never allowed to leave or, worse yet, dead? Would he have gone that far to make certain we were together forever? Red Flint had almost taken his obsession with me to that end—I still shuddered at the memory of him raising the flint knife to stab me; if not for Malinalli smashing him across the head with the incense censer....

Might that someday be Little Reed too? I wondered, and my insides curled up like tender vegetation in a cold snap. I'd started asking myself such questions even before Black Otter spiraled down the same road of obsession that Red Flint had. I wanted to believe it was only coincidence, an unnecessary and unfair connection in their behavior; and after Black Otter's end, I tried very hard to tuck that thought away and leave it in the past, while I looked towards the future. This freak occurrence had no bearing on my future with Little Reed. *He is strong where they were dangerously weak. He would never succumb to such...magic.* For lack of a better word.

Malinalli had turned away to look over my bags, so she didn't see the sickly frown on my face. I pushed it away again, replacing it with a smile, willing myself to be cheerful. "Do you realize this is the first time in two years that we'll go more than a couple of weeks without seeing each other?"

"I wish I were going with you," Malinalli admitted. "Promise you'll be careful when you're in the north."

"I promise. And we won't be gone that long, a few months at most. You and Mazatzin will do fine running the priesthood while we're gone."

"The other high priests are already grumbling about the new restrictions on sacrifices," Malinalli said.

"Let them. It's not as if we don't allow them any human sacrifices." At least not yet. Little Reed and I had instituted limits on the number of victims each temple could give to the gods each year, with the idea that we'd eventually narrow it down to a handful of willing sacrifices each year, or better yet none at all.

"Ozomatli has been quite vocal about his displeasure with the new laws."

"And I trust you to deal with him appropriately, even if it means punching him in the face, as you did to Lord Storm House."

She laughed. "Some men are completely baffled when we don't behave as feminine as they think we should, aren't they?"

"They'll learn. We must be patient, and not be afraid to show them what we can do."

Malinalli nodded. "You'd best get going before you're late. And get enough rest while you're traveling. You've been working so hard, you deserve the break."

"I will, and I'll write to you whenever I can."

¤

While I allowed myself to wander the halls unshadowed by guards, when I left the palace, I always took some with me; who knew if any of my uncle's loyal followers still remained in Culhuacan, waiting for the right moment to avenge their fallen leader? Tonight I took my normal four-guard complement with me.

We met Amoxtli at the temple where he was waiting next to the smashed remains of the giant feathered serpent heads that once framed the staircase. Replacing them was on our long list of projects to restore the city to her former glory. He took the basket of butterflies I'd picked up from the priestly menagerie on the way over and we walked behind the temple, through the gate at the edge of the precinct, and made our way down the overgrown path to the sandbar; it was the same place where, as a child, I'd picked the fight with Black Otter that led to him and his family being exiled from Culhuacan. The log I'd knocked him off had long since disintegrated; but with my perfect memory I could still tell exactly where it had been, the place I'd stood when my father slapped me for bloodying Black Otter's nose because he called me "just a little girl"; the spot where I'd thought my father would kill him when I let slip that his father was worshiping Smoking Mirror in the palace. So many phantom memories haunted Culhuacan; I looked forward to escaping it when we built our new city.

Amoxtli set the basket on the sand and looked out over the water. The sun hung low, bathing everything in fading orange light; soon it would disappear beyond the mountains and start its journey through the underworld. "Black Otter used to bring me here to spear ducks," Amoxtli said with a heavy sigh. "He once told me your father and our uncle Nochuatl used to bring him here too, but whenever I asked him to tell me about them, he said he couldn't say any more because I'd tell Father. No one was allowed to talk about either of them in Culhuacan; I didn't even know that the box my father asked me to take north contained Mixcoatl's bones until one of my men let it slip while we buried it."

Memories of Ihuitimal soured my mood, and with the sun sinking below the mountains, we had to hurry if we were to get back into the city before sunset. He nodded when I suggested that we get to the prayer, and we both bowed our heads as I recited the plea to Tlaloc:

"Guardian of the Drowned,
Tonight we honor he who fell into your watery embrace.
May he find happiness in the land of Tlalocan,
May you find nourishment in our tears of sorrow,
And turn our grief into the rain that feeds the living."

I cut my palm with my sacrificial blade and let the blood dribble into the water. Once a cloud of red hung in the water like smoke, I closed my fist and raised my hands to the sky.

"Most merciful Quetzalcoatl,
Lighten the burdens weighing down our hearts,
Show us the path forward without those we've lost,
Show us how to turn grief into hope,
And anger into forgiveness.

Show us how to leave the past behind,
Show us into the future,
Most merciful Feathered Serpent."

Amoxtli opened the basket and a flock of black and orange butterflies sputtered out into the open air. They bobbed out over the lake, spreading out and dispersing in the sunset. The sight brought me a smile, and I felt energized, just as I had for so many days after the god had taken possession of me; the tingle of magic had never quite left after that, but I rarely felt so aware of it anymore.

Papalotl! a soft, child-like voice whispered with awe. I looked around, startled that someone other than me, Amoxtli, and my guards might be watching this ceremony. But I saw no one else. And those who were there stood in silent contemplation; Amoxtli's eyes sparkled with tears. I thought to ask him if he'd been the one to speak, but it felt wrong to interrupt the moment.

And since we walked back to the palace in complete silence, I didn't ask him then either. My mind ticked over the strange coincidence that the voice had sounded startlingly like Little Reed had that first time he'd called me by my childhood name—the name he shouldn't have known since everyone who'd known me by that name had been dead for years before.

CHAPTER THREE

The caravan left Culhuacan while darkness still shrouded the land. There was no grand send-off, no crowds of noblemen bidding us farewell, no musicians playing drums and flutes; as with trade caravans carrying uncounted riches, we slipped from the city under cover of darkness and secrecy.

As usual I hadn't slept well, and with Little Reed sharing the royal litter with me, sleep remained ever elusive. Last night's dreams had been particularly unpleasant: I was back on the battlefield amidst the confusion as my uncle—possessed by Smoking Mirror—tore through the armies as a giant, smoking jaguar, trying to get at Little Reed. But instead of saving everyone, I floundered over the sacrifice I needed to make to harness Quetzalcoatl's power; I dithered and argued over whether never being with Little Reed the way my heart wanted was truly worth it for either of us, and by the time I'd made the right decision, it was too late—Smoking Mirror had already broken through the crowd of warriors protecting Little Reed and eaten him whole, as if he were nothing more than a fried grasshopper. Then the smoke jaguar had turned its fiery orange eyes on me.

Now, instead of closing my eyes to rest, I lay back among the pillows and blankets, watching Little Reed smoke his pipe in the dark as he looked out the curtain, no doubt thinking I was asleep. But I didn't dare close my eyes, lest I open them again to find he really wasn't with me anymore. Would the dreams ever end or would I live the rest of my days worried that reality was the true dream that someday I'd wake up from?

Once the sun rose newly-birthed over the mountains ahead of us, I finally gave up on sleeping. After a slim breakfast of fried fish and tlaxcallis, we sat with the curtain open, playing patolli. It was one of the few "manly" things my father had taught me—completely unbeknownst to my mother, who found such games unseemly—and I'd taught it to Little Reed when he was young. We didn't gamble with cacao beans the way most people did; instead we wagered secrets, with the person who lost their treasure divulging something the winner didn't know. My impression was that Little Reed was completely non-competitive about the game; he was as content revealing the bits and pieces of himself as he was to hear mine. I often mused that we never would have known each other so well if not for playing patolli after those weekend meals at Nimilitzli's house.

Though I'd bet he'd become competitive if I suggested switching out telling secrets for wagering bits of our clothing off, I thought with a smirk as I captured his first of six treasures. I expected the growling desire when I looked at him, but I felt only a tingling deep inside. It felt so much more pleasant, so much more natural than that intense, hungry desire that Black Otter used to bring out in me.

Little Reed thought for a moment, then he said, "I always preferred Nimilitzli's tlaxcallis to yours. But only slightly."

I rolled my eyes. "That's hardly a secret, Little Reed. You really think I never noticed that you ate twice as many tlaxcallis when Nimilitzli made them?" I sighed. "I liked them more too."

Laughing, Little Reed said, "Maybe we should wager cacao, since we already know all of each other's secrets."

"Hardly. I'm certain there are a lot of things I don't know about you, as there are a lot of things that you don't know about me."

"For example?"

I shook my head. "No, I won your treasure, so you're the one who must divulge."

He took a swig from his water skin then suggested, "How about this: the winner gets to ask the loser a question to answer, with complete honesty and no embarrassment?" He had a twinkle in his eye that made that tingling intensify.

"All right," I agreed.

"So, ask away."

"Did you take any lovers while you were in the army?" I widened my eyes as soon as I asked it; so much for that insistent desire keeping its mouth shut.

Little Reed raised an eyebrow. "We're answering those kinds of questions, are we?"

My cheeks burned. "I don't know why I asked that. You don't have to—"

"The answer is no," Little Reed went on with a lopsided smile. "Though I came close to breaking my priestly vows once, with an exceptionally beautiful woman; unfortunately, a pompous, loudmouthed royal brat barged in and stopped it. I still resent him for it."

The memory of that night brought a hot flush creeping down my neck and over my breasts. I couldn't hold Little Reed's gaze anymore, my heart thudding in my ears.

Little Reed set the bean dice in my hand. "Your turn." Judging from the intense look in his eyes, he had his own questions and no intention of losing this time. I tossed the beans, feeling suddenly numb. What if he asked me the same question? I couldn't lie to him and say I'd had no lovers besides Black Otter; would it devastate him to know I'd been his father Quetzalcoatl's lover, even if it never went beyond the Divine Dream? *Perhaps it's time to get all this out in the open,* I thought as I moved one of my red pebbles around the cross-shaped board.

Little Reed took his roll and moved his jade pebble, knocking mine off the board by landing on it. Now I had no markers on the board and he had claimed one of my treasures. He grinned at me, almost as if he'd planned all this rather than made a lucky roll of the beans. "My turn to ask a question."

I swallowed, hoping my nervousness wasn't obvious. "Ask away," I said, trying to sound relaxed.

But I didn't expect the question he actually asked. "Do you, on some level, still think of me as you used to, before Black Otter?"

I blinked at him, puzzled at first. "Are you asking if I still love you?"

"In a manner of speaking." His expression was completely calm, but a slight hitch in his voice betrayed his nervousness.

I sighed. "Little Reed, I never stopped loving you, and I never could. I could die and be stuck on the banks of the Black Lake in Mictlan for countless years and I'd still love you."

He didn't speak for a moment, a strange look on his weathered face, as if my answer had somehow surprised me. Could he have really thought I could so completely fall in love with another that I could never love him anymore? "Why...why did you say that, about Mictlan?" he finally asked, an inexplicable excitement in his voice.

Now I was even more puzzled. "I don't know...I suppose because it was on my mind. I died on the battlefield, after all, and Xolotl told me that because Smoking Mirror had no heaven for his sacrifices that I'd have to sit on the Black Lake for who knows how long, until Smoking Mirror actually gained a heaven for me and his other sacrifices to go to."

"And that's it?"

I nodded, but felt something tugging at the back of my mind. I tried to draw it in, to make it form a coherent image in my head, but as quickly as it came on, it vanished, lost again.

Little Reed seemed disappointed by my answer, but he quickly handed me the dice. "Your turn."

I tossed the beans, expecting my rotten luck to continue, but two of my beans showed their white dots, letting me move back onto the board. And knock Little Reed off the board at the same time. "Why would you think I don't love you anymore?" I asked.

He shifted uneasily. "When I asked you to marry me...I upset you," he said. "I know it was too soon after Black Otter died, but—"

"Black Otter had nothing to do with any of that," I said. "The man forced me into his bed, so how could I possibly love him as I've always loved you?"

Little Reed's eyes grew wide and hot. "He forced himself on you?" he growled, his voice quaking with pent-up rage.

"Gods no!" I grabbed his hand and gave it a reassuring squeeze. "No, no, he wasn't that kind of man, Little Reed. Not at all. What I meant is that...I didn't want to be in his bed, but under the circumstances...it was a matter of survival. And maybe for a while, I thought...maybe I might be able to find some happiness with him. But it was never like what we had, Little Reed. Nothing at all."

The rage faded to concern. "What do you mean by *had*?"

I stared at him a moment, uncertain what to say. The moment had come, but I still didn't want to tell him. "It's not your turn to ask a question," I said.

The hurt plain in his eyes, he picked up the beans and rolled them. We went through several silent turns and each landed all six of our markers on the board, working our way towards each other's treasure squares. The longer the silence held up—and the longer it took for one of us to finally capture the other person's treasure—the more my chest ached and my stomach twisted. It was on the tip of my tongue to tell him I didn't want to play anymore when he finally captured one of my treasures. He then looked up at me again, his face carefully controlled now. "What did you mean by *had*?" he asked softly.

I fought back tears. "I'm sorry, Little Reed. The Smoking Mirror was going to kill you, and I knew only the god could save you, and I had only one thing of value left to give in sacrifice...." I choked a moment and paused to regain my composure. "We can't get married, Little Reed. That's the sacrifice I made to save you. I'm sorry."

He sat straighter, his shoulders rising as if my words had lifted a burden off of them. "Is that all?"

Given the intensity of our conversation, his casual dismissal of this news startled—and hurt—me. "You say that as if it's no sacrifice at all," I snapped.

A crestfallen expression came to his face. "Not at all, Papalotl. You saved my life and I can't ever thank you enough for that, but what does it truly matter if we cannot ever marry? Marriage is but a social display, a political alliance for convenience sake. Certainly not something to get so upset about."

I shook my head. "You don't understand, Little Reed. I know I said marriage, but...I was speaking of it in the manner in which *we* intended to practice it—not as a political maneuver, but rather as an expression of our love for each other. All my life I've felt as if you were the string holding my sacrificial blade together, that we were meant to be together, and not merely to fulfill the god's religious plans, but to...and I know this will sound crazy and ludicrous, but...I always thought we'd make love important and vital, the way the gods intended it to be."

As soon as I said it, that same itch of inaccessible memory came upon me. None of what I said was supported by anything I'd learned in the priesthood; none of the countless tales of the gods said anything about love, and yet...it had felt so achingly true when I'd said it. I felt almost divinely inspired, and I was acutely aware again of the tingling in my limbs, in my blood, in my belly—burning sun-like inside me.

Little Reed didn't say anything for a moment but eventually he nodded, the look on his face inscrutable. "I have felt that way too," he admitted.

The pleasant tingling faded as I said, "That is what I gave up, Little Reed, to save you. It was what I wasn't strong enough to sacrifice—no, *refused to sacrifice*—on Red Flint's behalf, so instead Nimilitzli paid the price for me. I would have gladly given my very life to save you, but since Ihuitimal had already given that to Smoking Mirror, I had only my heart left to give. So yes, while I still love you as much as I always have—and always will—I've given up being able to act on that. And I don't regret it in the slightest; I would do it again without hesitation to save your life, Little Reed."

He pulled me into a fierce hug that scattered the pebbles on the patolli board between us. "And I would sit on the banks of the Black Lake in Mictlan until the end of time if it meant saving you," he whispered. He buried his face in my neck, holding me close a moment, then he gave my cheek a soft, warm kiss before pulling away, evidence of tears clouding his eyes. He looked at the board and sighed. "I suppose the game is over then."

"It is," I agreed, my heart heavy.

He looked out the curtain then said, "There's one last secret I want to share with you."

"All right."

"I dread to think of you enduring this sacrifice on your own, on my account, so I'm making the very same one for you, my love. I shall take no other into my heart—or my bed."

I shook my head adamantly. "I cannot ask such a thing of you, Little Reed—"

"You're not asking; I'm giving it, freely and without reservation. You might not have the freedom to act on your love for me, but I don't have that restriction, and this is how I choose to act on my love for you."

A few tears finally came, hot on my cheeks. He smiled at me and wiped them away with his thumbs, his hands warm and comforting. "I'm going to walk for a while, stretch my legs," he said, his voice barely above a whisper. "You should get some more sleep; you look exhausted." He gathered the game pieces and folded up the board made from a reed mat and put them away into his leather carrying bag. He called for the caravan to stop but he didn't say anything more as he left the litter, closing the curtain behind him. A moment later the the litter jostled as the porters got back underway.

I lay staring at the roof. In the dim light creeping in from the curtain's slivered opening, I could barely see the painting of Quetzalcoatl flying in his feathered serpent form among the blue clouds where the rain god Tlaloc poured rain from his sacred jars. He slithered towards the earth below, to the underworld where he traveled death's road to rescue the bones of humanity and bring them back to the world, to give humankind life with his own blood. It was so obvious who Little Reed inherited his self-sacrificing ways from.

Except the sacrifice he made puts him in the same predicament as your own father, I thought with a frown. *With no blood heir to carry on the god's wishes after us, how can any of this matter in the long run?*

I knew what Little Reed would say: *trust in the god.* And really, what else could I do?

¤

We reached the city of Chimalhuacan late in the afternoon, right before dinner time, and King Toztli greeted us in the courtyard along with his daughter Cornflower—another of my former husband's concubines. I was glad to see her looking well, and she greeted me with a hug and chattered earnestly the whole way to the great hall. We hadn't been close at all when she was in Black Otter's household—in fact we'd hardly spoken—but coming home to her family had allowed her to put our mutually painful past behind her and open up.

Toztli had a grand feast waiting for us, with all of Chimalhuacan's nobility in attendance; fewer than fifty people, which was understandable given Chimalhuacan's small size. Toztli's eldest son and heir Nahuacatl greeted us, and it annoyed me that he let his gaze linger on me longer than on Little Reed. When we sat to eat, Cornflower whispered to me, "Don't be surprised if he approaches your brother tonight about you. Father's been saying for weeks that we finally have a real chance at combining the royal families, and Nahuacatl is to make the best possible impression on Topiltzin."

I gave Nahuacatl a curt nod when he cast a furtive glance at me from where he sat next to his father. He was little more than a boy, probably hadn't even done a full year in the army yet. He turned away, his face darkening with a blush, and he looked as if he would get ill any moment. "I wouldn't think the former wife of a minor prince would be a fitting match for the heir to the throne," I told her.

"Ah, but to my father, you're not the former wife of a minor prince: you're the queen of a major city and an opportunity to meld two royal bloodlines. This isn't the first time Chimalhuacan has sought to merge with Culhuacan through marriage. Did you know that my grandfather named the city after your mother?"

"Truly?"

Cornflower nodded. "According to my mother, when your grandfather's only son came down with the Divine Sickness, he turned to his best friends to make a match for his eldest daughter. My grandfather changed his city's name to Chimalhuacan, hoping that would impress your grandfather into betrothing my father to your mother. He didn't know that your mother's father owed a blood-debt to your father's father: he'd saved your grandfather from being captured during the first battle they both fought against the Chichimecs. And even though your grandfather didn't betroth my father to your mother, he kept the city name, to honor their friendship. Or so my mother claims."

"That's fascinating," I told her as I held up a bowl of chile sauce for us to share. "I never knew any of that."

"It is funny to think that we might have been sisters had our parents married," Cornflower said, dipping her tlaxcalli into the sauce. "Of course, if your brother does marry you to Nahuacatl, that would make us sisters of a sort."

"Topiltzin won't marry me to anyone," I said, perhaps a bit more sharply than I'd intended, for Cornflower blinked at me, startled. "As priests of the god Quetzalcoatl, both Topiltzin and I have taken vows of chastity, so a marriage would really be pointless for either of us."

"But what about an heir for the throne?" Cornflower asked, confused. "If neither of you can marry...who will inherit Culhuacan after you're gone?"

"It is a dilemma we'll have to work out with the god," I admitted. "But enough about me. How is your daughter?"

◻

After dinner, Toztli invited us to sit with his war council to discuss political matters during the xocolatl service. Being the only woman present, I felt out of place, but was determined not to show any discomfort despite the not-entirely friendly looks from some of the men. Toztli avoided looking at me entirely, as if my very presence made him nervous, but he spoke with an eager friendliness with Little Reed as they smoked their pipes.

"So, Lord Topiltzin, what takes you into the north?" Toztli asked as he stirred his powdered heart flower into his chocolate with his wooden stirring stick, whipping it into the froth indicative of the best xocolatl.

"We're making a religious pilgrimage on behalf of the god," Little Reed answered.

"He has interests in the north?" Toztli asked, surprised. "Are you by chance looking to drive the Chichimecs farther into the desert? I know a good many good Toltecas would support such a venture."

Little Reed chuckled. "Actually, we're interested in improving our relationship with the Chichimecs. Wars between our peoples came about because life in the desert is difficult and the Chichimecs sought better lives. We, on the other hand, sought to deny them that merely because of their tribal affiliations. They have much to offer and teach us, if we're willing to listen and accept them into our communities and learn from them."

"But certainly the god wouldn't want them here in the valley, not after they outlawed his worship in Culhuacan and tried to conquer everyone in the name of their wretched Smoking Mirror god?" Toztli asked.

"Smoking Mirror may be a Chichimec god, but my uncle was not a Chichimec himself," I said between sips from my cup. Toztli flinched when I first spoke but then put on a strained smile. "So long as the Chichimecs honor Quetzalcoatl alongside their own gods, he considers them his people and will extend his blessings and protections upon them."

"But there's no work for them here," one of the war council members grumbled.

"Oh, but there is." Little Reed held up his hand and our scribe hurried forward with a stack of parchment. "I have a proposition for you, Lord Toztli; one that will put the Chichimecs to work and help them integrate into our society." He set the parchments down one at a time, placing them close together so they formed a large drawing of a precinct. "Now that Xochicalco has fallen, there isn't a market center large enough to handle all the trade coming in from the south. So we build a new one, right here." He pointed to a space of empty land slightly south of the halfway mark between our two kingdoms. "We've already invited the King of Chalco to participate as well and he's agreed to help. Together, our three kingdoms would run the market and share in the profits from the taxation, split equally among us of course. And we hire Chichimecs to do the work."

"But the Chichimecs aren't architects, Lord Topiltzin," Toztli pointed out. "They are a warrior society that lives in tents outside the city limits; they can't even weave cotton into cloth, so how can we expect them to build a market complex from stone?"

"We train them, of course, as the Teotihuacanos trained us hundreds of years ago. Quetzalcoatl's gift of civilization is for all his people, not only those who have already mastered the skills; if anything, it is our obligation to spread the god's teachings to every new people we meet, if only to bring them closer to the god himself. We will teach them that there is more to existence than suffering and warfare, and we too will benefit from the rewards that brings. After a hundred years of nonstop war, we can finally enjoy peace and prosperity."

Toztli gazed at the drawing, chewing his lip. "The last ten years have been grueling, with Toltecas fighting each other," he admitted. "And driving the Chichimecs back into the north would probably take another ten years—"

"And cost us many lives," Little Reed added. "We've already lost so many men to Ihuitimal's war—so many we probably won't ever fully recover. If we turn on the Chichimecs, they'll quickly realize they outnumber us, and with the troubles in the south, we can't rely on our trade partners to come to our aid; in fact, we should fully expect goods from the south to dwindle to a trickle within the next generation."

"Then why waste resources building a new market center?"

"Because while the south falters, the valley will rise and the south will need our trade goods the way we've long depended on theirs. The god has foreseen this."

Toztli looked at his war chief, a frown on his face. He was so easily flustered; it was little wonder my uncle had used him so readily. In contrast, his son Nahuacatl was studying the plans and whispering to one of the other war council members who nodded eagerly and whispered back, pointing out things in the drawings. If Toztli accepted this agreement, his indecisive tendencies would weigh down the construction efforts. I casually whispered to Little Reed, "Suggest that his son lead the construction effort."

Little Reed had been watching the young man as well and gave me a nod before telling Toztli, "And we believe that Chimalhuacan's heir Lord

Nahuacatl should lead the project as the chief architect. I understand he's an extremely bright man with an eye for beautiful architecture."

Toztli grinned. "He is indeed, Lord Topiltzin. When he was a boy, he used to complain about having to be the heir to the throne because he wanted to be a stone carver instead. I do indulge him a bit; he helped design Quetzalcoatl's new temple here, since Ihuitimal insisted I tear down the old one and replace it with a temple for the Smoking Mirror." He turned to his son, who was beaming now. "I'm certain he will relish a task of such magnitude."

"Then we have an agreement?" I asked.

Toztli gave me that hesitant look again—which was really starting to annoy me. "Yes, My Lady. I believe we do have an agreement. May I extend my humblest thanks for including Chimalhuacan in this venture?"

"Of course you may, My Lord. Topiltzin and I are very pleased that you wish to help us with this; it's a strong first step to reestablishing the friendship and trust our families enjoyed for generations before my uncle's bid for power."

His smile faltered ever so slightly, exposing an underlying sense of fear—not exactly the reaction I'd expected—but he quickly covered that again. "I'm eager to put the last twenty years behind us as well and to move into a prosperous future together."

"As am I," Little Reed said, rising and helping me up too. "Thank you for the delicious meal and the exquisite chocolate, but we should retire for the night. We're leaving for Acolman before dawn tomorrow."

But we didn't get more than a few steps down the hall before Nahuacatl called out to us. He looked nervous as he approached. "Forgive me for delaying you," he said with a bow. "But I was wondering if I might have a moment of your time, to discuss a...political matter with you, Lord Topiltzin?"

Little Reed's brow creased but I patted his arm, and said, "It would be better if I discussed this matter with him, My Lord, so go on ahead without me."

Nahuacatl looked at me with an expression of horror, as if he hadn't expected me to know what this was all about. Or perhaps that I'd be so bold as to suggest that he should discuss marrying me *with me* instead of with Little Reed.

Little Reed hesitated until I gave him a reassuring smile then he left, taking his guards with him. Mine remained nearby.

Nahuacatl cast his eyes down as he said, "Please forgive me if I've offended you, My Lady. I was only following traditional protocols—"

"I know you were, My Lord, but the fact that Topiltzin and I share the throne has made it necessary to...change the way some things have been done in the past. You understand?"

He nodded, his cheeks flushed with youthful embarrassment. "Then my sister told you of my intentions?"

"She did, and I'm flattered by your interest."

The desire scoffed. *Flattered? About being treated like an empty field in need of planting?* I felt it itching to take over my tongue, but I held it back. There was no need to be unduly harsh on Nahuacatl when he was just doing as his father told him.

"May I ask you something, My Lord?" I went on.

"Please do, My Lady," he said.

"How old are you?"

"Nineteen winters."

"Still so young yet. Forgive my asking, but why ever would you want to marry a woman eight years your senior? I said goodbye to my best childbearing years before you even went into your first battle, and Lord Black Otter never succeeded in begetting children with me—and not for lack of trying." I laughed, trying to sound embarrassed, but the desire seethed. "Surely Chimalhuacan's future king deserves better than his former ally's widow."

Nahuacatl started to speak, but when I added, "And surely this isn't some scheme to attach our kingdoms, at both of our expenses," he snapped his mouth shut.

"I didn't realize...the gap in our ages was so vast." He was suddenly sweating, not wanting to admit his father's ploy. "You appear much younger than twenty-seven."

The desire growled, fighting to take control, and take Nahuacatl to task for his evasion, but I held my ground. "You flatter me, My Lord. But even if not for my advanced age, I couldn't accept a proposal. I've taken a vow of chastity in Quetzalcoatl's name, so even if we did marry, I couldn't give you an heir. I cannot—in good conscience—trick you into an unconsummated marriage. And having already been one of several women in a man's household...well, as the joint ruler of the throne, I'm in a position to say I will not go through that again."

Nahuacatl nodded. "Forgive me, My Lady."

"There is nothing to forgive. These are interesting times, for everyone. We no longer need to mindlessly follow the old ways; not only can we make friends with our former enemies, but we can also determine our own futures, both men and women. Surely there is a lovely young woman that makes your heart ache like no other?" When he blushed, I chuckled and suggested, "She's the one you should be asking to tie your cape to, My Lord. And I can't imagine her saying no to such an intelligent, kind-hearted man such as yourself. Best ask her before someone else does."

The thought so appealed to him he started walking away, excitement on his face, but he paused to tell me, "Thank you for your time, My Lady, and your kind words."

I bowed my head as he hurried off. See? It wasn't always necessary to tear people apart.

No, the desire rumbled. *But if we did, next time he would have thought twice about toeing the same old lines of thinking. We already spent far too much of our life bending to the whims of self-important men.*

CHAPTER FOUR

It took two days to reach Acolman, but I remember little of the journey, for I spent most of the time sleeping in the litter. It was just as well anyway, as Little Reed was able to spend most of his time with his friend. But I wanted some time with Citlallotoc too; we'd developed a friendship while he helped me run the city during Little Reed's recovery, and I'd miss him, but not as much as Little Reed would. With Little Reed having lived far from home in the army for a ten-year stretch, Citlallotoc had likely known him as long as I had.

When I was awake I watched them from a distance, letting them have those final days together without distraction and not pretending that my friendship with Citlallotoc was as important as his with Little Reed. But when we reached Acolman and met Citlallotoc's younger brother, Huemac—who was holding the throne for him—the reality hit me hard. I wept when we gathered in the courtyard to go to Teotihuacan for the next few days while Citlallotoc did the penance and religious rituals necessary to take his rightful throne.

"Are you feeling well, My Lady?" Citlallotoc asked me when my turn came to say goodbye to him.

I nodded, the tears flowing freely. "I'm so happy for you. I know how difficult it is to be denied your rightful throne, and you and Topiltzin fought so long and hard to get it back...I'm so happy for you."

He smiled. "We did fight for it a very long time, didn't we?"

I hugged him tightly—the last time I'd be allowed to do such a thing—and whispered, "Thank you for everything you've done for us, Citlallotoc; for being Topiltzin's loyal friend, and for saving him from Red Flint, and standing for him on the battlefield when he couldn't do it himself. I shall never forget any of it."

He didn't answer at first, merely patted my back, and I imagined him shedding a few tears of his own, but I laughed that off. Citlallotoc wasn't a sentimental creature, and when I pulled away from him to wipe away my tears, he smiled back at me. But his smile looked unusually strained. "It has been an honor to serve you and your brother, My Lady, and I shall take to heart every leadership lesson Topiltzin taught me. And no god will be held above Quetzalcoatl here in Acolman."

I kissed his cheek before finally letting him move off down the line to Little Reed, who had been watching us with a proud yet sad smile. He embraced Citlallotoc as well and murmured his goodbyes while he gripped his arm. "We'll be back in time for the coronation," Little Reed promised. "The gods themselves wouldn't let me miss it."

Citlallotoc nodded but said little as Little Reed helped me up into the litter before following me inside. Little Reed sat at the curtain watching the city fade in the distance as we left, letting the mask he wore for everyone but me slip away. "Strange," he muttered, once he finally closed the curtain.

"What?"

"I'm so very glad for him, and yet...I feel as if I'm losing a piece of myself in all this."

I nodded and put my arm around his shoulder, hugging him. "I know what you mean. If Malinalli ever left...I don't know that I'd ever be all right again. After everything we've been through together...she's family to me."

"Yes, he's that important," he admitted. "I didn't expect that at all."

It took only a couple of hours to reach Teotihuacan, to the northeast of Acolman, and as with the previous journey, I slept for most of it. By the time I woke up, famished and grumpy, our men had already set up camp and Little Reed suggested I get something to eat before retiring for the rest of the day. "Tomorrow we start the fast, so best stock up now," he reminded me, handing me two tlaxcallis as he filled my bowl with stewed beans.

I avoided looking at him while I ate; hunger always brought on the desire, but it waned with the second bowl of beans. I ate yet more after that, finishing off the meal with a third tlaxcalli; I couldn't remember the last time I'd eaten so much and I went to bed feeling very full.

But I woke before sunrise, feeling intensely ill. I stumbled out of my tent and wobbled down the passageway to the water yard.

But once there, memories of the last time I'd been there set me into a panic; the high priest Ahexotl had found me alone, retching after a long night of ritual drinking. I remembered it all with a sickening clarity: his thick body pinning me against the water jars, the horrid taste of sour octli as he forced his tongue into my mouth, my nose touching the water as he held my head down over the water jar, threatening to drown me if I made a sound. *I'll leave you virginal enough,* he'd breathed on my neck. *And you can owe me again for that favor.* The shame and fear shooting through me brought up everything I'd eaten until my stomach couldn't heave anymore.

"Do you need help, My Lady?" someone called, and I nearly fled for the cover of the water jars. At the last moment I recognized my guard's voice, but I still shivered, crouched in the corner next to the water jars, feeling horribly exposed.

No hurt, another voice said—a child's voice, the same one I'd heard by the lake a few days ago. The tingling in my limbs intensified and a twinge of anger roiled inside me. *No hurt,* it repeated. The protectiveness in the voice made my heartbeat slow.

"Are you all right, Lady Quetzalpetlatl?" the guard called again. "Should we come in to help you?"

I finally found my tongue. "I'm fine. I just need a moment, thank you."

"We're waiting out here if you need us," my other guard said.

I rose, still shaking, but now because I felt as if magic were dripping off me. *If only I'd felt so powerful when Ahexotl attacked me,* I thought as I scooped handfuls of water from the rain jar, rinsing the foul taste from my mouth. *I would have set him on fire and watched him burn, to ensure he didn't get away.* My stomach clenched painfully, making me take deep, calming breaths, and I stood there, letting the anger drain from me until the tingling became little more than a background sensation.

We were supposed to start a two-day fast, but my stomach hurt so much that I took a tlaxcalli anyway, to help settle it. Little Reed didn't scold me but instead eyed me with concern. As we walked to the temple of the Feathered Serpent to pray, he said, "Your guards told me you got sick this morning."

"It's nothing," I said. "I think I over-ate last night."

"If you're ill, you shouldn't do a full fast," he insisted. "It's enough to give up chilis and salt."

"I appreciate your concern, but really, I'm fine." I hated the idea of not being as strong as him, especially about something I had years of practice with. True, hunger always aggravated my sexual desire, and I had no legitimate means of satiating that anymore. But if Little Reed could control himself, I could as well.

Except fasting probably doesn't affect him the way it affects you, I thought as we climbed the stairs. It was always on the tip of my tongue to ask Malinalli if she experienced something similar, but anytime I really thought about it, I couldn't bring myself to ask. It sounded so ridiculous that the two should have any connection to each other; they were both appetites, but I could choose to go without the latter while the former was a necessity. I had to blame myself for this conflation, for in my early years as a priestess, rather than feel the true pangs of hunger, I'd sought sexual gratification with the god as a distraction. And it had allowed me to vicariously be with Little Reed, since the god shared his face. My tendency to indulge one appetite to forget the other caused this bodily confusion and I'd have to work at un-training myself.

How amusing. It wasn't the same voice as earlier that morning; I knew the sound of my desire well, and while it often made me feel powerful, it also seemed depraved. *That's the stupid priestly training speaking,* it whispered with a laugh. *Leave it to humans to think it a good thing to feel shame for the gifts the gods give them.*

I'm not ashamed, I fired back, my temper rising.

You can lie to everyone else, but you can't lie to yourself. I'm the reason people listen to you at all; I am the fire burning in the bellies of all women, the flame that men—in their pathetic weakness—fear and try to control with their stupid little rules; they try to crush me and call me evil, and you only validate their stupidity by trying to silence me. Without me, you're only half a being, incomplete—exactly what they want you to be.

Those words reminded me of what Xolotl had told me that day on the battlefield, sending a chill through me: *You are the fire in women who won't bow to the whims of men or gods. Quetzalcoatl gave humanity life, but you give them reason to want that gift.* I felt more confused than ever. What did it all mean?

Stop playing the game by their rules and you'll understand.

¤

For a while I was able to sit with Little Reed, praying silently and meditating, but the single tlaxcalli didn't last long. The internal rumbling and gurgling grew steadily more distracting, but by noontime, it gave way to nervous fidgeting as I tried to quell the tickle of desire building inside me.

The day wasn't particularly hot, with blankets of clouds blotting out the sun, but I felt so hot that I thought—more than once—I should take off my priestly robe, to cool down. I usually didn't notice Little Reed's scent unless we were standing very close, but today it carried on the gentle breeze: spicy copal soap mixed with the pungent flowers he rubbed on to combat odor throughout the day. It was as enticing as the aroma of roasting venison. Soon I couldn't focus long enough to even think about meditating.

But when the voice started whispering that I should forget all this meditation nonsense and lay Little Reed on the stone platform and make him feel manly, I had to get away. Fearing the voice would take over, I tried to leave quietly, hoping Little Reed wouldn't notice, but as soon as I reached the stairs, he called after me.

"Where are you going?"

I didn't dare look back at him despite the concern in his voice. "I'm going somewhere else to pray."

"Really? Why?"

I floundered for an excuse that wouldn't raise more questions.

"Are you all right?" he asked. Hearing his sandals on the stone as he walked up to me, I finally took a deep breath and looked at him.

I expected the desire to roar up and take over as it had always done with Black Otter, but instead a different feeling rose in me; an aching in my heart that made me want to cry. I wanted to be in his arms, with him holding me and reassuring me that there was nothing wrong with me, that everyone fought these internal struggles just as I did, even if in my heart I knew they didn't. And that no matter how different—how abnormal—I was, he would love me regardless.

For a moment I thought of telling him everything. But how does one confess yearnings to sexually devour every man she sees as if they were food instead of people, and not seem a lunatic? I couldn't even convince *myself* that I wasn't sick and crazy. "I need to be alone for a while," I finally said. "The feeling here...it's not right for me, so I'm going to find somewhere where I am attuned to the god." Seeing disappointment cross his face, I asked, "You feel that sometimes, don't you? That having others around you can interfere with your spiritual connection to the god?"

"I do, and I understand. Please, don't let me keep you any longer. Go and find the place you need. I'll see you later tonight."

I kissed his cheek quickly—he seemed to need it as much as I did—then I fled down the stairs, fearing the desire would take over. I caught sight of my guards moving to follow me—*Two of them at once! Now wouldn't that be interesting?*—so I hurried on by, keeping a distance from them as I walked out onto the Avenue of the Dead, hoping I could outrun the incessant voice in my mind.

Uncertain where to go, I let my intuition lead me; to my surprise, it took me all the way to the opposite end of the huge precinct, to the Temple of the Moon. But I didn't want to be there either; that was where I'd cut off two of my fingers to summon Quetzalcoatl, to save us from attacking Chichimecs. The memory made my right hand sting where my two outer fingers used to be, prompting me to squeeze it with my other hand.

But this was where the gods had led me, so I took a deep breath and started up the stairs. After a few steps, I stopped to tell my guards, "Stay here. I'll be fine by myself." They looked ready to argue but nodded and let me go. As I continued up, I heard one of them suggest the other go keep watch on the other side of the pyramid. I was making their jobs harder, but I was afraid what might happen if I let them come with me.

When I reached the summit, I turned to look out at Lake Metzliapan. The clouds had cleared, letting the sun shine on the water's shimmering surface. I couldn't see Culhuacan in the distance, but Tultepec shone mirage-like on the opposite shore. To the northwest of the lake, scrub forest stretched for days before opening onto a grass plain bordering the desert.

As I stared at it, my breath caught. In the vision long ago, Quetzalcoatl had shown me temples, buildings, and a magnificent palace filling that land, but I recognized the underlying topography. *That's where we're to build the god's sacred city,* I realized, excitement igniting a righteous flame in my chest.

Home? the child's voice suddenly whispered in my head, startling me. I tried ignoring it, as I often did with the desire, but it asked again, *Home?*

Feeling foolish, I answered, *Maybe.*

Maybe? It didn't know the word.

If the god wishes it, I answered.

God?

I didn't even try to answer that one. But my mind wandered to memories of sitting in front of Quetzalcoatl on the platform outside the Temple of the Feathered Serpent in the Divine Dream, gazing longingly into his eyes—Little Reed's eyes—as the flakes of Love drifted lazily from the sky upon us, our relationship moments away from changing forever. How his touch had melted away my dress, the feathery tickle as he kissed my neck, and that feeling of excitement that, for a few years at least, had been enough....

Tatli!

I started again, unnerved to be interrupted in such thoughts. I should have been praying, not daydreaming about those bygone days when I'd been shameful enough to treat Quetzalcoatl as if he were no better than a mere mortal. I sat and closed my eyes. I didn't have the patience for whatever stupid game the desire was playing with me now.

Why would you play games with yourself? the familiar voice of my desire asked. The child-voice still babbled incoherently in the background with an occasional familiar word thrown in.

I opened my eyes, my heart faltering.

He is annoying, isn't he? the desire growled.

My mouth went dry. "He?" I looked at the front of my robe, to my abdomen hidden beneath the folds, but when I set my hand over it, I felt as if I'd been struck by lightning. *The exhaustion, the sickness this morning—* "No, no, no," I murmured, struggling to my feet. I hurried down the temple stairs, each step more desperate than the one before. *I must check my calendar journal!*

But I already knew what I'd find in there; my perfect memory made such a journal unnecessary, but Nimilitzli had taught me to keep it religiously and so I always did, out of habit. Still, I needed to see it, in ink, in tangible form, to confirm what my gut already knew: between nursing Little Reed back from his wound, handling city business during his recovery, and restarting Quetzalcoatl's cult in Culhuacan, I'd completely overlooked the fact that I hadn't bled for over two months.

Back at camp, I ducked into my tent and immediately emptied one satchel then a second, until I found the little stack of fig bark papers bound between buckskin covers. I'd made a new one when I first came to Culhuacan, since I'd lost my old one in the fires in Xochicalco. Most of the pages were empty, but when I read over my fine Mayan script on the last page I'd written on, my stomach clenched. "Dear gods, I'm pregnant!" I whispered, lips trembling.

And if the child-voice was to be believed, the god was the father.

I flashed back to that fateful day in Quetzalcoatl's temple in Xochicalco: my mother's face pale and drawn, Nimilitzli kneeling in a pool of her blood, trying to stop my mother from bleeding to death. *Bearing a child is dangerous enough without involving the gods,* my uncle had warned me. *She should cast it away or she'll never see her own grandchildren.* Would that be me too?

But why am I listening to some disembodied voice in my head? I scolded myself. *Who's to say Black Otter isn't the father?* Blinking back tears, I picked up the journal again and reread the notes I'd written on the last day I'd bled.

It was the week Black Otter had left to negotiate my release with Little Reed, and within hours of his return, his father's guards had shot him dead out on the lake. No, there was only one possible father, and I would end up dead like my mother.

I dropped the journal and covered my eyes, unable to breathe. *It must have happened when Quetzalcoatl possessed me on the battlefield,* I thought, shaking with rising anger. *He said we would be together in the real world someday, but who would have thought he was being so esoteric?*

Why angry? the child-voice asked, confused.

"Shut up!" I snarled. To my relief, it fell silent again. What would Little Reed think when I told him? He would think it was Black Otter's, of course, and Black Otter had insisted that Little Reed would kill any child of mine he thought came from my former husband—

That's nonsense. The child isn't Black Otter's, and even if it was...there's no way in Mictlan Little Reed would do something so horrible. He will love any child I gave birth to, regardless of its parentage.

But I didn't want children, and I certainly didn't want to die. I didn't ask for any of this, and Quetzalcoatl hadn't asked me if I accepted this risk; he at least gave my mother the choice, so why hadn't he granted me the same? I turned on my side and pulled my knees to my chest, struggling to hold back the sobs. *How could the god I love so dearly do this to me?*

When I finally left my tent, I went to the cooking fire to get something to eat. There was no use fasting; with a child growing inside me, stealing everything, it was only a matter of time before the desire took over and I broke my vow to heaven. Would it cost Little Reed his life? I didn't want to find out, but I was already eyeing my guards with a savage hunger that disturbed me.

As I sat next to the fire, filling my empty belly with one tlaxcalli after another, a new thought occurred to me. *I could cast it away.* Part of me cried sacrilege, but the other part gritted her teeth and barked about letting gods or men dictate my future. No, this would be my decision, my choice, no one else's. That voice I kept trying to silence was right; no more playing the game by everyone else's rules. This was my life, and I would choose my sacrifices myself, not have them foisted on me.

¤

After three days in Teotihuacan, we went back to Acolman for Citlallotoc's coronation. The kings of our various allied cities were already there, and everyone was atwitter with rumors. "The coronation ceremony has been pushed back two days," King Growling Monkey of Xochimilco told us at the feast the night we arrived. "I tried to get some answers, but no one will even let me talk to Huemac, let alone Citlallotoc."

After dinner, I sat in my private steam bath, soaking up the humidity and contemplating my next step. Nimilitzli had shown me long ago how to mix and administer the medicine for ending a pregnancy, but she'd also told me that the side-effects were troublesome: heavy bleeding, vomiting, and—depending how far along the pregnancy was—intense abdominal pains similar to those experienced during labor. If I took it tonight, by morning I wouldn't be able to leave bed for a least a week and, thinking perhaps I was dying, Little Reed might cancel our trip north, forcing us to wait until next spring before resuming the search for my father's bones. We couldn't afford to wait another year though; Smoking Mirror's cult could rise to power once more and war could break out again. The sooner we started building the god's new city, the better. We had to find my father's bones before the end of summer to keep on the path the god laid out for us.

We would only be gone for a few more months at most, but what if I didn't have even that much time left to act? Three months into her pregnancy with Little Reed, my mother was dead. What if this child was growing just as fast? The possession had happened a little over two months ago....

Except, when I looked at my bare belly, I realized I wasn't even showing yet; at this point, my mother had been very obviously pregnant. I didn't look as if I lived the austere life of most religious leaders—thanks to the daily feasting the last four months—but I didn't look pregnant either. This child wasn't growing at the accelerated rate that Little Reed had, despite their shared paternity.

I'll wait until we get back to Culhuacan, I decided as I dressed in clean clothing. I went to Little Reed's quarters, to walk back to the great hall together and wait for news with all our allies.

But shortly after I arrived at my brother's quarters, Little Reed's guards alerted us that Citlallotoc had sought us out.

To my surprise, he wasn't wearing royal regalia when he came in, but rather his usual cotton armor and eagle-feather shirt. He carried his carved wooden eagle knight helmet under his arm. He immediately went to his knees before Little Reed and bowed in supplication. Before he could say anything, Little Reed took him by the arm. "What are you doing? You don't bow to me, My Lord. You're going to be king in a few days."

Citlallotoc sat up but refused to rise any further. "Forgive me, My Lord, but I have given that honor to my brother."

I gasped. "Why in Mictlan would you do that?"

For a moment, Citlallotoc looked uncomfortable, but he said, "I have served with you a very long time, My Lord, and while I used to have aspirations to my father's throne, I found that, with the years, my heart was calling me elsewhere. Please forgive me for not being forthright about this when I first realized it, but I didn't want to disappoint you, for you kept your promise to return my throne. And I thought maybe if I came here and went through with the fasting and purifying ceremonies, my heart would follow me to the throne, as I thought it should."

"What are you saying?" Little Reed asked, gripping Citlallotoc's shoulder.

"You have taught me to listen to the gods, particularly Quetzalcoatl, and within the last two days, I realized he was telling me I don't belong on Acolman's throne. I belong at your side, defending you and your family, and seeing his good works come to fruition, the same thing I have been doing for nearly ten years."

Little Reed went to his own knees in front of Citlallotoc. "If you do this...it means renouncing any claim at all to your family's throne. You can't go back on it."

"I've already done so in private, to my brother," Citlallotoc said. "He's going through all the ceremonies now, and I'll make the formal abdication at the coronation ceremony in two days." Sensing Little Reed's hesitation, he added, "I'm positive about this, Topiltzin. The first time I met you...I knew you were a man destined for greatness, a man I could give my devotion to without regret or hesitation. Anybody can be a king, but it takes a special man to serve the son of a god, and I hope in my heart I'm that man."

Little Reed beamed as he rose to his feet and told Citlallotoc to bow his head. He motioned me to his side. "Do you pledge to defend and serve your king and queen with faith and loyalty?"

"With my life," Citlallotoc promised. "I also pledge to protect your children, and to treat them with the same love and respect I would give my own."

His words brought forth a torrent of guilt. Only days ago I'd worried about Little Reed having no heir because of his promise, and here I was planning to cast off a child who could be the next king. *You would throw your life away for some stupid tradition that thinks blood equals the ability to rule intelligently?* the desire asked, disgusted. *And only because the child is male?*

"Do you pledge that same loyalty and faith to Quetzalcoatl?" Little Reed went on.

"I do," Citlallotoc said. "And may the gods curse my tonalli should I fail in any of this."

Little Reed motioned for him to rise and when he did, he embraced him tightly. "From this day forth, I shall call you my brother, for that is what you've always been to me," he said.

CHAPTER FIVE

We stayed a week in Acolman celebrating Huemac's ascension before traveling north again, following the coast of Lake Metzliapan. I'd never been so far from home. There were no roads to follow anymore, only game trails winding through the forests and meadows. Black and orange birds shrieked constantly from the tall grasses, and we subsisted on rabbits our soldiers shot with their arrows. Occasionally we came upon quail nests or berry bushes to give a welcome reprieve from the steady diet of meat waging war on my bowels.

Since realizing the source of my exhaustion, I'd increased my food intake and found sitting in the litter tedious, and so took to walking with Little Reed and Citlallotoc among the soldiers. At first I struggled to listen to the conversations over the suddenly constant flow of babble in my head; it was especially bad at night, when I lay alone in my tent, staring up at the ceiling with nothing to keep me from listening. Those first few days I thought I might go crazy, but eventually it receded to the background, as with music I'd learned to tolerate if not enjoy; and by a week into our travels north, it had become a lullaby as I crawled under my blankets to fall asleep.

Eventually the forests opened onto a plain of golden grasses sprouting from black fertile earth. "Good for farming," Little Reed noted as he let the moist, black dirt break apart between his fingers. He rose and looked into the north again. "Do you recognize it?"

I nodded. "We're finally here."

"And there's the copal grove where we buried the king's bones," Amoxtli said, pointing to a large cluster of trees a quarter hour's walk away.

"Excellent!" Little Reed slapped his hands together to dust off the dirt. "We can have them dug up before nightfall."

Our caravan wound its way through the tall, golden grass, and once we reached the outskirts of the grove, Little Reed told Citlallotoc to set up camp. From there, Little Reed and I gathered a dozen soldiers, and with their digging sticks upon their shoulders, we set off into the trees, following Amoxtli. We picked our way over fallen logs and around clusters of thorny bushes, the layer of decaying leaves and twigs crunching under our feet.

After what seemed forever, Amoxtli finally stopped and looked around. He approached a gnarled old tree and leaned against it as he swept the mat of leaves and dirt away from its roots. "Right here," he said.

Little Reed motioned to the others and they hurried forward, their digging sticks ready.

The afternoon heat made my head pound as the child's voice babbled joyfully, so I sat on a log and watched, the anticipation of finally finding my father's bones making my stomach cramp. Little Reed brought me a water skin as the men chopped into the damp earth with their wooden blades. "Nervous?"

"A little." I swallowed the water, grateful for how fast it settled my stomach.

Smiling, he gripped my shoulder, reassuring. "I'm anxious too, but everything will be all right."

The moments spilled past in an endless march punctuated with the sounds of chopping through soil. I remained sitting on the log, waiting for the telltale thump of wood against stone; Little Reed paced, occasionally glancing over the men's shoulders to check their progress.

"Are you sure this is the right place, Cousin?" Little Reed asked Amoxtli after they'd been at it for an hour.

"I'm positive, Your Majesty. We should have hit it by now."

"There's nothing here," one of the soldiers grumbled, wiping the sweat from his brow.

I stood up, my legs stiff from sitting. "What's going on?"

"The box isn't here," Little Reed said.

Amoxtli shook his head. "I don't understand. I buried it myself!"

Little Reed set a hand on Amoxtli's shoulder. "I believe you, Cousin. It's just not here anymore."

Frustration vied with fear in my stomach. If we couldn't find my father's bones, how were we to know where to build the god's temple? "What are we to do now?"

Scratching his head, Little Reed said, "Let's go back to camp and regroup. After a good night's sleep, we'll decide our next step."

We traipsed back the way we'd come, following the path we'd made on the way in. But within a few moments, one of the guards hooted in alarm.

I looked to the right to see a group of men lurking among the trees a number of paces away from us. They wore bone jewelry and black tattoos decorated the faces peering at us around the sides of the trunks.

Chichimecs!

When the soldiers rushed to stand between the Chichimecs and me and Little Reed, Little Reed ordered them to halt. Our soldiers held their ground, their grips tight on their digging sticks. The Chichimecs showed us their obsidian-bladed spears.

Little Reed stepped slowly in front of his men. "We won't harm you," he called, holding his hands out in front of him to show he carried no weapons.

The Chichimecs eyed him before casting their gazes around at our soldiers. The tension in the air raised the hairs on my neck; the voice that had been babbling in my head all day had fallen quiet. Birds and locusts filled the nervous silence with their music.

"We intend no harm," Little Reed repeated.

The Chichimecs exchanged puzzled looks and one muttered to the others in a strange dialect I didn't recognize.

Little Reed must have known it though, for he immediately matched it when he spoke next. The Chichimecs' eyes widened, but then they started answering him, speaking at a staccato pace. Slowly their postures relaxed, and eventually the men—ten in all—stepped out from behind the shelter of the trees. After another exchange, they pointed to the north. Little Reed bowed and they returned the gesture, almost as an afterthought; obviously he told them nothing about us being royalty, and because he dressed like an ordinary soldier, his rank wasn't obvious.

Little Reed signaled everyone to lower their weapons. "It seems this area is not uninhabited after all. They've agreed to take us to their chief, Ten Spines."

The god hadn't mentioned anything about having to liberate the land from barbarians before building on it. *But the god didn't show you the entire battle plan, did he?* My hand wandered to my stomach as the child's voice resumed its nonsense in my head, the sound oddly comforting.

As we walked back to our own camp in the company of our new companions, I told Little Reed, "I didn't know you spoke Chichimec."

"It isn't so difficult; it's similar to our language, just different pronunciations. I can teach you sometime."

As soon as we emerged from the trees, the camp guards raised the alert and Citlallotoc hurried out to greet us, a look of concern on his face. Even when Little Reed assured him everything was all right and informed him we were going to see the chief, he still didn't relax and kept a close watch on the group of Chichimecs lingering at the outskirts of our camp. "Are you certain this is a good idea, My Lord? Their kind is prone to treachery."

"No more than our kind, my friend," Little Reed answered, giving him a pat on the shoulder.

"I should come with you."

"No, stay here and make sure our camp is secure. If things do go sour, I need you to get our people out of here quickly."

"If you believe there is danger, then I object to you leaving with them."

"I don't believe there is, but I don't make a habit of not considering all possibilities."

Citlallotoc looked as if he wished to continue arguing, but he knew when to follow orders. He said no more as we left, our personal guards escorting us.

We followed the Chichimecs down a winding game trail to a river. The path opened up onto a camp consisting of at least twenty deer-skin tents circling several cooking fires. The women washing laundry at the riverside looked up from their work, curious, and several children followed us from a distance. When we reached the center of camp, our escorts took us to the largest tent. They signaled us to wait then ducked inside.

I looked around, taking in this strange, primitive setting. The tents were clustered close together, and I caught sight of a few young boys watching us from behind the ones across the central fire. A bent old man sat outside his tent, dressed only in a ragged rabbit-skin loincloth, knapping a large chunk of obsidian into the smaller cores used for spears and arrow tips. He wiped his nose with his wrist when he met my gaze but went back to his work, uninterested. A girl sitting at the fire, though—perhaps fifteen, sixteen years old—watched us with open curiosity while the old woman next to her mended a buckskin shirt. When the girl noticed my gaze, she quickly turned to the woman, whispering; the old woman merely chuckled and pointed at the cooking pot, which the girl took to stirring earnestly while still casting furtive glances in my direction. I cast her a smile, which she returned with cautious friendliness.

The flap on the tent parted and a large, battle-scarred man wearing a bone-and-feather headdress stepped out, a broad smile on his face. The other men followed him out but started when he bowed to Little Reed. "Lord Topiltzin, the Revered Speaker of the Tolteca, it is an honor to finally meet you," the man said in our tongue. The others looked at each other, puzzled, but they soon followed suit, bowing to Little Reed as well.

Little Reed returned the gesture. "You've heard of me, Lord Ten Spines?"

"I may not live in the valley anymore, but I keep apprised of what transpires there. I congratulate you on your ascension to Culhuacan's throne; the stars say your reign will be the beginning of great things for all peoples, so it is an honor to host you here in my humble camp."

"The honor is all mine, and I thank you for taking our audience."

Ten Spines waved his words off with a laugh. "The pleasure is all *mine*." His gaze wandered to me standing behind Little Reed, and that familiar glaze men often got when they looked at me settled over his eyes. "And is this lovely blossom your wife, Your Majesty?"

Little Reed urged me forward by the elbow. "This is my sister, Lady Quetzalpetlatl. We co-rule, sharing the throne in Culhuacan."

I bowed to Ten Spines, and to my relief, he quickly shook off the distraction and gestured to the old woman at the fire. "My wife, Lady

Bitter Rabbit, and that is my eldest daughter, Mitotia." He finished introductions by pointing at the girl. To me he added, "They would appreciate whatever help you can give them preparing the noon meal while your brother and I speak business."

Little Reed cleared his throat, his posture tense, but I smiled and said, "I'd be honored to help, My Lord." When Little Reed looked at me, questions in his eyes, I whispered, "We're in his camp, so let's respect his ways. Besides, you can't make any actual treaties or alliances without me, so let's ease him into our way of thinking."

"You will join us once the meal is ready?"

"Of course."

Little Reed and Ten Spines retreated into the large tent, and I went to the cooking fire, my guards remaining nearby. I knelt on one of the ratty mats. "What are we cooking?" I asked Bitter Rabbit as I inhaled the aromatic steam above the boiling pot.

She showed me her gapped smile but said nothing.

"She doesn't understand your language," Mitotia replied as she stirred the pot.

"But you do," I noted, impressed.

Mitotia nodded. "My father spent his formative years traveling around the south."

"You speak it very well. Your father taught it to you?" Given how casually Ten Spines had dismissed me, it surprised me that he would do so.

"Sort of," Mitotia said with a blush. "He was teaching my brother and I asked him to teach me too, but he refused, saying it would ruin my disposition for marriage. So I hid outside his tent and listened in and learned as he taught my brother."

I burst out laughing. "That's something I would have done." I liked Mitotia already.

¤

Ten Spines and Little Reed were deep in discussion when Mitotia and I brought the finished stew into the chief's tent. Little Reed immediately rose to help me with the pot while Ten Spines remained sitting, smoking a long cylindrical pipe. Once Mitotia had filled two tortoise shell bowls for the men, Ten Spines tried to dismiss both of us, but this time Little Reed didn't hesitate.

"Forgive me, and I know this will sound strange and maybe even improper, but when I said that Lady Quetzalpetlatl and I co-rule Culhuacan, I meant that we share power equally. We make all political decisions together, and as the highest priests of the Feathered Serpent's order, we both lead our citizens in their spiritual lives. It's imperative we involve her in all treaty discussions, and I cannot proceed any further if that is an issue for you."

Ten Spines looked from Little Reed to me and back again, an amused expression on his face. It softened though when he saw Little Reed was serious. He cleared his throat before turning to me again. "Forgive my behavior, Lady Quetzalpetlatl. I'd heard that Lord Topiltzin's ways were...different than most, but I didn't realize...." He sat straighter, looking distinctly uncomfortable. "I apologize for insulting you."

I sat next to Little Reed, who ladled out some stew for me. "I was not insulted, My Lord. I'm quite used to these kinds of confusions, for as you said, my brother's ways are strange to many." Would there ever be a time when my worth would be judged by my own actions rather than everyone defining it by how Little Reed did things? *Someday,* I thought. *I'll make certain of it.* "Where are we in the discussions?"

"Lord Topiltzin was attempting to convince me that building a Tolteca city on our ancestral lands would somehow benefit us." Ten Spines set aside his pipe and picked up his bowl. "I'm concerned about the kinds of influences this project would bring to our people. The Tolteca have been in a near-constant state of warfare since before I was born, trying to keep the Chichimecs out of the valley, and yet now you seek to establish a Tolteca stronghold in the north."

I suppressed a smirk. He was worried about Tolteca influence after all the chaos and war his people had brought to us? In the days of my great-grandmother, women could be war queens, but the steady invasion of Chichimecs and their philosophies had worn that tradition away. It was little wonder that men such as Flame Tongue thought it perfectly acceptable to dismiss me. It would take years to undo the negative impact Chichimecs had brought to Tolteca culture.

"The valley is at peace for the first time since the fall of Teotihuacan," Little Reed pointed out.

"With all due respect, Lord Topiltzin, you've been on your throne a mere four months," Ten Spines said.

"That is true, but it's the goal of our new reign to keep it that way."

The tent flap burst open and another man came storming in. The stranger's hair dangled in greasy strands around his red-and-white-stripe-painted face, and bits of bone and string decorated his dingy black robe. He brought a wave of fury with him.

Our guards moved to intercept him. When Ten Spines assured them this new man wasn't a threat, they reluctantly retreated to their stations, but remained on alert.

"This is our shaman, Ueman," Ten Spines told us. "Please forgive his blustery entrance; he tends to the dramatic."

"Vile villains!" Ueman barked at us, his face livid.

"Pardon?" I asked, taken aback.

"They desecrated the sacred grove, My Lord!" Ueman told Ten Spines. "They were digging up the god's earth!"

The smile fell from Ten Spine's face, replaced with incredulity. "Is this true, Lord Topiltzin?"

After a tense pause, Little Reed said, "We were looking for something."

Ten Spines stiffened. "The copal grove is a sanctuary dedicated to the god of the hunt. It is a grave crime to disturb the ground."

"We meant no harm by it, My Lord," I assured him. "You see, we came north to retrieve my father's bones, which my cousin buried in the grove. If we'd known your people were here, and that the site was sacred, we absolutely wouldn't have gone forward with the search without consulting you."

Ueman's face turned even fiercer. "Bones? Bones!" He turned to Ten Spines. "They've come to steal the god's bones!"

"Well, they can't have them!" Ten Spines fired back, rising to his feet.

Little Reed stood too, holding his hands up for calm. "I'm afraid there's been a misunderstanding, My Lord. We seek the remains of a mortal king, not a religious artifact."

"Lies, My Lord!" Ueman hissed. "Tolteca treachery! They've come to take Mixcoatl away from us."

I blinked, startled, and puzzled. "Mixcoatl was my father."

"And now they call themselves children of a god? Blasphemy!"

They think my father's a god? I glanced at Little Reed; obviously bringing up his divine parentage now would be a mistake. To Ten Spines, I said, "My father's name was Mixcoatl, but he was not a god, I assure you. He was the king of Culhuacan, but my uncle Ihuitimal murdered him and usurped the throne. Topiltzin and I fought for nearly ten years to regain our rightful throne."

"We do not name our kings for gods," Ueman snarled. "That is the height of disrespect."

"And neither do we," Little Reed said. "The god Mixcoatl is unknown among the Tolteca. I'm sure there are gods we worship that are unknown to your people too."

"I can't believe you, Lord Topiltzin—of all people—can claim ignorance of who Mixcoatl is," Ten Spines said. "You claim to be Quetzalcoatl's high priest."

"We are the Feathered Serpent's high priests," I countered, my voice colored with growing irritation.

"Then you would know that Mixcoatl is Quetzalcoatl's father, My Lady."

I almost laughed but caught myself before losing control of my tongue. *What do these backwards, uncivilized people know of the gods?*

"At the beginning of summer, the god showed us where his bones were buried—inside the copal grove—and he instructed us to dig them up and take them with us when we left for the winter hunting grounds to the north." Ten Spines looked to Ueman for confirmation, and the shaman nodded firmly.

"That may well be," Little Reed said. "But I assure you that the bones you found were not the bones of any god; they belong to the mortal king of Culhuacan, and we've come to give him a proper burial, with full funerary rites. And Quetzalcoatl has instructed us to build a city upon the site where King Mixcoatl's bones are found—"

"Oh, so now they want our land too?" Ueman spouted. "Typical Tolteca scheming!" He barked something else to Ten Spines in their own language as well.

Little Reed said, "We would never dream of building anything without—"

"Enough!" Ten Spines sliced his hand through the air like a sword. "I'm sorry, Lord Topiltzin, Lady Quetzalpetlatl, but I must insist that you return to the valley immediately and not return."

I started to protest, but Little Reed stopped me with a gentle squeeze to my wrist.

"We shall do as you ask, My Lord, but may I beg your indulgence for just one night? We've been traveling almost nonstop for several weeks and our camp is already set up. Will you allow us one night to rest? We will leave before dawn tomorrow."

Ten Spines thought a moment, his face hard, but then he said, "We are not a pitiless people, so yes, you may have your one night." Ueman started to protest, but Ten Spines silenced him with a raised hand. "But remember that the gods know of any treachery you might be planning, and we will not hesitate to take every last one of you to the sacrifice if they command it."

"We promise no treachery," Little Reed replied. "And as a show of good faith, I invite you to station a patrol of warriors inside our camp, so you may rest easy with your decision to allow us to remain here tonight.

Nodding stiffly, Ten Spines said, "My men will escort you and your sister back to your camp."

ロ

Neither of us spoke as we returned to our own camp where our soldiers were busy working. Citlallotoc greeted us at the improvised fire pit our servants had made in the middle of camp. "How did the negotiations fare?"

"They are still not over. These men will remain in camp tonight—" Little Reed pointed to the Chichimecs who'd come with us—"so please let all of our men know they are to be treated as guests, with the utmost civility. Now, if you'll excuse us, Lady Quetzalpetlatl and I will need privacy for the next hour."

"Of course, Your Majesty." Citlallotoc eyed the Chichimecs though, the distaste plain on his face.

Little Reed and I retired to our tent. As soon as the flap was closed, I said, "I can't believe this! They have no right to take my father's bones like that! And I can't believe you let them!"

"I'm not *letting them*, Papalotl," Little Reed said with a chuckle. "This is where the god wants his city built, and I intend to convince Ten Spines to join us in this venture."

"Then why did you agree to us leaving tomorrow?" Would we return to Culhuacan and raise an army to take these lands by force? And could we even convince the valley's Chichimecs to mobilize against their own people still in the north?

"We won't be leaving. In fact, Ueman will convince Ten Spines that we are their friends."

"How?"

"He told Ten Spines he was going into the Divine Dream to get guidance from the gods on how to deal with us."

"Is that what he told Ten Spines when he started jabbering in their language?"

He nodded. "And we will go into the Divine Dream as well."

I hadn't visited the Divine Dream in almost three years, and much had changed for me since then; the last time I saw the god, we were still lovers, using the divine realm more for sex than religious inspiration, and after I thought I lost Little Reed forever, I swore off going back because it hurt too much seeing him in the god's face. But I was also haunted by how arrogant and disrespectful I'd been to the god, lying with him in the Divine Dream, selfishly using him as a substitute while my heart ached for Little Reed. It embarrassed me that I'd behaved so childishly, so pruriently.... I dreaded facing him again and having to answer questions about why I never came back after promising I would. "Must I go too?" I asked, trying to sound casual even as my stomach roiled. "I'm feeling very tired."

"I think it especially important that you go," Little Reed said. "Quetzalcoatl will assure Ueman of our good intensions, so we must be there to stand with the god, show Ueman we are united in our power and fealty to the god. And to each other."

I chewed my lip a moment before nodding. Little Reed was right. Now wasn't the time for timidity and childish embarrassment. I was the god's high priestess, professional in every regard, and I wouldn't let fear stand in the way of my duties.

I hadn't brought any teonanactl mushrooms with me, but Little Reed provided some from his own personal store which he kept in a plain, undecorated box. He mixed the dried mushrooms into two cups of octli— one for each of us—then we drank. I swallowed mine fast to make certain my fear didn't cause me to back down. My sinuses stung from the alcohol but it didn't quite mask the bitter taste of the mushrooms; my body reacted with heightened arousal, as if suddenly remembering why I'd so often drunk this concoction in the past. I squeezed my thighs together, positive that my desire was plain to see.

"Which mat do you want?" Little Reed asked, motioning to the two feathered prayer mats set up in front of our small idol of Quetzalcoatl. It was such a simple, courteous question and yet it made me sweat.

"Actually, I'm going to go to my room," I said. "I prefer to lie down while in the Divine Dream." I bit my tongue, mortified as soon as I said it, but quickly added, "I've fallen over before and hurt myself, so it's safer for me to lie down." I fumbled with the tent flap separating my sleeping quarters from the large anteroom, my cheeks aflame.

"Very well." Little Reed sat, oblivious to my embarrassment.

I ducked into my quarters and secured the flap behind me, breathing deeply. I stared at my bed, the desire rebounding—and bringing with it memories of the god's feathery touch, on my neck, my breasts, my thighs....

But I shook it off. I wasn't seventeen anymore; I had ten years on that foolish girl, and I was not only the high priestess, but the Queen of Culhuacan. I was stronger than this. I swallowed, calming myself, then lay on my bed and waited for the Divine Dream to take me away.

And waited. And waited. Eventually I drifted off to sleep, my body surrendering to the far greater desire for rest.

CHAPTER SIX

"Are you ready to go?" My eyes flashed open to find Little Reed kneeling next to me.

Except I wasn't in the tent any longer. I was in a room similar to mine in the palace back in Culhuacan, but bigger and more airy. When the breeze shifted the half-open curtains closing off the patio, the air smelled heady with flowers and heat; no hint of the brackish water smell of Lake Meztliapan or the cloying humidity that made the air feel thick in the lungs. "Where are we?" I asked, sitting up.

"The Divine Dream," Little Reed replied, taking my hand to help me to my feet. "We're inside the palace we will build in the god's new city."

"You've been here before?"

"The god has shown it to me often." Little Reed gave my hand a gentle squeeze. "Let's go and find Ueman."

As we went for the door leading out, I noticed movement off to my left, at a secondary doorway covered in a bright blue curtain. Embroidered dancing rabbits decorated the hem, but they moved as if alive, playing reed flutes and banging drums with their forepaws as they pranced and bounced about. The corner of the curtain lifted slightly and a real rabbit—tawny brown with glistening pine-pitch eyes—poked its head out. It peered at me, twitching its nose.

Little Reed and I stepped out of the room into a portico that extended in a square around a cozy garden choked with beds of bone flowers in full bloom. "This is our family garden," he told me as I looked around in awe. "Every council member's extended family shall have one in our palace, with their living quarters clustered around it, just like this; as will the priesthood as well." He pointed out the other doorways off the portico.

Opposite my own doorway, across the garden, the curtain on the doorway was light blue with a large white and green feathered serpent in the center—Little Reed's royal sigil. A walkway connected my side of the garden to his, meeting at a large flagstone patio in the middle. At the north end of the patio, a tall limestone statue of Quetzalcoatl in his feathered serpent form curled in a column up towards Heaven, watching over everything.

I glanced back at my own door curtain to find it was a strange murky grey color, as though smoke clung to it, obscuring its true color and pattern. I puzzled over that for a few moments as we left the garden for a hallway that led into the heart of the palace.

But catching a glimpse of our icpalli thrones in the great hall drove it from my thoughts. They looked so small in the giant room—it was at least three times the size of Culhuacan's great hall, and painted from floor ceiling with maps of our various allied cities. The ceiling itself was an illustration of the divine realm; the underworld loomed over the main doorway, and a winding stone staircase led up onto the mortal plane with its rivers and trees and mountains. That eventually gave way to the sky with Omeyocan hovering above our thrones. The various gods had been painted on the three planes, each doing the things they were known for: Tlaloc dumping pots of rain on the earth from the clouds, the Feathered Serpent moving the winds over the earth, Xipe Totec sowing the maize seeds with the blood dripping from his flayed skin, and Lord Death sitting on his throne of bones in Mictlan, his servant Xolotl sitting at his feet in dog-form. Even Smoking Mirror was in the mural, as a black jaguar rising from the smoke of a burning city.

Outside the great hall was a large vestibule whose roof was supported by columns of stone statues of all the gods. This opened onto a set of stairs overlooking a courtyard filled with boxes of flowers of every color and fragrance. The sacred precinct was also visible from the top of the stairs, and straight across from the palace was a large pyramid with an open-sided temple at the top.

"That's the Temple of the Feathered Serpent," Little Reed told me as we walked down the steps to the long walkway that opened onto the city itself. "That's probably where Ueman is."

And as always in the Divine Dream, fat flakes of Love fell from Omeyocan, covering everything and filling my nose with the sweet smell of bone flowers. It made my heart race with exhilaration.

The city wasn't empty either. The sacred precinct was teeming with people; tattooed Chichimecs walked among Tolteca nobles dressed in the styles unique to the various lake valley cities; some even walked and chatted together as if old friends—remarkably different to the dynamic between Tolteca and Chichimecs back in Culhuacan. No one bothered us as we cut through the crowds and made our way up the stairs of Quetzalcoatl's temple.

The platform was significantly larger than the ones on the pyramids in both Culhuacan and Xochicalco, but here the temple took up the entire area. As in the palace vestibule, large pillars—similar to the one back in the family garden—supported the roof. A gilded idol of the god—coiled upright with mouth gaping open, for the blood sacrifices—sat in the middle with feathered mats spread out in front of it. There was no altar as in the other temples.

Ueman was wandering around inside, gaping at everything in awe. When he noticed us standing under the roof at the front of the temple, he started. "What *is* all this?" he asked, coming to the front to stare at the city spread out below us.

Before either of us could answer, a familiar voice—deep and yet still so similar to Little Reed's—spoke up behind us. *This is the city I have asked Topiltzin and his queen Quetzalpetlatl to build for me.* When we all turned around, the feathered serpent column behind us began untwisting itself, dust and rubble flaking off as it moved.

Ueman gasped and nearly backed right over the side of the pyramid, but Little Reed grabbed his arm. "It's all right," Little Reed said. "He comes to me in such forms often."

Odd, for the god only came to me in such inhuman forms in the real world; in the Divine Dream, he was always a man, with quetzal feathers growing amongst his long black hair, and a touch that suggested his skin was covered in feathers even though he looked no different than Little Reed. My body ached with pitiful longing for the memory, and I hoped he wouldn't notice me as he slithered soundlessly across the floor to circle us.

But once he reached the stairs, he took to the air. The sleek stone feathers carved into his body ruffled in the wind, and when he fanned his long, glorious quetzal feathers around his head, I couldn't breathe. *He's so beautiful!* I thought, imagining him glowing brilliant white with a shimmering halo of emerald accenting his neck. My heart thudded, so sweetly painful.

Ueman went slowly to his knees, bewildered. "Forgive my reaction, My Lord, but the gods have never spoken so plainly to me."

There is no need for apologies, Quetzalcoatl said, hovering before us. *We gods do not often visit our followers in such ways, but this time I wanted to.*

Prostrating himself on the platform, Ueman said, "I am your humble servant, Most Precious Twin. What message do you wish me to bring back to your people?"

I understand your reticence in trusting Topiltzin, for he is but a mortal; but know that as my son he serves his father's will on earth, and together with Quetzalpetlatl will bring such peace as neither Chichimec nor Tolteca have known before.

Ueman started looking up, surprised, but he caught himself. "Lord Topiltzin...is your son, My Lord?"

Quetzalcoatl bobbed his head. *I placed him in the belly of a mortal woman so I might guide humanity out of the darkness and back into the light. He will bring an end to war, and enemies shall join together as friends and allies, and all shall reap the gift of prosperity and happiness. But they must open their hearts, for only then can they worship as their gods truly deserve.*

Ueman turned to stare up at Little Reed. "Forgive my doubting you, My Lord."

Little Reed shook his head. "It's quite all right."

Turning back to the god—but keeping his eyes downcast—Ueman asked, "Tell us what we must do, My Lord."

The god swam towards us, and for a moment I thought he was going to collide hard with us, stone crushing flesh and bone, but instead he passed among us as if he were wind, the tendrils of his essence reaching inside each of us; Ueman clutched his breast and wept while Little Reed breathed deep, smiling. The god's touch sent a tingling wave of pleasure rushing through me and I bit my lip to keep from moaning in ecstasy.

Build this very temple on the spot where you found the bones of the mortal king that shares the name of your tribal god; every odd stone shall be laid by a free Chichimec with earth upon their hands, for these are their ancestral lands; every even stone shall be laid by the hands of a free Tolteca, consecrated by each worker's own bloodletting, a small gift given in the name of the gods. For without both earth and water, nothing grows. The god's stone body returned inside the temple where it had started and slowly reformed the pillar it had once been. *Every temple to every god, every building erected, every street paved here in my sacred city will follow this same code, and the city will henceforth be known as Tollan.*

"And if we should fail in your task?" Little Reed asked.

Then the world shall fall further into the darkness already clawing for a foothold, Quetzalcoatl replied. *Nations shall rise and fall in endless war, spanning far and wide, and the temple steps will run slippery with the blood of countless victims, murdered to satisfy the hunger and power lusts of a few gods and their mortal allies. The bonds of brotherhood will fray, and when the Fifth Sun sets for the final time, it will be too late to keep them from snapping. A great shaking will reduce the cities and their temples to rubble, unleash plagues that devour my people from the inside out, and shatter all faith in the gods. The world will crumble, as will the memory of all that existed here.*

With those final words, the carved stone feathered serpent fell still, once again only a statue. The god had never been quite so ominous before, and hearing his predictions of the end of the world left me chilled.

"We shall not fail you, My Lord," Ueman promised. He looked around at the city with tears in his eyes.

"The god actually spoke to me!" he whispered. "All my life I've dreamed that Mixcoatl would come to me while I meditated with the peyotl and deem me worthy of providence—"

"But didn't Ten Spines say Mixcoatl told you to take the bones with you when you left for the winter?" I asked, trying to sound more puzzled than annoyed. Now I was certain he'd lied to us.

Ueman bowed his head. "A voice spoke to me in the Divine Dream, telling me to take the bones away, but I never saw the face of the one who said the words. I just assumed it was Mixcoatl himself."

Little Reed and I exchanged glances. I would bet my royal headdress it was Smoking Mirror who ordered the removal of my father's bones, to spoil our plans for the god's city.

"But now Mixcoatl has sent his son to bless me!" Ueman turned to look at Little Reed with eyes wide. "And Quetzalcoatl sent you for all of us!" He started to prostrate himself before Little Reed.

But Little Reed stopped him and instead helped him back up. "I don't seek to be anyone's god; I come to be a bridge between our peoples, to finally bring peace and a prosperous future for us all."

"We must speak with Ten Spines immediately!"

Ueman started down the temple stairs, but when my brother followed him, Little Reed became ghost-like; he walked down the stairs and yet he still stood at the edge of the platform, as if his tonalli had stepped right out of his body. The one still standing there turned to look at me and smiled, green quetzal feathers tucked between the folds of his long black hair. *Papalotl,* he whispered; it was Little Reed's face and his voice, but it was the god.

"My Lord," I whispered, that painful ache resurfacing in my chest. I didn't move to hug him—as I often had when we saw each other—but I didn't resist when he embraced me. Eventually the tension melted away under his feathery warmth and I leaned into him, savoring the feeling of safety and security that had brought me back to him as often as desire and need had. He stroked my cheeks with his feathery hands, sending an eager shiver through me, but rather than kiss me he gazed lovingly into my eyes. The way Little Reed often did.

Topiltzin showed you the city? he asked.

"Some of it." My voice hitched with longing but I cleared my throat, embarrassed. "I saw the palace."

Let me show you the rest. He took my hand and led me down the stairs, into the precinct and out into the broader city.

He showed me the artisan quarters filled with homes decorated with exquisite feathered banners and delicately painted flower boxes. Wind chimes of dried reeds played music in time with the clacking of the obsidian knappers making blades for shaving and the kitchen rather than for macuahuitl swords. He showed me the market overflowing with people selling goods from every corner of the world: cacao beans from the south, pottery and hides from the valley, dried fish from the eastern coasts, and medicinal plants from the northern desert. We walked through the various residential neighborhoods where the whitewashed houses were painted with images of the gods and animals, and Tolteca children ran with Chichimec children, laughing and playing.

Eventually we ended up back in the sacred precinct, and he took me to the calmecac where hundreds of children sat in large classrooms learning to read, write, and keep the calendar.

There's one more place I want to show you, Quetzalcoatl told me with a mysterious smile. We went to a gate that led into a vast garden hidden by high stone walls behind the calmecac. There were no people in here, only trees, flowers and bushes, and the sounds of birds and monkeys and bees. We said nothing as we walked along a gravel path, still holding hands; but when we reached a pond in the shade of an enormous oak tree, we sat in the grass to rest.

"Tollan is going to be magnificent," I said, soaking in the thick, sweet fragrance of bone flowers hanging over everything, setting my heart racing and my desire simmering. The unease and fear I'd felt earlier was forgotten, and when Quetzalcoatl leaned in to kiss me I eagerly welcomed his embrace, even more so when he lowered me gently onto my back, the grass prickling through my dress.

I shivered as he trailed his hand down my neck, the illusory feathers tickling as he rubbed his feathery hands over my exposed breasts; it wasn't unusual for us to skip the whole undressing distraction, particularly when we were impatient. Which one of us had banished our clothing, I wasn't certain, but we were both naked and entwined with each other as if it had only been a few weeks since last indulging in such pleasure, not almost three years.

I bit my bottom lip against the gasp as he eased himself into me, holding one of my legs up against his shoulder as he thrust slow and deep, gazing at me with intense eyes. I stared back, swallowed up by the mesmerizing depths there. Gods were supposedly unfathomable, so different from humans, and yet when I looked into his eyes, I knew he saw my very soul, understood me on that most primal level, as if we were kindred in some regard that I didn't yet know how to articulate. In him I saw everything I cherished; faith, love, Little Reed, all meshed together in a blur of breath and muscle and slow, sweet movement. I gripped fistfuls of grass as the pleasure cascaded over me, delicious and familiar.

Slowly the buzz of gratification wore away and the edges of reality began bleeding through the Divine Dream. The orange sky darkened and the ceiling of the royal tent became gradually visible. The teonanactl would only hold me here a few moments longer, but Quetzalcoatl rested his head against my leg as if we had all afternoon to bask in post-coital bliss. He rubbed his feathery fingers over my belly, reminding me of what he'd put in there—under circumstances far less pleasurable than this—and I wondered what he'd say about that, what explanation he'd give me for why he'd done it, and whether he'd assure me that it was all part of his grand scheme and that I would be all right.

But he merely sighed and kissed my calf before lowering my leg. *I missed you so much, my love,* he whispered. *It feels so good to have you back again.* He leaned over and kissed me, his loose hair a curtain around our heads.

His words brought dueling emotions rampaging through me; was that really all he had to say to me? And were we truly back together again? Now that I was thinking more clearly, the guilt and shame of having yet again treated the god as little better than a mortal man bit down on me.

I opened my eyes to find myself back in the tent, fully clothed, my body slick with sweat underneath my dress and my mouth dry from the heat. I went out into the anteroom to get some water, feeling woozy.

But when Little Reed came out of his own room dressed in the lightweight royal robes he'd brought along to wear to Citlallotoc's coronation, I tried to melt back into my own room. I was too slow though. When he saw me he smiled like a man who'd put a ball through the stone ring to end a highly contested tlachtli game. "A most gratifying afternoon in the Divine Dream, don't you think?" he asked, making my cheeks flare. "Ueman has spoken to Ten Spines and they both wish to meet with us immediately to discuss the terms of our partnership."

"Already?"

"It has been several hours since we went into the Divine Dream, and I was waiting for you to come back from it," Little Reed admitted. "Perhaps I put too much teonanactl into your octli." When I looked away, my face hot, he furrowed his brow. "Is everything all right, Papalotl? You look...." He scrutinized me, struggling to find the right word perhaps.

"I'm fine," I assured him. "The heat is a bit stifling. Let me wash up and changes clothes, and we'll get on our way."

He brought me a rag and a wash basin filled with water. "You're certain you're all right?" he asked again as I took his offerings.

I nodded, putting on a brave smile even though the guilt struck hard now. Here he'd forsaken all others because he loved me, and I'd spent the afternoon indulging in shameful lust with his father. Even now I couldn't believe I'd been so selfish and weak. The god's high priestess should be strong and faithful.

I considered confessing my bad behavior to him, but thinking about the god making love to me in the priestly garden set the wanton desire bubbling inside me. *I can't ever go back into the Divine Dream,* I realized. It felt weak to think it, but Nimilitzli had told me that sometimes the strongest thing we could do was distance ourselves from those things that tempted us most. I would have to find less personal ways to learn the will of the god and guide my people from now on.

He still looked troubled, so I repeated, "I am fine," and gave his hand a gentle, reassuring squeeze. "If you wait for me, I'll be out in a moment, my love."

My words brightened his mood again, and he gave me a curiously seductive smile before ducking out through the main tent flap.

¤

"How soon should we start building?" Ten Spines asked as he and Ueman escorted Little Reed and I around the Chichimec camp. The three men had brought their pipes along, indulging in a bit of smoking as they walked. All around us, men and women alike hurried about, preparing for the evening's celebratory feast.

"We should lay the foundation for the main temple before the end of summer, but work will continue through the winter months, as weather permits," Little Reed replied.

Ten Spines shook his head. "Food is plentiful here in the warm seasons, but we'll starve if we stay the winter."

"We'll have food brought in from the valley, enough to sustain all our workers and your tribe through the winter, and in the spring we'll plant maize, beans, squash, and chile, to stock up our stores for next winter."

"But our people have never farmed, Lord Topiltzin," Ueman pointed out. He'd taken to performing a slight hunch whenever he spoke to Little Reed, as if trying to maintain a bow. "Nor do we know about building the giant stone cities the Tolteca are renowned for."

"We will teach your people these skills," I assured him. To Ten Spines, I said, "Imagine the possibilities for your people in the future, My Lord: if they learn to farm, they can settle in one place, build permanent homes and establish schools where their children can learn a wide variety of skills, such as metallurgy and feather-working; skills they can pass on to their children."

"Having spent nearly ten years in the army, I know how difficult it is living out of a tent and moving all the time," Little Reed added. "Neither men nor women live very long in those circumstances, but once your people begin working the land and reaping the benefits of a settled life, they'll be happier, they'll live longer, and their children will be healthier and have greater opportunities."

"The older I get, the more difficult the winters become," Ten Spines acknowledged. "And I worry what will become of my family once I'm gone. My only son...he ran away to the valley because I didn't approve of the woman he wanted to take to wife, and though Mitotia is as bright as any man...." He shook his head. "I wish she'd been born one, for she has always been a better leader than even her brother. But because she is a woman, when I die, leadership will go to someone outside my family, and frankly, the young men of my tribe dream too ardently of war. I've seen my share, and there is nothing glorious about it."

"Sometimes war is necessary," Little Reed said. "But peace is even more so."

"And I have your assurances that my people will not be relegated to being slaves or persecuted because they were born in the desert?"

"All of our peoples will share in the power and wealth of Tollan, and we shall live in peace," Little Reed promised. "That is the will of the god."

When Ten Spines looked to Ueman, the shaman nodded, conceding the fact.

"And as a token of this promise, I would ask you to take command of the project once Lady Quetzalpetlatl and I return to Culhuacan after we've laid the temple's foundation."

"You aren't staying?" Ten Spines asked, surprised.

"Until Tollan is finished, we have ongoing obligations back in the valley."

"It is just as well, for Mitotia will need to learn the ways of the Tolteca royal court."

Puzzled, I asked, "And why might that be, My Lord?"

"Because she will marry your brother, of course."

Little Reed suddenly choked on his smoke and I had to thump him on the back as he coughed.

"She will make a fine wife, My Lord," Ten Spines added hastily. "She can be willful, but she is loyal, and she turned fifteen in the spring, so she hasn't lost more than a few of her best childbearing years."

Red-faced, Little Reed beckoned to his guards for a water skin and one immediately obliged. He gulped some down, coughing between drinks.

Ten Spines' brow furrowed in irritation. "I know Mitotia is not a beauty—"

"Actually, she is very beautiful," I cut in. "And Topiltzin would be so very lucky to have her at his side; I had the opportunity to speak with her while we prepared the afternoon meal, and she deeply impressed me. I see why you think she would be a great leader if only tradition wasn't standing in her way."

Ten Spines puffed up his chest and let a modest smile capture his lips. "She is so very astute; even more so than I. And yet your brother shows contempt for the thought of marrying her?" His smile vanished as he cast a hard glare at Little Reed.

"You mistake his reaction, My Lord. He is merely nervous about having to reject your proposal; he is already betrothed to another." I expected Little Reed to shoot me a questioning look, but he seemed not to hear me with all his coughing, so I continued on. "And while I'm certain you're aware that most Tolteca royalty keep concubines in their households, he's chosen not to take any himself. We're striving to create a more equal society for everyone, and since many traditions undermine such efforts, we've chosen to set the example ourselves. One set of rules for men and another for women—or one set for Toltecas and a different set for Chichimecs—doesn't promote the changes we aim to make."

Nodding stiffly, Ten Spines said, "There is logic to your words, My Lady, but I must admit disappointment. This is how we Chichimecs cement intertribal pacts, and your brother appears a good healthy match for her. I fear this means her last chance at marriage is over; she is obviously too old to interest anyone."

I nodded. "I understand your concerns, My Lord, but what does Mitotia want?"

"She wants to honor her family, of course."

"There are many ways for us to honor our families. In the past, the only way for most women was to marry and have children, but there was also the priesthood. Based on my brief discussion with her, I think Mitotia would excel in the priesthood, and you spoke earlier of what a good leader she would be. In the priesthood, she can be that, and more; she can help support your people in ways she never could as a king's wife, hidden away behind palace walls, risking childbirth one time after another with the possibility that none of those children will survive, let alone go on to do great things for your people. She can do great things for your people *now*; we Tolteca have no cult honoring the Cloud Serpent, so imagine if she helps establish that in Tollan. Perhaps she even becomes Mixcoatl's high priestess."

"That is compelling," Ten Spines admitted. "But what about having a family?"

"She can have both," I assured him. "That is one of the many reforms Quetzalcoatl seeks with our reign. Priests and priestesses will be allowed to take a spouse if they choose."

By now, Little Reed had finally recovered. "Please accept my apologies for this most inopportune moment to be taken by a coughing fit." He cleared his throat again, as if still bothered by a little smoke in his airways. "I have no doubts that Mitotia is as brilliant as my sister suggests, and we should encourage her to apply that potential in a way that will honor your family and herself. The priesthood will help her explore that potential to its fullest. So, if I might suggest, rather than sealing this pact with a marriage, let's bind it with a dedication to the priesthood, say until Mitotia reaches her nineteenth year. She'll attend the calmecac in Culhuacan where we'll teach her the art of writing, and reading the sacred calendar, as well as teaching her the stories and philosophies of the various gods. At the end of those four years, Mitotia can either take the trials to continue on in the priesthood, or she may choose to pursue a different lifestyle. Are these terms acceptable to you?"

"They are most adequate, Lord Topiltzin." Ten Spines grinned as he clamped his pipe between his yellowed teeth.

¤

"So, who is this mystery woman I'm supposedly betrothed to?" Little Reed asked when we returned to our tent to don our royal headdresses before the night's feast.

"I'm not the one who coughed up my lung at the suggestion of marrying our new ally's daughter," I said. "I had to say something to get Ten Spines to not grab his spear and avenge his dishonor."

"Yes, but now he'll expect me to marry someone."

What marry? the child's voice suddenly piped up. It had been thankfully quiet all afternoon and it annoyed me that it started bombarding me with stupid questions now.

"Don't worry, Little Reed. It will be several years before he'll start to wonder; plenty of time for you to find someone to fulfill that role."

Little Reed took a deep breath, his fists clenched. "I made a promise—"

"I didn't ask you to, so let's stop this foolishness," I fired back, more angry than I'd intended. I wondered if I would feel even half as guilty about this afternoon in the Divine Dream if he hadn't made that promise.

Seeing the hurt on his face, I sighed and pulled him into a hug. "Things didn't turn out as we'd hoped, but we can't let our feelings for each other trump the needs of our people. I can't give us an heir—" *An heir?* "—so you must marry someone. I won't let you end up like my father, with no one to carry on what we build here. There's more at stake than us, and we must never forget that."

"If only you understood," Little Reed whispered. "I *can't* love another the way I love you."

"This isn't about love; it's about your duty." Seeing the pain in his eyes

81

at this, I sighed and added, "Who's to say you won't find someone you can love. Maybe you already know her; maybe she's even in the priesthood."

"Like Malinalli?"

I looked up at him sharply, a surge of jealousy rising inside me. So many paranoid questions raced through my head—did he mention my best friend because he'd always liked her? Was there something between them and I'd never noticed because I'd been so focused on my own feelings? *There was that look she gave him when he came home to Xochicalco with Red Flint,* I remembered. Her blushing smile had raised my hackles but also shamed me; a feeling that started filling me now again. If they were attracted to each other, who was I to stand in their way? It wasn't as if I had anything real to offer him. And what kind of a friend would I be if I kept Malinalli from being happy because of my own selfish longings?

Friend? The voice was infinitely puzzled and I wished it would go away. My tongue felt dry as I asked Little Reed, "Do you like her?"

"I don't see her like that." His expression was unreadable.

Looking away again, I asked, "Well, is there anyone you could *see like that*...aside from me, of course?"

He shook his head, exasperating me.

"Well, you're going to have to make an effort," I said, returning to the flap to my sleeping quarters. "Now get your headdress on. We're going to be late."

By the time I returned to the anteroom with my white heron-feathered headdress in hand, I'd calmed the chaos of emotions fouling my mood. Little Reed appeared in better spirits as well and he gladly helped me with my own headdress when I asked. The silence between us felt oppressive though, so I sought to fill it with meaningless jabber. "What did you make of that story Ten Spines told us? About Mixcoatl?"

"What about it?"

"Do you think it's true, that he's Quetzalcoatl's father and your grandfather?"

"He is not the god's father."

"You've asked Quetzalcoatl this?"

"No," he admitted, amusement in his voice.

"Then how do you know?"

Little Reed didn't say anything for a moment. "Because my father would have mentioned it at some point in our conversations. We speak to each other in the Divine Dream at least once a week, often more."

I bit my lip, those moments in the garden today coming back to me, unwelcome. "What sort of things do you talk about?"

Little Reed moved around in front of me to check if my headdress was straight. "Religion mostly, and the future. We talk about the gods as well, sometimes even Mixcoatl."

"Then there is a Cloud Serpent?"

He nodded, adjusting my headdress with the care of a perfectionist. "But never as Quetzalcoatl's father."

"It is a fascinating coincidence," I remarked, "that the Chichimecs should believe that the two are related and your father chose to put you into the belly of the queen of a mortal king called Mixcoatl."

He chuckled. "It was all part of the god's plan; he knew where we'd build Tollan, and that we would need the help of Ten Spines' people, and that they worship Mixcoatl as Quetzalcoatl's father. It makes it easier to sway them to our plans."

"And it would incline them to see you as a god, by proxy," I said with a smirk.

"I consider that an unfortunate side effect, not a benefit. I'd rather people embrace what we do because it's a good thing, not because they fear divine retribution if they question it."

"I only hope that Ueman doesn't get out of hand with you being Quetzalcoatl's son. I won't abide anyone accusing you of being the kind of person who would elevate himself to the status of a god."

Little Reed caressed my cheek. "And you ask why I could never love another, Papalotl."

I took his hand in mine and gave it a squeeze. "I will always love you too," I whispered, a hitch in my throat.

CHAPTER SEVEN

The celebratory feast lasted well into the night, so we slept late into the morning. But when I woke, the meat I'd eaten last night—coupled with anticipation—left my stomach tied in a painful knot. Ueman had promised to bring us my father's bones this afternoon.

I barely touched my breakfast; given Little Reed's concerned glances, I knew he wanted to ask what was wrong with me, but thankfully our guards soon announced that Ueman and Ten Spines had arrived.

Ueman came into our tent along with two warriors carrying a rough-hewn, unpainted stone box. They placed it carefully at my feet as Ueman bowed low. "I humbly return your father to you, My Lady, and I beg forgiveness for my harsh words to you yesterday."

"It's quite all right." I eyed the box with trepidation; it didn't look nearly big enough to fit the bones of a man of my father's considerable size. "This is the box you dug up in the copal grove?"

"Everything is as we found it."

"That is the box I brought north," Amoxtli confirmed. He stood off to the side at a discreet distance.

Ten Spines stepped forward and pulled the stone lid off. He set it carefully against the side. "And as you can see, the bones are still inside."

Both Little Reed and I leaned in for a closer look.

A nest of disarticulated and broken bones filled the box, resting on a thick bed of decomposed tissue turned to sludge. A stale, rotting smell wafted out; a fragrance similar to the curiously alluring fragrance of a temple. Little Reed knelt to look in the box, a frown on his face as he poked among the bones with his sacrificial blade. "The skull is missing."

"It was probably on the skull rack in the temple," Amoxtli said, a deep frown on his face.

"Which means it's gone for good, since we cremated all those remains." Little Reed pulled away again. "And you're positive these are Mixcoatl's bones?" he asked Amoxtli.

"I can only go on what the guard said my father told him."

I continued staring into the box though, taking in every detail. The long bones of the legs had been snapped in half, to fit crosswise in the box, and an irresistible impulse drove me to move them aside. Under them I found the splintered remains of a ribcage, most of the ribs snapped in half along their midpoints.

The memories of what I'd seen that night in my father's quarters rushed back at me, a nightmare I could never fully escape: him lying on his bed mats, his throat hanging open in a grisly, bleeding frown, his already broad chest even broader than normal and showing off the ribs underneath, gleaming like a jaguar's bloodied fangs in the moonlight.

Though Quetzalcoatl's cult didn't practice heart extraction, I'd learned the method the priests of the Sun used, and it wasn't until now—seeing the snapped ribs again—that I realized that what my uncle had done shared nothing with that practice. Priests of Tonatiuh cut into the flesh at the bottom of the ribs, following their contour; then they reached up into the chest, to grip the heart from below to tear it out. What I'd seen that night in my father's quarters...it had none of the respect for the body of the sacrificial victim. Ihuitimal tore my father open like a mad animal, possessed of hate. It wasn't a sacrifice; it was the quenching of a personal vendetta.

"It's him," I managed before the bile and fear and rage bubbled up my throat. Horrifying images of vomiting all over my father's bones made me spring to my feet. I managed a couple of steps outside our tent before losing control.

A breath later, Little Reed crouched at my side, holding my hair back while I trembled and heaved. When he offered me a water skin to rinse out my mouth, I met his gaze and the desire geysered up inside me. I felt lightheaded and for a moment I thought it would take over, but I squeezed my eyes shut and took deep, calming breaths. *Get a hold of yourself, Quetzalpetlatl.* I got up and moved away from him before swigging several mouthfuls of water and spitting it out into the bushes behind our tent, rinsing away the foul burn. Embarrassment kept me staring into the bushes for a moment before turning back again.

Little Reed watched me, pity and regret on his face. "Feeling better now?"

I nodded. "I didn't expect it to overwhelm me so."

He came over and pulled me into a firm hug. "I'm truly sorry, Papalotl," he whispered.

I hugged him tightly in return, squeezing my eyes shut to keep from breaking down again. "Do you think burying him with full rites will finally let my heart mend?"

"I hope so."

◻

After Ten Spines and Ueman left, I retired to my bed, overwhelmed.

Hurt? the child voice asked.

I usually ignored it, but I desperately wanted to talk to someone, and Little Reed was busy with our new allies. *Very much so,* I thought back.

Why?

Because someone stole my tatli from me. I sniffled. *You're lucky; no one can kill your father as someone did to mine.*

What kill?

What is *kill,* I corrected him. *We ask, 'what is' when we have a question.*

What is kill?

It's when someone makes you die.

What is die?

It's when you don't live anymore. You stop thinking or speaking or feeling.

The voice fell silent, making me believe it hadn't understood anything I'd said—no surprise—but then it asked, *Why you kill me?*

My heart faltered and that nausea swept over me again. *I haven't killed you.*

Will you?

I stared at the ceiling, my heart hammering in my throat. I had no idea how to answer that. I didn't want to answer it.

Will you? it asked again.

"I don't want to die," I whispered. "If I don't...you might kill me."

I won't.

You can't promise that. My nantli let Little Reed live, and it killed her.

Nantli?

My mother.

You is my nantli, the voice whispered.

Tears wound down my cheeks, a tremendous ache swelling in my heart. What was I thinking, even talking to him? *You* are *my nantli,* I corrected him.

You are my nantli? he asked, puzzled.

I tried to hold in the sob but I couldn't stop it. With one word, he'd changed everything; changed my whole future. No matter how much I feared dying, I knew now that I couldn't go through with it; this wasn't some phantom voice in my head—it was the voice of my son, my flesh and blood, and nothing would ever be the same. I set my hand on my stomach, splaying my fingers, feeling the magic pulsing deep inside me;

the magic the god had given me, magic I hadn't asked for but was now mine to grow and nurture. I wiped my tears and whispered, "Yes, I'm your nantli, and I will protect you always; I promise."

◻

I slept late into the evening, waking to the sweet smell of tobacco. Little Reed, Amoxtli, Citlallotoc, and Ten Spines sat around a fire in the anteroom, set up in a small kettle brazier. They smoked their pipes and spoke in hushed voices, but everyone looked up when I came out of my room. "Feeling better?" Little Reed asked, concern on his face.

I smiled back at him. "I finally am feeling better." And it was no exaggeration; I felt as if a huge boulder had been lifted off my shoulders. I had such big news to share with him, but not around the others. "What are you discussing?" Hopefully my personal issues this afternoon hadn't slowed progress on our mission.

"We're going to start clearing the copal grove tomorrow," he said. "That should take a week, maybe two, then we can start laying the temple foundation."

"It will really take that long?"

Ten Spines chuckled. "My Lady is eager to get back to civilization."

I smiled gamely at him. "Not at all. There isn't much for me to do until the burial ceremony and the foundation dedication, but perhaps I could start training Mitotia."

Little Reed nodded. "I've been working with Amoxtli on his training, but we'll need more assistance during the burial ceremony."

"Mitotia is eager to go to Culhuacan with you," Ten Spines said with a sigh. "I've always known in my heart that she wasn't meant for the migrant life, still...it grieves me to let her go."

"We will take very good care of her," I assured him. "And she will come home again once she's finished her training, and she will make you most proud."

Ten Spines nodded. "My wife made a wonderful dinner and she's keeping it warm on the fire outside for you, if you're hungry."

"I'm starving," I admitted, and thanked him before ducking through the tent flap, out into the camp.

Amoxtli followed and called to me once we were outside. He was nervous as he approached.

"Is something the matter?" I asked.

"I wanted to...to tell you how very sorry I am for what my father did to your father," he said, wringing his hands, his head bowed.

"You're not responsible for what he did."

"No, but as his son, I share in his shame, and this afternoon...seeing how deeply his crimes affected you, it feels the right thing to do."

I gripped his shoulder. "You're a very good man, Amoxtli, and I'm so very glad you're my cousin."

"You accept my apology?"

"Whole-heartedly." I hugged him and he returned the gesture awkwardly, as if he didn't know what to do; but when I let him go, he was smiling. He gave me a nod goodbye before retreating back into the royal tent.

Bitter Rabbit and Mitotia sat at our camp's cooking fire, Mitotia mending a buckskin dress while her mother wove a basket from river rushes. The old woman gave me a gap-toothed smile and set her weaving aside to fill a bowl with soup.

"I was hoping I might see you tonight, My Lady," Mitotia remarked when I sat on the mat next to her. "My father says he's sending me south with you and your brother, to become a priestess." When I nodded, she said, "Forgive my asking, but what does a priestess do?"

"The various priesthoods make certain the gods are properly honored through sacrifice and prayer. But we also track the heavens and keep the calendars, both domestic and sacred, so we can tell the farmers when to plant and when to harvest. We also read omens for the king, and we lead the people in the monthly festivals. But most importantly, we share the gods' will with the people, so everyone know how to keep them happy so they will continue showing us mercy rather than destroying the world."

"That sounds very important," Mitotia said.

"It is. If you ask me, it's more important than even being queen, for while royalty comes and goes, the gods are with us always."

"So I will be learning only about the Tolteca gods?"

I shook my head. "We welcome all the Chichimec gods into the temples, so they may too enjoy the benefits of our peoples' shared prosperity." *Even the Smoking Mirror?* I wondered, but kept it to myself. "Actually, would you teach me about the Chichimec gods, particularly

Mixcoatl?"

"Mixcoatl? Well, he's the god of hunters; we bless our weapons in his name so they might bring down the deer easily and often. They say he came from the clouds as a great serpent, hence his name."

"Your father mentioned that Mixcoatl is the father of Quetzalcoatl."

Mitotia nodded. "The story goes that he journeyed south to conquer lands for the Chichimec people, and he came upon a savage war-queen who wouldn't bend to his rule. They battled for days, and finally he chased her into a cave and trapped her there. Demanding she submit to his rule, he pierced her with an arrow, impregnating her, and she gave birth to the Feathered Serpent, the one who gives us all life and who imparts knowledge upon us."

I bit my lip, horrified. I didn't know what to say that wouldn't be a complete dismissal of Mixcoatl's worship.

Bitter Rabbit said something in the Chichimec tongue and Mitotia answered, a look of bewilderment on her face. "Is it true my father wishes me to become some kind of priestess of the Cloud Serpent, in the new city you and Lord Topiltzin are building here?"

"That was the plan," I admitted. When she frowned, I added, "But plans can easily change. We will not force you to serve a god you wish not to."

She cast a furtive glance at her mother before leaning closer to me and saying, "Every winter, our shaman dresses as the Cloud Serpent and he picks one of the young women to battle, as Mixcoatl battled the war queen." She lowered her voice as she went on. "He drags her to his tent and sheds her maiden blood, so a child is conceived. The following summer, after the child is born, he sacrifices it, to honor the Feathered Serpent."

Without thinking, I set my hand on my abdomen as if to protect my son. I made myself take it away as soon as I realized what I was doing. "Quetzalcoatl doesn't want the blood of children," I said, unable to contain the outrage.

"The priesthood doesn't practice this kind of ritual?"

"Not at all...well, not anymore...or at least not for much longer. Topiltzin and I are on a mission from Quetzalcoatl, to reform the priesthood and how sacrifice is done. So no, such sacrifices will soon be a thing of the past. Nor will the ritual raping of Tollan's citizens be tolerated."

Mitotia let out a held breath. "Forgive me, for I know it is a sacred ritual, but I am glad to hear that. Ueman always picks older girls who haven't, for whatever reason, gotten married yet, and my mother has told me he's already talked to my father...about me. No one's allowed to marry a woman who's been had by the god, and once I had the baby, I would pretty much be useless to the village."

So that was what Ten Spines had been referring to, about this being her final chance. "I will not allow it," I assured her. "For the next four years you belong to the Temple of Quetzalcoatl, so you needn't worry."

She gave me a relieved smile and spoke to her mother again. Her mother nodded approvingly, reaching over to stroke her daughter's shoulder. "What can I ever do to repay you for saving me from such a fate?"

Smiling back at her, I said, "You needn't do anything, but I very much want to learn to speak your people's language."

She nodded. "I shall teach you."

"Tomorrow I'll begin tutoring you in the priestly arts. I'll need your assistance at the temple dedication ceremony in a few weeks."

¤

It was on the tip of my tongue to tell Little Reed my big news when I returned to the tent after dinner but, even though Ten Spines and Amoxtli had left, Citlallotoc was still with him and I didn't fancy saying anything in front of him either. I sat with them for the remainder of the evening, mostly listening; my mind was elsewhere, going over all the questions Little Reed would ask, and my stomach grew tighter and tighter with dread. How could I explain to him that I hadn't told him until now because I'd been planning to rid myself of the god's son? By bedtime, I didn't want to tell him at all, so I slunk away to my quarters and let my son's babble lull me to sleep. Since talking with him earlier that evening, he'd integrated the few speech rules I'd taught.

Come morning, Little Reed had already gone before I woke. Although we saw each other briefly at dinner, he retired early, exhausted from clearing the copal grove. I still said nothing to him about the baby, not wanting to add a worry on top of his exhaustion.

This became our daily routine. I passed my own days teaching Mitotia about the different gods and telling her the stories I'd learned as a child and perfected during my years in the calmecac. She was a highly attentive student, soaking up everything I told her, always asking questions; she reminded me of Mazatzin in intelligence and temperament, and I mused that someday she could be a very successful high priestess of whatever god she chose to serve. When I wasn't teaching her theology, she was teaching me to speak Chichimec.

And to my surprise—and pride—my son learned it right along with me. He babbled assorted Chichimec words the first few days but they quickly became full sentences. His Tolteca became mostly understandable as well, and I spent the evenings before bed singing the sacred songs for him in my head. By the day before the ceremony to bury my father's bones under the temple's foundation, my son could sing the songs back to me. I'd never thought it possible to feel so proud.

I want to give you a name, I told him. *I've been thinking about it for a few days now, and I've come up with the perfect one.*

What is it, Nantli? he asked, excited. I wished he was big enough for me to feel him moving around. *Can it be Quetzalcoatl?*

I chuckled aloud. *You can't have your father's name; if he were human, that would be fine, but you're not allowed to take the gods' names for your own.*

Why not?

Because the gods are special; they're one of a kind whereas we are many...so very many. And there is power in the gods' names, and to take them for ourselves would dilute that power.

I don't understand, he admitted.

It's all right. Someday you will. But I did get the idea for your name from Quetzalcoatl.

Will I like it?

I hope so.

Well?

Yamehecatl.

Warm Breeze?

Exactly. Because you are a wonderful, warm breeze that Quetzalcoatl blew into my life so unexpectedly, and I couldn't imagine you not being in it.

Yamehecatl was silent, and for a moment, I thought he'd gone to sleep, but he whispered, *Then you love me, Nantli?*

I slid my hand up the side of my dress, to set it against my bare stomach, as if to will myself to feel his hand touching mine the same way Little Reed used to touch my hand through our mother's belly. I felt nothing but my own firm guts underneath. *I do, my precious little breeze. Very much.*

I love you too, Nantli.

◻

In the morning, when I came out into the anteroom, Little Reed and Citlallotoc were on their way out of the flap, dressed for the final day of work. Today the men would lay the first foundation stones, dragged all the way from a limestone quarry Ten Spines' men found on the north end of the grasslands. It had taken them all day to get the dozen stones to the temple construction site, dragging the blocks with ropes and rolling them over logs. Little Reed hadn't bothered to wash up yesterday and still bore the scrapes and dirty smudges of a day of hard labor, but he was as handsome as ever. "Sorry to rush out, but we're already late," he told me, planting a kiss on my cheek that sent the desire simmering and growling. "We'll be back a few hours after noon though, to get ready for the ceremony. Can you put together all the things we'll need for tonight?"

"Of course." I swallowed back the desire, taking a deep breath when he finally turned to leave again. "There's something I need to talk to you about tonight, Topiltzin," I called after him, my stomach knotted with a mixture of anxiety and excitement. "After the ceremony."

He looked back at me, concerned. "Is everything all right?" Citlallotoc wore the same expression.

I nodded. "In fact, it's quite good news, but it can wait until tonight. I wanted to mention it, so I won't forget to talk to you about it."

He gazed at me a moment longer, his expression uncertain, but he said, "I'll see you this afternoon then."

I waved goodbye, the desire growling humorlessly, so I took some of the dried meat Little Reed had left for me on the plate on the floor next to the kettle brazier. I sat and chewed it slowly, my jaw already hurting. It was some kind of lizard, with the bones still in it. How did the Chichimecs survive with no maize to make tlaxcallis, and no beans for their soup?

We'd gone through our supply within the first week and I couldn't wait to get back to Culhuacan and enjoy nice hot, fluffy tlaxcallis again.

As I finished eating, my guard rattled the copper bells sewn into the flap of the tent and stuck his head inside. "There's someone here to see you, My Lady."

It annoyed me that he still called Mitotia "someone", having not taken the time to learn her name. Initially it surprised me how many of our men were hostile to our new Chichimec allies—not outright—but now it irritated me. Our guards and soldiers glared at the Chichimecs, a practice the Chichimecs returned with equal vehemence, and a few Toltecas addressed them as "Dog Men" in our tongue. Luckily no conflicts had broken out, though I sensed it was only a matter of time before one of the Chichimec warriors learned enough of our language to confirm they were being insulted and took it as a matter of personal honor.

"Just send her in," I snapped at him, and went to retrieve my priestly robe.

"It's not the Chichimec girl, My Lady." He looked over his shoulder before stepping inside and closing the flap behind him. "He claims to be your husband."

I stared at him, not amused. "My *former* husband is dead."

"I told him as much, but he insists on speaking with you."

Someone was playing a trick on my guard, and I didn't appreciate it. Despite my dreams to the contrary, Black Otter was dead in Tlalocan with all other drowning victims, enjoying a paradise of eternal green and plenty for having fed the Rain God with his death. Whoever thought this was funny would get a flogging. "Send him in," I growled.

My guard opened the tent flap and motioned outside. A breath later, a gaunt, harried-looking man stepped inside followed by my second guard. He walked hunched over, his clothes little better than rags—his cotton loincloth was dingy and tattered, as if he'd fished it from the lake and hadn't washed it since. But when he raised his head to meet my gaze, my breath caught. "Black Otter?"

"Quetzalpetlatl!" He took a step towards me, arms outspread as if to hug me.

But when I recoiled, horrified, the first guard snapped his spear out, blocking Black Otter. "No one touches the queen without her permission."

Black Otter threw a murderous glare at him, but said to me, "I nearly died, and this is the greeting you give me?"

I stared at him, trembling. "How...but I saw you die!" The moment Ihuitimal's guards shot him with an arrow and he fell into the lake played over and over in my head.

"I thought I would die too, but instead I washed up on shore at Xico," Black Otter said.

I hadn't seen him surface, but the guards *had* practically drowned me while trying to subdue me after sending Black Otter into the lake. I'd been in no condition to search for him after that, and for all I knew he'd been alive and they left him to die. "The gods spared you?" I concluded.

He nodded, his eyes teary. "It took me a few months to recover, but I came looking for you as soon as I was able, and so here I am!" He held his arms out again expectantly but when I still made no move to embrace him, he asked, "How can my own wife not be overjoyed to see me still alive?"

"I'm not your wife anymore."

"Says who? Topiltzin?"

"*I* say so," I fired back.

He stared at me, flustered before stammering, "You haven't the power to divorce me. Only a man can ask for that."

"Your father's rules are no longer the law in Culhuacan...or here. As far as I'm concerned, our marriage never existed."

"Never...!" Black Otter flexed his fists. "Your father tied your dress to my cape—"

"He declared that union void when he exiled your father."

"Yet we consummated it our first night together. You consented."

I stood straighter, glaring at him. *Let's devour him,* the desire growled. I pushed the voice aside but allowed the confidence to remain. "Don't mistake self-preservation for consent. Under your father's laws, a woman had no right to say no."

When he pressed forward again, furious, the guard pushed back with his spear. "Yet that never stopped you from moaning my name every time after, did it?"

I flinched. *Who does he think he is?* the desire growled. Images of him lying dead on the floor after I'd ravaged him sprang into my head, so similar to those dreams I had about Red Flint after he attacked me in the

Temple of Quetzalcoatl in Xochicalco. *If he wants it so badly, let's give it to him.*

But the guard belted Black Otter in the chest with his wooden spear handle, sending him sprawling at the feet of the second one. Both guards turned their spear points at his chest. "Shall I drive this filthy dog through, My Lady?" The first guard didn't take his intense gaze off Black Otter. When I set a calming hand on his shoulder, he relaxed his grip but kept his spear pointed.

"Try to belittle me all you want," I snarled at Black Otter. "But your words mean nothing."

Black Otter's gaze swung back and forth between me and the guards. "Forgive my cruel tongue, My Lady. These last few months, not knowing if you were even alive...it's been rougher on me than you can know. I survived only by the grace of the gods, and I understand you wishing to move on, thinking you'd lost me, but...the gods gave us a second chance, Quetzalpetlatl."

"They did give us a second chance, Black Otter; to undo the mockery of love and devotion your father thrust us into. I'm back where I belong, as the high priestess of Quetzalcoatl, and you...you have women and children who will rejoice to know you're alive." I almost added "and well", but reconsidered, given his shabby state.

"You...are you not happy I'm alive too?" His voice broke.

I frowned, stung that he'd even ask that. Did he think me an unfeeling monster? "Of course I'm happy you're alive, but I also know that what we had...that was not love, Black Otter, and I will not forsake my duties as high priestess to Quetzalcoatl for anything less than real love. Go home to Jade Flower and your children. They need you, and you need them."

"I don't need her," he spat like a petulant child. "I don't want her. I want you!"

I set my jaw tight, the stolidness creeping up on me again. "Then you leave me no choice." I motioned to the guards to stand him up and they did so. "I want him taken back to the valley and turned over to the King of Chalco, so he may be held accountable for at least one of the women he took an oath to keep and protect."

I turned back to him. "Black Otter, I hereby exile you from the cities of Tollan and Culhuacan. Should you choose to ignore my authority, I will declare you an enemy of the god and the guards will kill you on sight. We were once good friends, but you will forget about me. Go home to your women and make a new beginning with them."

Black Otter stared at me, pleading. "I'm in no condition to take care of four women and their children, Quetzalpetlatl. Look at me; I haven't a home, let alone a kingdom to support them."

"I'm certain if you agree to tie your cape to Papantzin's or Cornflower's dress, their fathers will be quite happy to give you a position in their court and means enough to support your family." I told the guards to escort him out.

"But I love you, Quetzalpetlatl!" he cried as they dragged him from the tent. "Why is that not enough for you?" He continued yelling and crying as they led him away.

Mitotia had appeared at the tent flap, and stood watching the commotion. Amoxtli was with her, staring at his brother as the guards dragged him away. When he turned to me, disbelief in his eyes, I nodded and said, "Go. Maybe you can talk some sense into him."

He hesitated while my words sunk in, but then he hurried after the guards, calling, "Brother!"

"Who was that?" Mitotia asked.

"Nobody important." I frowned, setting my hand over my stomach pensively. It was a good thing I wasn't visibly pregnant or that situation might have turned uglier.

"Are you feeling all right, My Lady?" Mitotia asked, noticing my gesture.

I dropped my hand. "I'm fine." I motioned her inside and fetched my priestly robe and my satchel. "We have a lot to do today, so let's get going."

CHAPTER EIGHT

I tried to put Black Otter out of my mind as Mitotia and I left the camp, but the memory of his wildness followed me down the winding game trail through the tall grasses. I imagined him breaking free of my guards and looking for me again, and several times I contemplated going back, just to be safe; we'd left without my guards, after all. But once we forded the small river, helping each other across the rocks, and made our way along the line of trees, to a ravine that opened onto a plain of scrub brush and hundreds of maguey plants, I decided it was pointless to turn back. *We'll get this done quickly,* I decided, as we picked our way down the steep incline.

When we came to the nearest maguey, whose broad, spongy leaves grew taller than either of us, I cut off one of the smaller leaves growing close to the heart of the plant. "The spines on the larger leaves are too thick for our purposes," I told Mitotia as I handed her the leaf and cut off several more. We sat on the ground, our knives out. "The thorns at the end of the leaves are the best ones, for they are the thinnest. So cut the end off, about this far down—" I demonstrated it on the leaf in front of me and she followed my action—"then you shave off the excess until it resembles a needle." I held up my finished thorn before starting on a second leaf.

"What do you use these for?" Mitotia asked as she worked on her first.

"Bloodletting rituals," I said. "Women pierce their tongues—symbolic of the breath of life—while men pierce their genitals, on the testicles or the foreskin."

Mitotia cringed. "We don't have to pierce ourselves...down there, do we?"

I chuckled. "We already give enough blood from there every month."

"Will I have to do any of this bloodletting at tonight's ritual?"

I shook my head. "You must learn proper technique first, so Topiltzin and I will do the bloodletting tonight."

"Will there be a sacrifice too? Father told me people die at the sacrifice daily back in the valley."

"No human sacrifices," I assured her. "Quetzalcoatl prefers the blood of his priests, given in earnest devotion."

Mitotia nodded. "We sacrifice maybe two or three people a year, in honor of the most important gods. In the winter, we take a chosen warrior out into the desert, away from camp, and dress him as the Cloud Serpent, and all the warriors shoot him with arrows. And in the spring, we appease the Rain God by drowning the weakest child in the river. That happened to my youngest sister; she was older than most of the sacrifices, but she fell out of a tree and hit her head, making her no better than a baby. Father said her sacrifice was a mercy, and she would have been honored to help her people."

I shuddered at the thought of my little Yamehecatl drowning. *But what if he was suffering?* No, I didn't want to think about that. I reached to clasp my stomach but stopped myself.

Are you all right, Nantli? Yamehecatl suddenly asked me, and I nearly jumped.

I took a deep breath before replying, *I'm fine, my little warm breeze. I have a lot to do right now, so go back to sleep and we'll talk later? All right?*

Will you sing me a song, Nantli?

Smiling, I gave in, singing aloud one of the many songs about Quetzalcoatl as I carved out the rest of the thorns. He sang with me a while, but eventually his voice became a sleepy drone. Mitotia listened the first few times then joined in, her voice a nice deep complement to my own. We sang as we packed up our supplies and climbed up the incline to the trees. I was relieved to finally be going back to camp.

Mitotia went first, nimble with youth, but when I went up after her, trying to keep pace, the ground at the top gave way. I yelped and tried to sit as I went down, but instead I bounced off a rock and tumbled head over feet down the side of the ravine. I heard Mitotia's cry but otherwise everything was a blur of colors and sound. When I landed at the bottom, I slammed down belly-first, my breath gushing out of me. I gasped for air, pain radiating through my chest and abdomen. *Yamehecatl! Yamehecatl!* I called in my head but he didn't answer. When my lungs finally filled with air again, my first outbreath came out as an agonized wail.

"Are you all right, My Lady?" Mitotia called as she skidded down into the ravine to me. When she rolled me over, I cringed and grabbed my belly, feeling as if a rock shifted inside of me. "What do I do, My Lady? You're bleeding through your dress!"

I tried to sit up, but dizziness and sharp pains changed my mind. *You got your wish after all.* Tears burned my eyes.

"What should I do?" Mitotia asked again, tears in her voice.

Her panic brought my years of midwife training to the fore. "Run and fetch the first strong man you see."

She blinked at me. "And leave you here?"

"No time to argue. Now go, and hurry back."

She scrambled back up the side of the ravine, slipping a few times before making it to the top. She ran off down the game trail, back the way we'd come.

I shielded my eyes from Lord Sun, cursing myself. *This is what you get for questioning the god's plan. He gave you a child to ease your aching heart, but you thought it was a curse and schemed to rid yourself of it. Are you happy now? You'll never get to hold Yamehecatl; you'll never get to talk to him again.* I broke out into hiccupping sobs.

But tears wouldn't help me. I'd probably broken bones and had internal injuries that I might not survive. I was alone and exposed, and my fears about Black Otter getting free came back to me fresh. What would he do if he found me completely helpless and injured? Why hadn't I waited for my guards to return?

Stop it, immediately! The voice of my desire came without all the usual hunger and embarrassing tingling; it was all confidence and command. *Keep your wits, and don't give in to the fear. Take a deep breath and pull yourself together.* I took several breaths until the sobs stopped. *Now you wait, and stay calm.*

It will help to pray, I told myself. *And make an offering to the god. Whatever keeps you strong.*

I looked for my bag only to find it tangled in some scrub brush. I tried sliding over, but the pain swelled anew in my abdomen. After catching my breath I stretched my arm as far as I could, but the strap remained beyond my reach. *Just a little farther.* My fingers began tingling deep inside....

Suddenly the ground rumbled under me. I looked around, my calm forgotten. Was it an earthquake?

Behind me, the maguey plant's thick, fleshy leaves waved as if caught in a great wind, yet none of the plants around it moved, and no wind was blowing. The rumbling focused between me and the maguey plant, as if something large and sinister was burrowing towards me—

Despite the intense pain in my gut, when lime-white roots burst from the ground next to me, I yelped and rolled away. They wound towards the bush, wrapped themselves around my satchel and dragged it out, shredding multiple branches. When they moved towards me, I started clawing away, but they dropped the bag right in front of me and then withdrew. I watched—mouth hanging open—as they slithered back into the ground and the maguey plant fell still again.

Did I really see that?

Shouts shattered my awe and I turned on my side to see Amoxtli approaching the ravine at a run. Mitotia followed close behind, panting and sweating.

"Quetzalpetlatl!" he called when he reached the edge. "Stay still. I'm coming down to get you." I clutched my bag, tears of relief welling in my eyes. Thank the gods it wasn't Black Otter.

When he reached me, his eyes widened at the blood on my dress, but he didn't question. He slid his arms under me and lifted me gently, straining under my weight; he wasn't a very large man, built thin and wiry the same as his father. I held onto him tight, afraid he might drop me. "Everything will be all right, cousin," he whispered, sweating as he struggled back out of the ravine, his own legs shaking under him.

¤

When we reached the royal tent, Amoxtli laid me on my bed. "Fetch the surgeon for her," he told Mitotia, who was pacing like an anxious deer. "He's down by the river, tending to a man who smashed his foot under the foundation stones." He turned to me, his face ruddy from exertion. "I'll fetch Topiltzin." He left, and Mitotia started to follow, but I called her back.

"Forget the surgeon," I told her. "He won't know what to do anyway. I need a midwife."

Her gaze wandered to the bloodstain on the front of my dress. "You're pregnant?"

Who would have thought such a small question could so thoroughly break my heart? When I tried to answer, it came out as a choked sob.

"I'll hurry back," Mitotia assured me.

And so I waited again, staring at the ceiling, preparing for the inevitable.

She returned shortly with her mother. "She knows the most about this," she assured me. "She helps all our women in their childbed, so don't worry. She'll take care of you."

Bitter Rabbit told Mitotia to fetch the water jar as she knelt at my feet and pushed my dress up over my hips. "How long since your last bleeding?"

"Four moons." I returned to staring at the ceiling, horrified. I'd never minded performing my midwife duties for others, but it was frightening being on the other side of the mat.

"This is your first child?"

I nodded, and cringed as the old woman felt my stomach none too gently.

"Any abdominal pains that begin small but grow very painful?"

"No, though it hurts when I move or try to sit up." I gritted my teeth when she bent my knees and checked me for signs of labor.

"You've leaked water," she murmured when she finished.

"And the baby?"

"If the baby died, you will give birth by nightfall, early morning at the latest. Time will answer your question."

Mitotia returned with a deer's bladder of water and a buckskin rag. "Is she going to be all right, Mother?" she asked as she wiped the dirt and blood off my face and arms.

"The gods willing." Bitter Rabbit cut my dress off with a knife and with Mitotia's help put me into a clean one. Gritting my teeth again, I settled in, physically drained and emotionally raw. Bitter Rabbit pulled my blanket up to my chin and tucked me in as if I were her own daughter.

As the numbness started whisking me off to sleep, Little Reed burst into the room, out of breath and wide-eyed. Amoxtli followed him in. "Omeyocan blind me, what happened?" he asked, kneeling next to me.

"I fell down a hill," I said.

"Are you all right?" He turned to Bitter Rabbit. "Did she break anything? Is she going to be all right?"

"She will be fine, but it remains to be seen whether the child will survive the night," she answered.

Little Reed turned to me, bewildered. "You're with child?" Behind him, Amoxtli's eyes widened too.

"I wanted to tell you," I stammered. "But I didn't know how to...."

"You were afraid to tell me?" Shock and hurt played across his face.

As I struggled to find the right words, Bitter Rabbit motioned to Mitotia, and her daughter followed her to the tent flap. "I'll come back later to check on you, but if the pain becomes worse, send for me right away."

Once they left, I asked Amoxtli, "Would you mind letting us talk alone?"

"Of course, My Lady." He looked overwhelmed as he ducked out of the flap as well.

Little Reed stared at his hands. "Was this the good news you wanted to tell me tonight, after the ceremony?"

I nodded. "I'm sorry, Little Reed. I should have told you sooner."

"How long have you known?"

I shrugged, hesitating, but admitted, "I started to suspect it when we were at Teotihuacan."

"Nearly a month?" Little Reed looked as if I'd struck him through with an arrow. "Why didn't you tell me, Papalotl?"

I covered my face, not wanting him to see how torn up I was. "Because I was planning to end this pregnancy once we returned to Culhuacan."

He didn't say anything, and I was afraid to look at him. But when he finally spoke, his voice was calm. "I know you said you didn't want children, and I understand, but I hope you weren't planning this out of loyalty to me. It doesn't matter that Black Otter is the child's father; I would love your child regardless."

"Black Otter isn't the father."

"But who else's could it—"

"It happened that day on the battlefield."

Little Reed's puzzled look continued only a breath before realization lit his eyes. "You mean the god—"

I nodded. "When he took possession of me. Which makes what I was going to do all the worse."

Little Reed gave my hand a gentle squeeze. "You thought it would mean your death."

"I don't want to die. And I didn't ask for this...and it infuriated me that the god would do this to me, with no warning or explanation. Does he expect me to merely accept it?"

My raw, unfettered emotions left him looking bewildered. "I'm sorry," he said, trembling.

I squeezed his hand back. "I know I sound angry, but I'm not anymore. I realize now it's a blessing I didn't know I wanted, but I was clumsy...and now the gods have truly taken my son away from me."

"We don't know that for certain."

"I know it," I sobbed. "Yamehecatl hasn't spoken to me since I fell."

"Yamehecatl?"

"That's what I named him."

"It's a good name," Little Reed conceded. "But what do you mean by him speaking to you?"

"I can hear him, in my head. That's how I know he's a boy. And he's so clever, Little Reed; I taught him all the sacred songs and he's been learning Chichimec as Mitotia's been teaching it to me. And he calls me Nantli." That last statement completely broke me. Little Reed stroked my hair as I rested my head in his lap. "Do you think I'm crazy, hearing voices in my head?"

"Not at all," he said, with no hesitation.

I peered up at him, hope building inside me. Maybe I wasn't as strange as I thought. "Do you hear them too?"

"No." For a moment I thought that was all he had to say, but he added, "At least not anymore. There was a time, long ago...but not anymore."

So the insistent desire might someday go away and leave me in peace? I thought to tell him about the other voice but the notion of discussing something so embarrassing, so sexual with him was too much to contemplate; even if we were lovers, I doubted I could. "Yamehecatl hasn't spoken to me since I fell, even when I try to wake him."

"He may be sleeping," Little Reed offered. "Let's see what time tells us, and think positively."

"Thank you, Little Reed." I hoped my smile wasn't actually a frown. "I'm truly sorry for keeping all this from you."

He stroked my hand with his. "I want you to know that you're not alone in this, and I will be with you every step of the way." After making certain I was tucked comfortably under my blankets, he said, "I will speak with Ten Spines about delaying the ceremony a few days while you recover."

But I latched onto his hand, keeping him from standing. "There's something else I must tell you about."

His look of concern returned.

"Black Otter came to see me today."

Little Reed blinked, startled. "But he's dead."

"I thought so too, but somehow he survived."

A new intensity showed in his eyes. "Where's he been all these months?"

"In Xico, I think."

"With Flame Tongue?"

"I don't think so. Flame Tongue would have told us." Xico's king was desperate to please Little Reed, after all. "Black Otter looked as if he'd slept under bushes and hadn't washed his clothes in months. He's a complete ruin, Little Reed."

"Did he threaten you?"

I shook my head. "My guards dealt with him swiftly when he became angry, but mostly he begged me to take him back. It was rather sad."

"Sad is too generous a term," he muttered. "Did you say anything to him about the baby?"

"Of course not. He'd have every reason to believe he was the father, and with the mental state he was in...."

"Where is he now?"

"I sent him to Chalco, to make amends with Jade Flower and Papantzin."

He contemplated the tent wall. "Did he say anything about the throne?"

"Only that he couldn't take care of the others without a kingdom to support them, though it was more an excuse to not go and find them. Come to think about it, he never even mentioned his father, or Amoxtli." I would have to ask Amoxtli about what Black Otter said when he spoke to him.

Little Reed tightened his jaw. "It wasn't a good idea to let him go, Papalotl."

Frowning, I said, "Would you want to be the one to tell Amoxtli that his brother survived, but we executed him because he once was a contender for the throne?"

"Of course not, and we both know that's not what I'm talking about."

"He needs time to heal; I broke him, so I owe him the opportunity to restart his life with the others. I'm surprised Cornflower would talk to me at all after everything that happened."

"Don't blame yourself. He made a decision that a strong, moral man wouldn't have, and now everyone pays the price for that. If anyone owes those women an apology, it's him."

"That may be, but that doesn't change the fact that they need him. And if it makes you feel better, I exiled him from our lands, under penalty of death."

"Very well. But now I really must go and talk to Ten Spines." He kissed my forehead before rising. "Now get some sleep and I'll be back soon." He disappeared through the tent flap.

I pulled the blanket up to my chin, letting the exhaustion wash over me. That was two heavy stones off my conscience, but an even bigger one remained. *Please talk to me, Yamehecatl.* He still didn't answer, so I closed my eyes and muttered a prayer, promising to never again doubt Quetzalcoatl's plan if only he wouldn't take my son from me.

ꙮ

When I woke again it was dark and the smell of food set my stomach gurgling. I tried to sit up, but the pain of bruised muscles made me dizzy, so I lay back again, out of breath.

Little Reed parted the tent flap. "Good, you're awake." He held it open for a young man who brought in a small kettle brazier and set to lighting the branches it contained. The fire cast a pleasant orange glow over my quarters. Little Reed brought me a steaming bowl of soup, and I cringed as I sat up again.

"Let me help you." He sat behind me and let me lean against his chest, providing firm, strong support for my back. "How are you feeling?"

"Very stiff," I said between sips. It tasted wonderful in spite of the lack of salt and chile in it. "But the pain isn't so bad anymore."

"Good. Bitter Rabbit says if you'd lost the baby, you'd be in labor already."

"True, but...he's still showing no signs that he's alive."

"I'm certain he will, Papalotl." Little Reed gave me a gentle squeeze with his elbows—the best hug possible while holding my bowl as I rested between sips. "She also said if you don't lose the baby, you shouldn't travel until after you deliver, so we're staying here for the winter. I've already sent word to Acolman, requesting a hundred stonemasons to build permanent houses before the weather turns cold. I won't have our son born in a drafty tent."

I paused, my heart thudding. "*Our* son?"

He nodded. "I know you said we couldn't marry but—and hear me out first—but maybe we still can. You said that you sacrificed the chance for us to be together, and I think we both can agree that our reasons for wanting to marry aren't traditional."

"No, they aren't."

"So, what if we marry for traditional reasons? This is a stroke of luck for both of us; the people expect me to marry and produce an heir, and you're already carrying a child. If we marry, no one can legally question Yamehecatl's parentage or his status as heir."

I gave him a good-natured scowl. "Not to mention all your allies will stop pestering you to marry their daughters."

He grinned. "An added bonus."

I went back to my soup. "It does make good political sense, but...we can't ever consummate this marriage, Little Reed. You understand that?"

He nodded. "I accept that it's a marriage of convenience, for both of us."

"And you can keep a concubine or two, so you have the things I cannot give you."

Little Reed sighed. "Sex is not so important that I can't be faithful to you, Papalotl, so please stop making such suggestions."

Funny how it didn't pain him at all to give up what felt to me like denying my very nature. "I'm sorry," I murmured. "I'm trying to be fair to you."

"I know, but that doesn't mean being unfair to yourself. We'll face the challenges together, with faith in the god."

Smiling, I let myself recline further back against him. But my pessimism didn't allow me peace for long. "But what if Yamehecatl doesn't survive? We shouldn't even talk about this until we know for certain."

"Or maybe we shouldn't talk about *that* possibility until we know," he suggested, a gentle ribbing in his voice.

"It does feel better to be positive." I set my empty bowl back into his hands, and he put it aside before wrapping me in his arms. "But what about Ten Spines?"

"What about him?"

"I told him you were betrothed."

"You didn't say to whom, so why couldn't it be you?"

"True. But when he discovers I'm pregnant, he'll think badly of us."

"Let's not worry about what he thinks."

I watched the shadows dance on the canvas walls. I couldn't remember the last time I'd felt this content, this safe, and I didn't want it to end.

But when I started drowsing off, Little Reed laid me down and pulled the blanket over me. I felt so cold, so alone, and desperately wanted not to be. "Little Reed?"

"Yes, my love?"

"Please stay with me." When he looked towards the tent flap, an indecisive look on his face, I stammered, "Only until I fall asleep."

Nodding, he stretched out next to me and laid on his side, propped up on his elbow so he could look down at me.

I moved onto my side, hoping it would wake me enough to keep him talking—and stay at my side. "If we can't go back to Culhuacan, who's going to marry us? We're the only priests of Quetzalcoatl here, and we can't perform our own wedding ceremony."

"We could ask Ueman—"

"I will not get married in front of anyone but a priest of Quetzalcoatl, Little Reed." The flint to my voice made him raise an eyebrow, so I said, "It was bad enough enduring a wedding ceremony performed by Ihuitimal; he poured blood on me, Little Reed. I still get sick thinking about it."

"That doesn't mean Ueman will do that. I spoke to Ten Spines about their gods, and they don't worship the Smoking Mirror. He says Tezcatlipoca is a far northern god."

"Yes, well, this Mixcoatl god isn't much better. Mitotia told me Ueman reenacts the vile story of Quetzalcoatl's supposed conception by forcing himself on one of the tribe's young women, and Ten Spines was going to give her to him for the ceremony at the end of summer. I can't even imagine.... Ueman is no better than Ahexotl was."

"It's a very good thing you talked Ten Spines into committing her to the priesthood instead." Little Reed sighed, his brows furrowed. "I know the god talks mostly of stopping human sacrifice, but it's also these kinds of exploitations he aims to stop."

I squeezed his hand with mine. "We will stop it."

Little Reed nodded. "We'll summon a priest of Quetzalcoatl to marry us."

"Let's ask Mazatzin. He's been a good friend to both of us for many years."

"He would be a very good choice." He kneaded my hand gently in his, never taking his gaze off me as silence descended between us.

The look in his eyes reminded me of the first time I'd met Quetzalcoatl in the Divine Dream; we'd gazed at each other as Love drifted down on us from Heaven. Back then, Little Reed and Quetzalcoatl had looked exactly alike—except for the emerald green quetzal feathers that grew amongst the god's long black hair. But while his father remained forever the same, never changing, Little Reed had changed a great deal. His silver hairs outnumbered the black ones, and when he laughed, the crinkled skin at the corners of his eyes didn't smooth out the way it once did. Yet he still turned my heart into a war drum, and when I thought of Quetzalcoatl's kiss, of his feathery touch, of making love in the grass in the Divine Dream, it wasn't the young face of the god I thought of, but rather the one that gazed at me now.

Tatli! Yamehecatl piped up, startling me so much I gasped aloud.

Little Reed sat up, suddenly alert. "Are you all right?"

I could only answer him with tears. Bless the gods, they had spared my son! *Are you all right, Yamehecatl?*

Of course, he laughed. *Why wouldn't I be?*

I wanted to scold him for scaring me so, but the joy of hearing his voice again overwhelmed everything else. All I could do was cry harder.

Little Reed held me close even as he trembled against me. "Should I fetch Lady Bitter Rabbit?"

I shook my head, finally finding my voice. "You were right; our son's fine."

"He's talking to you again?" When I nodded, he asked, "What is he saying?"

Smiling, I said, "He's calling you his tatli." And I was so very glad he did, for that's exactly how I wanted him to think of Little Reed.

CHAPTER NINE

Little Reed spent the entire night lying next to me, and, at some point someone brought him a blanket—my own serving as a buffer between us. When I woke, I savored the warmth of his body against mine in the morning chill, and marveled at how wonderful it was to wake up next to someone again. Neither of us said anything about it when Little Reed woke and went to fetch us breakfast, but as we ate in distracted silence I knew last night's special intimacy wouldn't be repeated. There were some things we couldn't do again because they tempted fate.

After breakfast, Little Reed composed a message to Mazatzin and sent it with a runner to Culhuacan. He spent the day out at the worksite, overseeing the construction of the temple's foundation while I remained in bed, following Bitter Rabbit's orders. At lunch time, I sent for Amoxtli and invited him to eat with me.

"I still can't believe that Black Otter is alive," I said once we were deep into the meal of roasted prickly pear. "Did you get to talk to him before he left for the valley?"

He frowned as he nibbled. "I did."

"And?"

"He's...I don't know that he even recognized me." Amoxtli put down his unfinished food.

"I'm sorry I had to send him away—"

He shook his head. "No, I completely understand. He reminded me of some crazed wild animal. I thank you for sparing his life though, My Lady."

"We've lost too much family as it is. Maybe he can recover and find happiness again with Jade Flower or one of the others."

"Let us hope." After a pause, he said, "But what about the child?"

I knew it was only a matter of time before the question came up, and now I was glad Little Reed had given me an easy means of explaining it without having to reveal Yamehecatl's true parentage. "Actually, the child is Topiltzin's." I bowed my head, avoiding his gaze in a show of embarrassment that wasn't entirely faked. "We're going to marry soon."

Amoxtli nodded, looking relieved. "That's a good thing, for my brother certainly can't handle more responsibility right now. And Topiltzin will take good care of you and the baby; his devotion to you is not only obvious, but refreshing as well."

¤

Once I'd rested for several days, and gotten permission from Bitter Rabbit to leave my bed, Little Reed took me to the construction site in the royal litter. I hadn't been back since that first time, when we'd dug for my father's bones. Much work had been accomplished.

All the trees were cleared, even the giant that had sheltered my father's original burial site. A layer of limestone blocks covered the area, with the middle stone removed to reveal a hole large enough to fit the box of bones inside. Amoxtli held my mother's urn while Little Reed and I scooped her ashes into the box.

We consecrated the grave with prayers, sprinkled octli and waved copal smoke over it with a clay censer. Little Reed slit the throat of a small dog, spilling its blood over my father's bones and our mother's ashes, and he laid its body in the box, murmuring a prayer to Xolotl before sealing it again. Citlallotoc lowered the box into the hole.

"We witness the birth of a new, brighter era, built upon the bones of those who came before us." Little Reed motioned to the men to backfill the hole with dirt, and when that was finished, workers laid the heavy stone over the top. It had been a rainy, dreary day when I'd watched Cuitlapanton lay my mother's ashes under the tree in Xochicalco's royal gardens, but today the sun blazed, casting a stifling heat over the entire ordeal; I didn't even cry, but was merely relieved that it was over at last.

But by the end of the ceremony, the short, dull pains came back. "If you don't wish to lose this baby, you need to stay in bed," Bitter Rabbit warned me when I summoned her. "The fall dislodged the child's tonalli and it's trying to leave. Stay still and it will settle back into place once the child is born."

But that's five months away! But I bit my tongue. How many times did I lecture Cuitlapanton's wives about the things they needed to do if they didn't want to miscarry? I didn't want Yamehecatl's soul to wander off, forever lost after the gods gave me a second chance; if that meant sacrificing months to the childbed, then so be it.

The stonemasons arrived within a week and Little Reed put them to work building permanent houses not only for us, but for the workers staying the winter. Mitotia moved in and set up her sleeping mat in my quarters, to look after me during the night while I continued teaching her during the day. Little Reed made an icpalli for me to recline in bed, so I didn't have to lay on my back or side all the time; a nice gesture, but I missed leaning on him.

By the end of the month the stonemasons finished a small royal villa to house us, Citlallotoc, Ten Spines and his wife, and Ten Spines' war chief. The unit consisted of four domiciles and a large storeroom and kitchen, all sharing a common courtyard. A tall stone wall surrounded it all, ensuring privacy. Each house had three rooms—a large anteroom for eating and entertaining guests, and two cozy sleeping quarters, each with its own hearth. Little Reed built a wooden screen for my room, to block any drafts and lock the heat in around my bed, making my sleeping area an ideal place to pass the winter. He also built me a special bed that could be lifted on poles, so he and Citlallotoc could carry me out into the anteroom.

Within a few days of moving into our new quarters, Mazatzin arrived and we all sat down to a hot meal in the anteroom. He looked concerned when he first saw me reclined on my bed while everyone else sat on their mats, but he waited until the evening pipes came out before leaning over and whispering, "Are you injured?"

I laughed. "In a manner of speaking." To Little Reed, I said, "Perhaps now would be a good time to make our announcement?"

Both Citlallotoc and Ten Spines were there as well, stuffing their pipes. "Is it good news, I hope?" Ten Spines asked once he got his tobacco smoldering.

"It's very good news." Little Reed took my hand. "Lady Quetzalpetlatl and I are getting married."

Both Citlallotoc and Mazatzin raised their eyebrows in surprise, but Ten Spines roared with hearty laughter. "You Tolteca are a strange lot, bedding your sisters and all. Is there a shortage of women back in the valley?" After a puff on his pipe, he added, "But a lesser man would have conquered and left. You, My Lord, are an honorable man."

Little Reed had the same look in his eyes as when Red Flint had besmirched me as a whore. He'd taken Red Flint to task for it, but now I set my hand on his and gave it a gentle squeeze, to snap him out of it. I told Ten Spines, "We are but following the path the god laid out for us, My Lord."

Ten Spines nodded. "The gods are mysterious, and we cannot comprehend their ways. I ask you forgive me if my original suggestion for binding our alliance trod on your toes, My Lady, though why did you not tell me then?"

"It was a private matter that we'd chosen to keep such until we returned to Culhuacan, but circumstances necessitate revealing our intent early."

"A wedding is always a welcome occasion. When is the ceremony, so I can set my men to gathering the food supplies necessary?"

Having regained his composure, Little Reed answered, "The tying ceremony will be tomorrow night."

"That's too soon, isn't it? It will be impossible for my hunters to kill enough deer by then."

"Traditional Tolteca wedding ceremonies last four days, so there will be time to gather meat," Little Reed said. "And the stonemasons brought a large supply of maize, squash, beans, and chile with them, so we'll have enough food. Do you think Lady Bitter Rabbit would be willing to coordinate the cooking efforts?"

"She would be most pleased to, though our women know little about cooking with the maize," Ten Spines said.

"We'll train them." Little Reed rose. "Perhaps we can go and speak with your wife and get the details solidified while my fire priest rests from his long journey?"

While Little Reed, Citlallotoc and Ten Spines left I finished my last tlaxcalli, savoring it. After two months of meat, wild roots, and prickly pear, even Mitotia's burnt attempts at tlaxcallis were delicious. As Mazatzin finished his plate, he asked, "What did you mean by 'circumstances'?"

"I am with child."

Mazatzin sat taller. "Really? Congratulations! I had no idea you and Topiltzin were...so close. Though I suppose that explains why the two of you lifted the prohibitions against marriage in the priesthood."

I didn't like the idea of he—or anyone else—thinking Little Reed and I had been secretly breaking our vows of chastity, but that was a small price to pay to make sure no one questioned Yamehecatl's parentage.

¤

Unlike my first wedding, no one paraded me around on a litter, showing me off, nor did hundreds of people attend the tying ceremony in our house; only Ten Spines, his wife and daughter, Citlallotoc, and Amoxtli were present while Mazatzin tied my dress to Little Reed's cape. We didn't exchange gifts of clothing either.

But in other ways the ceremony was exactly the same as when I was a girl; we retired to my quarters for days of prayer, something much easier to accomplish with my priestly training and cultivated patience. I wasn't made to fast during the first evening—Little Reed insisted I was in far too delicate a condition to be expected to do that, but I forewent salt and chile, as ritual practice dictated.

And as with that first wedding, after the final feast, Little Reed and I retired to our separate quarters, leaving the marriage unconsummated. *But I will be far happier in this marriage than I ever was with Black Otter,* I told myself. Yet as I lay alone that night, trying to fall asleep, I couldn't quite escape the bitter knowledge that I was so very close to complete happiness but would never fully hold it.

¤

As the weeks passed, my body began showing signs of its condition, and it grew increasingly difficult to find a comfortable position to sleep in. Yamehecatl stayed awake longer and longer, chattering like a parrot into the early hours of the morning, and he resisted going to sleep as if he were already a toddler.

He'd taken to watching the world through my eyes and asking all sorts of questions, from what were the green things all over the trees, and why did they change colors as the weather changed, to why did the sun and the moon chase each other across the sky. *Is the moon trying to catch the sun and kill it?* I answered everything as best I could and mused that when he was born, he would have an immense vocabulary that would make the young me—who had developed language quite early in life—look plain stupid.

But to my sorrow, his interest in the gods and priestly knowledge quickly dwindled to nothing. He slept whenever I taught Mitotia. He declared my interest in weaving "boring". He loved it though when Little Reed and I played patolli—the traditional way now, for we'd soured our taste for betting our secrets. He also enjoyed music and would sing along to any song he heard. Sometimes his beautiful singing voice choked me up, and I wished Little Reed could hear our son as I did.

Tonight though he was quiet. I'd let Mitotia have the day off to help her mother mend her father's winter clothing, so Yamehecatl chattered most of the day, letting me go to sleep with little trouble.

But sometime in the middle of the night, I awoke with a start, thinking someone had prodded me. I looked over at Mitotia, but she was fast asleep on her mat, at my feet. I closed my eyes, praying I'd find sleep again soon. Yamehecatl woke me earlier every day.

But I felt it again: a strange, ticklish fluttering traveling from one side of my abdomen to the other. Now wide awake, I set my hand on my belly, my heart pounding. Had I felt my son move for the first time, or was I merely imagining it? Yamehecatl was silent, something he rarely was when awake. I didn't dare wake him up to ask though; I wouldn't get back to sleep for hours if I did.

When it came again, a bulge slid under my hand. My heart skipped. *I must share this with Little Reed!*

I prodded Mitotia with my toe a couple of times until she roused. She looked up at me, barely awake. "Is something the matter, My Lady?"

"Please fetch Topiltzin. I must see him immediately."

She stumbled from the room but didn't return when Little Reed came in a moment later, looking far from awake. "Is something wrong?" he asked, kneeling next to me, blurry-eyed.

"Nothing's wrong," I assured him. I took his hand and slid it up under my night dress, setting it palm-down against my abdomen.

"Umm." He cast me an uncertain glance—undergarments were too difficult to tie around my swollen belly anymore—but when Yamehecatl moved, his face lit. "Is that—?" When I nodded, he whispered, "Ayya!" He moved his hand across my abdomen, following our son's movements. "Amazing!"

"Truly." I seemed incapable of not crying these last few months.

"Are you all right?" he asked, his concern returning.

I nodded. "I feel so...happy."

He leaned his head against mine, smiling. "Me too, my love."

His words, his closeness—his bare skin against mine—sent a shiver of desire through me. I felt as if I were floating when our noses brushed against each other, teasingly, until he moved his mouth to mine and the passion engulfed me. I pulled him down onto the bed, the moment wrapping around me like the delicious heat of the steam bath on a cold day.

He bellied up to me, hand moving lower, creeping, caressing. The desire lurched, desperate and oh so glad to have broken free at last....

What are you doing? Yamehecatl suddenly asked, innocent and curious.

Not now, the desire growled. I wanted to pull away, embarrassed, but the desire was in command. I slid my hand down the front of Little Reed's sleep xicolli, finding him already hard despite the thin layer of fabric between his body and my hand. A hunger food couldn't quell spread inside me—

But a sudden, sharp pain radiated through my lower abdomen, cutting through the desire like an obsidian blade. I gritted my teeth against the tight, knotting sensation in my guts, the pain paralyzing.

Little Reed pulled away. "Are you all right? Did I hurt you?"

I shook my head, cursing myself. How could I have been so stupid to let the desire take over? "I'm sorry, I shouldn't have...we can't let this ever happen, Little Reed."

"No, I'm sorry," he stammered. "It's my fault; I shouldn't have kissed you."

I frowned. "No, I should exercise more control; I'm not a slave to my impulses. I made the sacrifice, not you, so the onus is on me to remain faithful to it."

"And I don't expect you to endure it on your own. You made that sacrifice on my behalf; I'd be dead now if not for you, so the least I can do is help you keep the path."

I smiled at him. "I am thankful to Quetzalcoatl every day for giving you life, Little Reed."

"As am I," he replied with a chuckle. He stared into the hearth a moment, an indecisive look on his face. "You know, when it gets to be too difficult, you can always go and see the god in the Divine Dream."

I stared at him, uncomfortable heat traveling up my neck. "What's that supposed to mean?" Little Reed shrugged, bashful now, and my insides curled up. "He...he told you?"

"He never outright stated anything," Little Reed hastily answered. "It's just...why don't you go see him—"

I tried to sit up, cutting him off as he rushed to help me. "I don't go into the Divine Dream anymore because my relationship with Quetzalcoatl.... This is embarrassing to admit, but it was wrong and I never should have done any of it. I was young, and he looked so much like you...and I feared you would never return. I behaved childishly, and selfishly. I disrespected his power and sacredness, to appease my own lusts. But even worse, I disrespected *you*."

Little Reed shook his head. "You didn't disrespect me—"

"I did, because I wanted you, not him, but I was perfectly willing to use him to that end. Quetzalcoatl isn't like us, Little Reed, and it's hugely arrogant to treat him as if we're his equals, or for me to treat my title of his wife as literal, the way we might treat our own if I'd never made this promise to Heaven. I've sworn to never go down that path again, and that means learning to get along without a direct connection to Quetzalcoatl, the same as everyone else. I love him, but he's an unknowable god, so how could I ever really love him the way I love you?"

Little Reed looked baffled. "You speak your true feelings about this...about the god?" When I nodded, he looked strangely wounded. "He would thank you for your honesty. He values that more than anything." He kissed my forehead and stood. "I hope I didn't upset you with my prying questions."

I shook my head. "It's weighed heavily on me, especially now that Yamehecatl thinks you and Quetzalcoatl are one and the same. I hope I haven't disappointed you, Little Reed."

"You could never disappoint me, Papalotl." He left to return to his own bedroom, a wave of regret following him.

¤

In the morning, Little Reed went next door to Citlallotoc's house for breakfast without me. At dinner, he ate with Ten Spines and the other men, leaving me and Mitotia to eat our meal alone, and he didn't come back to the house until after I'd fallen asleep. I wondered how long he'd known about me and his father; likely not long given his sudden distance. Perhaps he'd hoped I would deny the whole thing.

He stayed home for breakfast the next day and I watched him clandestinely, not wanting to be caught staring at him. I desperately wanted everyone else to leave so I could talk to him.

But halfway through the meal, a runner from Culhuacan arrived with a letter from Blood Wolf.

"King Meconetzin of Chalco has died and his sons are brawling for the throne," Little Reed announced once he finished reading. "Several of them banded together and are intercepting the trade caravans traveling to Culhuacan. Matlacxochitl went to negotiate a peaceful ending, but they took him captive and are threatening to maim him if I don't support their chosen candidate for the throne."

"They've already cut off his ear and sent it along with their demands to Lord Blood Wolf," the runner informed him.

"And what of our other allies?" I asked. "Why aren't they helping in this?"

"No one seems willing to step in without Lord Topiltzin to lead."

Little Reed stared at the letter a moment longer, chewing his lip. "What happened to Meconetzin's legitimate heir?"

"He was executed the same night the king died," the runner explained. "They even killed the queen and her daughters."

I gasped. "What about Lady Papantzin and the baby?"

The runner bowed his head, frowning. "I'm sorry, My Lady."

You should have convinced her to stay in Culhuacan, I thought, my appetite gone. The King of Chalco had become one of our staunchest allies since our claiming Culhuacan's throne; even Meconetzin's heir had declared his dedication to maintaining that alliance once he became king. There'd been no reason to believe her life—or the baby's—would be in jeopardy by going home. "What about Lady Jade Flower and her children? Certainly they were spared, not being blood relatives of the King?"

"I'm sorry, but I have no information on your sister."

I prayed Black Otter had arrived there safely and gotten her and the children out before all this transpired.

Little Reed folded up the letter and motioned to Mazatzin. "We'll leave immediately."

Citlallotoc rose to his feet as well. "Don't you mean me as well, My Lord?"

Little Reed shook his head. "I need you to stay here and oversee my affairs."

"But My Lord—"

"And I need you to guard my wife and son." Little Reed set a firm hand on his shoulder. "I trust only my very best man with such an important task."

Citlallotoc looked sullen, but he nodded.

"And move into my quarters while I'm gone, so you're within easy reach of the queen," Little Reed told him.

Amoxtli rose as well. "I ask permission to accompany you, My Lord.

My brother was sent to Chalco and I must know what became of him."

Little Reed nodded. "We welcome you to join us, Cousin."

The rest of the meal passed in a whirlwind of instructions and planning, but once it was over, Little Reed went to his quarters to pack. Citlallotoc lingered and only left once I asked him to go so I could have a private word with Little Reed. Eventually Little Reed emerged from his quarters, wearing cotton armor under his heron-feather xicolli emblazoned with the Feathered Serpent, his macuahuitl sword hanging from his belt. He looked striking in his army uniform.

"Will you hurry back once this is finished?" I tried to keep my voice steady.

"If I could fly back, I would," he assured me. When I looked away, he said, "I know this is really bad timing, with the baby due in a few more months, but things could deteriorate if I wait."

I nodded. "I know you must go, but...I'm afraid I upset you and we haven't made amends, and what if you're not back in time, or something happens in the childbed, and I never get to see you again?"

Little Reed knelt and took me into his arms. "I'm sorry I made you believe I was angry, Papalotl. I was working out my feelings about some things, but I shouldn't have kept you at a distance. Your personal relationship with the god...it isn't my business, and you don't need to explain yourself. I'm sorry I made you believe you had to. Can you forgive me?"

I hugged him tighter. "Of course, Little Reed. Just promise me you'll do your best to get back here before the baby comes."

"I *will* be here," he assured me. "And we'll wrestle Yamehecatl from the gods together." He kissed my cheek then moved his mouth towards mine, but after a hesitation he withdrew, leaving my heart hammering. "And don't worry, Citlallotoc will take care of you, and I'll write to keep you apprised of everything."

"I'll miss you." I held onto his hand a moment longer before finally letting go. "And come home safely to me, and Yamehecatl."

"I promise I will," he said with a smile, before going outside where Mazatzin and Amoxtli waited for him.

I sighed. "The last time someone made that promise to me, I never saw him alive again," I muttered.

CHAPTER TEN

The weeks turned into months, punctuated with an occasional letter from Little Reed painting grim pictures of life back in the valley. He'd tried negotiating Matlacxochitl's release, but when the reply consisted only of Matlacxochitl's severed nose, Little Reed sent troops into the countryside where the band of villains had taken refuge, and killed the lot. He marched on Chalco and seized control of the city, allowing the remaining sons to come out of hiding to make their petitions to inherit the throne. He listened to each man's case and picked two of the strongest and brightest candidates to co-rule, then installed his own advisor on the new war council to monitor affairs going forward.

He'd planned to return to Tollan at that point, two months after he'd left, but riots broke out in Culhuacan. A mob of Toltecas attacked and killed a Chichimec woman selling cotton cloth in the market, claiming she'd stolen it from another woman's inventory—for everyone knew that Chichimecs knew nothing about weaving "like civilized people". The woman's death spurred her husband to gather his friends and they hunted down and killed her murderers, though not before cutting out their tongues, gouging out their eyes, and slicing off their ears. From there the violence escalated, with mobs hunting any and all Chichimecs, killing the men and enslaving the women and children. Fear and anger ran rampant, and finding and punishing the ringleaders proved more than a little taxing.

But when Little Reed announced the need for workers to go north to help build Tollan, the Chichimecs—tired of being treated as animals—migrated to Tollan in droves, bringing their wives, their children, and their dreams with them.

"This place was already crawling with too many Chichimecs," Citlallotoc growled as he stood at the doorway overlooking the courtyard, watching the women working around the fire pit. He complained at least once a day about the women cooking outside rather than using the hearths in the kitchen. "A bunch of barbarians, the whole lot of them."

"We all want the same things," I told him as I worked on my weaving in front of the anteroom hearth. I'd become very round the last month and found it difficult to lie down all the time, so I sat as often as I could; occasionally, with Mitotia's help, I walked around the house.

"We won't have enough food to last the entire winter," Citlallotoc grumbled. "I'll have to request more from my brother and hope he has enough to spare. Things will turn ugly if we run out, and we'll be the first ones these Chichimec dogs come to looking for relief. You know what they say about Chichimecs and their own children?"

I pinned him with a glare. "My father used to tell me that if I kept crossing my eyes and making faces at my sisters that the gods would freeze my face. I've never witnessed any of our Chichimec allies feasting on their own children." I was grateful Mitotia wasn't here, though had she been, Citlallotoc never would have said anything; she made him uncomfortable and so he rarely spoke around her. I'd initially thought it attraction but I grew increasingly sure it had more to do with his stubborn distrust of all Chichimecs.

Why does he distrust them, Nantli? Yamehecatl asked.

Because they are different from us in many ways. Differences frighten people.

Do they scare you?

Most men frighten me until I get to know them and realize they're safe. Though even that had proven a mistake on more than one occasion.

Why?

It's complicated, my dear. I don't want to mistrust people immediately, but experience has taught me that it's safer to do so.

You're not scared of me, are you? Yamehecatl asked, concerned.

I chuckled aloud. *No. I love you, and trust you implicitly.*

"What's so funny?" Citlallotoc leaned against the doorway as the rain came down beyond the porch.

"I was talking to myself."

He gave me a silly grin. "You do that a lot these days. Am I insufficient company?"

I grinned back at him. "Quite sufficient, thank you."

He closed the heavy door curtain and sat on one of the reed mats in front of the hearth, next to me. He stared into the fire, knees drawn up, arms across them. "You needn't spare my feelings, My Lady. I know I'm no substitute for Topiltzin. I really thought he would be back by now." His gaze rested on my huge belly, concern painted on his face. "I'm certain he'll be back any day now."

Every day I told myself, *only one more day;* but with few weeks remaining until the birth, I worried. If matters went sour in the childbed, Citlallotoc would sit and guard me from the Black Dog, but it wasn't the same. I had so much to tell Little Reed; private things I couldn't imagine asking Citlallotoc to pass on to him after I was gone.

Why do you think you're going to die, Nantli? Yamehecatl asked, puzzled.

I don't think I'm going to, it's only...the childbed is dangerous. Sometimes things go wrong. That's life.

But what does it matter if you die? You'll come back again, as in the stories you tell me about Tatli and the other gods.

I'm not like your father, Yamehecatl. But I had already died once and came back to life....

Citlallotoc chuckled. "I am definitely not adequate company. You're 'talking' to yourself again."

I blushed. "Sorry."

"My father once told me my mother was so scatterbrained in her last month with me that she couldn't hold a conversation at all."

It wasn't unusual for women to become distracted and forgetful in the final months of their pregnancies; Nimilitzli had said it was because they carry two—sometimes more—tonallis in their bodies at once, and they knocked each other around. Though I suspected that it was because they were constantly distracted by the curious chatter of their unborn children.

Mitotia opened the door curtain, her long hair dripping water. "My Lord, my father asks to see you immediately." She looked agitated.

He glanced at her over his shoulder. "Is something wrong?"

"Strangers have arrived out of the north, and their leader...." She paused, as if reconsidering what to say. "Father asks you come right away."

Citlallotoc donned his cloak and went out into the rain.

"What's wrong with their leader?" I asked.

She glanced back at the doorway before whispering, "Lord Citlallotoc is the tallest man I've ever met, until now. This Chichimec is twice his size, and his face...I shudder to remember it!"

"What was wrong with it?"

"Half of it is blue, and not only his face; the whole left side of his body—arm, leg, and chest. I've never seen that color of paint before."

"Where is he?"

"The guards made him and his men wait at the gate."

Then I could see him from the doorway. I motioned her for help up and she did so. I shuffled to the door and peeked out of the curtain.

Citlallotoc and Ten Spines stood at the gate with several armed guards. Beyond, as Mitotia had said, was a giant of a man—he would have to bend down to step through the corbeled arch, if the guards would let him. And the left side of his body was painted the same shimmering color of the blue-throated hummingbirds that haunted the forests around the valley. The arch blocked any view of his face, but his deep, throaty voice boomed. "This is the illustrious Topiltzin everyone speaks of?"

"This is Lord Topiltzin's war chief, Lord Citlallotoc," Ten Spines answered, a quaver to his voice.

"I said I would speak only to Topiltzin."

Citlallotoc glared up at the other man and asked Ten Spines, "An ally of yours?"

The stranger laughed. "I require no allies."

"This is Lord Mextli of the Mexica," Ten Spines replied.

"I despise repeating myself," Mextli growled. "I demand an audience with Topiltzin."

"It's too late for an official visit," Citlallotoc fired back.

"It's never too late for matters of war. Or does the dark scare you, little lord?"

Citlallotoc stiffened. "If you were hoping for shelter tonight, I'm afraid we haven't room for your kind."

"I have no use for your pathetic stone buildings. I'm here to counsel Topiltzin, but he's too afraid to come out and speak to me."

"The *king* has no use for loudmouthed Chichimec dog-shit, and he'd hand you your own tongue if he weren't such an understanding man. Now, if you're finished preening, I'll gladly toss you out on your asses."

Mextli laughed. "I admire your gall, so I won't crush your skull...yet. But hear this: I won't allow you to build a temple to the Feathered Serpent on Smoking Mirror's lands. Quetzalcoatl kicked Tezcatlipoca out of the lake valley, and now his insidious influence infringes on our brother's territory. You will begin deconstructing the offending buildings immediately and leave here forever."

None of the sacred stories spoke of Quetzalcoatl having any brothers, but Smoking Mirror had called him "brother" when we'd faced off in

Culhuacan. And now this Mextli made the very same claim. I could accept that the sacred stories were only part of the truth—Quetzalcoatl had told me as much—but I'd never heard of any god called Mextli.

Citlallotoc laughed. "And why should Topiltzin bend to your bawling?"

"If I told you, it would wipe that smirk off your face," Mextli replied. "Refuse my request, and I will do the work myself—and Omeyocan help you, little man, if you get in my way."

"You're asking me to leave you and your men's bodies as scraps for the coyotes!" Citlallotoc roared.

"Such adorable threats. Pity you're not man enough to fulfill them."

Citlallotoc launched himself at Mextli, but Ten Spines held him back. "Let us not spill blood on Lord Topiltzin's doorstep."

"Oh, the blood will spill," Mextli said. "It's only out of respect for your better judgment, Ten Spines, that I will spare your people when everything turns bad—and trust me, it will. What is happening here in the heart of Smoking Mirror's realm is an affront to the gods, and everyone involved with this sacrilege will pay with their lives."

"Big talk for a man flanked by a mere fifteen warriors!" Citlallotoc shouted at him over Ten Spines' shoulder.

Mextli laughed. "Your superior numbers are meaningless. I could defeat the whole lot of you on my own."

"Then stop your strutting and draw your sword!" Citlallotoc reached for his, but again Ten Spines interrupted him.

"This is not the place, My Lord." Ten Spines cast a discreet glance in my direction. "Think of those we swore to protect."

Citlallotoc didn't follow his gaze but nodded, relaxing finally. To Mextli he said, "You and your men will leave. And if you return, there will be bloodshed."

"I wouldn't have it any other way." Mextli turned to his wet and bedraggled men. "Let us go and allow the little lord to sleep. He will need it." The strangers departed from the gate.

Ten Spines and Citlallotoc kept their place, leaning past the archway to watch them go. "It isn't wise to upset that man," Ten Spines said.

"He's a puffed-up grouse who squawks loudly," Citlallotoc growled.

"Perhaps, but his face...he's a monster."

"I don't care how he decorates himself; I won't tolerate anyone insulting my king at the gate to his own house. And his ludicrous demands that we tear down the temple—"

"What are we going to do?"

"He talks big, but he doesn't realize Quetzalcoatl has his own defenses." He finally looked back at me.

I shut the curtain and went back to my bed mat, feeling as if someone had squeezed my heart. Would duty have me call on Quetzalcoatl's powers again? *But I've already given so much.* As I felt Yamehecatl kicking around, a chill ran through me. *Maybe Mextli will go away,* I thought, determined to stop the rising tide of panic. *He's all bluster and I won't have to sacrifice my son.*

Who's Mextli, Nantli? Yamehecatl asked.

I have no idea, love. I shook my head. *And I hope we don't find out.*

◻

Shouts in the courtyard woke me before dawn. Bare feet slapped on the stone floor of the anteroom and I heard Citlallotoc tear aside the curtain to Little Reed's quarters. "What in Mictlan is going on out there?" he demanded.

A guard answered, out of breath. "My Lord, the temple is under attack!"

I tossed aside my blanket and went to the door, Mitotia at my side. I opened the curtain to find Citlallotoc donning his cotton armor while a nervous guard stood at the doorway outside. "It's Mextli's men, isn't it?" I asked, my stomach knotting up.

"Undoubtedly." Citlallotoc threw a cloak over his armor. "He will pay with his life for this." He took a long spear from the corner near the front door and told me, "Stay here for now. If I need you...?"

"I will." I tried to sound brave. "But please, it costs me a great deal."

He nodded and disappeared into the dark.

"I thought we increased patrols around the sacred precinct, to make certain the Mexica didn't come back," Mitotia said.

"Apparently those patrols weren't sufficient."

I looked into the courtyard. Screaming and yelling came from beyond the wall, from men and women alike. Bitter Rabbit lurked in her doorway, looking into the sky and muttering under her breath. "Pack us a bag with some clothes and food, and pack one for your mother as well."

"Why?"

"If Mextli kills your father and Citlallotoc we'll need to leave quickly, so don't hesitate any further."

Mitotia raced across the courtyard to talk to her mother. Bitter Rabbit's worry became distress, but she nodded and disappeared inside. When Mitotia returned, she went immediately to my room while I remained at the doorway, watching the outer walls. Oddly, I felt stronger than I had in ages.

With our bag packed, Mitotia suggested I change out of my night dress into some traveling clothes; but as I turned from the doorway, a flaming arrow stuck into the ground next to the cooking fire. The already terrified servants fled screaming through the gate when a second arrow bounced off the stone wall of Ten Spines' house and skidded across the ground onto the reed mats near the cooking fire.

"No time!" I grabbed a cloak off the peg next to the doorway. "We're leaving now. Get your mother and meet me by the gate."

But five guards stood outside the gate, blocking our way. "Lord Citlallotoc ordered us to keep you here," the lead guard replied, nudging me back with the handle of his spear. "You'll be safer in your house."

"When it's on fire?" I demanded. "The Mexica are shooting flaming arrows over our walls!"

"There's enough mayhem out here without worrying about where you are, My Lady."

Losing patience, I snapped, "Step aside or I'll call on the god to clear the path for us!"

He must have been at the battle for Culhuacan, for he paled and immediately stepped aside. "I'm coming with you, though," he said, keeping pace with me. "If I'm to die for disobeying orders, then let it be because I stepped between you and an enemy spear."

Despite the danger of the moment, I frowned. Evidently the orders of my war chief counted more than my own orders as queen.

After months of virtual captivity, I felt exhilarated at being out among the people again. And even better, no pains hounded my movements; in fact, I felt as energetic and strong as at twenty, when I spent my days running up and down the vast staircases of Xochicalco. The further I walked, the better I felt. Had it been a mistake to spend so many months lying in bed when I was perfectly capable of getting up and walking around without pain?

But that good feeling abandoned me when we reached the sacred precinct, where most of the fighting was concentrated. *What madness leads me here, to the middle of a pitched battle?*

We're exactly where we need to be, the desire answered, so confident and sure.

The guard grabbed my arm. "You can't go in there!"

And yet every fiber of my being screamed that if I didn't, I would regret it for the rest of my life. I pulled away from him and ran into the writhing mass of death, feeling light as a feather.

He fought his way through the crowd, shouting after me, "My Lady! You must come back! It's not safe—"

The din of battle swallowed his words when I spotted Citlallotoc sparring with several Mexica warriors at the foot of the half-built temple. Above him, Mextli—massive and hulking—was ripping up blocks of stone and hurling them into the crowd. Finally seeing his face, I was mesmerized. He wore no cotton armor, no elaborate headdress; if not for the simple white loincloth, he would have been completely naked. Blue paint covered him head to foot on the left side, but none of it rubbed off onto his pristine white loincloth. He carried himself as if a spear-thrust to the gut or taking an arrow to the chest meant nothing. He tore apart the Feathered Serpent's temple as if this were a typical day's work.

At the temple's foot, Citlallotoc dispatched the two remaining warriors then charged up the steps, his spear ready. Ten steps up, he launched it, putting his whole body into the throw. He had magnificent form that spoke of a lifetime of training.

But Mextli batted the zipping spear aside as if it were an annoying insect. "Certainly Topiltzin's best warrior can do better than that!" he roared, laughing. His words brought much of the fighting nearest the temple to a halt as both sides watched their leaders face off.

Citlallotoc drew his sword. "Let us decide this like honorable men. Just you and me, to the death, winner claims these lands; for Topiltzin if I win, for Smoking Mirror if you do."

"When I win, I will sacrifice the whole lot of you and scatter your children to the desert," Mextli said. "But with you, little lord, I shall teach my people the art of making tlaxcallis using your ground-up bones for masa." He beckoned to Citlallotoc with one hand.

Citlallotoc charged up the steps, bellowing like a bear.

Mextli scooped up the spear and swung the butt of it around, bashing Citlallotoc in the face. Citlallotoc rolled down the stairs, dazed, but caught hold of one of the stone steps to stop from tumbling all the way down. Blood gushed from his broken nose.

Snickering, Mextli tossed the spear to him. "I think you'll need this too. Maybe you'll fare better if I'm unarmed."

Citlallotoc snatched up the spear and got to his feet. Wiping blood from his mouth and chin with the back of his hand, he climbed the stairs, leading with the spear.

Mextli didn't move, only stared at him. But when Citlallotoc tried to jab him with the spear, he side-stepped and grabbed it one-handed, lifting Citlallotoc off his feet. He swung him around and let go, flinging him down the stairs. Citlallotoc hit the bottom, landing chest down with a gushing grunt.

Mextli descended the stairs and yanked him up by his cotton armor. "How dare Topiltzin come here to exploit the hard labor of Smoking Mirror's chosen people, and make them forget their gods with false promises of peace and prosperity?"

He threw Citlallotoc back to the ground and faced the crowd. "Their real aim is to exterminate every last Chichimec and expel you from your homelands! Tolteca fathers tell their children that you eat your own sons and rape your daughters; they raise generation after generation to hate and despise your people because they know their time is coming to an end, and they are terrified. The Chichimec people are meant for greatness, so stand strong against your Tolteca enslavers and seize the robes of power for yourselves! You will live in their lavish palaces as kings, with them scraping an existence at your borders, paying you tribute to keep you from crushing them. Someday they'll quake in fear before the very name of your people!"

Cheers rose from Mextli's men, but Ten Spines' men exchanged mistrusting glances with the Toltecas they'd fought next to moments before. A heavy, contentious silence settled over the precinct.

Citlallotoc swiped Mextli's left leg with his sword, and a cloud of blue flakes drifted off the wound, like feathers from a sling-shot bird. *That's not paint at all!* I realized.

Mextli roared in pain, but when Citlallotoc tried to roll away, Mextli stepped his right foot onto his hair, pinning his head to the ground. Citlallotoc swung again, but Mextli kicked the sword away. He stamped hard on Citlallotoc's right forearm with a sickening crunch. Citlallotoc howled in agony.

"Now we'll have our fun, little lord," Mextli snarled, pinning him with his knees, gold dust sputtering from the wound on his leg.

Just as when I injured Smoking Mirror during the battle for Culhuacan, I realized with a gasp. *Great Feathered Serpent, he* is *a god!*

And as if to confirm my conclusion, a flint knife suddenly materialized in Mextli's left hand. *Citlallotoc never had any chance at all against this man.* The only way he would survive—that *any of us* would survive this— was if I called on the god.

I set my hand on my swollen belly, thinking of all the things I'd miss: getting to hold Yamehecatl, seeing him with my eyes, not only my heart, to see if he resembled the god as Little Reed did. Had all of it been for nothing? I couldn't breathe, but I'd learned the hard way to have the courage to make the right sacrifice when it mattered most.

I felt physically ill, but I took a deep, calming breath, trying to separate myself from my emotions as I reached for my sacrificial blade at my hip.

Forget the knife, the desire chided. *Remember the maguey.*

I hadn't thought about what I'd done since that day; I'd dismissed it as a hallucination. But now that same tingling returned to my fingers, coursing up my arms, and into my chest, a powerful, rhythmic pulsing begging for release.

Mextli waved the knife in Citlallotoc's face. "I'm going to peel the skin off your face and wear it as a mask," he hissed. "And when you beg me to end your suffering, I shall cut out your heart and eat it while you watch, little lord." Smiling, he traced the tip of the blade across Citlallotoc's forehead. "But we're going to take a while to get to that point."

This is crazy, I thought, bending down and setting my hands on the ground. The magic vibrated inside me, so I flexed my arm muscles and pushed.

As in the field, the ground rumbled, softly but with growing intensity. A murmur rose as everyone looked at each other—even Mextli stood, towering over everyone else.

But when the ground bucked, panic erupted. Men fled, falling over each other. I remained where I was, hands to the ground, focused on the magic surging through my arms. The crowd thinned enough that I saw Citlallotoc dragging himself away from Mextli, his right arm dangling useless at his side.

Mextli looked around, bewildered. "Is that you, Brother? Have you come to face me?"

No, Mextli, I *have come to face you.* I felt powerful, in control in a way I never had before. It was intoxicating.

Suddenly, lime-white roots shot out of the ground under Mextli's feet, striking like rattlesnakes and lashing onto him, cutting like obsidian blades. "*What in Mictlan...?*" He tried to yank them off, but they coiled around his chest like a boa constrictor suffocating a tapir. He slashed at them with his knife, slicing them off, but I willed more to spring from the ground, weaving over him into a net. He ripped through the mesh with his bare hands, spewing gold dust as they laid open his fingers and palms. But he was making headway against my trap.

Oh no you don't! I pushed more tingling magic, imagining thousands more roots spearing out of the hard ground to drag him down into the belly of the earth monster. The ground began swallowing him a bit at a time; first his feet, then his knees. Soon he was up to his hips in dirt, clawing to keep from going under. *Squeeze and crush him,* I thought, an intoxicating thrill coursing through me; not very different than when Black Otter got the desire going.

But when Mextli sank to his chest, the roots went up in flames, engulfing him completely. I jolted from my near-trance-state and fell over onto my rear, staring horror-struck into the flames. He looked right at me through the throbbing yellow and orange, but then the flames went out and he was gone. Only the charred roots remained.

With the sacred precinct nearly empty, the guard who'd followed me finally reached me. He helped me to my feet, but I shrugged him off when I spotted Citlallotoc hunched on the ground, surrounded by several Chichimecs who were either trying to help him up or were calling for help.

I hurried over and gasped when I saw the spears of arm bone piercing the skin. He would never use his sword arm again.

CHAPTER ELEVEN

I held Citlallotoc's hand as our men carried him back to the house on a stretcher. Thankfully the compound had suffered only minor scorching around the courtyard, and I welcomed the quietness after the chaos in the sacred precinct.

A surgeon arrived shortly and shooed everyone from Little Reed's quarters so he and his assistant could tend to Citlallotoc unimpeded. I lingered in the anteroom, pacing to work off the distress that Citlallotoc's cries of agony built inside me. I should have stopped Mextli sooner, before he could so injure him. *I shouldn't have even let the two of them face off.* My abdomen tightened unpleasantly but I ignored it; I was too anxious about Citlallotoc to sit still.

Mitotia and her mother came to the door from the courtyard; both looked relieved to see me. Mitotia rushed to hug me. "I've been searching everywhere for you! When you ran off into the fighting...I was certain you'd be killed."

"I'm fine, but Citlallotoc is badly injured. I fear they might have to amputate one of his arms." I flinched when he started a new bout of agonized howling. This time an intense pain gripped me and I winced, clutching my swollen belly.

"You're having pains?" Bitter Rabbit asked.

"A few, but they aren't that bad."

"Do they all feel the same as that last one?"

"I should get back into bed," I conceded.

I crawled into my bed and tried to sleep once Citlallotoc's cries subsided—no doubt thanks to a healthy dose of yauhtli—but my own pain continued to steadily grow. *No, I'm not ready for this yet,* I thought. *Little Reed isn't here. The baby can't come now. What if things go terribly wrong?* I tried to talk with Yamehecatl, to take my mind off of the pain, but he remained distressingly silent.

The hours melted together as the pains came longer with less respite in between. Bitter Rabbit stayed with me, checking my progress time and again while Mitotia kept damp rags on my forehead. The surgeon came to tell me about Citlallotoc, but his words were gibberish to me. I begged him for yauhtli, so I could sleep and forget the pain for a while, but Bitter

Rabbit forbade it, saying, "You must be able to follow my directions when the time comes." I despised her.

With no chance for sleep, I scrambled for ways to make the hours bearable. I focused on my breathing, meditated, ground my teeth down on deer-hide straps, but nothing really helped. I prayed for Little Reed to get here soon. I constantly searched the dark corners of my quarters for signs of the Black Dog, waiting to mark me a second time. *At least if I die again, my soul won't belong to Smoking Mirror,* I thought, as sweat poured off me. *I'll go to Teteocan, where Mother went. Maybe I'll get to see her there?* That thought brought me some comfort.

Shortly before midnight, when the pains grew so bad that I screamed when they squeezed me, the gods answered my prayers. Little Reed was suddenly at my side, holding my hand. "I'm here, Papalotl," he whispered. I thought I was hallucinating, but he caressed my sweaty hair away from my face. "Forgive me for being so late."

"Where were you?" I wailed, overcome with a choking mix of despair and joy.

"One thing after another kept coming up back in Culhuacan. But now is hardly the time to bore you with those details," he said with an anxious laugh. "I came as fast as I could; I wore my men out trying to make the journey in ten days."

"I'm so glad you're here," I said, taking his hand with mine. But another bout of pain attacked and I knew only pressure and agony for an eternity before it finally left me alone again. Lying still was delicious bliss.

"Now you go," Bitter Rabbit told Little Reed. "The childbed is no place for men."

But when he tried pulling his hand from mine, I found the strength to tighten my grip. "No, please stay with me," I begged. "If everything goes wrong, I need you to hold me when the Black Dog comes."

He squeezed my hand reassuringly. "I'm not going anywhere."

Bitter Rabbit glared at him. "If you're staying, you will help. Take her under the arms and hold her up, so she can crouch, and don't dawdle; it's time to battle the gods and claim your son."

Little Reed hurried to follow orders, lifting me up.

The pressure came again with numbing intensity and this time I screamed not from pain but determination; I was a warrior charging into battle, sword drawn. The gods had my son but I would capture him and bring him home. They tried to knock me back with another wave of pressure, but I pushed and pushed back, refusing to retreat.

A sudden rush of relief ended the battle at last and I turned limp in Little Reed's arms. He still held me up though, and I heard no crying. "Is he here?" I panted, feeling drunk after so much struggling. "Is it over?"

"The difficult part is," Bitter Rabbit said. "The baby's head is out. One more good push and you'll have the rest of him."

I wept; I was too exhausted to face the gods again. I could barely move. I couldn't do this.

But when the next wave of pain came on, my body forgot its exhaustion and I bore down harder than ever, too focused even to scream. This time the pain left quickly, taking the intense pressure with it. Little Reed gently lowered me onto my bed and sat behind me, letting me recline against him, and he held me tight as Bitter Rabbit washed the blood and afterbirth off our son.

I expected Yamehecatl to be overly large and fat, as Little Reed had been upon his birth, but he was normal in proportions. He had Little Reed's fine black hair, and once Bitter Rabbit dried him off, the curls on his forehead resembled the pictograph for the word "wind". She wrapped him in a blanket of rabbit furs and laid him in my arms. "Your son, My Lady," she said with a smile.

He didn't make a sound during any of this, and I was terrified that he was in fact dead, but then he yawned, showing off two surprisingly long front teeth. Not entirely unheard of, Nimilitzli had told me, but a rare occurrence I'd never seen in my years as midwife to King Cuitlapanton's wife and concubines.

"He's beautiful." Little Reed's voice was choked with emotion. He fingered one of the curls and laughed. "You gave him a most appropriate name, my love."

"He is beautiful," I agreed, kissing Yamehecatl's forehead. He sighed.

"And the birth went well? Nothing we should worry about?" Little Reed asked Bitter Rabbit.

"It went perfectly; in fact, I've never had a birth go so smoothly—I didn't even have to cut her to help the baby pass, and the afterbirth came out immediately." To me, she said, "You must be truly blessed by the gods."

I gazed down at Yamehecatl, my heart breaking with joy. "Quetzalcoatl has indeed blessed me."

"I shall find a warrior to bury the afterbirth on a battlefield for you," Bitter Rabbit said, drying the placenta and umbilical cord between cotton cloths. "So the prince will grow up to be a brave warrior."

I frowned; not that I didn't appreciate the offer, but when I looked down at Yamehecatl—so tiny, so precious in my arms—imagining him as crushed and injured as Citlallotoc curled my stomach. "Actually, we're going to bury it at the foot of Quetzalcoatl's temple." Nimilitzli had done the same with Little Reed's afterbirth, in a solemn ceremony at the foot of the god's temple in Xochicalco a few days after his birth, so his tonalli would always gravitate towards the temple. As was customary, my mother and father had buried mine under the hearth stones in the great hall in Culhuacan, so my tonalli would remain near the home.

Bitter Rabbit nodded. "There was a battle fought there yesterday, so it will do." She rose to leave. "I'll be back in a moment with a fresh fur for your bed."

"What does she mean by a battle?" Little Reed asked, concern in his voice.

I looked up at him, resting my head against his shoulder. "A man named Mextli came looking for you, and he and his men attacked the temple. You should have seen this Chichimec, Little Reed; he was gigantic and he had glued something blue—feathers, I think—on the entire left side of his body, and...I know this is going to sound crazy, but I don't think he was human."

Little Reed furrowed his brow. "Why not?"

"Citlallotoc cut him, but he bled gold dust, as Smoking Mirror did when I wounded him. He even pulled an obsidian dagger right out of the air and he shattered Citlallotoc's arm with a single stomp. Have you gone to see Citlallotoc yet? The surgeon spoke to me about him earlier but I wasn't in any condition to listen."

"No, I heard you and came here immediately." Little Reed gazed towards the door, fidgeting, so I told him to go and see his friend. "You're certain?"

"Of course. I want to know how he's doing too."

He ran his hand over Yamehecatl's head once more then left, the copper bells on the door curtain tinkling softly in the late night silence.

Bitter Rabbit came back with a blanket of wolf pelts and a basket for

Yamehecatl; while he lay quiet in his new bed, she washed me from head to toe. She helped me into a clean night dress and brought in my reed-woven recliner, so I could sit up and nurse. She started to teach me the basics of getting him to latch on, but he did it immediately, as if on instinct; in a matter of a moment, he lay comfortably in the crook of my arm. I'd worried about his long teeth, but he nursed with surprising care, making me wonder why so many women struggled with this most basic task. "I swear you were born for childbirth and motherhood," Bitter Rabbit said with a smile.

I swallowed the bitter compliment. *And to think I'd planned to cast him off....* It felt right and natural cradling him in my arms, feeding him; first time mothers often panicked and worried about everything they did, but I felt no apprehension, only a strange confidence that usually came with the birth of the second child. For the first time, the world felt completely in harmony.

As Yamehecatl fell into milk-drunk sleep, Little Reed returned. He looked pale and worried. "How is he?" I asked.

Little Reed shook his head. "The surgeon says there's no fixing his arm, so we're amputating it tomorrow, once the light is good."

"They can't let it heal as it is?"

"The injury will poison his blood and he could die, so we must remove it." He gave Yamehecatl a sad smile. "He did manage to tell me what happened out on the precinct...about why he's not dead right now."

My heart skipped. "What did he say?"

"That before Mextli could dress him like a deer, some sort of plant roots broke out of the ground and dragged him away; the kind of roots that attacked Ihuitimal and dragged him under the ground."

"How do you know about that?" I asked, startled. "You were knocked out during that battle."

"This was what Citlallotoc told me."

That made sense; Citlallotoc had been at both battles. "What else did he say?"

"That the god saved the city as he did in Culhuacan." Little Reed met my gaze, concern in his eyes. "Did you call on Quetzalcoatl again?"

"I thought about it," I admitted.

"But?"

I breathed deep to slow my heart rate, so I didn't feel so scared. "When

I was alone after falling down the hill...I wanted to give the god some blood, but my bag was out of reach, and I...I made one of the nearby maguey plants bring it to me, with its roots...with magic!"

I expected suspicion and disbelief, but instead, Little Reed's face lit up. "Why didn't you mention this months ago?"

"I thought I'd imagined it, having fallen and possibly hit my head. And it sounded crazy. But when I saw Mextli out on the precinct—"

"What were you doing out on the precinct in the middle of a battle?"

"They were shooting flaming arrows over the walls, so I took Mitotia and Bitter Rabbit and we left. The god led me to the sacred precinct, and when I saw Mextli battling Citlallotoc...I thought I would have to call on Quetzalcoatl by giving the only thing I had left to give." I peered down at Yamehecatl, hugging him tighter, ever so grateful I could hold him at all. "But then I remembered the maguey plant and decided it was worth trying."

Little Reed stroked Yamehecatl's head. "I'm so very glad you did. I could never forgive myself for not being here to make certain you didn't have to make such a sacrifice in the first place. I'm sorry I didn't get here sooner."

"It's all right. I'm grateful you're home again."

"It's good to be home."

I watched Yamehecatl sleeping. "At first, I thought I might only have had these abilities because of Yamehecatl, but I can still feel the magic inside me. Maybe Quetzalcoatl gave it to me as a gift, just as he gave me Yamehecatl."

"Or perhaps the possession awakened magic asleep inside you," Little Reed suggested. "We should cultivate it, see the full extent of what you're capable of."

I laughed. "I would have thought if one of the two of us would have magic, it would have been you. You're the one with a god for a father."

"Heaven's ways are unknowable."

Seeing him gaze longingly down at Yamehecatl, I held the baby out to him. "You haven't even held your son yet."

He hesitated, but after I insisted, he took Yamehecatl into his arms. He relaxed when the baby didn't stir or protest. "He is a miracle, isn't he?"

Watching him hold Yamehecatl, I realized we were a family with a shared future, and I ached with joy. Maybe this wasn't how I'd imagined true happiness before I made that sacrifice, but this felt just as real and precious. It settled my bitter heart. "He most definitely is."

◻

Yamehecatl never cried when he was hungry; I instinctively knew it was feeding time and would wake to find him already awake and patiently waiting for me. After being such a chattering monkey all of these months, his silence now startled, and worried me. The first time he woke up for more than a few moments to feed, I tried to talk to him, much as we talked when he was still inside me; but I saw no recognition in his eyes, no evidence that he understood anything I said. He looked completely uninterested in the world—and, most upsetting, in me as well. I'd loved those bedtime conversations, teaching him about language and emotions, but now that was gone, and I missed it terribly. I'd lost the Yamehecatl I'd grown to love these last several months and I feared he'd never come back.

But I kept talking to him always, determined to find my boy again. *He's forgotten everything before he was born but someday he'll remember, and that cheeky, curious boy I knew will return.*

The day after the birth, Little Reed and the surgeon amputated Citlallotoc's arm above the elbow. At Citlallotoc's request, Little Reed wielded the sword. I sang loudly, hoping to drown out Citlallotoc's screams as they cauterized the wound. He remained in bed for a week after that, growing increasingly depressed, so Little Reed and I sat with him often, trying to keep him engaged in conversation.

"I was going to leave him here when we left, to watch over the city's progress for us, but I don't think that's a good idea anymore," Little Reed confided to me as we took a tour of the sacred precinct to assess the full damage of Mextli's attack. "He's taken losing his arm really hard; I can see it on his face."

"Well, he *is* a warrior and now he can't even wield a sword," I pointed out.

"He doesn't need to anymore, for we're going to live in peace from now on."

"Be that as it may, he's spent most of his life in the army, Little Reed, and being a warrior is an integral part of his identity. Imagine if you couldn't ever again perform a proper sacrifice to the god because someone cut off your...." I cast my gaze towards his crotch but promptly met his eyes again, my face burning.

Little Reed grinned at me. "That would indeed be tragic."

"Perhaps it's not quite the same thing as losing an arm, but don't underestimate how devastating this is for him. And saying he doesn't need to wield a sword anymore isn't going to help him feel better."

"No, it won't."

That night, after dinner, as the three of us sat in the anteroom drinking xocolatl, Little Reed told Citlallotoc, "I've sent for Matlacxochitl to come and oversee the city's development, and once he arrives in a few weeks we'll travel back to Culhuacan. The weather's warming up nicely."

"I thought I was staying here to oversee the city's construction," Citlallotoc said, his voice flat. He stared into his cup of xocolatl. "Do you no longer trust me to protect the city?"

"I trust you implicitly, which is why I want to entrust you with something even more precious to me than a mere city."

Citlallotoc finally looked up at him, mild curiosity in his eyes. "What would that be, Your Majesty?"

"You're the most skilled and accomplished military man I've ever met, so I'd be honored if you would oversee my son's weapons training. I want him to learn from the best."

Hope burned in Citlallotoc's eyes, but when he glanced at his missing arm, it dimmed. "But I can't even wield a sword anymore—"

"I will help you relearn with your other arm," Little Reed assured him. "I've seen you use your left hand in battle; you might not be as accurate as with your right, but you're still absolutely deadly with it. The only reason you aren't already ambidextrous is purely the lack of need." He gripped Citlallotoc by the shoulder. "We'll get you back in fighting shape in no time. That is a promise, my friend."

Citlallotoc smiled stiffly. "Thank you for your confidence in me, My Lord. And My Lady."

Smiling, I said, "It's easy to have confidence in a man of your quality, Citlallotoc."

◻

Once Matlacxochitl arrived—bringing still more Chichimecs from

Culhuacan with him, along with some poorer Toltecas looking for work—we packed up our house and prepared to journey back to Culhuacan. After nearly nine months in Tollan, leaving was bittersweet; while we would be more comfortable in Culhuacan, my son had been born here, and I didn't relish returning to a place where memories of brutality and loss lurked around every corner. I begrudged that my son should have to spend his most formative years in that kind of place. But it wouldn't be safe here for our family until the city and her defenses were finished.

Matlacxochitl greeted us in the courtyard as we gathered to leave. I hadn't seen him since he arrived, so his mask took me by surprise. It was molded fig-bark paper painted the same tone as his skin and it covered the top half of his face, disguising his lack of a nose. He also wore a jaguar skin, with the head for a cap, concealing his missing ears. He smiled, surprising given all he'd been through, and the curious looks Ten Spines' men gave him. "You will take good care of Tollan while we're gone?" I asked him, hoping my own smile didn't look as forced as it felt.

He bowed. "I shall take the very best care of it, My Lady. And allow me to congratulate you on the birth of the prince. I promise when he returns, it shall be to the most luxurious palace you've ever seen, in the most beautiful city in Tolteca lands."

While he spoke with Little Reed, I turned to get inside the royal litter but stopped when I noticed Mitotia saying goodbye to her parents. Her mother—teary-eyed—hugged her tight, but to my pleasant surprise, her father made no effort to hold back his own tears. "I know you will do many great things, not only for our family, but your people as well."

"I promise I will make you proud, Father."

He laughed, his whole belly shifting as he did. "You already make me tremendously proud." He kissed her cheek. "Have a safe journey, and we will see you when you return home."

She waved goodbye and hurried to the line of soldiers and servants waiting to depart. Ten Spines held his wife while she wept.

As I started climbing inside the litter again, Citlallotoc stepped up to help me, offering me his good arm to balance on. When he handed me Yamehecatl in his basket, it warmed me to see him finally smiling again.

Little Reed climbed into the litter after me and we sat at the open curtain, waving as we wound our way through the humble beginnings of our god's city and out into the countryside. It was so small—only two neighborhoods and a sacred precinct with a single temple a quarter finished.

"Glad to finally be going home?" Little Reed asked.

I shook my head. "I won't be home until we're back here, with our days in Culhuacan done and over." Feeling a tug at the back of my attention, I turned to see Yamehecatl rousing, waving his arms around. I asked Little Reed to fetch him while I untied the front of my dress. "Don't you think it's odd that he never cries?" I asked as I put Yamehecatl to my breast. He latched on immediately, sucking boisterously. For all I worried, he never lacked for appetite.

"Well, he *is* the son of a god."

"*You* cried. In fact, for the first few weeks, you would only stop crying if I held you."

He laughed. "I remember."

I looked at Yamehecatl, furrowing my brow.

"What is it?"

"I'd hoped that, like us, he would remember all those evenings he kept me awake talking late into the night, but when he looks at me now...he has no idea who I am."

"Yes, but what we remember of those first days is all filtered through our life experience, which gives it meaning it didn't have for us back when we first experienced it. It was all a mystery at the time."

"I suppose. But I miss it."

Little Reed slid over next to me and put his arm around my shoulder. "And I bet he misses it too."

I watched Yamehecatl nurse while Little Reed lay napping before the day's heat caught up with us. I waited for Yamehecatl to fall asleep as well, so I could nap too, but he nursed slowly and methodically, showing no signs of going to sleep. Eventually he decided he'd eaten his fill and looked up at me, blinking as if he hadn't even noticed I was there until now. I smiled at him as I dabbed the milk from his soft lips, and my heart skipped a beat when he smiled back at me. "You remember me now?" I whispered. He smiled again, this time making a small cooing noise that made my heart ache. He laid in my arms a long time, smiling up at me and moving his mouth, as if trying to make the words we used to speak to each other.

Yes, everything was going to be fine.

PART TWO
THE YEAR TEN HOUSE

CHAPTER TWELVE

I found the silver hair during my morning brushing; it fell into the water bowl on the pedestal in my bath yard, and when I looked at the bristles of my brush, I found a second one. *Has Little Reed been using my brush?* Though how could he, when he wasn't even in Culhuacan right now? When I glanced into the obsidian mirror hanging above the bowl, something caught my eye, so I leaned closer for a better look.

I appeared dark and murky in the mirror, but something was out of place. I reached up and yanked a long, silver hair out of the front of my head. I stared at it, puzzled. I wasn't yet thirty and already I was silvering?

Being the queen of Culhuacan wasn't a relaxing job, and with the move to Tollan less than a month away, there was so much to do and take care of. My mother had been only a few years older than I was now when she died, but she'd had no silver hairs. I took after her in many ways, except this, it seemed. I tossed the hair aside and checked the mirror again, but I found no more.

"What are you doing, Nantli?" Yamehecatl asked, startling me. He wore only wrist and ankle bands with little copper bells on them—we fully dressed him only for the temple or market—but somehow he'd slipped into my bath yard without making a sound.

Taking him into my arms, I said, "Nothing, my dear. But what are you doing here? I put you down for a nap."

"I want to go to the field with you," he said, sweeping back his unruly black hair from his eyes. His curls still reminded me of wind glyphs.

"You know you can't come with me."

He frowned, tears queued. "But I like watching you do magic!"

I sighed. "I know you do, but it's not safe. Nantli doesn't have the best control, and I don't want you to get hurt by accident."

"I'm not scared."

I laughed. "I know. You're a brave warrior, like Citlallotoc."

Yamehecatl grinned. "Yesterday he showed me how to throw an arrow with the atlatl. I'm really good."

"I know you are, my love." It both amazed and disheartened me to see him growing up so fast, a fact exacerbated by his early language development. For his first few months, he developed at the same rate as normal children, babbling and testing out sounds to hear himself speak, but those soon turned into words, and he progressed quickly after that. He learned new words after just hearing them a few times and moved from two-to-three word sentences to full-blown, complex ones within another few months, just as Little Reed had at that age. Luckily that was the only unusualness they shared. Physically, Yamehecatl was growing at the same rate as any normal child, and he was as clumsy as anyone his age, which meant his perception of his own skills with weapons—or staying far enough back while I practiced my magic—were skewed.

He gave me pup-eyes and I tried to resist, but it was futile. "All right, but only if Citlallotoc comes with us, to watch over you while I practice."

Yamehecatl ran in a circle, squealing, but then he stopped, holding his knees together. His cheeks darkened as a small puddle of urine collected on the flagstone under him—one of the reasons we rarely bothered with his clothing at this age. "I should water your flowers," he whispered and tiptoed out into my garden.

Chuckling, I tossed down some copal ash to soak up the liquid. When he returned, I washed his legs off and he led the way to the nursery across the hall to fetch his toy sword.

My uncle changed many things about the palace during my years in exile—most of them foul and self-serving—but he'd left the royal nursery untouched. The birds and butterflies and snakes still adorned the walls, and the family baby basket hung from the ceiling. Yamehecatl tucked his toy sword in there every night. The room looked smaller than in my girlhood memories, when I'd slept in here alone; maybe because Little

Reed and I had stuffed it full of toys for our only child. I was Yamehecatl's age when I started noticing that everyone but me had a brother or sister and I began pestering Mother about correcting that. She'd given me a sad smile but always told me, "Maybe if we pray hard enough...." Yamehecatl seemed content by himself, so hopefully he and I would never have to have that conversation.

He tore into his wicker clothes basket, tossing aside xicollis decorated with feathered serpents or birds or geometric patterns. "This one! This one! This one, Nantli!" He held up the rumpled full-body rabbit suit I'd made for him. "Because I'm going to be a rabbit warrior when I grow up!" he'd informed me when I asked him about the peculiar request. Every time I saw it, I remembered the last time I'd been in the Divine Dream and saw the rabbit poking its head out from under the door curtain, to what I presumed now would be Yamehecatl's nursery in Tollan. He wore the suit around the palace a couple of times, and threw a fit about wanting to wear it to temple services, but I hadn't seen him in it for a few weeks now.

I sniffed it—making certain it was clean enough—then helped him into it and tied the many laces up the back. It came with a rabbit-head hood with ears made from lacquered maize-leaves that stood at crooked angles from his head. He grabbed his play sword from the baby basket and stood expectantly in front of me, his chest puffed out.

"My, what a mighty rabbit warrior we have here."

He beamed and took my hand, leading me from the nursery. "Let's get Citlallotoc and go!"

Citlallotoc sat in the great hall, smoking pipes with the other war council members. Three months ago, Little Reed and Amoxtli went to Tollan to oversee the palace's completion, leaving me and Citlallotoc in charge of Culhuacan. Things were quiet, with most city business finished before noon, so the men often gathered in the afternoon, making jokes and talking over their pipes before begging off the rest of the evening.

But with all the fire priests set to move to Tollan in two days, my own free time was scarce. Yesterday I helped Mazatzin prepare the codices for the journey and tomorrow I would help Malinalli pack up her meditation room. And I had my own packing to do as well. But I always practiced my magic at least once a week; who knew when I might need it again.

Once inside the great hall, Yamehecatl sprinted across the room, yelling for Citlallotoc. Citlallotoc handed his pipe to the servant behind him and started to stand, but my son leaped on him, knocking him over. "Well, if it isn't the illustrious rabbit warrior!" he roared. "You must grow faster than your father, for I swear you weren't so heavy yesterday!"

"I measured myself on the door this morning," Yamehecatl said. "I haven't grown at all."

Citlallotoc gathered him up with his one good arm and rose. "You'll catch up to me someday." He turned to me with a self-deprecating smile. "What brings you here, My Lady?"

I motioned him to follow me away from the others, who went back to their vulgar jokes and laughter. "Are you busy this afternoon?"

"I was going to sit in the steam bath for a while, but otherwise no. What do you have in mind?"

Yamehecatl furrowed his brow crossly. "I want to watch Nantli do her magic, but she won't let me unless you come along. Will you come with us?"

"I can't watch him and practice at the same time," I explained, feeling guilty for asking such a favor.

Citlallotoc set Yamehecatl down and nodded. "I can do that."

Yamehecatl hooted and bounded around the great hall, but when he turned back to us, he slipped and landed bottom-first with a yelp. He glared at the floor, rubbing his behind.

"I see why you'd need help with him," Citlallotoc said with a chuckle. "The boy's feet are quicker than his head."

¤

"Do you ever dream you're a rabbit, Nantli?" Yamehecatl asked as we followed the path along the lakeside.

"I never have," I admitted. "Is that what you dreamt about last night?"

"I dream it all the time. I'm a giant brown rabbit, big as Tatli, and I run all over the mountains, and everything spins around me, like when I do this—" He spun in circles, giggling, and Citlallotoc grabbed his arm to keep him from falling. He swayed on his feet as if drunk. "If you don't dream about being a rabbit, Nantli, what do you dream about?"

"A lot of different things." I still dreamt of Mictlan and Lord Death, but not as often anymore. But two new ones joined the ranks of the recurring dream; in the first, I was trapped in a garden whose walls I could never reach the top of when I tried climbing them. It reminded me of the vision I'd had in Teotihuacan years ago, before I became a priestess, except that in the dream, Little Reed wasn't there. I was all alone, and scared.

The other dreams were more pleasant. I'd make love with Little Reed on the temple altar in Xochicalco, or under the giant copal tree in the main gardens. Sometimes he was his father instead, though often I wasn't positive which of them I was with at any given time. I'd wake questioning my decision to avoid the Divine Dream rather than indulging my desire for the god's feathery touch. *He's a god and you have no business treating him as a mere mortal,* I always reminded myself. My dreams had other ideas though.

The lakeside path veered away from the water and climbed a small incline, up to a tall stone wall with a wooden gate. Citlallotoc and I left our guards there and went inside, sliding the latch shut behind us to make certain no one barged in and saw me performing magic. Only a few people close to me knew of my abilities.

Inside was what Yamehecatl called "the field", though it was hardly large enough to be rightfully called that. Inside the gate grew two large oak trees that shaded a shed filled with tools to care for the thirty-odd maguey plants the priesthood cultivated for ritual use. The plants varied in size and maturity, and the field's position atop the highest hill ensured no one could see over the walls—thus why I chose it for practice.

The rows of maguey started ten paces beyond the shed. The biggest ones—near the back wall—had giant leaves standing taller than Citlallotoc, and a few sported the tall yellow flower stalks marking the last months of their lives. Some of these plants were older than me.

Yamehecatl ran towards the maguey, oblivious to the ultra-hard daggers jutting from the tips of their leaves, but Citlallotoc brought him back. "You don't go near the maguey unless you're holding someone's hand," he lectured. When Yamehecatl frowned, he asked, "Don't we have a duel to finish?" He pulled a digging stick out of the shed, and Yamehecatl squealed, fumbling his tiny play sword in his pudgy hands.

With Yamehecatl occupied, I walked out to the edge of the maguey and knelt in prayer.

Lord Quetzalcoatl,

Protect me while I practice your gift,
Show my head, my heart, my hands the way,
Help me cultivate this power to best serve you.
I'm forever your faithful servant.

Keeping my eyes closed, I focused. With the help of prayers, meditation, and much practice, I'd learned to build the magic's intensity slowly, to feel it move through my belly, my arms, and finally my hands. My flesh tingled as if asleep, but my skin pulsed with heat. I rested my hands flat on the ground in front of me.

The closest maguey plants flexed their leaves like a bird's wings. I changed speeds slowly, regulating the flow of magic through my hands by sheer will. After a few minutes of this, my mind started drifting and the world seemed to flex around me, like the beginnings of octli intoxication. As I worked more with the maguey, I felt a strange, indescribable connection between us, as if they spoke in waves of vision and memory; I'd learned from experience that if I stayed too long, depression would threaten to swallow me. I let the magic flow a while longer but soon broke it off, not wanting to press it.

As I knelt resting, I noticed a group of three rabbits peering at me from between the rows. When our gazes locked, they sat up and stared at me with liquid black eyes. How strange that such normally skittish creatures would dare come so close. They looked so soft, so warm.... *I wish I could touch them.*

Suddenly they loped towards me, stopping within easy reach. I stared at them agape, but froze when one of them came closer still. It set its front paws on my knees, staring back up at me, nose twitching. I couldn't bring myself to speak aloud. *Did you come because I asked?*

Another rabbit bobbed its head and rubbed its nose with its front paws. I gasped. The loud noise should have scattered them, but they stayed. I raised my hand slowly, afraid the one on my knee would bolt, but instead it leaned its head into my hand. I ran my fingers through the soft fur behind its ears, my heart thudding with joy.

We learned in calmecac that everyone has a nahual—an animal spirit that followed us throughout our lives—and having been born on the day-sign of Tochtli, mine would be a rabbit. But in my experience, only the gods had actual, physically-manifested nahuals—

"Rabbits!" I turned to see Yamehecatl running towards me, a look of glee on his face. This time the rabbits bolted back into the maguey.

"No! Wait!" When they didn't stop, I pressed magic into the ground, hoping that would draw their attention.

But instead the maguey whipped their leaves around in a frenzy. Something swiped my cheek, leaving it stinging, and when I reached up, my fingers came back bloody. More sharp pain bit my arm; a maguey spine stuck out of my robe sleeve, a blossom of crimson growing around it.

Yamehecatl's laughs turned to screams, and I didn't think; I turned and leaped at him. Scooping him into my arms and burying my face in his hair, I shielded him from the stinging attack spreading pain over my back, my neck, and my calves. Someone grabbed me from behind and shoved me towards the shed.

I didn't look up until Citlallotoc told me we were safe, but Yamehecatl continued clinging to me like a baby monkey, weeping. Maguey thorns marked the head of hundreds of tiny rivers of blood running down Citlallotoc's bare shoulders and back. "Are you all right?" he panted.

"I'm fine." I was more worried for Yamehecatl, and immediately checked him over. He clutched his knees to his chest, rocking back and forth. Tears shimmered in his eyes when I held his chin up to find a single cut on his cheek, but otherwise he wasn't injured. I finally breathed. I'd gotten to him in time. Overcome with guilt, I pulled him into a desperate hug. "Thank the Feathered Serpent you're all right, my darling little breeze. I'm so sorry."

Citlallotoc knelt next to me. "You're not all right, Quetzalpetlatl. You have at least twenty thorns in your back."

I glanced over my shoulder and cringed. "You've got quite a few of your own." Gritting my teeth, I pulled one from the side of my neck and pressed my thumb against the wound to staunch the bleeding; luckily it had missed anything vital. "Will you help pull these out?"

Citlallotoc extracted my thorns for me and I returned the favor. My dress soaked up most of my blood, leaving only a few stains on the sleeves of my robe; those I could explain away as from my daily bloodletting.

Citlallotoc's back was far messier. "I'm so sorry about this," I murmured as I dabbed the blood with a length of cloth I tore off my dress.

He glanced at me over his shoulder. "What exactly happened?"

"I let go of too much magic and the maguey went crazy." I shook my head. "I should know better than to bring anyone with me. I can't properly control this power."

"Things could have been far worse if you were alone."

"I shouldn't have ever brought Yamehecatl though. He could have been hurt, and I would never forgive myself—" A choke rose in my throat and I peered watery-eyed over at my son where he sat in the corner, knees still drawn to his chest. One of his rabbit ears lay crumpled over the side of his head.

"I shouldn't have let him get so far away from me," Citlallotoc said, following my gaze.

"This isn't your fault. It happened so fast...and you got us out of there. I owe you my life." I hugged him and kissed his cheek.

"Good thing I haven't any children of my own, for I'm completely unfit for the task," he muttered, unconvinced.

"Nonsense! Yamehecatl adores you; he loves his father, but he wants to be like you. And what are good fathers if not inspirations to their children?" I tossed the bloodied linen into the garbage heap in the corner. "Certainly you want to marry someday, right?"

"Of course."

"So why haven't you yet?"

He chuckled. "I'd think it would be obvious."

I furrowed my brow at him. "It isn't."

He sighed, and raised what was left of his right arm.

"Because you're missing your arm?"

"Not many women consider a stump appealing."

I almost laughed and declared him ridiculous, but bit my tongue. Honor was everything to him, so it was no surprise he worried what others thought of him. I'd seen the young noblewomen snicker and whisper at the feasts, and imagining what such women might say—or show—in their most private of moments, when a man was at his most vulnerable.... "They're self-absorbed wretches," I snarled, hot with indignation. "And though they might be beautiful, their tonallis are empty black mirrors."

Citlallotoc contemplated his stump. "Sometimes I still think it's there, and I can actually feel my fingers moving. But every time I look, my arm is still gone."

I looked at my own three-fingered hand. "I know what you mean. Sometimes it still throbs, as it did right after the surgeons sewed me up."

"I often feel as if I'm being burned again." He sat in silence a moment before muttering, "And I wonder how much longer I can stand feeling this way."

My mind reeled with his admission. I wanted to say something to comfort him, to assure him the pain goes away, but I still suffered ghost pains years after losing my fingers. I'd never received more than a superficial burn—and those had all been due to carelessness around a hot cooking stone—so what did I know about his pain?

Before I could find the right words, one of the guards called from beyond the gate. I donned my robe, covering up my blood-stained dress, and left the shed.

The guard bowed when I opened the gate. "My Lady, Lord Toztli of Chimalhuacan is here, and he demands to see you immediately."

CHAPTER THIRTEEN

I didn't meet with Toztli immediately. If Little Reed were here, he wouldn't have "demanded" anything, but because he must deal with me, he made his irritation clear.

And as the queen, I could make him wait.

Back at the palace, I asked my handmaiden to set a warm bath for me while I took Yamehecatl to his bed. He sucked his fingers while I sang, still clutching me tight with his free hand, but eventually sleep whisked him away. When I left the nursery, I spotted Malinalli in the vestibule down the hall and called to her. "Can you help me with something?"

Usually I preferred to bathe myself, but my back ached so badly I wasn't certain I could do it this time. Nor did I want my handmaiden seeing all my wounds and asking questions. Malinalli knew of my magic, so it was easier explaining it to her as she helped me peel off my dress and get into the bath.

"Is Yamehecatl all right?" she asked, scrubbing off the dried blood between my scabbed-over wounds.

I nodded. "Thank the Feathered Serpent." Though the god proved deaf to my prayers today. "Citlallotoc took the worst of it."

"Some of these hit very close to your spine. You're lucky you can move still." She dabbed my back dry, wiped salve over the wounds, and wrapped me with a roll of cotton cloth, so I wouldn't bleed through my dress again. "Lord Toztli is pacing the great hall like a dog in need of relieving himself," she told me while she fixed my hair and applied makeup to hide the cut on my cheek.

"The man hates talking to me." If Little Reed were here, I'd have worn one of my finer court dresses and my royal diadem, but I decided my high priestess robe and headdress would serve me better today; men took me more seriously when I did. Everyone knew how I'd summoned the god to confront the Smoking Mirror outside of Culhuacan, and it paid to remind men such as Toztli that I was the god's chosen high priestess, capable of harnessing his power. And my robe's silver and emerald embroidered feathered serpents and the headdress's brilliant white heron feathers demanded attention. I needed to feel powerful facing Toztli.

Over the last few years, I'd learned to exercise better control over my often impulsive desire, but I appreciated how powerful I felt when it came on, so I'd devoted effort to nurturing and encouraging that particular aspect of it. The desire enjoyed being let off the rope and it came to relish politics almost as much as sex. It knew precisely how to deal with haughty men such as Toztli, who thought it right and proper to disrespect or dismiss me. I let the desire seep in as I walked to the great hall with my head held high. I took my time settling onto my icpalli while Toztli and his bodyguards stood waiting. My war council remained bowed until I was fully seated.

I breathed deeply, marveling at the calm inside me. "You asked for an audience with me, Lord Toztli?" I began, beckoning him forward.

Chimalhuacan's king came to the dais and granted me a cursory bow. His gaze fell on my robe as he straightened, and when he met my eyes, a careful smile slid to my lips. "Thank you for agreeing to see me, Lady Quetzalpetlatl."

"It's always a pleasure to see you. You look quite well."

"You flatter me, My Lady, but I'm far from well." Indignation tinged his words.

"Is something wrong?"

His face darkened as if I'd flung a crass insult. "Something is indeed wrong. My son is missing."

"Nahuacatl?"

"I haven't any other legitimate sons."

Insolent little man, the desire growled but after a silent warning to remain focused, it went on, "Do you wish me to send men out to help you find him?"

He cast me a scathing glare unseen to the men sitting behind him. "That would be ever so kind of you, My Lady. He was last seen in the market, in the company of Chichimec warriors, so I fear for his safety."

"I shall dispatch search parties immediately."

"I hope he's found before you and Lord Topiltzin abandon Culhuacan next month."

"No one is abandoning Culhuacan," I said, barely holding back the snap. "Lord Ixtlilxochitl will assume control of the city once we move to Tollan, but Topiltzin and I are still her king and queen."

Toztli took to pacing in a small circle. "It's just very convenient that as you prepare to leave, the Chichimecs start making trouble. If you recall, I asked Topiltzin to send them back north years ago, and now Chimalhuacan and the other lake cities are left to deal with the problem you leave behind."

"Problem?"

"The Chichimecs, of course."

"There is no 'Chichimec problem'. They've adapted well to city life, and they've contributed to the prosperity we all enjoy. We couldn't have built the market without them. They've earned the right to be here."

Toztli laughed. "And now they've earned the right to rule over us? You're leaving a barbarian in charge of Culhuacan when you leave."

A general grumble rose from the men sitting on the floor behind Toztli, and the council member seated next to Ixtlilxochitl muttered something to him, but Ixtlilxochitl maintained his normal scowl, his gaze like thrown arrows at Toztli's back.

"Lord Ixtlilxochitl earned this kingdom's trust through his loyalty and honor, and both Topiltzin and I agree he is the best candidate. Our decision is not open for debate."

"And yet a good ruler is mindful of how his allies view his choices,"

Toztli fired back. "Or whom he lets influence his decisions."

Now my war council members came to their feet, those grumbles turning to shouts. I motioned for them to sit again. "As I said, I'm happy to send troops to help your men locate your son. Chimalhuacan has always been a close and trusted ally, and because we look forward to a long friendship, if anything tragic has befallen Lord Nahuacatl, I personally promise that the culprits will be put to the sword, be they Chichimec or Tolteca."

Toztli stared me down a moment—a gesture only a man of his status could get away with—and he bowed, sweeping his fingers across the ground at his feet. "I thank you for your assistance, My Lady, and I pray we can find my son in time."

"As do I. I shall have troops out searching within the hour. If you wish to stay the night, I will have quarters prepared for you."

"You are most gracious, but I should return home immediately."

"Good journey to you then."

Toztli swept from the great hall, guards in tow. My tense body ached, and with the tight bindings around my chest and the rising clatter of indignant conversation, I couldn't breathe. The desire wanted me to go after him and make him pay for his insolence, but I shushed it. Before anyone could approach, I departed out the back doors to the garden patio.

I peeled off my headdress and exhaled loudly, the buzz of insects a welcome respite. "If you knew what I was capable of, Toztli...." I growled under my breath, letting the desire spit one last time.

"He'd quake in his sandals." Citlallotoc lurked near the doorway, a smile on his face.

When the anger started giving way to arousal, I shoved the desire back into its box. "I didn't see you inside."

"I had to call on the surgeon about some of these wounds, so I was late. I didn't want to be rude, so I listened from out here." He joined me at the edge of the patio. "I commend you on your patience with that pompous monkey ball-sack."

I sighed. "After three years as queen and ruling equally with Topiltzin, you'd think I'd have earned some respect from our allies."

"Many do respect you, My Lady, and not only because they respect Topiltzin. But others—such as Toztli—feel threatened."

I chuckled, but it was true. When we toured our allies' cities, women came out in droves to see me, bringing their young daughters with them, all smiling with fresh hope. Female enrollment in the calmecac had risen sharply since Little Reed and I took the throne, particularly since lifting the prohibition against marriage in the priesthood. And we'd passed laws restricting the authority of husbands and fathers over their wives and daughters, bringing an end to legal forced marriage in Culhuacan. Kingdoms such as Xochimilco and Tultepec followed our lead.

But a good number of our allies grumbled about destroying the fabric of Tolteca society. It was bad enough we educated barbarians, but allowing women and girls to share power with their husbands or fathers was borderline treasonous. "They'll stop having children, and the Chichimecs will out-breed us! In a generation, the Tolteca world will crumble!" Many noble fathers refused to enroll their daughters in the calmecac in Culhuacan; and in Chimalhuacan, women weren't permitted in the calmecac at all. Their existing priestesses were nothing more than figureheads standing in the shadows of the priests, parroting traditional rules at the behest of the king. I dreaded to think of Cornflower and her daughter living under such restrictions, treated no better than dogs bred for the dinner table.

"Being a ruler is thankless work," Citlallotoc said. "But to also be a woman...I do not envy your struggles, My Lady, but I admire your strength and grace in dealing with them."

I wasn't certain how much longer I—or the desire—could deal gracefully with the likes of Toztli. "Thank you. Would you mind assigning the search teams?" This whole day had left me exhausted, but Nahuacatl was Chimalhuacan's best hope for a good future, so the sooner we found him, the better.

◻

No news came with the dawn, but I welcomed the distraction of packing up Malinalli's meditation room with the help of Ixchell and Mitotia. In a matter of hours, everything was in wicker baskets, ready for the journey north, and all that remained was to clean.

"Why don't you come to Tollan now?" Malinalli asked Mitotia as they swept the floor. "Mazatzin and I can continue your training until the calmecac opens in a few months."

"I have to stay here until I take the trials and become a full priestess," Mitotia said.

"That's not a requirement of our agreement with your father," I pointed out as I ensured all of the basket lids were tied securely.

"No, but if he discovers I'm not taking vows to Mixcoatl, he'll be furious."

"He can't force you to; we never even promised you'd take the trials to become a priestess."

"No, but he'll pressure me, and he's very good at that. Why do you think my brother left in the middle of the night and told no one where he was going?"

"But you're still coming to Tollan after you take your vows?" Malinalli seemed unusually anxious.

"Of course. He is pushy, but he is my father."

Malinalli nodded, pleased.

"It's amazing how quickly times change," Ixchell said as she ran a wet cloth over the face of the hearth, cleaning the dust and soot off. "If I'd had more say in my own future when I was a girl, I probably wouldn't have ended up in the priesthood; my father put me in calmecac to keep me out of trouble."

I laughed. I couldn't imagine Ixchell ever being a misfit. "What trouble could that be?"

She gave me a lopsided smile. "Oh, the kind fathers always worry about. My mother died when I was young, and he knew nothing about raising daughters, so I followed my brothers everywhere instead of learning to weave and cook. But when he caught me kissing the neighbor boy when I was seven, he feared he would be a grandfather much too soon, so off to calmecac I went; we were very poor, but he indentured my older brothers to the king for three years to pay my way. My life probably would have been very, very different if not for that."

"You might not be the next high priestess of Quetzalcoatl in Culhuacan, of all places," I said with a chuckle.

"And you might never have met Tlanextli," Malinalli added. Ixchell blushed.

As soon as we lifted the prohibitions against priests and priestesses marrying, Ixchell and Tlanextli—a priest of Tlaloc—married in the great temple. Neither was young and they looked at each other with a fondness grown of many years together; it filled me with joy to know they needn't keep their love secret anymore. If only Nimilitzli and Mother were here to see the changes we'd made because of them.

Bells jingled behind me and I looked back to see Citlallotoc hovering in the doorway, a grave expression on his face. My stomach dropped. He usually spent the afternoons in the practice yard with Yamehecatl, teaching him about weapons, and now grisly visions of accidents filled my head. "Is everything all right?"

"The search teams found Nahuacatl."

I let slip a sigh of relief. Why was my first instinct always to think something terrible had happened to Yamehecatl? It was silly. "Good news then."

He shook his head. "You should speak with the soldiers who found him."

The room fell silent as I rose and followed Citlallotoc out.

A group of four soldiers stood waiting by the cistern behind the Temple of Quetzalcoatl. They bowed to me, sweeping their fingers across the ground, but I motioned them up, impatient. "You found Nahuacatl?"

The highest-ranking soldier stepped forward. "Yes, My Lady, in the copal grove. Someone had removed his heart."

I gasped. After two years of slowly whittling away at the number of sacrificial victims permitted, Little Reed and I had finally outlawed most human sacrificial practices. We still allowed the sacrificing of willing victims, for who were we to deny a person the right to give their life in the name of the gods if they so wished? But we required they registered their wishes before myself and the king, to make certain it was indeed true willingness, and we completely outlawed the sacrificing of children under the age of sixteen. At first the other high priests grumbled, but that lessened as the city prospered and grew as never before, suggesting the gods approved of the new law. There hadn't been any unauthorized sacrifices in Culhuacan in the last year.

"Any other injuries?" I pressed.

He shook his head. "Lord Toztli's men found him first and were wrapping him up to take back to Chimalhuacan when we arrived, so we didn't get a close look at the prince's body."

I sighed. With Toztli already railing against the Chichimecs, this was the worst possible outcome. I cast a glare over at the temple of the

Smoking Mirror—a small, ground-level structure more resembling a house than a temple. Oddly enough, of all the priests I thought would take issue with our dramatic curbing of human sacrifice, Ozomatli had been the most compliant and least argumentative. Was that because he was sacrificing people in secret to his demon god? Only Smoking Mirror's high priest would dare to defy the Feathered Serpent's will.

I dismissed the soldiers and motioned Citlallotoc to follow me towards Smoking Mirror's temple.

◻

The odor of burnt tobacco greeted me at the temple doorway, covering a musty, rotting smell that sometimes made my stomach gurgle. All temples shared that smell, from the blood offerings poured into the idols, and I'd rested easy this last year knowing little of it came with death. But in here I swore the stink was more rotten than in any other temple.

The Smoking Mirror's high priestess—a Chichimec woman named Yaretzi—knelt on a reed mat in front of an array of polished obsidian mirrors on the wall, muttering prayers under her breath. Another mirror lay on the floor in front of her, holding the smoldering pile of tobacco leaves that emitted the cloud of gray smoke that gave everything a murky appearance. She looked to be in a trance, but when I turned to leave— obviously Ozomatli wasn't there—she turned and asked, "Can I help you with something, My Lady?" She spoke with a heavy northern accent.

It baffled me that any woman would willingly serve the Smoking Mirror, so when I'd demanded that Ozomatli find a high priestess—and not some docile mouthpiece for himself—I really thought he wouldn't be able to find anyone and I'd have a good reason to convince Little Reed to disband the cult in Culhuacan. But in fact he found someone not only capable but also strong and willful. She shared none of Ozomatli's pandering politeness, and when I spoke with her, she listened with a pointed intensity, assessing and judging for later; a skill she undoubedly picked up during her days as a slave in my uncle's court. I both liked yet feared her the way I used to fear the old matrons who took a switch to my behind for bad behavior when I was little. "Do you know where Ozomatli is?"

"At home, sleeping. He was up late performing a ritual." She inclined her head when I thanked her and went back to her prayers, the smoke swirling around her like a lover's caress. I couldn't leave fast enough.

"Wonder what this *ritual* was," Citlallotoc muttered.

"Let's go ask him." I went across the precinct to the priestly quarters, north of Quetzalcoatl's temple.

In Xochicalco, the only children who ever ran around the priestly quarters had been me and Little Reed, but here quite a few young boys and girls played together in the streets or behind the houses' walled courtyards. A few boys bouncing a rubber ball together paused to watch us pass, and though I usually had smiles for children, today I couldn't muster the will to put on a false face.

Ozomatli's house sat at the end of the main row. Most of the high priests and priestesses lived in the palace, in what had been the nobles' suites when my father and uncle had ruled, but Ozomatli chose to live here among the other priests and priestesses. "I want to be readily available to those in need of assistance at any time of the day," he told me. A noble reason, yet I suspected his true purpose was a need for privacy for forbidden rituals. The house was the largest in the priestly quarters, for it once belonged to the high priest of Tlaloc, and the rain god's statues still dotted the colorful flowerbeds of the courtyard garden. A cord attached to a set of copper bells dangled outside the front doorway curtain.

I momentarily considered not announcing our arrival—the better to catch Ozomatli at whatever evil he practiced in secret—but my better sense prevailed. We were here to find out where he was and what he was doing last night, not to throw around baseless accusations supported only by my gut. I pulled the cord, ringing the copper bells.

A young, soot-covered novice answered the bells and quickly ushered us in, bowing to me the whole time. The house's anteroom was clean, a stark contrast to the boy, who had been cleaning out the hearth, and the air smelled of copalli and sweet tobacco. The whitewashed walls bore murals of the gods—the same ones that came with the house—and cut flowers filled numerous vases.

"I wish to speak with the high priest," I told the boy, and he hurried away into a side room closed off with a plain blue curtain. Citlallotoc moved around the main room while we waited, peeking in to side rooms and examining the religious artifacts on display.

Ozomatli emerged from his room, looking sleepy, his priestly robe tied sloppily closed in the front. "Greetings, My Lady," he said, giving me a sluggish bow.

"Up late last night?"

He nodded. "I was performing a ritual for the Offering of Flowers."

"A ritual requiring the shedding of human blood?" Citlallotoc asked.

Grimacing at him, Ozomatli said, "All rituals require blood, My Lord, but since we have no willing sacrifices at the moment, I fear you're insinuating something illegal."

"As you may have heard, two days ago the heir to Chimalhuacan was kidnapped from the market center," I said. "This morning our soldiers discovered his body in our copal grove."

Ozomatli blinked. "He's dead?"

"Sacrificed, with his heart removed in the fashion practiced by your god's cult."

Citlallotoc stepped right up to Ozomatli so the man had to crane his neck to meet his gaze. "Where were you last night?"

"In the temple, performing a sacrifice to the Smoking Mirror," Ozomatli replied, looking to me rather than meeting Citlallotoc's challenging gaze, "but completely in accordance with the rules and regulations set down by the law. I burned the ritual tobacco leaves, partook of the sacred teonanacatl, and slaughtered a juvenile jaguar. You can ask the ritual game keeper; he provided two slaves to handle the beast in the temple for me."

"What about after the sacrifice?" I asked.

Ozomatli shifted uncomfortably and didn't meet my gaze. "I attempted to commune with the god and gain inspiration, but he didn't oblige me." He stepped away from Citlallotoc to approach me. "My Lady, if any of my people broke the law, I have no knowledge of it or who did it. If I did, I'd immediately turn them over to you to face justice, for they taint the good name of the entire cult."

Your cult's good name is tainted by the very god it honors, the desire growled.

"I trust that you would," I said. "But you must admit that the situation is very concerning. When Tozli learns the circumstances of his son's murder, he will call for heads, and he's going to come first to those cults that still practice heart extraction and other such barbarities."

"We keep all our practices strictly within the boundaries of the law—"

"That you are aware of. Every priesthood has at some point had to contend with an outlaw among its ranks, and how the rest of us deal with those criminals colors the perception of the entire cult."

"We are in agreement about that, My Lady."

"Then you will not object to accompanying me to Chimalhuacan, to assure Lord Tozli that you are doing everything in your power to make sure the culprits are brought to justice."

After a brief hesitation—in which he cast an uneasy glance at Citlallotoc—Ozomatli said, "I'm happy to assist, Lady Quetzalpetlatl."

"Good. Be ready to go by dawn."

As Citlallotoc and I left the house, Citlallotoc strode to keep up with me. "We're going to Chimalhuacan?"

"*I'm* going to Chimalhuacan, for Nahuacatl's funeral," I corrected him. "You're staying here to watch over the kingdom in my absence."

"After how Toztli behaved during his last visit...I'd feel much better if I came with you, to make certain he doesn't forget himself."

"He's not going to forget himself; instead, he'll be overjoyed that I'm bringing him his son's murderer."

"Who?"

"Ozomatli, of course."

"But we have no definitive proof—"

"He might not have done it with his own hands, but that's not his style," I said. "He gets others to bloody their hands for him, so he can deny involvement, which makes him even worse than my uncle."

"Then you think he's been orchestrating murders for his cult?"

"It wouldn't be the first time." When Citlallotoc stopped short, I said, "Let's just say that in the past, he hasn't always acted honorably towards his king and high priest."

"You mean Ihuitimal?"

"Yes, but as you said, I have no definitive proof, just stories and...intuition."

"Nothing I can actually bring charges against then," Citlallotoc finished. "This convinces me all the more that I must come with you. If Ozomatli is dangerous, I must be there to protect you."

"And I'm asking you to stay here and protect the one thing in this world that is most precious to me," I countered. "I know it isn't as glamorous as staring down haughty kings and following around treacherous priests, but I trust no one but you and Topiltzin to watch over my son."

Citlallotoc frowned. "I'm honored by your faith in me, My Lady, but you are as important as the prince—even more so. Someone should go with you, for protection."

"I'll have my guards with me." He started to protest again, but I cut him off. "I appreciate your concern, Citlallotoc, but I'm not some weak noblewoman who's never been outside the palace walls. I have my own means of protection that is stronger than any sword."

Citlallotoc bowed his head. "You are perfectly capable of taking care of yourself," he conceded. "Please forgive my thoughtlessness."

I took his good arm with mine and smiled up at him. "And I thank you for caring enough to worry about me."

CHAPTER FOURTEEN

"**B**ut I want to go with you, Nantli!" Yamehecatl sat on my bed next to my travel bag, and when I tried to place a dress inside, he blocked me with his pudgy little hands. "I want to go with you!"

I gave him a sharp glare before moving his hands. "You can't come, my precious little breeze."

"Why not?" he whined, looking pained.

"Because this isn't a casual visit. The women will cry nonstop for several days, and Lord Nahuacatl's body will be laid out for everyone to see."

He gaped at me. "There's going to be a real dead body?"

"It will be wrapped in paper."

"Ayya! Now I really must go!"

I glared at him. "That's precisely why you're not going. Lord Toztli lost his son and you gawking at the body as if it's some colorful lizard is terribly disrespectful. These are delicate matters, and this isn't the appropriate time or place for small children."

He crawled to me and sat up on his knees, wringing the front of my dress with both hands. "Please, Nantli! Please!"

"No."

He yanked on my dress, nearly pulling me over, then he leaped off the bed and stomped towards the door. "You're so mean!" He disappeared out into the hallway.

I let him go, but once I finished packing, I went to the nursery to find him curled up on his bed, fingers jammed in his mouth, brows furrowed. I pulled him onto my lap. "There will be other times—better times—to go. You'll be happier here with Citlallotoc and you'll have the other children to play with—"

"I hate the other children!" he barked.

"Why?"

He frowned, tears dribbling down his cheeks. "All the ones my age are so stupid—they can barely even talk, but the older ones, who talk as well as me...they say I'm still a baby because I'm so small, and they won't let me play their games."

I hugged him. "Sometimes it's difficult being special."

Yamehecatl snuggled against my breast, wetting my dress with his tears. "I miss Tatli."

"Me too." I kissed the side of his head. "He'll be back soon though."

"But when?"

"A few more weeks, maybe a month at the most."

"And you promise you'll only be gone a couple of days?"

"I'll come back as quick as I can."

He rubbed his tears away. "But who will feed me before bed, and sing to me?"

I still nursed him every night; most noblewomen never nursed their children, hiring out the task so they could resume their normal routines quicker, but I'd chosen to stick with it. Most peasant women nursed as long as possible, especially when they desired no more children, and I hadn't missed the inconvenience of monthly bleeding these last couple of years. I cherished those quiet moments holding my son while he drowsed off to sleep with a milk-drunk smile on his face.

But he'd gain his third summer soon, and there wasn't any real need to continue nursing him; he ate and drank with the rest of us, and if the other children were teasing him....

"Maybe it's time to end the nighttime feedings," I suggested. When he looked ready to cry, I added, "You are getting older, and you said you don't like it when the other boys call you a baby."

He looked away, his jaw set, his brows furrowed again. "I hate them all but...they do say mean things...about you feeding me like that."

"Then the time is right." I hugged him and he clutched onto me.

"Will you still tell me stories before I go to sleep?"

"Of course, my dear sweet breeze."

"Tell me one now?"

I leaned back against the wall and he settled into my arms. "Which one do you want to hear?"

"One about the Feathered Serpent."

"How about how he gave maize to the people?"

Yamehecatl scoffed. "You always tell me that one."

"Then how about the one where Quetzalcoatl journeys into the underworld to bring back the bones of humanity?"

"That's Tatli's favorite, and he does better voices than you."

I chuckled. "He is very good at sounding like a god, isn't he?"

He nodded.

"How about the one about the creation of the Sun and the Moon?"

Yamehecatl screwed up his face into a pout. "Aren't there any new ones? Ones you haven't told me yet?"

I thought a moment. "Well, I haven't told you the one about the Feathered Serpent and the goddess Mayahuel."

"Who's Mayahuel?"

"She was the granddaughter of the Earth Monster Tzitzimitl, who held her captive in Omeyocan."

"Why?"

"Because she had powerful magic the Earth Monster didn't want given to the world, so she guarded Mayahuel jealously. But the other gods wanted to give a gift to humanity, to make them happy and bring them closer to the gods. Quetzalcoatl—in the guise of Ehecatl, the Wind—stole Mayahuel from the Earth Monster's garden and took her to Earth, letting her ride upon his shoulders."

"That was very nice of him," Yamehecatl said. "If someone was holding you prisoner in a garden, I bet Tatli would come rescue you."

"I'm certain he would too." Little Reed pretty much had done as such when Ihuitimal brought me to Culhuacan after Xochicalco's destruction.

"What happened next?"

"Ehecatl and Mayahuel went to the earthly paradise of Tamoachan and they came together to form a tree with two branches; one was called Quetzalhuexotl—the Feathered Tree—and the other was Xochicuahuitl—the Flowering Tree.

"But when the Earth Monster discovered Ehecatl had taken her granddaughter, she was furious, and she flew down to earth to find Mayahuel and destroy her."

Yamehecatl frowned. "But why would she do that?"

"Because Mayahuel defied her and left the garden."

"But you said that Ehecatl stole her, so why didn't the Earth Monster want to destroy him instead?"

When I'd first heard this version of the story in calmecac when I was a handful of years older than Yamehecatl, I'd asked Mothotli the fire priestess several similar questions, which caused her to become more and more flustered and culminated with her wrapping me on the knuckles with her switch for daring to question the sacred stories. She convinced me to keep my tongue quiet but my brain had refused to follow suit, and the years in between had taught me an answer to that question. Quetzalcoatl had told me that he and Mayahuel had been lovers—much as he and I had been—so it stood to reason that making this tree was a sly way of saying they'd had sex, and that Tzitzimitl focusing her wrath on Mayahuel was a lesson to young girls that terrible things happened when they gave in to the lusts of men.

But I didn't want to talk so frankly to my three-year-old son, whom we hadn't even mentioned sex to yet. "It's what she chose to do because earth monsters aren't known for their kindness or understanding. When the ground shakes as she stretches, she doesn't care if good boys or girls get hurt with falling rocks, or even die. She's a creature of wrath and chaos."

The look in Yamehecatl's eyes told me my answer didn't satisfy him, but he was eager to get on with the story. "Did Ehecatl fight her when she came?"

I shook my head. "No. The Earth Monster savaged the tree and destroyed the branch that was Mayahuel, killing her. Ehecatl's branch was spared though, and when the Earth Monster left, he changed back into his godly form and buried Mayahuel's remains. And from that grew the maguey plant, which we use not only for cloth and rope, but as our sacrificial thorns. But most importantly, we make the sap of the maguey into the sacred octli, which allows men and women to commune with the gods."

Yamehecatl sat listening for a couple of breaths after I finished, expecting me to go on; when I didn't, he cocked his head and asked, "Is that it?"

"That's it," I confirmed.

He looked downright cross. "That was a terrible story, Nantli! Where's the adventure, the fighting? Where is the Feathered Serpent's trickery, like when he convinced Lord Death he could play a rock like a flute?"

"There wasn't any."

"No wonder no one ever tells this story. There's nothing fun about it."

"The sacred stories aren't meant to be fun. They teach us about the world."

"Don't ever tell me that story again, Nantli. I like stories where Quetzalcoatl is heroic, like Tatli."

I chuckled. "Very well. I won't ever subject you to Mayahuel's sad story again."

He asked me to sing him a song and I did so, letting him curl up against my breast, fingers in his mouth as he sucked his way to sleep, but I couldn't stop thinking about the story. Yamehecatl was right; it was depressing, and my heart couldn't reconcile the Ehecatl of the story with the god who had given humanity life with his own blood, who'd brought us civilization through knowledge and kingship, and who used to make love with me in the Divine Dream with such passion.

It was a terrible story, but not for the reasons Yamehecatl thought it so. For all she went through, no one ever honored Mayahuel. *Though maybe we ought to*, I thought as I tucked Yamehecatl under his blanket and kissed him on the forehead. *If we can make room for Smoking Mirror—of all gods—in our temples, why not Mayahuel too?*

¤

Ozomatli was waiting in the courtyard with all the fire priests when I came out of the palace before dawn. I'd spoken to the ritual game keeper yesterday and he confirmed Ozomatli's story about the jaguar, but that didn't exonerate him from ordering Nahuacatl's murder. I would have to watch him very closely.

To my surprise though, Ixtlilxochitl was there as well, with a pack on his shoulders. When he saw me, he greeted me with his usual grim countenance. If I hadn't seen him laughing and performing slight-of-hand tricks for his daughters once, I would have thought him incapable of smiling. "Did Citlallotoc put you up to this?" I asked, casting an annoyed glare back at Citlallotoc, who was watching from the stairs.

"I rather agree with him that you shouldn't go alone," Ixtlilxochitl replied, his voice gruff.

Pointing to the soldiers assembled for the journey, I said, "I'm hardly going alone."

"Lord Citlallotoc says I'd make the ideal companion since Toztli would rather speak to you than me."

Or he'll think I'm insulting him by bringing my only Chichimec council member with me, I thought but held my tongue. That was unfair to Ixtlilxochitl. And if he was to govern Culhuacan when we moved north, Toztli would have to learn to deal with him on cordial terms.

Still, would there ever be a day when men realized I didn't need their protection unless I asked for it? I let it go and instead thanked Ixtlilxochitl as he helped me into the royal litter.

Once I settled among the pillows, I leaned out of the curtain and waved goodbye to Yamehecatl, who dangled half-asleep in a servant girl's arms. He waved back sleepily and I blew him a kiss as the caravan moved slowly out of the courtyard.

It only took a few hours to reach Chimalhuacan, so I caught up on my sleep while the procession of soldiers and priests moved east along the road. Malinalli stopped by the litter with some cold tlaxcallis for me midmorning, but other than that, I kept to myself, planning out what to say to Toztli, and hoping this dull ache in my breasts wasn't a sign of things to come.

I'd sent a runner ahead the day before, informing Toztli of my impending visit, but only his head steward greeted me when the caravan stopped in the palace courtyard. The mousey little man groveled about how the king was otherwise detained; understandable, but he could have acknowledged the value of our cities' alliance by sending someone important—his war chief perhaps—to greet me. The head steward showed me to the guest quarters and promised to see to accommodations for the rest of my company.

"Lord Toztli wouldn't dare to not personally greet Topiltzin,"

Ixtlilxochitl growled as he investigated the adjoining rooms, making certain all was safe.

"I'm aware of that." I dropped my bag and flopped down on the bed, my aching breasts leaving me irritable.

"You should make it clear to him that it's unacceptable to treat you differently than he does your husband."

"I know!" He didn't react to my outburst but I still felt bad as soon as I said it. "Forgive my foul mood. I know you're trying to help."

"I'm trying to keep him from treating you like a dog rather than a queen," he corrected me. "Toztli is the kind of man who tests for weaknesses to exploit, and if you show the least bit, he will wring your neck with it. He tried that once with Ihuitimal, and Ihuitimal had his second son killed and warned that his heir would be next if he tried it again."

I scrutinized him more closely now, my throat constricting. "You worked for my uncle?"

"I was one of the king's personal guards. I fell into Topiltzin's hands and instead of sending me to the sacrifice, he asked me to carry peace terms to Culhuacan." He glanced out into the hallway as he finished his survey of my quarters. "He didn't ask me to divulge any of Ihuitimal's secrets or plot against him despite my having direct access to him. He was more interested in suing for peace to free you. That's why I pledged my loyalty to him once the war ended." He turned to me. "If you require nothing further, I should investigate my own quarters. The head steward was giving cowardly looks to the palace guards when we passed by them. They may be lying in wait and will require that I correct their behavior with a few broken noses."

◻

Toztli wasn't at dinner, though Nahuacatl's wife took a break from the ritual lamentations to host the meal. Already she looked as if she'd run out of tears to shed.

Cornflower was there as well and I embraced her when she greeted me with a brave face. She was heavy with child—she'd found a place as a concubine in the household of one of her father's advisors—and I hoped this ordeal wasn't taxing her too much. She offered to sit with me and play hostess, but I insisted she sit with her family and not concern herself with entertaining me. Mazatzin and Malinalli sat with me, as did Ixtlilxochitl. Apparently he hadn't been ambushed when he went to his quarters, but he still watched the room with keen eyes.

"Of course something such as this would happen when we're ready to leave for Tollan," Malinalli noted as she dipped her tlaxcalli into our shared bowl of chile sauce.

"The timing is very suspicious." I cast my gaze over at Ozomatli, who was sitting with his fire priest and those of Tlaloc and Xipe Totec. He looked irritatingly relaxed, and even chuckled at the conversation; inappropriate for a mourning feast. But to priests of the demon Smoking Mirror, death wasn't a serious matter, and people were merely dogs waiting for the cook to pick them.

"If war breaks out, it could be years before the seat of power moves to Tollan," Mazatzin noted, watching Ozomatli as well. "Especially if our allies see this as a warning from the gods about Quetzalcoatl's reforms."

"Which is why it's all the more important we produce the culprits. Let them sacrifice themselves until Smoking Mirror has devoured himself into obscurity."

I didn't sleep well; the women's laments carried as far as the guest quarters, and I lay awake thinking about the last time I'd heard such a ritual. I wondered where Jade Flower was now. When I'd returned to Culhuacan, a letter from her awaited me, thanking me for sending Black Otter back to her and the children, and assuring me that they left Chalco before the struggle for the throne broke out; Papantzin's father kicked them all out when Black Otter refused to marry his daughter, and so they were going to Xico to stay with Flame Tongue and Anacoana. I hadn't heard anything from her since, and I only knew they'd moved again when Anacoana told Citlallotoc as much on one of his official visits a few years ago. I often joked that she was infatuated with him—for she took every opportunity to talk to him despite her father's lectures about proper ladies not doing such things; but if not for her affinity for Citlallotoc, I wouldn't know much of anything about my sister anymore.

I managed to drowse off once the cries ended, but I woke at dawn soaked in milk, thanks to engorgement. I finagled a clean night dress from one of the servants and wrapped my chest with extra layers of cloth before joining Malinalli and Mazatzin for breakfast before they continued on to

Tollan. By the time I returned to my quarters for a nap, my breasts throbbed so badly I wanted to cry, so I asked my servants to draw a hot bath for me. A few moments in the heat worked magic, relieving the pain and pressure so I could finally relax.

The bath in my quarters in Culhuacan was laid into the ground and tiled with shells imported from the south, but this bath sat aboveground and was lined with beaten bronze, the better to retain the heat. I'd had a similar one in my old quarters, and Black Otter and I had made love in it at least a dozen times....

Those thoughts of Black Otter soon melted into memories of that night so long ago with Little Reed in his tent at the army encampment. I still remembered the taste of salt and chile on his tongue, the callused flesh where his fingers met his palm, the heat and hardness of his tepolli against my belly. I'd sacrificed any possibility of real physical intimacy with him, but I could freely carry on an affair of the imagination. And this time Red Flint wouldn't interrupt us, and there wasn't any chance of Yamehecatl wandering in and asking embarrassing questions....

But the laments started up again, soft at first but growing steadily louder and increasingly mournful. They created a grim litany of devastation and loss that chewed away at the desire until nothing remained. If only it were always so easily quelled. I finished washing and remained there until the heat was sapped, then I dressed in my fresh nightdress for a nap.

I gasped when I came into my quarters to find Toztli standing in front of the hearth, staring into the flames. He turned around at my startled cry, and the look on his face was as dark as any I'd ever seen. In only my nightdress, I felt horribly naked, and I swallowed back the shameful desire that feeling provoked inside me. "Lord Toztli," I stammered. "I realize these are trying times for you, but it's highly inappropriate to barge in on the wife of your closest ally."

He laughed. "Don't flatter yourself, My Lady. I'm not interested."

"I should hope not." Anger and embarrassment heated my cheeks, but I tried to appear strong. "How can I be of assistance?"

"My son's death...." But instead of finishing, he returned to glaring into the hearth.

"I'm deeply sorrowed by your loss. Nahuacatl was an exceptional man, and he would have been a most honorable king. His death is a great loss to all of us." When he said nothing, I pressed on. "When I heard of the circumstances of his death, I immediately knew one of Smoking Mirror's followers was responsible and brought his high priest to account. Ozomatli has pledged to do everything in his power to expose the rogue priests who perpetrated this terrible act, and together, he and I will deliver them to justice for you."

Toztli picked up a small bag resting at his feet and dumped its contents on the floor in front of me: five green quetzal feathers, a desiccated snake carcass, and a handful of dried-up butterflies. He stared back at me, anger seething in his eyes. "Then explain these things my men discovered with my son's body."

I stared at these objects that priests of Quetzalcoatl often used in conjunction with sacrifices, and my jaw set tight. *That demon-worshiping lake scum, trying to frame Quetzalcoatl's cult for this atrocity?* "These were placed with the body to make it look as if the god's priests committed this crime. We don't make human sacrifices; not even willing ones."

"It wasn't always that way," Toztli said. "Even as little as four years ago, criminals still died in the Feathered Serpent's name."

"When they did, the priests never took out their hearts."

"That's your official stance, but you've opened your ranks to heathen Chichimecs, so how can you be sure they aren't bringing their bloody rituals to Quetzalcoatl's worship? You blithely lay the blame at the feet of Smoking Mirror's followers, so why not your own as well? The evidence is right there, at your feet, and as the high priestess, you're responsible for controlling your priests and followers. Even if Smoking Mirror's people did this, the blame lies on you as the queen; you allowed that Chichimec cult to continue in your midst. No matter how you look at it, you and Topiltzin are culpable for my son's death."

I clenched my jaw. *I told Little Reed that tolerating Smoking Mirror's cult would come back to bite us,* but my being right gave me no satisfaction. "We did allow the cult's continuance, so yes, we bear part of the responsibility for what happened. I promise you that I will address this issue with Topiltzin again as soon as he returns from Tollan."

"Not good enough!" Toztli snarled. "The future of my kingdom is now in question!"

"And Topiltzin and I will help you, whether it's assisting you in arbitrating the choice of a new heir from among your other sons, or helping you identify a good candidate from among the city's noble class."

He laughed, incredulous. "I lose my favorite son, whom I raised from birth to be my voice once I die, and this is all you offer me?"

"What do you wish of me, Lord Toztli?"

"Your son, of course, you dimwitted woman!"

I stepped back. "Outrageous! How dare you even—"

He bridged the gap between us in three mighty steps, backing me into the wall. "You cost me my kingdom's future! The only proper reparation is for you to suffer the same fate, and I will accept nothing less!" He pointed to my stack of papers sitting with the jar of ink and a goose quill on the floor next to my bed. "You will write to Lord Citlallotoc, ordering him to bring the prince to me."

"You're delusional if you think I'd let you anywhere near my son!"

My years as the most powerful woman in Culhuacan had trained me to believe no one would dare touch me without my permission, so it took me completely by surprise when Toztli grabbed me by the hair and dragged me across the room to the bed. All his assurances that he had no interest in bedding me screamed, *lies!* as he forced me down on the mats and blankets.

But he picked up the papers and shoved them into my face. "You will write that letter and call him here!" he bellowed.

But then he let me go. When I looked back at him, tears blurring my vision, he stared at me with wide, disbelieving eyes. He ran his fingers through his long hair and muttered, "What have I...?"

Only once my heartbeat slowed did I become aware of the magic pulsing in my fingertips. What good were such powers if I couldn't remember them when they could make a difference? I pulled my hands close to my chest, gathering my magic. I wouldn't make that mistake twice.

He turned away from me, tears in his voice. "I deserve justice, My Lady. I didn't ask for this!"

"Neither did I." I held my breath to keep from screaming at him.

"I begged Topiltzin to drive those animals back into the desert but *you* talked him out of it, and now you've destroyed my kingdom—"

"You've done that by declaring war on Culhuacan, Tollan, and the god," I retorted.

"None of this would have happened if you had done the right thing back then. And only doing the right thing now can make any difference."

I flexed my fingers, the tingling burning, my mind growing distant as the desire supplanted me. "I will devour you before I let you touch my son."

Toztli stared at me, taken aback. "Have it your way. Remember it's your stubbornness that forced my hand." He strode from the room, rattling the bells on the curtain's hem.

I flew after him—*how dare he turn his back on me!*—but two of his guards pushed me back inside. "Ixtlilxochitl!" I shouted.

"Your Chichimec dog can't help you now," one of the men said and ripped the curtain closed. I stared at the fabric, panting as I came back to myself. *I never should have agreed to let Ixtlilxochitl come; I should have known they would hurt him.*

But now I was on my own, which meant saving myself. I hurried out to the bath yard again, tearing aside the vines on the walls, searching for a way out. But there were no secret doorways, only smooth, plaster walls. I tried pulling myself up and over using the vines, but they snapped easily, dried out from the hot weather. I tried again and again, determined to scale it—and not think of my recurring dream of the endless high walls—and I nearly made it to the top at one point, but the vines ripped and I hit the ground with a grunt, my tailbone aching. I sat there stewing, tears of frustration creeping up on me.

"All that magic at your disposal and yet you let him manhandle you," a voice suddenly spoke up behind me.

I scrambled to my feet to find a huge man looming in the doorway to my room, leaning casually against the jamb. He wore an amused smile and a feathered xicolli that hung to his thighs, with the tail of a blue and red loincloth visible under the jagged hem. And his entire left side was painted blue. "Mextli?"

"You remember me? But then it's hard to forget a face like mine, isn't it?" He laughed.

"What are you doing here?"

"Reconnoitering," he answered with a grin.

Already twice in one day I stood practically naked in front of someone I hardly knew. I came back to the patio and snatched up my high priestess robe and slipped it on over my shoulders, relieved to be less exposed. "Why would you be at all interested in Chimalhuacan?"

He raised his one eyebrow—there wasn't one on the left side of his face. "Who says that's the interesting thing here?"

Catching his meaning, I edged away while trying not to be obvious. "What's so interesting about me?"

He laughed. "Let's not play games with each other. We both know what happened that night in Tollan. Personally, I found it very...illuminating."

My heart pulsed fear through my body. "I did what I had to. You were going to kill my friend."

"I was." After a tense silence, his gaze shifted to my quarters, the casualness returning. "Don't worry, I'm not bitter. The element of surprise is a time-honored battle tactic, and it was my own fault for not anticipating that Quetzalcoatl would bring his own powerful allies. You won that round. But you won't fool me again."

I looked away too, attempting to match his nonchalance despite the pit in my stomach. "Are we to battle again then?"

"I haven't decided yet. But I warn you, I'm not someone you want declaring war on you."

His annoying arrogance overrode my fear. "Toztli has already done as much, so what's one more?"

"You really haven't any idea who I am, do you?"

"I don't really care," the desire spat.

That arrow hit a sensitive spot; he maintained his smile but the slight narrowing of his eyes betrayed him. "I am the god of war, and I don't lose."

The desire always drove the fear away, so I let it stay. "Tonatiuh is the god of war; you're a little desert quail who's attached himself to a worthless sorcerer."

This time the whole left side of his body puffed up, like a grouse. *He is covered in feathers!* I realized, unable to help staring at the comical yet gruesome display. "You foolishly dismiss me, but I would be stupid to do the same with you." He smoothed his arm-feathers with his right hand. "I will find out who you really are, so I'm better prepared the next time we match powers."

"You don't already know me? I'm Lady Quetzalpetlatl, Queen of Culhuacan and High Priestess of Quetzalcoatl. That is all you need to know."

He laughed again. "I think you're the one who doesn't know who you really are. The Feathered Serpent has convinced you of your own mediocrity, and it's such a shame; so much potential, and yet you allowed that man to slap you around like a dog. Maybe you aren't the worthy opponent I first thought you were."

His words unexpectedly stung. "No, *you're* not worth *my* time, nor do I need your approval, or even your respect."

"Because it's so much better being the Feathered Serpent's plaything?"

A whirlwind of embarrassment and anger raged inside me. "Quetzalcoatl is twice the god your pathetic Smoking Mirror could ever hope to be," I snarled, "so crawl back into that dung-heap you came out of and leave divine matters to *real* gods, little hummingbird boy." It felt both terrifying and exhilirating to say it, to a god of all things!

Mextli still grinned, amused. "Big words for a little *thorn bush*."

The puzzling insult so took me by surprise—and the desire too—that suddenly I was back in control again. And that comfortable confidence had fled. I choked back the fear though, determined not to show it. "Why...why in Mictlan are you here anyway?"

"As I said, I'm learning more about you, seeing what I'm up against. And I was hungry; fortunately the right meal presented himself and now I get to see you and your magic in action."

I stared at him. "You killed Nahuacatl?"

He shrugged. "I would have preferred a warrior's heart, but delicious nonetheless. He served his purpose; you're here, after all."

"You planted all that...that other stuff? The butterflies and feathers and snake—"

"I'm not exactly proud of that," Mextli admitted, contrite. "I prefer to wage honorable war, but sometimes the rules must bend. A good war chief exploits his enemy's weaknesses; Toztli fears your power—both spiritually and politically—and he desperately wants everything to be as it was before you took the throne." He rubbed his chin. "As for your weaknesses...well, that I cannot say yet; I must know the full spectrum of your magic first. Though given how easily he manhandled you, this probably isn't worth my time."

My cheeks burned. "He took me by surprise."

"I can afford to be taken by surprise; you cannot. Topiltzin can only sacrifice so much to keep you from Lord Death."

"Sacrifice?" I thought back to when Xolotl marked Little Reed for death right after I'd come back from the dead. I'd tried hard—futilely—to forget that image, as well as what the fact of his still being alive meant, but I couldn't run from it forever. Somehow I'd cheated Heaven of its sacrifice, and what price would Little Reed pay for that?

Mextli looked into my room again, distracted. But then suddenly he loomed over me, covering me in his shadow. I cowered. "Human life is a fragile, finite thing, and once it's gone, there's no coming back. Never forget that." He disappeared with a sound like snapping sticks.

Toztli stormed into the bath yard, his guards with him. His men grabbed me by the arms. "Time to do the right thing, My Lady."

CHAPTER FIFTEEN

I expected Toztli to try to make me write the letter again, but instead he and his guards escorted me out of the palace. Curious citizens gathered at the sides of the street, held back by guards as we passed.

Eventually we came to the sacred precinct, to the temple of Quetzalcoatl. Crowds flooded in after us, pressing close to the base of the pyramid as we climbed the steps. To my confusion, Mazatzin and Malinalli were at the top, both bound and gagged. Ixtlilxochitl knelt behind them, only bound and looking unperturbed; he wasn't a man prone to verbal outbursts. Ozomatli was there too, but he was free. I stared him down as the guards pushed me by him.

"Don't blame him for your folly," Toztli said, noticing my vehement gaze. "You tried to push responsibility for my son's death on his cult when all the evidence points to your own priests as the culprits. It's only fitting he should witness justice being properly meted out."

"My priests didn't do this either. We're all being played against each other for a god's amusement—"

"Lies!" Toztli shouted. "The law of the land in Chimalhuacan is a life for a life. Culhuacan swore to uphold the laws of its allies and yet you shun that promise now. Hypocrite!"

"My son did not murder your son—"

"Enough! Will you give me the justice I ask for, Lady Quetzalpetlatl?"

I glared back, carefully articulating each word, "I will kill you before I let you harm my son."

"Then your priests will pay for your arrogance." Toztli nodded to his guards.

They seized Malinalli and wrenched her to her feet.

But Mazatzin launched at one of them, butting him in the side of the head with his own. They both fell to the ground as the other guard dragged Malinalli towards the sacrificial stone. Ozomatli stood watching stupidly but stumbled aside when Ixtlilxochitl—he'd somehow freed himself of his bindings—rushed past him. Ixtlilxochitl grabbed Malinalli's guard by the neck with his arm and squeezed.

Seizing the distraction, I rushed to grab Malinalli and get us out there, but a third guard intercepted me and tried to wrestle me back. Magic gathered in my fingertips and this time I didn't hesitate. I latched onto his bare arms and let it go.

He stumbled backward, weaving around like a drunkard, shouting incoherently. He shuffled past me, towards the edge of the pyramid and stepped over as if he didn't see it. The crowd below screamed as he fell head over feet to his death.

I stared, baffled. What had I done to him?

Toztli stared over the edge too, the color drained from his face. When he turned back to me, his eyes went wild with panic. "Witch!" He fumbled at the dagger on his belt.

"Don't make me hurt you," I warned, backing away. "Topiltzin will come for you. Think of your people—do what's best for them. Don't let this devolve into all-out war." I nearly unleashed my magic when I ran into Malinalli behind me. The guard had let her go in a last-ditch effort to free himself of Ixtlilxochitl's stranglehold.

"Don't just stand there!" Ixtlilxochitl shouted at Ozomatli. "Defend your queen!"

Ozomatli met my gaze, panicked, then fled down the back steps, abandoning us.

"Coward!" Ixtlilxochitl snapped the guard's neck, ending his struggle; but when he moved to intercept Toztli, the other guard—whom I'd thought Mazatzin had knocked out—buried a knife in his ribs. They went down in a heap.

Toztli finally freed his own knife and advanced towards me.

"Go!" I shouted over my shoulder at Malinalli. "Get off the temple!" When she hesitated, I squawked, "Now!" and she finally ran, disappearing down the steps.

"You're nothing but a filthy witch!" Toztli screamed, and leaped at me.

He knocked me over but I grabbed his upraised arm and pushed magic into him. Nothing happened, and my arms strained under his superior strength; if anything, he'd gotten stronger and wilder. I pushed harder, the magic burning in my blood like fire. He huffed and puffed, red-faced, as he strained to stab me. His breath turned foul and pungent, making my eyes sting.

Then my strength gave out.

The blade pierced my shoulder, all the way to the hilt. The pain didn't register, but the look of drunken glee in his eyes did and I pushed out all the magic I had left in one last attempt to get him off me.

His eyes immediately clouded over, as if he'd gone into the Divine Dream. He let me go at last and tried to stand, but he stumbled away instead, dropping to his knees again. He tried again to stand but this time he vomited all over the stone no more than an arm's length from me. The stench of rancid alcohol stabbed my sinuses, threatening to empty my own stomach. Toztli broke into violent shakes, falling face first into his own vomit. He stared back at me with one blank, empty eye as the convulsions slowed, and his breathing along with it, until he lay dead.

I tried to move, but my body refused to obey. I was a sack of stones, so weak I couldn't even blink. Screams and drunken shouting came from all around me; people were throwing stones that buzzed in and out of my field of vision like birds in flight. *What have I done?* I wondered as my mind slowly drifted away.

¤

I was back in Xochicalco, right after the confrontation where Ahexotl sliced my heel and tried to burn me alive. Despite knowing Little Reed was dead, I kept asking everyone where he was, but no one would answer me; Malinalli behaved as if she didn't hear me talking at all and instead forced me to drink something that reminded me of chewing on bronze jewelry. Yet I couldn't get enough of it and I begged for more and more.

After a while I wasn't in Xochicalco anymore, but rather in my own bed in Culhuacan. Little Reed sat next to me, holding my hand and looking harried. My muscles took their time waking up too, moving with aching sluggishness. A stale, sticky residue coated my mouth and tongue, begging for water to wash it away, but when Little Reed helped me sit up and put a cup to my lips, it was that same taste from my dreams. An inexplicable eagerness took over and I finished it in one long gulp, warmth and strength spreading through me. I wiped the corner of my wet mouth with the back of my hand and started when I saw crimson on it. "What in Mictlan—?"

"It's blood."

My stomach twisted right along with my mind. Why on earth did he feed me blood?

Little Reed took the cup and handed it to Malinalli—who stood behind him, looking tired and worried. "I think she's ready for some water." Once she moved off, he told me, "You used too much magic."

"So you fed me blood?" My stomach threatened to heave.

"It's what the god said to do," Malinalli supplied, stopping at the doorway to the bath yard. "When I found you, you looked half-dead, and you stayed asleep for days. Mazatzin and I feared you would never wake up, so we asked the god for help."

"And he told you to feed me blood?" Now I noticed the cuts on her bare arms from the bloodletting.

"We all took turns feeding you," she said. "Mazatzin, Citlallotoc, myself, even Ozomatli—"

"You told Ozomatli about my powers?" I tried not to sound indignant; she'd saved my life again after all.

She shook her head. "I didn't tell him what it was for; I said he needed to give me some each day, and he did, no questions asked. I think he feels guilty for running away instead of defending you."

The events on the temple top came back to me. "Ixtlilxochitl! Is he—?"

"He's all right," Little Reed assured me. "He's recovering, slowly. It was bad enough he'd been stabbed, but he appeared to have been poisoned too. Mazatzin was very sick for a day or two also."

I clenched my jaw. Had I poisoned them when I'd released all my magic on Toztli? Was that why the city sounded like a drunken revel right before I passed out?

When Malinalli disappeared into the bath yard, I asked Little Reed, "Did you give me blood too?"

"Of course."

"But why blood?"

"Remember how you always needed blood to call on the god? Well, your magic uses your own blood, but the small amounts you typically use don't take a toll on you. This time, you used more in one burst than your blood could sustain; you're lucky you didn't kill yourself."

"I didn't even think about what I was doing. I only wanted to stop Toztli."

"What happened?" Little Reed asked.

"Someone murdered Nahuacatl in ritual fashion in our copal grove, and Toztli blamed us, because we allowed Smoking Mirror's cult to continue. I went to Chimalhuacan to pay our respects and to promise we'd find the culprits, but he demanded I hand Yamehecatl over to him. He was going to kill our son, Little Reed...." I started to choke up but worked my way past it. "When I refused to comply, he took Malinalli, Mazatzin and Ixtlilxochitl hostage, and threatened to sacrifice them. And when Toztli attacked me...I unleashed everything I had at him."

Malinalli returned with my cup of water. "Whatever magic you used was potent. I felt as if I'd drunk three cups of octli instantly. Everyone was out of control after that, throwing rocks, breaking things, setting houses on fire...."

"I must be very careful with this. If Ixtlilxochitl or Mazatzin had been any closer to me when I let it go, they might be dead now."

Little Reed gripped my hand. "They're both fine, but yes, care is needed. You almost killed yourself."

I nodded, guilt eating me as I swallowed the cold water.

"Did we ever find out who actually killed Nahuacatl?" Little Reed asked.

"I don't think so," Malinalli answered. "We rather forgot about the investigation in light of Quetzalpetlatl's condition."

I finished my water and asked her, "Could you fetch Yamehecatl? I'm desperate to see him."

"Of course." She ducked out of the door, leaving the copper bells on my curtain jingling.

"It was Mextli again," I told Little Reed, keeping my voice low. "He came to see me while Toztli held me prisoner."

Little Reed sat up straighter. "What did he say?"

"He wanted Toztli to think the god's priests were responsible, so he left some of our sacrificial items with Nahuacatl's body."

"But why?"

"So Toztli would blame me for his son's death."

"So he'd kill you?"

I shook my head. "Mextli knows I attacked him on the precinct in Tollan, and he...wanted to see 'the full spectrum' of my powers."

"That son of a demon god!" he swore under his breath.

"As terrible as it may sound, I learned a great deal about my magic in all this. And Toztli effectively declared war on us, so he reaped the fate he deserved. He'd wanted an excuse to challenge me for a long time, and Mextli played into his fears to make it happen sooner rather than later."

Little Reed nodded. "I must apologize. I knew Toztli had grown uncomfortable dealing with you these last few years, but he and I always got along very well, and I thought that would keep him from behaving horrendously. I should have been far more mindful of it. I'm so sorry."

"I didn't think he was the kind either, Little Reed." I squeezed his hand. "What will we do about Chimalhuacan now?"

"Blood Wolf will run the city until Toztli's remaining sons come of age and one of them proves himself. But until then, Chimalhuacan will be a tribute state to Tollan."

I embraced him. "I'm glad you're home again. These last few months felt like years."

"The next time I leave for Tollan, you and Yamehecatl are coming with me, and we won't return."

"Then the palace is ready?"

He nodded. "And the city is already ten times larger than when last you were there. This year's crop yield promises to eclipse any here in the valley." He brought me another cup of water when I asked. "Tell me more about what Mextli told you."

I shrugged. "He thought I should have dealt with Toztli when he grabbed me by the hair and threw me down—"

"Toztli put his hands on you?" Little Reed started rising to his feet, but I grabbed his hand.

"It's all right. It's over now, and I'm none the worse for it. But Mextli's right; I need to learn better focus and practice more, so my magic becomes a part of me. I was lucky my hesitation didn't get me killed." I chuckled. "I'm actually quite glad Mextli came to talk to me."

Uncertainty crossed Little Reed's face. "He seems to have impressed you."

"Impressed isn't the right word. It's more...it's so unusual for a man to not only think I'm capable of more, but to actually encourage me—"

"I encourage you," Little Reed said with a hint of hurt.

"Of course you do, and so do Citlallotoc and Mazatzin, but...the first time I go on a solo visit to one of our allies, he thinks he can knock me around and bully me. Not many men outside our small circle of friends take me seriously, either as a leader, or as a threat. I'm that loudmouthed woman married to Lord Topiltzin."

"You're not loudmouthed. And how do you know that I'm not that decrepit old man married to the beautiful Quetzalpetlatl?"

"You're not decrepit." I stared at his hands sitting on the blanket so close to mine. "As for Mextli...it was nice for once to not be underestimated and instead be taken seriously."

"I might think he was being nice if he didn't have such a reputation for ruthlessness," Little Reed admitted.

"Well, we aren't always what we seem, are we?"

He smiled. "That much is true of anyone."

"Can I ask you something?"

"Of course."

"Did you save me that day on the battlefield...by sacrificing your own life?" A sudden rush of fear made me bite off the last word, barely getting it out.

He didn't answer right away, and he didn't meet my gaze when he finally did. "It upsets you that I would do such a thing for you when you'd readily do the same for me?"

"What upsets me is that you're still here...."

"You wish I was already gone?" he asked, confused.

I shook my head. "Of course not, but....this means Heaven may decide any day now to collect on your debt. I lost you once, and I can't bear the thought of losing you again." I dabbed my eyes, trying to catch the tears before they fell.

He hugged me again, stroking my hair. "Rest your heart, my love. Where you see a curse, I see a gift. Yes, my time here will be short—everyone's time is finite—but that means I have every reason to make the most of every moment. And without that sacrifice, Papalotl, I wouldn't have you, and I wouldn't have a son I love more than life itself."

I breathed deep, the heaviness dissolving into relief and acceptance. "I love you so much, Little Reed."

"I've never doubted it for a moment."

"Nantli!" Yamehecatl ran to me from the doorway in a blur and leapt into my arms, almost knocking me over. "Nantli! Nantli! Nantli!" he squealed, squeezing me with his pudgy little arms. "Are you all better now? You're not going away again, are you?"

I laughed and pushed his curls aside to kiss his forehead. "I'm fine, and no, I'm not going anywhere without you."

"You promise?"

"I promise."

He sighed and rested his head on my bosom. "I missed you so much, Nantli. Did you miss *me*?"

"Terribly."

"Oh! Oh! Guess what, Nantli! Citlallotoc taught me a new move with my sword and I can't wait to show you!"

"I can't wait to see it."

Little Reed let me lean back against his shoulder. Yamehecatl moved back and forth between our laps like an ant that had lost its way as he told me about everything I'd missed while I was gone. I sighed and closed my eyes, treasuring this moment with all of us together as a family.

CHAPTER SIXTEEN

Little Reed insisted I rest some more, but after sleeping for nearly four days, come dinner time I needed real food in my stomach. I stuck to tlaxcallis and water, but ate with a ravenous hunger that would certainly make me sick. Such dire hunger always brought out the desire, but it remained mysteriously quiet, letting me carry on conversations with both Little Reed and Citlallotoc.

The latter seemed unusually withdrawn and nervous. Guilt perhaps for not insisting on accompanying me to Chimalhuacan himself? By the end of dinner, I was too fatigued to approach him about it and instead begged off the after-meal activities in favor of putting Yamehecatl to bed and getting some more sleep.

Yet Yamehecatl proved hyperactive and adamantly opposed to sleeping. He hugged me repeatedly and laughed hysterically during all the songs. He begged me to tell him the story of Mayahuel again, "But make Ehecatl more heroic this time, Nantli! Make him take a sword to the Earth Monster and save Mayahuel." I hadn't the patience to go through with that again, and considered nursing him, for that always worked to get him to sleep. But my milk supply had finally dried up enough that I wasn't uncomfortable anymore, and nursing him now would set back that progress. Eventually he wore himself out and drifted off to sleep.

Back in my quarters, Little Reed was waiting for me with another cup of blood. "Must I really drink more of this?" I grimaced into the cup.

"Just once more, for good measure," he told me as he tried to wrap a tourniquet on his left arm to stifle the bleeding.

Yamehecatl's mention of Mayahuel reminded me about things I wished to discuss with Little Reed. "I have an idea, for a new religious policy," I said, helping him tie on the cloth.

"Oh?"

"What would you think of designating a feast week to honor the goddess Mayahuel?"

He blinked at me, surprised.

"Yamehecatl had me tell him the story about her the other day, and it struck me how unfair it is that we don't honor her, despite everything her death gave us; we give all the honor and credit to Quetzalcoatl, as if her part were of no consequence—"

"Her role was far from inconsequential," Little Reed said.

"Exactly, so why don't we honor that by giving her a feast week, where people can make offerings of octli and maguey fiber?" I finished tying the tourniquet and looked up into his bright eyes. "It's the least she deserves, don't you think?"

"I think it's a wonderful idea." As he leaned in closer to me, his warm, tobacco-tinted breath on my cheek set me shivering with longing. "It's a grievous oversight we must correct."

"Very grievous," I murmured, my train of thought drowning in the ebb of desire and want flowing over me.

Someone rang the bells on my door curtain, but Little Reed still didn't move away, perhaps fearful of breaking the moment. "Come in."

Citlallotoc entered, closing the curtain carefully behind him. "Sorry to disturb you, My Lord and Lady, but there's something I need to speak to you about." He was more nervous than at dinner.

Little Reed finally moved away, leaving me disappointed. "Is everything all right?"

Citlallotoc shifted his feet. "I should have brought this to you as soon as you returned from Tollan, but with caring for the queen, you already had so much on your mind...."

His evasiveness scared me. "What's going on?"

My words finally broke his hesitation. He hurried over and prostrated himself at my feet. "Forgive me, My Lady, but I failed you."

"What is that supposed to mean?"

"The day you left...that night...the prince got into some octli."

"Where in Mictlan did he get that?"

"I don't know. I checked your quarters—"

"I don't keep octli in my quarters."

He nodded. "I didn't find any in here, or in Lord Topiltzin's quarters either."

Little Reed furrowed his brow. "Did you ask him?"

"I did, but he denied everything."

"Are you certain he wasn't merely misbehaving?" I asked. "He was very high-strung before bed tonight."

"I smelled it on his breath, My Lady."

I cast a worried gaze over at Little Reed. "You don't think someone tried to poison him, do you?"

"I'll question all the guards and servants," Little Reed assured me, heading for the door as if to go and do it right now. "I don't want you to worry; I'll get to the bottom of this. You still need to rest and recover."

Laughter drifted in from the hallway, followed by bare feet pattering on the stone floors. Yamehecatl tore open my curtain with his hand as he ran by, shrieking in delight.

Citlallotoc poked his head out of the doorway. "What are you doing out of bed, young man? Come back here this instant!" He disappeared through the curtain. Both Little Reed and I followed him.

Yamehecatl stood in the doorway to Little Reed's quarters, grinning at us with the curtain draped over his head like a cloak. It might have been cute were he not swaying on his feet like a drunkard. "I'm a magical rabbit and you can't see me!" He jumped up and down.

Little Reed took him firmly by the arm. "We can see you just fine, Yamehecatl. What are you doing out of bed?" He wrinkled his nose as he lifted our son into his arms. "Who gave you octli?"

"Heaven gave it to me," Yamehecatl said with a screechy laugh. But when he locked gazes with me, his jovial mood darkened. "Why won't you feed me anymore, Nantli? Don't you like me?" Before I could say anything, he suddenly spat, "Of course she doesn't like us; she didn't want us in the first place!"

His words cut me like a knife.

"That is enough!" Little Reed rarely raised his voice—and I'd never heard him do so with our son—so I wasn't the only one to flinch. Yamehecatl stared at him, shocked, but then he buried his face in Little Reed's chest and cried.

I moved to comfort him, but Little Reed held his hand up to stop me. "I will speak with him." He took Yamehecatl back to his nursery.

Citlallotoc shook his head. "I don't understand how this happened. He was sitting with us the whole night, and you put him to bed yourself no more than a handful of moments ago. Even if someone did sneak into the nursery after you left, certainly there wasn't enough time for it to affect him so? Could there be?"

His questions were vital and worthy of serious investigation and discussion, but all I wanted to do was curl up in my bed and cry myself to sleep. Yamehecatl had obviously began remembering conversations we'd had before he was born, things that I thought we'd worked out long ago, but I was wrong. I dreaded our conversation tomorrow morning.

Unable to hold in the tears any longer, I shook my head and retreated back into my quarters.

¤

In the morning I stayed in bed until Little Reed brought me breakfast. "Yamehecatl is still asleep," he told me when he set the tray on my lap. "Are you feeling all right?"

I shrugged, too drained to look him in the eye. "I never expected to hear that from him. How can I ever fully apologize to him?"

"You don't need to apologize. You had your own survival to consider."

"That may be, but that doesn't change the ache in my heart."

"I don't suppose it does," he admitted. "No more than it soothes the one in my heart, knowing that if not for me, our mother would still be alive."

I frowned. "She made that choice of her own free will, Little Reed."

He set a hand on mine. "As did you, and it was only yours to make."

While I ate, Little Reed filled me in on his investigation into who might have tried to poison our son. "No one confessed to giving him anything last night or any other time, so we shouldn't allow anyone access to him until we work this out. It means extra tasks for us, preparing all his meals, but until we find the culprit we shouldn't trust anyone."

"Not even Citlallotoc?" I asked.

Little Reed shook his head. "He wouldn't do such a thing, but the fewer people who have contact with Yamehecatl, the better. Citlallotoc will understand."

I would feel slighted if asked to stay away from one of our allies' children, but Citlallotoc's devotion knew no limits. He accepted his new orders with no question and focused on investigating the servants and guards.

I kept Yamehecatl at my side day and night, preparing all his meals and testing all his drinks before allowing him to partake. At first he relished my sudden constant attention, and didn't mind sitting in my quarters watching me weave instead of playing with his friends. He never mentioned what he'd said to me that night, and I avoided bringing it up;

he was as affectionate as ever, curling up in my bed with me at night, sucking his fingers while I sang him to sleep.

That contentment couldn't last forever. After two weeks, it started with whining when I wouldn't let him go play with the other children; four days later, he pushed over and broke the small idol of Quetzalcoatl in my quarters. "You're so mean!" he shrieked, his cheeks glowing brighter with each ragged breath. "Why do you hate me so much?" Already the heady smell of octli oozed off him like too much perfume, as if he'd fallen into a vat of the stuff.

I rose from my loom, my heart pounding. He hadn't eaten or drunk for several hours, but he turned increasingly intoxicated right in front of me, stumbling around the room, punching things with his fists and kicking them with his bare feet. I ran to the door and shouted for Little Reed.

He rushed from the great hall, his guards following, and when he saw Yamehecatl raging, he tried to grab him.

But Yamehecatl lashed out at him, pummeling him with his fists. "It's not fair, Tatli! Why won't she teach me how to talk to rabbits? I'm the one who dreams of being one!" Little Reed took hold of him and he struggled a moment before going limp, passed out.

Little Reed laid him gently on my bed while I stood by the door, shaking. "What in Mictlan is wrong with our son, Little Reed?"

He shook his head. "What happened?"

"He was fine one moment, but the next.... He's had nothing to eat or drink since breakfast, and I wasn't doing any magic. It just came from nowhere. And now he reeks like a drunk—" I gasped when a new idea occurred to me. "Do you think someone put a curse on him?"

"We should check." Little Reed smoothed Yamehecatl's sweaty hair away from his forehead while I fetched my divination pouch from the wicker basket in the corner.

I murmured a prayer to Quetzalcoatl and emptied the bag of maize kernels onto Yamehecatl's chest. We both chanted various incantations that reveal divine curses, watching the kernels closely, but I saw nothing out of the ordinary. I shook my head, frustrated; I could deal with curses, but I had no idea what was wrong with him.

"Maybe you should talk to the god," Little Reed suggested.

I fumbled the kernels back into my pouch, trembling. "I don't want to see him. Going to see him will only invite questions about things I'd rather not talk about."

"The god won't pressure you to talk about anything you don't—"

"I'm not comfortable talking to him, for my own reasons, and I ask you to respect that."

Little Reed bowed his head. "I'm sorry. I will talk to him myself. But we should consider the possibility that there isn't anything wrong with Yamehecatl."

I creased my brow. "Meaning what?"

"He has divine parentage, which comes with a cost. I age fast, so maybe this is his price."

"Spontaneous intoxication? What about his future as king? Who would follow a man who smells like one of those old men who spend all day deep in their cups of octli?"

"It could get better with time; my aging has slowed in recent years. And maybe something triggers it—Citlallotoc told me Yamehecatl was very upset and cried himself to sleep the first time it happened."

I stared at Little Reed, appalled. "Why was he crying?"

"It was the first time you'd been away from him for a whole day."

I swallowed back yet more guilt as I gazed at Yamehecatl sleeping so peacefully on my bed. "He was agitated right before this, but what about the last time? He wasn't upset; if anything, he was overjoyed."

"Maybe it's linked to intense emotions and we need to teach him how to better control them so this doesn't control him." Little Reed took my hand and pulled me closer. "Everything will be all right. We'll do it together, as a family."

¤

With the departure for Tollan imminent, I cleaned out my meditation room and packed everything into wicker baskets. As I set about the cleaning, someone rang the bells on my curtain.

"Forgive my intrusion, My Lady." Ozomatli stood in the doorway, looking remorseful.

"What brings you here?" I asked, focusing on dusting off my shelves to keep from looking at him. Remembering his cowardice in Chimalhuacan made the desire want to tear him apart.

"I wanted to see if you needed help with your packing, but you appear to have everything well in hand."

"I do, thank you. I trust you've packed up your own meditation room?"

He nodded. "Smoking Mirror's priesthood is ready for the move to Tollan, My Lady."

I wished it weren't moving there, but after much discussion with Little Reed, I still didn't have a good excuse to forbid it. And though it made me seeth inside, I was no closer to having evidence that Ozomatli had conspired against Amoxtli. "You and your people are leaving tomorrow morning?" I asked. When he nodded, I said, "May you all have a safe trip," and went back to my work, signaling the end of the discussion.

He lingered in the doorway a moment before turning to leave, but then he turned to face me again. "I must apologize for my behavior that day in Chimalhuacan. You needed my help and I abandoned you."

I cast my gaze back at him, searching for signs of insincerity, but he was exceptionally good at hiding it.

"Some would find it amusing that the high priest of Tezcatlipoca is afraid of violence, but I joined the priesthood to avoid facing battle. Hardly a manly admission, but times are changing, as are the expectations of men and women, and I no longer must hide the truth. I thank both you and Topiltzin for ensuring I never again have to fear being dragged off the battlefield to be sacrificed." He bowed and turned to leave again.

But I called out, "If you're so thankful, why are you still a priest of the Smoking Mirror? Those dragged off in battle feed the very god you serve, and he would have your heart as willingly as any other."

Ozomatli thought a moment. "I've always been a priest of Tezcatlipoca, just as you've always been a priestess of Quetzalcoatl. My father gave me to the temple when I was a baby, and in Culhuacan, no god was more revered for many years. The other cults have adapted, and I aim for Smoking Mirror's cult to adapt as well. Who better to do that than someone who knows the god's ways but was never comfortable with the means?" He smiled and left.

Someday I would get the evidence I needed to wipe that false smile off his face for good.

¤

The morning I'd waited three years for finally arrived. Yamehecatl—

dressed in his rabbit outfit—skipped around the servants and soldiers gathered in the courtyard, excited about his first long journey since his infancy. I feared he'd fall over drunk, but he kept his excitement low enough. Citlallotoc was to remain behind until Matlacxochitl arrived to replace him as Culhuacan's assistant governor, so he stood with the priests and priestesses and various war council members staying behind.

Normally we started our journeys under cover of darkness—the better to slip out unnoticed—but since we weren't returning, we took our caravan through the streets. We sat at the open curtains of the litter, Yamehecatl in my lap, and we waved to everyone as we passed. I was so glad to leave Culhuacan for good, and yet an unexpected heaviness fell upon me.

Even though painful memories haunted most of the palace halls, with the years the good memories had come back: the days spent in the women's hall where my mother had taught me to weave; sitting on my father's lap on his throne while he laughed and tickled my nose with feathers from his headdress; or running through the gardens with Black Otter. And new memories I treasured stacked upon those too: Yamehecatl taking his first steps in the great hall, walking from me to Little Reed who encouraged him with outspread arms; or sitting with Malinalli in the gardens, talking through the troubles of the day as the stars grew brighter in the night sky; or watching Little Reed and Citlallotoc playing at the ball game like a couple of boys in the exercise yard. Together, we'd made Culhuacan into a home, and I had to admit: I was going to miss it.

PART THREE
THE YEAR THIRTEEN FLINT

CHAPTER SEVENTEEN

"You and Tatli have too many houses," Yamehecatl told me as we walked hand-in-hand through Tollan's merchant quarters. Two guards cut a path through the crowd ahead while four more protected our sides and backs. Most people stepped out of our way, but some priests in black robes glared at us as the lead guards forced them to step back against the buildings. It was bad enough seeing those filthy, blood-smeared priests of Smoking Mirror as part of my priestly duties, but they seemed to be everywhere whenever I took my son around the city on my free days.

I ignored their stares and swung my arm in time with Yamehecatl's as he skipped at my side. "We need many houses to hold all of Tollan's riches," I told him. "If we kept all of it inside the palace, we'd have nowhere to sleep."

"Where do we get it all?"

"Some is tribute from the valley, but we found most of it here, while building Tollan."

"You mean like the gold and silver and jade?"

"All from the mines east of the city," I confirmed. "Along with the obsidian and turquoise deposits."

"I like the seashells!" Yamehecatl dragged me ahead, pointing up to the nearest tall, limestone treasure house. "Tatli says Citlallotoc brought them from over the mountains, where there's so much water you could never find the end of it."

"It's called the ocean," I told him. Citlallotoc traveled often, negotiating trade agreements with the peoples beyond Tolteca borders, and he'd told me in detail about the ocean; how in some places it shone like a pool of jade stones, but was royal turquoise in others. I envied his freedom to travel and see such magnificent sights. Maybe someday I would get to see it too.

"When I grow up, I'm going with Citlallotoc on his travels," my son piped up. "And we're going to fight great battles and monsters." He slashed the air with a pretend sword.

"Citlallotoc would welcome your company, but you won't find many battles. Tollan is at peace with its neighbors, and that's good for everyone. That's why our allies declared your father Emperor of the Toltecs." A title extended to me as well by virtue of being his wife, but I preferred the title of Queen.

"Peace is so boring." Yamehecatl pouted, but before I could scold him, his attention shifted again and he pulled me along to the next building. "This is the Serpent House, where we keep the animals for the sacrifice. And over there is the Feather House, filled with birds of all colors!"

"How do you know so much?" I asked, inviting him to show off, something he loved doing.

He stood taller. "Tatli brings me here a lot. He says someday it will all be mine."

"Well, you will share it with your queen."

"Why would I do that?"

"Because husbands and wives share with each other."

Yamehecatl stuck his tongue out. "I'm not getting married."

"Why not?"

"Because girls are boring."

I creased my brow at him. "Oh, we are?"

He giggled, suddenly shy. "Well, you're not, Nantli, but most girls aren't like you. They can't talk to rabbits, or make maguey plants shoot their thorns off."

"Neither can most men. If you think girls are so boring, it's because you only learn about them from other boys. Maybe you should try befriending some girls; when I was your age, my best friend was a boy."

He gazed up at me, puzzled. "You're very strange, Nantli."

Laughing, I pulled him back on track for the market. "Now you know where you get it from."

◻

Yamehecatl loved the market almost as much as I did because he knew he could manipulate me into buying him something. I loathed spoiling him—nothing was worse than a self-important prince—but as the only son I'd ever have, I found him difficult to resist. I had strategies though: I bought him a small rubber ball at the first blanket we came to and hoped that would keep him distracted while I shopped.

And it was working well today. While I browsed ceramic blood bowls, he bounced his ball back and forth on his knees, as Little Reed had shown him. Yamehecatl's aspirations weren't only to someday be the greatest warrior alive, but also be the best ritual ball player, though he had a long way to go before being anywhere as good as his father. Little Reed had inherited his own father's preternatural skill but only ever played for fun with our council. He once tried to teach me but I found the whole thing tedious, and my one experience with the game in Xochicalco had forever soured it for me.

Tollan's market was twice the size of any in the empire—even the one we'd built between Culhuacan and Chimalhuacan—and it took half the day to walk the entire thing. Hundreds of vendors hawked wares from in and outside the empire, and the aisles were always crowded. Today was no exception. The smell of roasting meat and fried maize permeated the air, making my mouth water. I bought some honey-glazed maize cakes for us, to make certain the pesky desire wouldn't start nagging me. Every salesman and woman smiled and rushed to help me, and a few even tried to sweet-talk Yamehecatl, knowing he could convince me to buy anything. But he was focused on practicing his ball skills, completely oblivious to them.

But while I was busy examining a particularly pretty bowl painted with serpents, Yamehecatl kneed his ball too hard and it flew past the guards, hitting a man standing nearby. The man yelped and rubbed the back of his head as he turned around.

I scrambled to apologize for my son's clumsiness, but when I locked gazes with the man, I nearly dropped the bowl in my hands, my heart hammering. "Black Otter?"

He stared back at me, panic cresting in his eyes.

Oblivious to having done anything wrong, Yamehecatl slipped past the guards to fetch his ball, running right for Black Otter. My panic boiled over. "Grab him, now!"

The guards immediately brought Yamehecatl back to me while he shouted about his ball. I drew him to me, protecting him with my arms as I continued to glare at Black Otter. "What are you doing here? I told you never come back, under penalty of death!"

When the guards turned their hard stares on him, Black Otter held his hands up, the color draining from his face. "Please let me explain, My Lady!" But two of my guards seized him and forced him to his knees, one holding him at spear-point.

It was on the tip of my tongue to have them run him through right there, but a young girl elbowed her way through the crowd and flung her arms around Black Otter's neck. She couldn't have been more than eight or nine. "Please don't hurt my tatli!" she cried.

This girl reminded me of myself at that age, tossing water on my anger before it could flare up. I nodded, and the guards withdrew their spears but stayed close to him. "Please do explain yourself." The sight of him hugging his daughter made my voice choke with emotion.

Black Otter rose slowly and the girl clung to him, her face buried in his side. "I know you exiled me under threat of death, My Lady, but I didn't know what else to do. Jade Flower was very sick, and no one back in the valley would help her because of me—because of who my father was. In a few of the western shore cities, they forbade us from even entering. So we traveled north, trying to find anyone who would help us. Eventually we came upon a family of Chichimecs moving to Tollan. They took us in and brought us to their shaman once we got here, but it was too late for Jade Flower. They helped me care for her until the Black Dog came for her earlier this summer."

The pain in my chest intensified. "Jade Flower is dead?" My sister had been in Tollan, dying, and no one told me? *Because they feared what you'd do to Black Otter.* I bit my lip when he nodded, and I tried to say more, but I was frozen.

"You're squeezing me too tight," Yamehecatl whined. He gave me a puzzled look when I finally loosened my grip. "Are you all right?"

I smoothed his hair with a faint, reassuring smile, but I dropped it when returning my attention to Black Otter. "I'm very sorry, Black Otter."

He didn't look at me as he nodded, tight-lipped.

"You're alone with the children now?"

The little girl—called Tiny Flower when I'd last seen her, though she'd have a real name now—peered at me with cautious eyes. "Are you going to take my tatli away too?" Her voice trembled.

I gave her a reassuring a smile, but Yamehecatl tugged at my sleeve, whispering, "Can we go? I'm bored." I shushed him, so he folded his arms and pouted.

"I should have left after Jade Flower died," Black Otter finally went on. "But this is the first place we've been in two years where no one seems to care who I am, and my children are treated with respect."

"Some of us do care who you are, Black Otter," I said. "And not because of your parentage."

He nodded. "The last time we talked...I cringe to even think about the nasty things I said to you. I know this changes nothing, but I'm sorry I frightened you. My behavior was inexcusable."

"It was." My gaze wandered back to the girl, now crying against Black Otter's side. Her terror hurt my stomach. "I'm pleased you've embraced your fatherly duties. All children should have the opportunity for a good, safe life."

He took a deep breath and bowed his head. "Yes, My Lady."

If I wasn't going to go through with the death sentence because of the child, how could I exile them instead? The desert was no place for children. But what should I do? "The king and I will call on you, to discuss where we go from here. Where do you live?"

"In the shacks outside the city walls." The poorest people lived out there, where we handed out food rations daily because so many of them were too new to Tollan to have found work yet, or they had disabilities preventing them from working. "You can ask anyone out there and they can show you to my hut."

Turning to the guards, I said, "We should get back to the palace."

We started to leave, but Black Otter picked up Yamehecatl's ball. "Don't forget this, young warrior." He held it out to him.

I tensed as Yamehecatl broke away to snatch the ball. He barely gave Black Otter a sideways glance as he murmured, "Thank you."

"You're the young prince?" Black Otter asked, a kindly smile on his face. "And you're what, three summers old now?"

Yamehecatl cast him an irritated glance and piped up, "I'm going to be five come winter."

"So you were born not too long after your mother became queen."

"I suppose. Who are you anyway?"

I shuffled Yamehecatl back to my side. "We really must get going, my dear. Your father's waiting." I motioned the guards to take Yamehecatl ahead, and once they were out of earshot, I snarled at Black Otter, "Before you get any stupid ideas, you're not his father. He's Topiltzin's son, and yes, I am married to Topiltzin as well. Keep that in mind when we call you to court."

"Of course, My Lady," Black Otter said. "I thank you for your mercy."

I nodded and left, my guards flanking me. I wanted to look back, to see if he was still watching me, but I didn't want him thinking I cared.

¤

When he wasn't dealing with civic matters at the palace, or performing his high priest duties at the temple, Little Reed spent his spare time meditating at the priestly sanctuary behind the sacred precinct. It sat in the middle of the private gardens—the ones Quetzalcoatl had shown me in the Divine Dream—on an island in the middle of the river that fed the canals at the southern end of the city.

The garden walls encompassed vast lands, including the maguey fields where I'd fallen when I was pregnant, and when Citlallotoc wasn't traveling he brought Yamehecatl out here to practice with his sling against the many rabbits living near the walls. A sturdy wooden bridge provided access to the island and its walled compound, which was divided into twenty meditation rooms designated for the high priests and priestesses of the various religious orders. We left our guards at the main garden gates, relishing the bit of freedom we enjoyed here.

When Yamehecatl and I reached the bridge, Ozomatli greeted us on his way out. I wrinkled my nose at the smell of the rotting blood on his body—ignoring the quiet rumbling in my stomach—but Yamehecatl stuck his nose in the air and sniffed like a dog catching a scent. "Good day, My Lady," Ozomatli said with a smile. "I hope all is well with you today."

I gave him a feigned smile. "It's fine, thank you."

Yamehecatl bared his overly large front teeth, looking so much like a rabbit that I could laugh. "Why do you smell like the temple?"

Ozomatli turned his gaze to Yamehecatl, his smile strained for patience. His discomfort with children amused me, and I'd briefly entertained the notion of assigning him to teach the youngest calmecac students, just for amusement. In the end I decided it wasn't worth exposing them to him. "It's the way of Smoking Mirror's priests to wear the blood of his sacrifices," he answered.

"Why?"

"Because he enjoys the smell, I suppose."

Yamehecatl sniffed the air again, an uncertain look on his face, but he shrugged and returned to bouncing his ball, all interest in the conversation lost.

"Your god might enjoy the smell of death, but the people don't," I said. "We've had complaints about your priests smelling like a butcher's refuse pile." Not precisely true, but it was hard to ignore the wide berth and disgusted looks people gave them as they walked through the streets. I wanted to outlaw all grotesque displays—such as the high priest of Xipe Totec wearing the skin of a virgin girl, or the cult of Tlaloc's practice of pinching children to make them cry, to feed their tears to the rain god— but the time still wasn't right for outright bans on such things. "Small steps," Little Reed always said, "lest we look as strident as the despot we dethroned."

Ozomatli stood taller. "My Lady, I have made a great many changes to accommodate our new laws; we sacrifice one warrior a year, as the god's double at the Toxcatl festival, and give only our own blood during the rest of the year, the same as Quetzalcoatl's priests."

It was true that we'd approved only one sacrifice last year—for only one man came forward willing to offer himself in Smoking Mirror's name— but the desert would turn into an ocean before I believed that Smoking Mirror's priesthood wasn't secretly practicing the old ways. The sorcerer god's power-hunger and greed infected all those near him, turning his priesthood into a den of liars and murderers. Someday I would find the evidence to finally bring justice to my family which this terrible god and his cult had torn apart.

"Wearing the sacrificial blood is an ancient tradition—the way the god knows the wearer is not only a follower, but one who does his will on Earth. And so long as there isn't a law forbidding us from wearing our own blood on our arms and legs to show our devotion, the god's cult will continue to honor that," Ozomatli finished.

"Careful, or we will oblige you with a law banishing you and your demon god, priest," I snarled. And immediately snapped my mouth shut, horrified that I'd said it aloud. Usually I was very good at not letting the anger take over, but ever since Chimalhuacan, I'd found it increasingly difficult to do so when dealing with Ozomatli. I often imagined a restless, deadly jaguar lurking within me, waiting to pounce and devour anything it could get hold of. And it had a particular craving for Smoking Mirror's followers.

Ozomatli blinked at me, startled; but rather than speak again, I grabbed Yamehecatl's hand and hurried past him. When I reached the tall wooden doors, I glanced back, expecting to find him glaring at me. But he was already gone.

I'd lived with this frightening voice in my head for much of my adult life—even harnessing its power for my own use when needed—but at times like this, I couldn't help but wonder if I was slowly going crazy.

From the sanctuary doors, we walked down a short hall with storerooms on either side—for wood, gardening tools, and food—out into the central gardens. The meditation rooms formed a circle around it, with a small kitchen near the entrance where each high priest and priestess pair took turns making communal meals for the weekly administrative meetings. Murals of the various gods decorated the plaster walls outside each meditation room, identifying which order the room belonged to. A plethora of Feathered Serpent statues decorated the flowerbeds, while the stone rain spouts on the roofs were carved in the likeness of the goggle-eyed rain god Tlaloc, the second most worshiped god in Tollan.

Little Reed sat under the large avocado tree at the center of the garden, dressed in a simple white robe and meditating in the shade. When my heart soared at the sight of him, I knew I couldn't be as ill in the head as I feared I was.

"Tatli!" Yamehecatl broke free and sprinted down the path towards his father, and Little Reed laughed when Yamehecatl tackled him with a hug.

"I swear you get stronger by the day." Little Reed set the boy in his lap and swept aside his own fully-silver hair to better see him. "You're what, almost two years now?" he asked with feigned ignorance.

Yamehecatl folded his arms crossly. "You know how old I am, Tatli." He turned to me. "I don't look two, do I, Nantli?"

Stifling a giggle, I said, "You look at least twenty, my little breeze."

Yamehecatl beamed.

Laughing, Little Reed said, "Of course I know how old you are. I could never forget the happiest day of my life."

"What day would that be?" Yamehecatl asked.

"The day you were born, of course." He kissed Yamehecatl on the forehead.

"I remember that day too." It didn't surprise me that Yamehecatl remembered such things—I remembered my own birth as well—but he'd only started talking about it within the last couple of months. Sometimes I pressed him, to see if he remembered any of our conversations before he was born, but thus far that part of his life seemed lost to him. Much as my own was lost to me.

"But who was the woman with no teeth?" he asked me.

"That was Lady Bitter Rabbit, and she did have some teeth," I corrected him. "She was Mitotia's mother."

"The one who died last year?" When I nodded, he asked, "And who was the man we talked to in the market?"

Little Reed looked up at me too, casually curious.

I told Yamehecatl, "Why don't you take your new ball and go over there and practice your knee bounces." I pointed towards the far corner of the gardens.

Yamehecatl scurried away, laughing and bouncing his ball on the grass as he went.

I sat next to Little Reed in the shade. "We ran into Black Otter in the market."

Little Reed tensed. "What's he doing here? Is he in the stockade now?" When I shook my head, he blinked, taken aback. "Why not?"

"He and Jade Flower brought their children here because she was very sick and no one would help them, because of his father. She died a few months ago, and now he's left caring for their children all on his own. You should have seen how terrified his daughter was when the guards grabbed him...." I shook my head. "He did right by his family, as I told him to, and I can't blame him for wanting to stay here; the alternative is living in the desert, and that's no life for children."

"It isn't," Little Reed conceded. "But it's not his children I'm worried about."

"I told him that he will have to come and speak with us soon, so we can decide how to proceed. I will say though that he showed no interest whatsoever in getting me back."

"What about our son?" He watched Yamehecatl jumping up and down, trying to knock low-hanging fruit from the tree. "Did he ask about him?"

"He did, and I assured him you were Yamehecatl's father."

"And he accepted that?"

"I don't know. But it doesn't matter because we married before Yamehecatl was born, so by law you are his father."

"Our laws calls most human sacrifice illegal, but that doesn't necessarily stop it from happening."

"Trying to claim Yamehecatl won't do him any good; he won't suddenly be the rightful king, nor will it get him a job, or bring him out of the shacks outside town."

"You think we should give him another chance?"

"I think we should talk to him and find out what he was doing these last five years, and what his plans are for the future. And then go from there."

Little Reed nodded. "A most excellent idea."

CHAPTER EIGHTEEN

Little Reed wasted no time waiting to size up Black Otter. When we gathered for dinner with the council in the great hall, the guards ushered Black Otter in, along with his two children. The girl held his hand, taking in the maps all over the walls with apprehension; walking slightly behind them, the boy—who was probably no more than seven— stared up in awe at the ceiling with its paintings of the gods and the divine realms. He looked exactly as Black Otter had at that age.

Amoxtli sat in the council's circle, next to Mazatzin, and he started to rise, but caught himself. When he glanced over at Little Reed, questions in his eyes, Little Reed nodded and motioned him to go and greet his brother.

When Black Otter saw Amoxtli standing among the others, he froze; but the girl cried, "Uncle!" and she ran to Amoxtli, her arms wide. Amoxtli scooped her up, laughing while the boy hung back with his father, curious but unwilling to follow his sister. After he'd hugged her, Amoxtli set the girl down and knelt in front of her, holding her hands in his. "You've grown up so much since I last saw you, Cuicatl, and my, how much you look like your mother." He turned his gaze to the boy and asked, "Your mother used to call you Little Water Bug, but what do the gods call you now?"

"Night Wind," the boy replied, scrutinizing Amoxtli.

"Go and embrace your uncle," Black Otter chastised the boy.

But Amoxtli shook his head. "It's all right. He probably doesn't remember me, he was so young the last time I saw him." He came to Black Otter and stopped a handful of steps away from him. "But it feels even longer since last I saw you, Brother."

Black Otter hesitated, but then bridged the gap between them, pulling Amoxtli into a crushing hug. He squeezed his eyes tight as if holding back tears. "It's so good to see you again, Amoxtli."

Amoxtli hugged him back hard. "Sometimes I was certain I'd lost you forever, especially after that last time we talked."

"I'm sorry, Brother. I wasn't well, but I've gotten better, and I promise I won't let anything come between us again."

In spite of myself, a hitch formed in my chest and I had to clear my throat to be able to breathe properly.

Little Reed left his throne to stand with our cousins, setting a supportive hand on each of their shoulders when they finally separated. "Family is such a wonderful thing; we're all the stronger for it." To Black Otter, he said, "Let me be the first to welcome you to Tollan." When Black Otter started to kneel, Little Reed stopped him. "That isn't necessary, Cousin, for we are family." He motioned to the mat where Citlallotoc normally sat. "Please join us for the evening meal."

Black Otter blinked, but thanked Little Reed as he took his place on the mat. Mazatzin moved to Amoxtli's mat so Amoxtli could sit next to his brother, and the children sat behind Black Otter, the same way

Yamehecatl sat on the mats behind my throne. When I glanced back, Yamehecatl chewed thoughtfully on a turkey leg and stared at Night Wind, curious. Night Wind didn't return his attention.

The servants served everyone, saving me and Little Reed for last, as was our way, and we settled into our meals. No one said anything for the first few moments while we ate—and Little Reed held the sauce bowl for him and me—a task usually relegated to a man's wife—but eventually he told Black Otter, "Please accept my condolences on the loss of your wife, Cousin."

Black Otter bowed his head. "Thank you, My Lord." After a tentative bite of his roasted dog, he added, "May I extend my compliments on everything you and Lady Quetzalpetlatl have created here in Tollan? The city is magnificent, and the peace and prosperity are a welcome change from how things were in the valley for so long."

Little Reed smiled. "That's kind of you, but so long as our people must come to us for daily rations to feed their children and elders, our work is still incomplete. Have you been able to secure work for yourself yet?"

Black Otter cast an uncertain glance over at me before answering, "A kindly Chichimec family has been helping me, but I took a position as an apprentice obsidian knapper last week."

Nodding, Little Reed said, "Tollan's Chichimecs are selfless and industrious. We're grateful for their help building this great city and improving the lives of thousands through our mutual respect and friendship."

Half of our royal council was Chichimecs—and half of them women—and they all nodded their heads approvingly.

Little Reed set aside his empty plate and lounged back in his icpalli. "I'm eager to hear all you've been doing these last few years, and about your plans for the future."

Black Otter cleared his throat, looking anxious. "Well, after leaving Tollan that first time, I went to Chalco, and under Jade Flower's care, I recovered from my near-death ordeal." To me he added, "I must again apologize for my rough behavior when I first came to Tollan five years ago, My Lady. I was still a shambles after everything that transpired that day on the lake, but Jade Flower helped me move on. I don't know what I would have done without her. She was so patient...so caring." He turned to poke absently at his food. "Honestly, I don't know what I'll do without her now."

"Know that you have family to lean on in your time of need," I said, feeling guilty for my earlier suspicion. Sometimes my own egotism shamed me.

"I thank you for that, My Lady." Black Otter's strained smile broke into a frown when Amoxtli set a hand on his shoulder. Amoxtli whispered to him and Black Otter nodded, looking ready to break into tears, but he pulled himself together. "As for the future, my only wish is to provide stability for my children, especially during this trying time. I believe Tollan is the ideal setting for that. However, I recognize that my past may make our staying impossible, and if Your Majesty insists we leave, I will do so, without argument, this very night if you ask."

"I appreciate that, Cousin, but I'm not inclined to rush to judgment," Little Reed said. "If I might ask, to what god do you give your prayers these days?"

Black Otter averted his eyes, looking uncomfortable again. "I must admit that, in recent years, I haven't done much praying, and I've fallen away from honoring any particular god. My father's religious issues caused me a great deal of heartache and pain, and I haven't regained any sense of personal faith in the gods. Yet I often wonder if my questioning has led to my children's suffering."

Little Reed nodded solemnly. "It is perhaps the way of other gods to punish a crisis of faith, but the Feathered Serpent understands your reticence. Earned faith is strongest. I hope you'll consider exploring a renewal through the teachings of the Feathered Serpent. And now that you're in Tollan, trust you're under his protection, no matter the current of your heart."

"That is good to know, My Lord."

So it appeared Little Reed was leaning towards letting Black Otter stay. The maelstrom of joy and fear rolling through me left me uneasy, and I found myself staring at Black Otter more than was proper. Sweaty memories of frantic flesh crushing against flesh in the heat of intimacy made the desire purr and laugh. *He was a luxurious feast laid out for us. So delicious, so varied, so willing....* When he caught me staring, he looked away, uncomfortable, and I scolded myself for doing the very same thing so many men did to me that I despised. By the end of the meal, I wanted him gone from my sight, so I could relax again.

But at least the children got along fine. Over the course of the meal, Yamehecatl edged closer to them, until he sat right with them. The girl paid courteous attention but he said little to her, and whereas Night Wind had shown Yamehecatl no interest at all before, now the two talked intently and laughed. I couldn't hear their conversation but Yamehecatl was delighted. It warmed me to see my son enjoying himself so.

But then came time for Night Wind to leave. Yamehecatl hadn't suffered one of his drunken fits in several months now, but when Little Reed said Night Wind needed to go home, Yamehecatl stamped his feet and cried. "But I never get to have any friends stay the night!"

"The other noble boys can stay in the nursery with you anytime you want," I corrected him.

"But they aren't my friends! They don't even like me!"

His concern wasn't easily dismissed. The older he got the bigger the gulf between him and the other boys grew; because he was so clever, Little Reed and I had considered starting him in calmecac already, but his lack of emotional maturity made us hesitate. He might be able to speak as coherently as someone twice his age, but his tonalli was still that of a four-year old. For now Little Reed and I privately tutored him in our spare time, and I worried he'd never be truly ready for the discipline of calmecac. Little Reed had endured years of torment from the likes of Red Flint and his friends, but he'd rarely let it get to him; Yamehecatl, however, felt every invisible dart, and if he became too upset....

Already he began swaying so I summoned one of his guards. "Take him to his room and stay with him until I get there."

The guard hefted Yamehecatl into his arms, and my son started screaming and pounding his fists against the guard's shoulders. The man didn't flinch as he carried him from the great hall, the vague aroma of octli lingering.

My cheeks burned to see Black Otter looking uncomfortable on my behalf. "Please excuse him. He's a highly emotional boy," I murmured.

"Children can be." Black Otter gave me an understanding smile then turned to Little Reed again with a bow. "Thank you for your hospitality tonight, My Lord. And for your mercy, and this opportunity to redeem myself, not only in your eyes, but in those of your wife."

Little Reed set a hand on Black Otter's shoulder. "The Feathered Serpent believes everyone is worthy of a second chance. If this job with the obsidian worker doesn't meet your needs, please let me know and I shall see what I can do to help you find something better." He moved his gaze to the girl, who half-buried her face in Black Otter's side, embarrassed. "Have you enrolled the children in school yet?"

Black Otter shook his head.

"Education is compulsory in Tollan for all children at least eight years of age, though we encourage starting them even younger, so bring them by the palace registrar in the morning and we'll place them into temporary classes at the telpochcalli until they are properly tested for formal placement. An educated population makes for a strong empire."

"Thank you, My Lord. I will bring them by first thing in the morning." Black Otter bade us each good night and left.

Once he was gone, Little Reed asked me, "Your impressions?"

"Well, it is only one meal, but I didn't see anything to raise concerns. He does appear deeply affected by Jade Flower's death."

"And deeply uncomfortable around you," Little Reed noted, frowning. Had he seen me staring at Black Otter with lust in my eyes? Gods I hoped not!

"That's very different than how he was before we exiled him," I admitted.

"Then you believe him a changed man?"

I shrugged. "I'm still not entirely comfortable, if that's what you're asking." Though my own discomfort had more to do with my reactions to him than anything he'd said or done since running into him in the market today. But I didn't want to admit as much to Little Reed.

"You want us to send him away again?"

"Not at all; I think we should give him a chance to prove himself, one way or the other."

Little Reed thought a moment then motioned Amoxtli over to us. "We want to make certain that Black Otter integrates well with our ways here in Tollan. Would you keep watch over his progress and help guide him in the right direction? As a personal favor to myself and Lady Quetzalpetlatl?"

"Of course, Your Majesty," Amoxtli said.

"And if you should have any reservations about his ability to adapt—"

"I shall tell you immediately."

Little Reed clapped him on the shoulder. "Your loyalty to the realm is commendable, Cousin." Once Amoxtli walked away, Little Reed told me, "It's a start. Perhaps we can also find some means of testing Black Otter...give him a chance to prove his new good nature in solid fashion."

"What do you have in mind?" I asked.

He shook his head. "I'm not certain yet, but let us both think on it."

I nodded, but hearing Yamehecatl screaming down the hall, I said, "I should go tend to him."

"Do you need my help?"

I laughed. "Thank you, but you have temple duties tonight, remember?"

He sighed but planted a gentle kiss on my cheek. I returned the gesture but lingered a breath longer, wishing—as so many other times—that it could be more. But as always, it had to end. "Goodnight, my love." I hurried to the nursery, not looking back. No matter how guilty I might feel for gawking at Black Otter all night, I had no business indulging myself when my son was in the grips of one of his episodes.

But when I reached the nursery in the royal quarters, Yamehecatl fell silent. I looked inside to see the guard carefully tucking him under his blankets, fast asleep. When the guard saw me, he said, "He screamed himself out, My Lady."

I knelt to stroke Yamehecatl's sweaty hair back from his forehead. "I'm sorry Night Wind couldn't stay tonight, my darling, but maybe sometime soon," I whispered. *Once I know I can trust his father again.*

¤

Worrying about Yamehecatl kept me up most of the night as I checked on him once an hour. It wasn't a long journey to his nursery—it was right behind that same blue curtain in my quarters that I'd seen in the Divine Dream—but eventually I carried him into my room and laid him in bed next to me, to save myself the trip. The next morning he woke in better spirits and we lay in bed singing songs of Quetzalcoatl until my handmaiden came to warm my bathwater.

"Must you go to the temple, Nantli?" Yamehecatl whined. "Can't we lie in bed all day and you can tell me stories and we can sing songs and eat sweet maize cakes?"

"I'd love nothing more than to do that, but yes, I must go to the temple." I stroked his head soothingly. "I have many responsibilities, not only to you, but to the city and to the god."

"Maybe Tatli will sing with me," he said, petulance in his voice.

"Let your father sleep; he was up all night doing his duties to the god. Leave him be until at least the noon hour."

"But no one's here to play with me, Nantli," Yamehecatl moaned. "They're all gone at school, but even if they weren't, they still wouldn't play with me. When can I go to school too?"

"Well, your father and I have discussed it, and we want to put you into school—so you can make new friends—but...."

"But what?"

I had to tread carefully here. "The teachers at the calmecac have high expectations of their students, especially about behavior. We don't feel you're...ready to handle it."

He furrowed his brow. "What do you mean?"

"You struggle controlling your emotions, like last night, and when you get upset you quickly become out of control. I don't think it's your fault; inside each of us is a voice that tries to get us to do things or behave in ways that aren't in our best interest."

He gasped. "You know about the voice?" When I nodded, he asked, "But how?"

"As I said, all of us have one."

"Mine wants to always have fun. And he gets really upset when you tell me it's time to do something else. And I start feeling really strange."

I nodded. "Growing up means learning to recognize whom we should listen to and how we choose to behave. It's difficult, but with work, we learn to control ourselves, and we don't let the other voice rule us or our lives."

"What does your voice tell you to do?"

To devour and enjoy every mortal in sight! the desire cackled. "Just things I shouldn't."

"I wonder what Tatli's voice tells him."

I'd wondered the same thing ever since Little Reed mentioned having his own at one time, but since he never offered to talk about it, maybe he didn't want to anymore than I wanted to discuss my ferocious desire.

When the handmaiden returned from the bath yard, I asked her to dress Yamehecatl and told him I would see him again at dinner. I feared he might break down again, but he merely sighed and climbed off the bed. As they went out of the door, he scowled and said, "Stop saying that! Why are you always so mean?"

The young woman cast me a startled look—no doubt thinking he was talking to her—but Yamehecatl turned to me and said, "I want to go to school, so I'll work hard on it, Nantli."

I gave him a kiss on his forehead, which he promptly wiped away with the back of his hand, but he still beamed at me. "And I know you will do so very well at it because you're strong."

He leaned in closer and whispered in my ear, "Like you, Nantli."

¤

Yamehecatl's words warmed me more than the bathwater, and that glow followed me out of my quarters, ready to start my day.

Upon reaching the Hall of the Gods—the foyer decorated with the statues of the gods—I met Malinalli, on her way from her quarters in the priestly wing where all the highest-ranking priests lived. She had temple duties as well and wore her long, white fire priestess robe embroidered with feathered serpents breathing flames; they bore a striking similarity to the fire serpent I'd summoned long ago in Teotihuacan, and I wondered how much that incident had influenced her choice of the pattern.

When she reached me, she smiled and hooked her arm with mine as we walked side-by-side. "You're looking very happy this morning," I noted with a smile of my own.

She shrugged. "It was a good night."

After watching her grin for a moment, I worked it out. I stopped short. "Did you meet someone?"

After a brief hesitation, she blurted out, "Maybe."

I laughed and hugged her. "That's wonderful! Who is he? You must tell me everything!"

Her smile wavered. "Well...this is all very new, and I don't know if it's going anywhere...."

"You're not going to tell me?" I asked, teasing her with an offended gasp.

A flush crept into her cheeks. "You never told me about you and Topiltzin."

I hadn't, and now I felt guilty. "No, but I didn't tell anyone...except Nimilitzli, but she'd already presumed as much." After an awkward pause, I added, "I'm sorry."

Malinalli shook her head. "We were supposed to be devoted to the god in body and spirit, so I understand why you wouldn't tell anyone. Which is why I know you'll understand when I say I'm not ready to say more yet."

I nodded. "I respect that." As we walked again, I asked, "But you will tell me eventually, right?"

She hesitated again but soon gave me a smile. "I promise I will, when the time is right."

I patted her arm. "I'm happy that you're happy, Malinalli."

She beamed. "I really am. I hope it lasts."

"Maybe you'll get married and have children, and our children can grow up together."

"Maybe," she murmured, distracted. "Will you and Topiltzin have more children soon?"

Surprisingly, no one had ever asked me that before; it was assumed we would have more, and whenever I fell ill for a few days, rumors circulated that I'd miscarried. But in truth, my body had stopped its monthly bloodletting a year ago, not long after weaning Yamehecatl. Most women remained fertile into their forties, but my childbearing years ended before I'd passed my thirty-second summer.

I'd always thought I'd be happy to be rid of that inconvenience, but when it came far sooner than expected, I felt an acute sense of loss. Did this mean that, like Little Reed, I was aging faster, and I hadn't that many years left? That hadn't been the case for most of my life, and though I'd found my first silvered hair only two years ago, that had been easy enough to dismiss—it took a lot out of a person to run a kingdom. But the end of my monthly cycles seemed a warning that things weren't as they appeared.

After much contemplation, I'd decided there was only one possible cause: the magic coursing through my veins was prematurely aging my body. And here I'd once thought carrying the god's child was the thing that would kill me, when in fact it was the other unexpected gift he'd given me.

But there was a certain peace in knowing that now Little Reed and I could grow old and die together. For years the thought that I would have to sit by and watch him wither away while I remained behind all alone haunted me; the notion that once he was dead I could move on to marry—and be intimate—with someone else held no appeal for me. *Nimilitzli warned you about building your entire life around someone else,* I thought with a bitter laugh under my breath.

It was depressing enough to think about all this let alone speak aloud of it, and though Malinalli let me have peace while I mulled, I felt obligated to give an answer. "I've had all the children my tonalli will allow. Yamehecatl is challenging enough on his own, and this lets me to divide my time between family and the god, so it worked out well, to be honest."

Malinalli patted my arm. "That's good to know."

¤

Malinalli had class to teach at the next hourly bell at the calmecac, so I walked her there, on the north end of the precinct. Neither Little Reed nor I taught any classes, but Little Reed led the yearly pilgrimage to Teotihuacan with the newly-graduating novices. There was enough religious interest in Tollan that each order took their own pilgrimage on different weeks each summer, but it had become common practice that everyone preparing to take their vows to Quetzalcoatl—from all over the empire—would meet in Teotihuacan during the last week of summer, to be tutored by the god's highest priest. Little Reed had returned from this year's pilgrimage just a few week earlier.

As we approached the calmecac's courtyard with its cistern guarded by a statue of Tlaloc submerged in the water, Mazatzin and Mitotia came out of the alleyway that led to the priestly gardens, deep in conversation. As always my eyes were immediately drawn to the black tattoo of a feathered serpent along Mitotia's jawline on the right side of her face. Tradition among her tribesmen dictated that every man—and woman—take a tattoo to mark their entrance into adulthood. "Men get tattooed when they take their first war prisoner, and women on their wedding night," Mitotia had explained to me. "But since I'm never going to marry, and my vows to the god are the closest I'll get, this should be the pattern." It took me quite a few weeks to overcome the urge to stare whenever I saw her.

But I wasn't nearly as shocked as her father, who'd roared at her about taking vows to the wrong god. "You were supposed to lead the cult of Mixcoatl in Tollan!" But when he'd blustered to Little Reed about their "deal", Little Reed had listened patiently and explained he couldn't make anyone join any particular cult.

"Our deal was to educate Mitotia, which we've done. Beyond that, as a citizen of Tollan, she's free to choose her own path." Ten Spines called Little Reed a treacherous little snake and talked of gathering his people and leaving, but Mitotia herself spoke sense into him. He came back to Little Reed with much groveling and tears and Little Reed accepted his apologies without hesitation. Little Reed had a far easier time forgiving slights than I did; a quality I envied in him.

Mazatzin smiled and bowed in greeting. "Good morning, My Lady." I'd told him more than once that such a greeting wasn't necessary, but he was a man of formality, and I doubted I would ever change that. We all walked into the calmecac together, Mazatzin filling me in on the status of the priesthood before he went home for the day. When we reached the main hallway, I asked Malinalli about joining me for lunch, but she stumbled over her words before telling me she'd already made plans with someone else. "Maybe tomorrow?" she offered hopefully, and I told her that would be fine. I bade her and Mazatzin a good day and they set out on their separate ways as the first warning bell rang, sending students scrambling through the halls.

Mitotia followed me into my meditation room and immediately took up a goose quill at my desk. To soften Ten Spines's hurt pride, I'd agreed to take her as my apprentice and train her to replace me as High Priestess when I passed out of this world. I'd worried Malinalli would feel slighted, but when I spoke with her, she confessed that she had no ambitions to the position. "After you being the god's chosen high priestess, I'd be a dismal disappointment. That's too big of an expectation to have to live up to." At least my decision wouldn't challenge our friendship.

"You have the final planning meeting for the festival of the Maguey Goddess with the rest of the high priestesses at noon," Mitotia informed me, reading off the parchment calendar she wrote on every day. "Ozomatli requested funds to commission a new obsidian mirror for Smoking Mirror's temple; apparently one of his priests knocked it off the wall while polishing it last night and broke it."

"I'd like to break his stupid god," I muttered under my breath as I poked among the papers on my desk, seeing if there were any letters needing my attention. "Tell him I'll get his funds from the treasury when he has his priests wash more than once a week."

Mitotia allowed herself an amused smile. "Very well. Several women have come asking for your fertility blessing, to help them conceive this month—" Something I always enjoyed doing "—and several farmers have asked for either you or Lord Topiltzin to come and bless their new fields."

"The high priests of Xipe Totec are supposed to do that."

"I told them as much, but they want the Feathered Serpent's blessing on top of Xipe Totec's. I told them I would give you their request." She counted items on her list silently, pointing to each with the quill. "Oh, and we're also out of snakes for the afternoon sacrifice."

"We should visit the royal game warden then. Let me make my offering and we'll be on our way."

She bowed out of the doorway, closing the curtain to give me privacy.

I pulled my string of maguey thorns from my robe pocket and knelt on the reed mat in front of the wooden Feathered Serpent idol in the back corner of the room.

"My most Great Lord,
Today I give thanks for all you've bestowed upon me;
For the faith you instill in my heart,
For the strength you woke in my blood,
For your son who shares my life,
And for my son who is our future.
May he always know your love,
Your understanding,
And your pride.
I honor you, oh Great Feathered Serpent,
For my family,
For my friends,
For my life."

I poked the thorns through my tongue, one after another, coating the maguey fiber with my blood. I was so used to the practice that I hardly noticed the sting anymore. I set the string into a ceramic blood bowl and held it above my head as I prayed silently. Once finished, I dumped the string of thorns into the idol's open mouth, put a small wad of cotton over my wounded tongue, and closed my mouth to hold it in place while the bleeding stopped, giving more silent prayers.

And I thought of all those times I'd spent with the god in the Divine Dream, of the shared pleasure and feathery touches; no matter how long ago I'd stopped indulging that desire, my mind always went back to it when I prayed. Some great chosen high priestess I was.

"It still baffles me that anyone would willingly shove thorns through their tongue," a voice spoke up behind me, slinging my heart into a run.

I nearly knocked over the idol as I hurried to my feet and spun around. When I saw Mextli grinning at me, hunched over to keep from hitting his head on the ceiling, my fear gave way to anger. "What in Mictlan are you doing here?" I demanded after spitting out the cotton. I hadn't felt the desire take over, but I didn't push it back. Right now it was the best shield to protect me. Especially since he was blocking the only way out of the room.

He gave me a mock frown. "It's a pleasure to see you again too, little thorny one."

"Don't call me that!"

The grin returned. "But it's the perfect name for someone so...prickly."

"If I'm prickly, it's because you're a dog's ass!"

"Oh, am I?"

"You forced me to kill two people the last time I saw you!"

"And that's such a bad thing?"

"Says the the delusional dimwit who fancied himself a war god."

He laughed. "Now I understand why he finds you so fascinating."

"Who?"

He answered only by grinning wider.

"What do you want now, little hummingbird boy?"

"I come on behalf of my Lord Tezcatlipoca, with a proposition for you."

The desire guffawed. "What could he possibly offer me?"

"You might be surprised."

"This is all very precious, but I haven't time for your demon lord and his games. I have an empire to run." I started towards him with grim purpose, expecting him to step aside. A crazy notion yet so very solid in my gut; when the desire took over, I wasn't a woman to be trifled with.

And yet he didn't move. "You mean an empire that won't last another ten years?"

"It will last forever."

"Is that what the Feathered Serpent tells you?"

"It's what I *see* when Tollan's crop yields can feed the entire empire, and the ground spits up gold and turquoise for us to find without even digging. There's no more war, no more hunger. No one lives in fear anymore, because we've shown the people they have nothing to fear."

"No more war?" Mextli laughed. "And you say I'm the delusional one. You and Quetzalcoatl have brought only a temporary peace to these lands. The other gods haven't fallen asleep; they've noticed this power-grab, and they won't sit idly by while the Feathered Serpent grows fat. War is coming, and you're on the wrong side of the conflict, my dear."

His threats brought to mind Nimilitzli's warnings about involving myself in the power struggles of the gods. As usual, she'd been right. But the desire was unperturbed. "I'm not the one on the wrong side. Anyone who follows Smoking Mirror is but a pathetic scoundrel interested only in his own power. I would ban that demon's cult in Tollan—"

"If only you didn't have to bend to Quetzalcoatl's will?"

My face burned. "I *choose* to follow the Feathered Serpent's lead because his way is the right way."

Mextli shook his head. "You're so well-trained. The Feathered Serpent has a special gift for emotional manipulation, but you make it so easy. You must enjoy being manipulated."

Surging anger brought tingling magic to my fingertips, and next thing I knew, I stood a breath away from Mextli, barely containing the impulse to unleash it all at him. "You know nothing about Quetzalcoatl. Or me."

"I've made it a priority to get to know you." His voice was casual but the fluff of his feathers told the real story: I'd scared him. "You should let your inner monster out more often; when you do...you're magnificent."

His breathless whisper brought the flush of lust and longing creeping up on me. *Finally! Someone who appreciates the goddess within!* My gaze wandered over him, taking in every curve of muscle, every flash of feathery iridescence, a fire long dormant suddenly reigniting. His feathers met flesh in a precise line down the center of his body, and even the fingernails of his left hand were covered in miniscule blue feathers. *I bet he's feathered on the left half of his tepolli,* the desire mused, my gaze lingering at his loincloth as the heat threatened to overwhelm me. *And if it's even half as big as the rest of him—*

A shiver of excitement broke the desire's hold and I turned away, disgusted and disturbed. *How can you even think of this evil man—or whatever he is—like that? That's as bad as lusting after...after Smoking Mirror!* My desire recoiled like a severed worm; apparently there were things even it couldn't stand.

"Anyone can be fooled once," Mextli said. "But don't let him fool you twice. You're better than that."

My magic retreated from my limbs, leaving me cold and vulnerable. "What's that supposed to mean?"

"When you're ready for the truth, come and speak with Tezcatlipoca."

"What truth?"

But without another word, he vanished.

CHAPTER NINETEEN

It was on the tip of my tongue to tell Little Reed about Mextli's visit, but when I saw him that evening, helping our son tie on a clean loincloth before dinner, I was overwrought with guilt. This wonderful man loved me and our son, had forsaken all others to share in my sacrifice and build a peaceful family life with me, and I'd spent all afternoon dwelling—and sometimes daydreaming—on a moment of lust for some stranger who plotted against our chosen god. This, on top of my uncouth thoughts about my former husband.... I didn't deserve this loving, faithful man.

Little Reed smiled when he noticed me lurking in the doorway, but my expression must have troubled him. "Is everything all right?"

Before I could say anything, Yamehecatl shoved past him and launched himself at me, latching both arms around my legs in a hug. "You're home, Nantli! I was afraid you wouldn't come back!"

I kissed his cheeks, the joy on his face melting me inside. "I always come home." I swept his bangs aside to kiss his forehead too. "Why would you think I wouldn't?"

"I had a bad dream this afternoon, that you and Tatli left me next to a lake in the dark, and you never came back for me. Promise me you won't ever leave me by a lake."

His words inexplicably troubled me, as if I'd had the same dream once but couldn't draw forth any images, just a suffocating feeling of sadness and fear. I shivered as I said, "I promise never to leave you by any lake, my dear."

Yamehecatl hugged me again then rushed back to Little Reed and grabbed his hand. "Let's go! I'm starving!" He tugged his arms, encouraging him to his feet.

Little Reed obliged but took my hand too. My heart danced, the worries of the day dissolving under his loving gaze. "Is everything all right?" he asked again.

I kissed his cheek and leaned my head against his shoulder, welcoming his embrace. His strong, solid muscle brought on my own body's familiar, reassuring reaction and I smiled, basking in the heat between us. It didn't matter what the desire wanted; I was the stronger one, and I had everything I needed right here, in the arms of this man I loved. "Everything is perfect," I whispered.

¤

Sometime in the middle of the night, I woke up to the sound of bells tinkling. At first I thought they were mine, but when I heard Little Reed's voice followed by Mazatzin's, I rolled out of bed. They stood in Little Reed's doorway across our small family garden. "What's going on?" I asked, stifling a yawn as I crossed the flagstone path to the other side.

"So sorry to wake you at this early hour, My Lady," Mazatzin said with a bow. "But I suppose this should be shared with both of you."

"Let's speak in my quarters, so we don't wake Yamehecatl," Little Reed suggested, holding the curtain open for us. Mazatzin waited for me to go in first before meekly stepping in himself.

Little Reed's quarters differed from my own only in decor; wooden screens carved with images of the Feathered Serpent separated his sleeping area from the main anteroom with its walls painted with frescos of birds, snakes, and butterflies. He gestured for us to sit on the mats in front of the hearth and tossed some new logs on the fire to get better light. He also put some copalli incense on a clay burner before settling down on one of the vacant reed mats. "What do you have for us, Mazatzin?" he asked.

"A man came into the temple with a very disturbing report. His son vanished from the fields this evening, at sunset, but the man tracked him into the woods on the northern end of Tollan. Once there, he witnessed a man in a black priest's robe attempting to sacrifice his son. He tried to stop it, but someone struck him from behind. He awoke a few hours later to find his son's body half-buried in a shallow grave nearby, but when he dug it up, he found other bodies as well. He led soldiers to the grave and they pulled a dozen bodies out."

Every bone in my body shouted this was the handiwork of Smoking Mirror's cult, but I'd been wrong the last time. And Mextli was snooping around, causing trouble again. "This newest victim...was his heart removed?"

Mazatzin nodded.

"Was there sign of ritual sacrifice on the other bodies found?" Little Reed asked.

"Some of them, yes. Others were too decomposed to be able to tell at a glance. I should also tell you that the farmer positively identified Ozomatli as the man he saw in the forest."

Finally! The break I need to stick a thorn through him.

But Little Reed wrinkled his brow. "Was it truly light enough to make such a positive identification? It takes at least a quarter of an hour to reach the forest from the most northern fields, and he said his son disappeared at sunset, so it was dark when he finally found him. Did he bring a torch with him?"

"I didn't think to ask," Mazatzin said.

Little Reed sighed. "If this turns out to be true, I'm highly disappointed. I believed Ozomatli was bringing real change to Smoking Mirror's cult, so we could all coexist peacefully."

"Smoking Mirror isn't interested in peaceful coexistence," I said. "We should arrest Ozomatli immediately."

But Little Reed shook his head. "We must avoid rushing to judgment. An accusation is a place to start, but further investigation is warranted. These are serious charges, and Ozomatli deserves the right to defend himself against them."

I grudgingly nodded. "I have been wrong about him before." *He better not slither his way out of this one too.*

"What is obvious is that someone is murdering people in the name of some god, and has been for a while now," Little Reed went on. "We should look through the missing persons reported to the city registrar; perhaps we can identify some of the dead and alert their families. But first, I want to see this mass grave."

I rose to my feet. "As do I."

Mazatzin rose too—paying respect to my social position—but added, "I should warn you that the scene is quite gruesome, My Lady."

"I can't imagine it's any worse than what we saw in Quetzalcoatl's temple after my uncle spent twenty years defiling it," I said with an unintended snap. Mazatzin bowed his head, looking shamed, but I gave his hand a reassuring squeeze. "But thank you for the warning. I appreciate your concern."

Little Reed rose too. "We'll meet in the Hall of the Gods by the next hourly bell. That should give us ample time to dress and locate someone to watch Yamehecatl while we're gone."

I returned to my quarters and dressed in one of my longer, heavier priestly robes; the nights were getting colder as the winter season approached. I ran a brush through my hair but didn't bother fixing it, opting instead to put on a hooded cloak, to protect my ears from the wind.

Little Reed waited outside on the portico and we walked to the Hall of the Gods together. "We should keep all this quiet for now," he said. "We don't want to scare the culprits into hiding. Let them think we're unaware."

"How are we to keep the farmer quiet?"

"I'll discuss it with him. He won't want his son's murderer disappearing without facing justice."

"We need to make certain we act quickly and decisively."

He nodded. "It would be useful if we had someone trusted inside Smoking Mirror's cult. Do you know the high priestess well?"

"We don't talk much, so no." If anything, I avoided her; inexplicably, she made my skin crawl.

When we reached the Hall of the Gods, Citlallotoc came in through the front gate followed by his guards, looking bedraggled. He'd been away for a month, visiting our allied cities and collecting their issues and concerns to bring before us. He smiled when he saw us. "Greetings, My Lord and

Lady." He gave us a sweeping bow.

Little Reed embraced him with a hearty hug. "Welcome back. We weren't expecting you for another week at least." Once Little Reed finished, I granted Citlallotoc the same token, but had to stand on my tiptoes to reach his neck even as he bent over.

Citlallotoc unslung his pack. "You'll be happy to know I bring only good news from our allies. All is well throughout the empire."

"If only I could report the same here." Little Reed quickly filled him in on tonight's grim discovery.

Citlallotoc handed his bag off to one of his guards. "Let us go and see the scene then."

"Certainly you're weary from your journey," I said.
"Justice within the city is my purview, My Lady. And after hearing only domestic cases most days, this is an exciting change."

¤

Crime was rarely an issue in Tollan since we'd started providing free food to anyone who needed it. Theft and crimes of desperation were few and far between these days, and violent crime was almost nonexistent. With the years, Chichimecs and Toltecas slowly learned to live together in a semblance of peace, especially the younger generation who attended school together and learned to speak both Tolteca and Chichimec.

And because of Tollan's decidedly anti-war stance, we didn't have a "war council", and we'd changed Citlallotoc's title to "Justice of the Peace". Instead of planning and strategizing war for us, he now negotiated and maintained peace between our neighbors and allied states, and fostered Tollan's internal peace by acting as the city's magistrate. He listened to cases of land boundary disputes, missing livestock, or issues of offended honor. There hadn't been a murder trial for over a year now; it was so rare an occurrence that both Little Reed and I had sat in on that occasion and had been the ones to hand down the sentence of exile. There were no capital crimes under Tollan's laws.

In light of this newest mystery, Citlallotoc forgot any fatigue from his trip and walked with purpose down the trail leading into the forest. Guards greeted us inside the trees and one of them led us through the underbrush to a small clearing blanketed with leaves, in the middle of which lay a triangular stack of logs. More guards held torches, bringing the scene to late-afternoon brightness.

The royal surgeon hunched in the center of the peculiar log formation, muttering to himself. Behind him, lined up one next to the other, were at least a dozen bodies, all covered with blankets. When Citlallotoc called to the surgeon, he hurried over and bowed, brushing his dirty hands off on his cloak. He took Little Reed and Citlallotoc to see the bodies.

I circled the clearing, taking in the rest of the scene. Tension formed in my shoulders and the hairs on my neck stood upright, as if something powerful lurked nearby. The whole area reeked of dark magic; the ground throbbed with it, much the way Quetzalcoatl's temple in Culhuacan had when I'd first stepped into it after so many years. A dark memory clung to this place, a thousand screams of lives lost, families destroyed; and underneath it all, the ground pulsed with a sinister laugh. I shivered.

But there wasn't any outward signs of ritual sacrifice here; no blood-stained stone, no sacred markings carved into the trees, only leaves, logs, and trees. *Ozomatli must have used the logs in place of the sacrificial stone,* I decided, stepping closer to the log formation. The rounded shape was effective for expanding the chest for the incision. The ground in the middle was muddy and smelled of stale blood mixed with pungent earth. Despite my best efforts to suppress the rumbling in my stomach, I started salivating and had to step away. My reaction to such things had only grown stronger since learning I could rejuvenate my magic by drinking blood.

The feeling of being watched intensified and I squinted into the darkness beyond the torchlight, unsettled. Numerous guards cluttered the periphery, oblivious to the oppressive air. The preternatural whisper of *Mine! Mine! Mine!* played on the breeze. Chills raced up my back.

Someone touched my shoulder and I jumped. "I'm sorry, I didn't mean to frighten you," Little Reed said, looking guilty.

I shook my head and rubbed the raised flesh on my arms under my robe sleeves. "It's all right. This place is...." I looked around a moment, hearing the whispering again. "Do you hear that?"

Little Reed called for silence, but after a moment of listening, he shook his head. "What do you hear?"

I listened again, but I didn't hear it either. In the past we'd shared experiences of the divine in ways unnatural to normal human beings, so if

221

he couldn't hear it, it must have been my imagination. "I thought I heard someone whispering, but it was probably the wind."

He too scanned the dark beyond the trees, letting his gaze linger.

"You examined the bodies?" I asked, eager to change the subject.

He nodded. "It's as we suspected; the hearts are missing. The burying is unusual though; sacrifices are only buried when one intends to construct a temple, to make the ground sacred to a given god."

"Someone's building a temple here?" That idea had Mextli's feathers all over it.

"We'd definitely notice a new temple," Little Reed said. "Instead, they're treating this area as if it's already a temple. Come, look at this."

I followed Little Reed over to the pit where the bodies had been buried. He bent next to one of the logs and pointed to scorch marks in the rotting bark. "Someone burned something here, on a round object."

I bent for a closer look, and when I rubbed the ash between my fingers, I detected the faint odor of burnt tobacco. "Smoking Mirror's followers burn tobacco on an obsidian mirror," I pointed out. When Little Reed nodded, I added, "Ozomatli put in a requisition for a new obsidian mirror this morning. He claims one of his priests broke it, but I'd bet he broke it himself, out here."

"Perhaps, but that's not what concerns me."

I furrowed my brow. "Then what does?"

"There's no idol."

"He takes it with him. It would look suspicious to leave it out here for anyone to find."

"The idol would have to be large enough to place a human heart inside of it, and it would look suspicious lugging a large stone idol back and forth between the city and the forest. Someone would have seen it. And one man alone couldn't carry it on his own. It takes six strong men to move Quetzalcoatl's idol."

"But there was a second person; he knocked out the farmer from behind." Someone Mextli's size could heft a boulder onto his shoulders without sweating.

"All true, but there's no evidence that a heavy stone statue sat on the ground anywhere here, even for a short time; no indentations, no scrapes, nothing."

His determination to chew this bone exasperated me. "What does it matter if there's no idol?"

"The idol is the conduit between this world and the divine realm, to feed the sacrifices to the god it represents. If there's no conduit, one of two things is happening: the god is already in corporeal form and is being fed directly—"

"Smoking Mirror is walking around Tollan as we speak?" The hairs on my neck stood up again.

"It's possible, of course, but I doubt it. What did he do the last time someone summoned him?"

"He came as a giant smoking jaguar and he tried to kill you."

"Exactly. If he was corporeal, he would have attacked already; not to mention that we would have heard it happen. Remember how loud it was whenever you summoned Quetzalcoatl, or when Ihuitimal summoned Smoking Mirror at Culhuacan? This close to the city, we definitely would have heard it."

I nodded. "So what's the other option?"

"Someone is attempting to summon Smoking Mirror, and has failed twelve times."

Visions of that giant smoking jaguar tearing through Tollan, searching for me and Little Reed, made the magic roil in my belly. If Ozomatli succeeded, I'd have to call on Quetzalcoatl to fight Smoking Mirror again.

And the only thing I had left to sacrifice was my son.

I said, "We must stop Ozomatli before he tries a thirteenth time."

¤

I wanted Ozomatli arrested immediately, but Little Reed disagreed. "We need to proceed carefully and discreetly. We don't know that Ozomatli is the one behind this, and if he isn't, we risk sending the real culprit into hiding, and we lose the chance to give justice to the victims' families."

I grudgingly agreed, but I lay awake the rest of the night, thinking of ways to catch Ozomatli at his duplicity.

By dawn, Yamehecatl was up and begging me to dress him in his rabbit suit; he could dress himself, but he'd taken to mimicking the other noble children and insisted a servant do it for him. And for now, that servant was me.

"I'm going to be the king one day, and kings don't dress themselves," he declared.

"Your father does." I'd convinced him to at least slip into the outfit himself, but he still struggled with tying knots so I helped out there.

"That's because he only ever wears that ratty white robe," Yamehecatl insisted. "I'm going to dress so elaborately that I'll need an army of servants to dress me every day."

I laughed. "Why would you want that?"

"So everyone will look at me when I'm talking to them. Everyone ignores me when I talk now."

"I don't ignore you. Nor does your father or Citlallotoc."

He scoffed. "That's because you're my family. I'm talking about all those noble boys who pretend I'm not even there when I ask them questions; someday I'll be their king and I can't have them ignoring me, so I need to wear things that will make them want to pay attention to me."

"If all you worry about is wearing beautiful clothing, they will pay attention only to your dress, not to you," I told him. "If you wish them to truly pay attention to you, speak with wisdom and understanding; give them a good reason to listen to you. Your father dresses plainly and yet when he speaks, everyone listens because what he says is important."

Yamehecatl sighed. "I wish I could speak as well as Tatli, but I can't, so I need better clothing."

"You don't need better clothes; you need time to grow wise, and to find better friends than those noble boys."

This time Yamehecatl nodded. "Like Night Wind. *He* gets me, Nantli. Can you fetch him to the palace, so we can play today?"

"He's in school."

He frowned but nodded. "I want to go to school with him, Nantli."

"Night Wind goes to the telpochcalli, and as the prince, you can't go there."

"Why not?"

"Because a prince needs to know how to read and write, and you'll only learn that in the calmecac."

"I don't want to go to the calmecac!"

"A good king knows how to honor the gods for the good of his kingdom."

"I don't care about honoring the gods," Yamehecatl said, growing increasingly vexed. "Why should I anyway? What makes them so special?"

I suppressed the urge to lecture him about blasphemy and respect. When his own mother used magic, why wouldn't he question the usefulness of gods who exercised their own power in vague ways? "Because we owe them our honor, Yamehecatl. They created the world for us by their own deaths, and Quetzalcoatl made painful sacrifices to give us life. Remember all the trials he endured to rescue the bones of our ancestors from Lord Death?"

"I suppose that's something," Yamehecatl conceded with a grumble. "Still, I want to go to the telpochcalli, not the calmecac. I'm not sticking thorns in my tepolli as Tatli does." He shielded his groin as if I'd threatened to prick him with the rope of thorns I kept in my pocket.

I sighed. "Sometimes we have to do things we don't want to because we have obligations."

He balled his fists and stomped. "I won't go to the calmecac, and you can't make me!" Already I smelled the first hints of octli in the air.

But suddenly Citlallotoc pushed aside the curtain and poked his head in. "What's all this noise I'm hearing?" he asked, innocently surprised; his tactic for defusing Yamehecatl when he began getting out of hand.

Yamehecatl pushed past me and latched himself around Citlallotoc's legs. "You're home!"

Laughing, Citlallotoc hefted him up with his one good arm. "I'm surprised you even noticed I was gone."

"Of course I noticed!" Yamehecatl crowed. "I missed you!"

"Why? Did you throw something at me?" Citlallotoc grinned when Yamehecatl giggled at their private joke. "And I missed you, little man. I look forward to the day when you're old enough to come on these confounded trips with me; everyone else is so average with their swordplay, and I don't find them a challenge at all."

"I've been practicing! Let's go to the exercise yard, so I can show you my new moves!"

"Not until you've filled your belly, little warrior." He set Yamehecatl down and crouched in front of him. "And I have some inquiries to make around town—criminals to investigate, spies to unmask, monsters to slay, those kinds of things—but I will be back before lunch and I'm expecting you to be ready to meet swords at that time. You have until then to prepare yourself. And you'd better prepare well, for I intend to show no mercy."

Yamehecatl bounced up and down, giddy. "I'll be ready, I promise!" He wrapped his small arms around Citlallotoc's neck and squeezed, trying to show off his strength. He always saved his fiercest hugs for him.

Why can't it always be that easy for me? I wondered, frustrated. By comparison, our relationship was rocky and contentious. I knew Yamehecatl loved me, but why did he question everything I told him, while always doing whatever Citlallotoc told him to, no questions asked? I supposed that was the lot of a mother; I'd tested my own mother's patience more than once, and I cringed to think of some of the things I'd said to Nimilitzli in the heat of anger.

But at least Yamehecatl had two good men to admire and learn honor and nobility from.

¤

After breakfast, Citlallotoc left to snoop around the sacred precinct and watch some of Smoking Mirror's priests, looking for leads. Little Reed went to speak with Ozomatli; I wanted to go with him, so I could interogate the dog, but Little Reed insisted he conduct the questioning himself. "If I can be frank, my love, when it comes to Ozomatli...you have a hard time keeping an open mind. While I vehemently disapprove of his poisoning Ihuitimal to depose him—if he indeed was doing so—whatever proof we might have had is long gone, and short of him confessing to it, there's nothing we can do about it."

"To Mictlan with Ihuitimal; what about him trying to get you to kill our cousin?" I spat.

"He did put him into my hands, but that was a good thing; even Amoxtli himself says so. Whatever Ozomatli hoped to accomplish by that, he alone knows; and again, short of a confession, what are we to do? Put him on trial for betraying the illegimate king?"

Arguing such things always fatigued me, but even more so today, after so little sleep. Once Little Reed left, I retired to the patio in our family garden to sit down to some weaving.

Yamehecatl sat on the portico in front of his nursery doorway, half of his toys dragged out onto the flagstones, and his dramatic mutterings and imitations of animal sounds blended well with the drone of bees and cicadas, letting some of the day's worries slowly unwind from my shoulders. A breeding pair of quetzals had carved a nest hole in one of the copal trees, and despite this year's young having already left, the parents had stayed behind, fattening themselves on the fruit the servants left out for them every day. I'd brought some melon from breakfast, hoping they'd come down from the tree so I might watch them eat, but they stayed up in the branches, filling the morning air with their melodious *kyow! Kyow! Kyow!*

I'd finally settled my mind and found my focus, but then one of my personal guards came from the hallway. "Lord Citlallotoc wishes to see you in the great hall, My Lady."

"Citlallotoc is back?" Yamehecatl asked, springing to his feet.

If that was the case, he would have come instead of sending for me. I motioned to Yamehecatl's nurse as I stood, and she stepped out of his doorway where she'd been lurking, in case I needed her. "Nelli will watch you while I'm gone, so be on your best behavior," I told my son.

Yamehecatl kicked aside a wooden coyote on wheels but settled back down, resting his head on one hand while he fiddled with a carved warrior, his maize-leaf rabbit ears dangling over his brow.

I followed the guard to the great hall to find Citlallotoc pacing. Black Otter was with him, surrounded by four guards and looking terrified. He clutched a buckskin bag to his chest. "Forgive my interruption, My Lady, but I was in the sacred precinct and look who I found skulking about near the temple." He grabbed Black Otter by the shoulder then shoved him forward, so he tumbled to his knees on the flagstones. He drew his sword with the ease of someone who always had been left-handed. "Shall I carry out his death sentence now?"

I grabbed the handle of the sword, my heart hammering. "Gods no! It's all right; we know Black Otter is here and we've agreed to waive his exile. Forgive me for not informing you of this right away."

Citlallotoc scowled but put his sword away before helping Black Otter back to his feet. "My apologies for being unduly rough with you," he mumbled.

Black Otter shrugged but kept his eyes downcast, like a dog anticipating his master's whip. "I'm not hurt, My Lord."

Noticing him clutching the bag a little tighter now, I asked him, "What were you doing in the sacred precinct?"

"I went to visit my brother before going to work." He darted a nervous glance at me. "He asked me to meet him for lunch today and I wanted to make certain I knew where to go, since my new employer carefully monitors my time during the day."

"And what's in the bag?"

He looked at it as if he'd forgotten about it. "Oh, it's a gift for the temple. I've decided I should start tithing a portion of my income to the order." He opened the bag and produced an obsidian blade. "I made it myself, at work. I was planning to give it to Amoxtli to give to the Temple of the Smoking Mirror, since he's a priest, after all."

A wave of suspicion swept over me but I reminded myself that here in Tollan we didn't tell anyone which god they should devote themselves to, so long as said worship respected the laws of the city. Still, I couldn't keep the sharpness from my voice as I said, "Amoxtli is a priest of Quetzalcoatl, not of the Smoking Mirror."

Black Otter stood a little straighter, surprised. "Well, he was always the more independently-minded of the two of us...and undoubtedly would have been a better king than I would have." He fidgeted. "Will my choosing to resume worshiping Tezcatlipoca make you reconsider my exile, My Lady? Let me reassure you that I will not engage in any of the prohibited methods of worship; I will give my prayers and burn the tobacco as I used to, but nothing more. I'm relieved to have finally put those days behind me when I was expected to take my father's place as the next high priest; as I told you before, that was a life I never wanted to begin with."

I nodded. "I'm sorry for your detainment. Topiltzin and I should have made the reversal of your exile public knowledge. I'll make certain that an official announcement is made at this evening's public services, so this never happens again."

"I thank you, My Lady." Black Otter returned the blade to his buckskin bag.

"Let me keep you no further. I'm certain you're eager to deliver that fine obsidian spearhead to the high priest of Smoking Mirror. His name is Ozomatli, and you can probably find him at the calmecac."

Black Otter looked up sharply. "Ozomatli? My father's former fire priest?"

I tilted my head, my interest piqued. "Yes, that's him. Is something the matter?" I tried not to sound overeager.

"I'm surprised; he was quite close with my father, one of his most loyal supporters in the priesthood, but I was never very comfortable with him. My father respected the god's power, but Ozomatli...he constantly pestered my father to train him to be the next high priest of the Smoking Mirror, saying I wasn't made for the job. He begged my father to teach him the secret knowledge the god had taught him in the desert, but my father refused, saying he'd share it only with those the god deemed worthy."

"And what did Ozomatli think of that?"

"He tried to convince me to teach him what I knew, so he could better serve me when I was king. Naturally, I refused. I suppose he also tried to manipulate information from Amoxtli, but my father wasn't far into training him, so he probably didn't know anything useful. Ozomatli continued beating that particular drum all the way up to my father's death, so he got his wish to be the new high priest."

This sounded full of possibilities to help us with our current troubles, but I needed to talk it over with Little Reed before going any further. "Perhaps you should allow me to deliver the blade for you," I suggested.

Black Otter handed me the bag. "Actually, maybe it should go to the Feathered Serpent's cult. I don't know if it's an acceptable gift, but it's what I have to give, and perhaps it's best to put all of the past behind and start over anew, with a new god and a new outlook."

"We don't require that of you at all, Black Otter," I reminded him. "But the god accepts your gift and thanks you." I fingered the obsidian blade through the bag as I watched him go, Citlallotoc leading him out. I hissed when I pressed too hard and the blade sliced through the hide and cut my finger. "But your future might depend on you keeping some of that past in the present, at least for surface appearances, Cousin," I muttered under my breath.

◻

Once Citlallotoc returned to take Yamehecatl to the exercise yard for their afternoon weapons lesson, I went to the sacred precinct looking for Little Reed. I found him in the calmecac courtyard with a group of our youngest students gathered around the cistern, telling them the story of

229

Quetzalcoatl and Mayahuel, for today was the beginning of the Maguey Goddess's festival. Each child wore a rabbit, a monkey, or a maguey flower mask they'd made themselves in class, as part of the celebration.

I'd never heard Little Reed tell the Mayahuel story. He did different voices as usual, but this one lacked the joy and excitement he usually brought to Quetzalcoatl's stories. The young ones gasped when he described the Earth Monster destroying Mayahuel, and a few even cried when Quetzalcoatl buried her remains. The more times I heard the story, the more it depressed me.

Little Reed knelt and beckoned everyone closer. "Mayahuel's story is tragic, but out of it came something truly important, something that makes us all very happy. Can you tell me what that is?"

"Octli!" the children shouted.

Little Reed shook his head. "Something else."

I shared the children's puzzlement as they looked at each other and whispered. "The maguey plant?" a boy asked.

"Yes, she gave us that, and octli; but most importantly, she gave us love. For on the tree she and Quetzalcoatl created in Tamoachan bloomed flowers whose fragrance brought love into the hearts of everyone. And that is the greatest gift Mayahuel brought to us." When he noticed me listening from the far side of the cistern, he smiled, melting me inside. "For the next week, while we celebrate the Maguey Goddess and honor her for all she's given us, think about how different our world would be if not for her greatest gift."

After the priests and priestesses led the children back inside the calmecac, Little Reed came to me. "I thought you were spending the afternoon with Yamehecatl."

"He'd rather spend it with Citlallotoc, of course," I said with mock offense.

Little Reed laughed. "Well, Citlallotoc has been gone for a whole month." He took my arm and started walking with me.

"Is that always how you tell that story?" I asked as we walked towards the priestly gardens. "That's not exactly how we were taught it in calmecac."

He shrugged. "Perhaps my father has told me a different version."

"Except that it makes it all the more tragic."

"I suppose. But certainly you didn't come here to listen to me tell the children stories."

"No. I had an idea about how we might flush out our renegade priest. Have you met with Ozomatli yet?"

"Not yet."

"Good. I spoke to Black Otter this morning and he told me—"

"You spoke to Black Otter? Why?"

I'd never known Little Reed to be insecure, so the edge to his voice took me by surprise. And irritated me. "We didn't tell Citlallotoc we overturned his exile, so when he saw Black Otter in the sacred precinct this morning, he arrested him and brought him to me for sentencing. I promised Black Otter we'd announce the rescinding of his exile today so that this doesn't happen again."

Little Reed nodded, chastened. "I'll be certain to do so this afternoon at the temple service. So, what did he tell you?"

"When I mentioned that Ozomatli was our high priest of the Smoking Mirror, he had much to say, and not much of it positive. Ozomatli was open about his ambitions to be the next high priest, even going so far as to beg Ihuitimal to tell him the secrets he'd learned about the god in the desert—secrets such as how to summon Smoking Mirror—but Ihuitimal refused to teach such things to anyone but his own sons."

"That would give Ozomatli motive to dispose of Ihuitimal," Little Reed conceded. After we walked through the gate into the privacy of the gardens, he went on, "How do you suggest we use this new information?"

"We have Black Otter join Smoking Mirror's order, and because his father taught him those secrets, maybe he'll be able to draw Ozomatli out with the promise of finally getting the knowledge he needs to actually summon Smoking Mirror."

"We don't know that Ozomatli is the true conspirator," Little Reed reminded me.

I shrugged. "Either way, we dangle Black Otter as bait, and whoever is doing it won't be able to resist, especially after so much failure."

"This could work, and we were searching for a means for him to prove his loyalty." He nodded. "Excellent idea, Papalotl. I shall speak with him about it."

"I should be the one to talk to him. You barely know him whereas he and I spent our earliest years as friends, and we were married and shared a bed...." My cheeks blazed, but I quickly made myself go on. "He will be more comfortable talking to me about it." *And we know how to get him to do what we want,* the desire cackled but I bit my tongue. That wouldn't sound proper at all.

Little Reed hesitated, still uncertain, but eventually he nodded. "Fine. You speak with Black Otter. I will let Ozomatli know that our cousin will be joining his ranks soon."

CHAPTER TWENTY

Little Reed wanted me to summon Black Otter back to the palace later that same day, to discuss the job under the watchful gaze of the guards, but the rebellious part of me scoffed. Besides, Ozomatli might have spies watching the palace and if Black Otter kept showing up, he might suspect deception. Instead, I waited until after the work day's ending bell, then I put on a priestly robe and a festival mask. My formal one was gold and silver, in the shape of a maguey flower, but I didn't want to be recognized out among the people, so I borrowed the paper rabbit mask I made with my son last week.

The palace guards wouldn't let me walk the halls with a mask on, and I didn't want them coming with me, so I packed it into a bag and went out into my private garden. A doorway in the back wall led into an open-air passage, similar to the one in Culhuacan, only this one led to the priestly gardens. Guards still manned the corners—to keep unauthorized persons from coming in from the gardens—but once I closed the final gate behind me, I didn't have to worry. I slipped on the mask and followed the path towards the main gate.

Some way down the winding path through the trees and shrubs, I heard women's voices up ahead, near the large secluded pond where Quetzalcoatl and I had made love in the grass. I hid behind a large oak tree that blocked the view of the path and peered around the side.

Malinalli and Mitotia sat next to the pond, both of their backs to me as they ate tlaxcallis and talked. I knew Malinalli didn't have priestly duties today—it was her rest day—so I found it curious she would be out here, sharing dinner with a lower-ranking priestess. Their idle chatter soon turned into laughter, and they leaned their heads together, giggling like young girls over a secret. But it soon faded into a silence rife with tension as they looked at each other....

Like when you look at Little Reed. Suddenly everything I'd said to Malinalli yesterday punched me in the chest. How many times had I thrown around "he" when asking who was making her so happy? I'd been so careless, so full of assumption. What kind of a best friend was I to not know this about her?

All of those dismissed hints made sense now—how uncomfortable she was when we talked about men and marriage and children, as if that was what women and girls were supposed to talk about. Or those distant looks she used to give me when we were younger—the kind of looks I always garnered from men but chose to ignore as meaningless in my best friend. And there was that time in the garden, with Black Otter, when I'd nearly asked her to join us in my bed....

Even the desire knew, you idiot, I scolded myself. No wonder she was hesitant to tell me. We'd grown up learning that such impulses were unnatural and unlawful; codes in both Xochicalco and Culhuacan had strictly forbidden such relationships, and one could have been sent to the sacrifice as a criminal for acting upon them. And though Tollan had no strict rules against same-sex coupling, the general sentiment in the streets was that it was an abomination against the gods; last year's murder had been of a young man stoned to death by a mob of angry noblemen when his lover's father caught him with his son, so I understood her desire to keep quiet.

But certainly she didn't think I would turn on her for this? *I should have seen it, and been supportive, and maybe she wouldn't have felt it better to hide the truth from me. She's always listened and supported me, but I haven't done the same for her.*

I pushed back my mask to wipe the tears clouding my eyes. For years now Malinalli had seemed unhappy, haunted by an emptiness that I'd always assumed she'd fill once she found the right man, so at least I wasn't completely out of touch with her emotions. And I was exceedingly happy she'd found someone who made her laugh, and feel not so alone.

I slipped the mask back over my face and hurried up the path, treading as quietly as possible so as not to draw their attention.

◻

The smell of frying maize and roasting chile peppers filled the crowded, muddy streets outside the city wall. The noise was loud but joyous, children shrieking in delight as they greeted their fathers or mothers returning from the fields or the market. The old men played patolli and sipped cups of octli—a privilege they'd earned with their many years of life—while mothers barked at their children to come to dinner. Somewhere a flute kept time with a drum. It had been a very long time since I'd been out in the city alone, and the crush of bodies moving every direction unnerved me until I was confident my disguise was effective.

Most of the people living outside the city walls were Chichimec, but what they lacked in wealth they made up for in community. Priests of various Chichimec gods went around to the houses, delivering fabric or food, and neighbors helped mend crumbling stucco facades on each other's homes. A few tussles broke out over patolli games, and young women with their teeth dyed red with cochineal lingered at street corners, their high-cut dresses announcing sexual services for the right price. Definitely not the refined palace culture I was used to, but it also made my daily life seem predictable and shallow.

I wound through the crowd, hoping I'd see Black Otter, but with so many people living in close quarters, I would be there for hours trying to find him. I could ask someone, but what if they recognized my voice?

But then I saw Black Otter's daughter Cuicatl come out of one of the side streets, a duck carcass slung over one shoulder and a bag of masa over the other. I hurried and stepped in front of her, so that she had to stop. "I'm looking for your father."

She stepped back, fear in her eyes until I bent closer and lifted the mask enough to show her my face. "You know who I am?"

"I do, My Lady." She tried to bow, but I stopped her.

"No bowing. I don't want to draw undue attention."

"Sorry, My Lady."

"I need to speak with your father. Will you take me to your house?"

She inclined her head to the right and led the way when I motioned her to do so.

I followed her down several side streets until we were one row of houses away from the fields. The houses this far out were small but still constructed of stone and plaster; we provided warm, sturdy housing built by the city's stonemasons for everyone regardless of economic status, and city workers whitewashed every new house to give residents a clean canvas to decorate their exterior walls with designs and murals of their own choosing. Eagles and coyotes were particularly popular. Black Otter's house was plain white, with a log for beekeeping hung from the eaves over the front door. A heavy reed mat hanging across the door kept the wind and bees outside.

Black Otter sat next to the hearth, tying a new obsidian blade to a worn handle. He smiled, until he saw his daughter wasn't alone. Night Wind sat against the wall, looking bored, but his expression turned to curiosity when he saw my rabbit mask.

"Who have you brought home with you, Cuicatl?" Black Otter gripped the half-finished knife tighter than before.

I pulled off the mask. "It's me, Black Otter."

"What are you doing here?" He looked towards the doorway, as if expecting guards to come in too. "And why are you wearing a mask?"

"I've come on behalf of the kingdom to ask something of you. Can I speak to you in private?"

He hesitated before telling Cuicatl, "Take Night Wind to the cistern and fill the water jars while Lady Quetzalpetlatl and I talk."

Cuicatl rolled her eyes and dropped the bag of masa to the floor. She tossed the duck into her father's lap. "Let's go," she told Night Wind, grabbing his hand and dragging him out of the door.

Black Otter hung the duck from a hook on the wall. "Please forgive Cuicatl's temper. Losing her mother has been hard on her."

That wasn't a road I wanted to explore with him, so I moved immediately to the point of my visit. "Topiltzin and I need you to do something for us."

"Whatever I can do."

"We want you to join Smoking Mirror's cult here in Tollan."

Black Otter blinked at me, taken aback. "But, My Lady—"

"I know that's not the life you wanted, despite your father's insistences, but you know useful things that could help us solve a mystery and bring justice to a dozen murder victims."

"Murder victims?"

"We found a mass burial site not far outside town and it bears all the markings of Smoking Mirror's cult. We believe that one of the priests is trying to summon the Smoking Mirror."

Black Otter went back to tying on his blade, uneasy. "That is serious. Who is your suspect?"

"Ozomatli. And given everything you told me this morning, he's even higher on our list now. So far he hasn't succeeded in summoning anything, but he's certainly not giving up. We must put an end to this, before more people are murdered—or, worse yet, he actually succeeds."

"But how would my joining the priesthood help in any of this?"

"Because he'll want you to share your knowledge of the Smoking Mirror and his secrets, so he can finally complete this ritual properly."

Furrowing his brow, he asked, "You want me to show him the proper ritual for summoning the god to corporeal form?"

"Of course not. We can't let it go so far. But you'll need to earn his trust and convince him that you're open to the possibility of sharing. Tell him you're seeking revenge for your father."

Black Otter chewed his lip, debating. "So you want me to pretend to conspire against you and Topiltzin?" When I nodded, he said, "And I suppose that your coming here today is a courtesy, not a request."

"Let's say that your doing this will go a long way to rebuilding trust between us again," I said.

He stared at me with veiled annoyance. "Then I graciously accept this mission from yourself and the King."

"Topiltzin will be most happy to hear it. Rest assured you're doing the right thing."

"I hope this doesn't see me joining Jade Flower on the road into Mictlan. The children have lost so much already."

Smirking, I said, "It takes more than mere arrows or knives to kill you, Black Otter. It's obvious you have the gods on your side."

He tried to laugh but it came out awkward.

"Do well on this task, and your future will be bright again. It would be nice to have an actual blood relative back on the throne in Culhuacan, don't you think?"

Black Otter wrung his hands. "That's a generous thought, My Lady, but those days are far behind me now. My father's name is a curse in many cities, but none so much as in Culhuacan. If I did return—even with your's and Topiltzin's blessing—many would never accept me as their ruler, even if it's merely as a governor."

"Regardless, know you will be handsomely rewarded for your efforts. That is a promise." I slipped the mask back on and added, "At the very least, you'll get your noble title back and won't have to live out here anymore."

"It's not so bad out here. There's something freeing about not being followed everywhere you go."

"Indeed there is," I muttered. "Tomorrow morning, come by the calmecac and see Topiltzin. He'll officially name a position for you in Smoking Mirror's priesthood." I ducked out of the door, leaving the thick reed mat swaying in the growing dusk.

CHAPTER TWENTY-ONE

Black Otter reported to us every couple of days, filling in the details of his efforts to ingratiate himself with Ozomatli, which seemed to be going well. Within the first week, he'd supplanted the fire priest in Ozomatli's confidences, and by the second week, even the high priestess was pushing for him to take over the position. Several times I caught her watching him from afar with the infatuated look of a young girl; when I teased him about it, he reddened and mumbled about how he had no time for such things.

We always met in Little Reed's quarters, so there was no chance of Ozomatli walking in on us. Black Otter brought Night Wind with him, so he and Yamehecatl could play out in the garden while we talked; our meetings often lasted a couple of hours, and since the boys were inseparable, it was easier to let Yamehecatl run himself to exhaustion. I thought it would be uncomfortable spending so much time with Black Otter again, but instead it felt as if this was how things should be, with family all together again.

But not long after Night Wind and Yamehecatl became friends, I started worrying about the kind of influence Night Wind exerted over my son.

Little Reed and I began to talk again about enrolling Yamehecatl in calmecac, and decided we could start sending him there for a couple of hours a day. But when I told Yamehecatl, he said, "I don't want to go to school anymore, Nantli. Night Wind says it's a waste of time."

That struck me as odd; Black Otter had been quite proud when the teachers at the telpochcalli suggested moving Night Wind up to the calmecac. I heard nothing negative about the boy from the other priests, just that he was intense and quiet but always knew the answers when asked.

"Why would he say such a thing?" I asked, puzzled.

Yamehecatl shrugged. "He says they teach pointless things that I'm not going to need at all when I grow up."

Well, Night Wind must not be as intelligent as I thought. "Or maybe he knows that you're cleverer than him and he doesn't want you showing him up in class. You're going to school, regardless."

"So I will be in school with Night Wind?" When I nodded, he perked up. "Can I start tomorrow? Please, please, please!" My boy's temperament was so fickle.

I suppose every mother worries about her child the first time they go off to school, but I was so nervous I couldn't eat breakfast or lunch. I expected someone to come and tell me that I had to take him home because someone claimed he'd gotten into the sacred octli or that he was uncontrollable. But instead he came home bubbling with stories. He couldn't wait to go back, and asked when he could move into the dormitories with Night Wind and the other boys.

"Everyone eats and sleeps together, and everyone knows so much, Nantli! Much more than those stone-headed noble boys who live here in the palace. And the priests don't talk to me as if I'm a baby. When can I move into the dormitories, Nantli? When? Please!"

I laughed. "It's only your first day, my dear. And you've only attended for a few hours. When you're a full-time student, you have daily duties, such as gathering copal wood from the grove, or trapping snakes and butterflies for the sacrifice. When I was in calmecac, the girls used to do all the sweeping and cleaning, but now the boys do that too, and trust me, there's nothing more mind-numbing than sweeping the temple floor day in and day out."

My warnings had little effect on his opinion though. He begged day after day for us to put him into school full time, but I resisted. A mother got to hold her children close for only so long, and Yamehecatl hadn't even reached his fifth summer yet. He might share Little Reed's accelerated mental growth, but he was still small enough for me to carry in my arms—with some difficulty, admittedly. As long as I could do that, he was still too young to be sent off to school full-time. The day would come when I'd have to let him go—maybe next year—but not now.

¤

At any given time, there were numerous students working in the temples or the kitchens, doing their chores, and while it wasn't often that I had the job of watching over them, I did occasionally find myself in the temple with one or more students. Today, when I walked in, Night Wind was at the Feathered Serpent's idol, cleaning the splattered blood and dirt from around the mouth and base.

He didn't make a sound, as intense in his work as he was in everything else, but eventually he looked over at me, a nominally curious expression on his face. It was customary for others to bow when I entered a room— even in my capacity as High Priestess—but he remained knelt on the floor, still rubbing the cloth over the idol while he casually watched me walk around, determining the cleanliness of the temple. I could have chided him for his lack of attention to protocol, but he'd done an excellent job of cleaning, so I ignored the oversight.

I stepped up next to him, watching him scrub for a moment before saying, "Quite fine work, Night Wind."

"Thank you, My Lady." He bowed this time, still on his knees, but with hands out at his sides, so his head nearly touched the ground. "You're most gracious."

"I believe in pointing out the good wherever I see it. Tell me, how do you find the calmecac? Are you settling in well?"

"Well enough." He went back to work. He was a boy of few words, it seemed.

I asked him to work on the other side of the idol for now, so I could do my daily offering. He moved without argument.

I knelt on the reed mat in front of the idol and did my normal routine, bleeding my tongue with the rope and maguey thorns, praying aloud over the blood bowl before tipping the contents into the idol's open mouth. But as I started settling in for silent prayers, I noticed Night Wind watching me. "Yes?"

"Why do you still honor him, after everything he did?"

Furrowing my brow, I asked, "Why would I...what?"

"Why do you still worship Quetzalcoatl when he killed your mother, and your father?"

I gaped at him, a wave of fury rising inside me. "Why would you ask me such a thing?"

"But isn't it true that the Feathered Serpent put the King in your mother's belly and that killed her?" He gazed at me with innocent curiosity, as if he didn't understand why I was so upset. "Aren't you angry about that?"

Why you slimy little— The magic rushed to my fingers but I caught myself. Would I really strike out at a child? The rage brimmed just inside my consciousness, a kind of pulsing that matched my heartbeat, making the world vibrate. I breathed deep to steady myself. *Be careful lest those powers cause you regrets.* "Did your father tell you that?" I carefully modulated my voice so not to scare the boy.

Night Wind shook his head. "He doesn't talk about grandfather, or the others. Ozomatli said it the other day when I was cleaning the temple of Smoking Mirror. He thinks I don't listen when I'm working, but I always do; it makes the work go faster."

Who would have thought a small boy could be such an effective spy? "What else did he say?"

"That if not for the Feathered Serpent, my grandfather wouldn't have killed your father, and that it would have spared many lives in the war that came after."

"Or maybe even more lives would have been lost, sacrificed in temples in honor of that honorless Smoking Mirror," I countered. "There are many what-if games one can play about many things, but it doesn't mean that what happen wasn't for the best, regardless of the sacrifices that came with it. Everyone makes sacrifices."

"Not the gods," he said.

"Of course the gods make sacrifices. Quetzalcoatl gave his own blood so we might live—"

"Yes, but that was so long ago."

"It's a debt we can never fully repay."

He nodded. "So, the god is like my sister, who once saved me from falling into the lake, and now she makes me do things for her."

"That's not how it is at all. Do you even listen in class?"

"I always listen; but people tell so many lies that it's better to listen to the whispers, since those are things they don't want you to hear."

"Has Ozomatli been whispering about other things?"

Night Wind shook his head. "But Yamehecatl whispers to his invisible friend when he thinks he's alone."

I stiffened. I'd been so happy at the thought that my son finally found a friend who would accept him, but perhaps that was a delusion I embraced because I hated seeing him so alone, as I had been.

Night Wind went back to his work but continued, "I've talked to his friend too."

"When was this?" No one had told me that Yamehecatl had had one of his episodes.

"Last week. Yamehecatl says when his friend gets angry, he scares him, so I made him go away, and he hasn't come back since."

And here I'd thought the worst of Night Wind. "Thank you for helping him." My voice cracked despite my best efforts to stay calm.

Night Wind shrugged. "It's good to be around those that understand you."

I nodded, struggling to keep the tears back; I had to leave—the temple's air was suddenly stifling.

As I leaned against one of the feathered serpent columns at the temple's entrance, I traced my fingers over the stone scales, remembering the last time I'd seen the god, and how when I'd gazed into his eyes, it wasn't like looking into the unfathomable cosmos. I'd seen a kindred soul, one who saw and knew everything about me, and understood, and loved me for it. I'd sought that same look in Black Otter's eyes every time we'd made love, but he'd always been so disconnected—so focused on his own pleasure— as to make me feel that we must not even be in the same place. What transpired between us wasn't the sharing of selves and souls that I desperately missed from those times with the god, but rather something as pedestrian and everyday as eating breakfast.

But I can't go back to the god, I thought, the tears coming fast. *It's sacrilegious to see him like that, or to believe on any level that we are equals; I might have powerful magic, but if I were anything other than a true human woman, the god would have told me so long ago. It's no secret that Little Reed is half-divine, so what reason would he have to keep a similar secret from me? To even entertain such a notion is blasphemous, and that's a step I can't take, no matter how confused my heart might be.*

Citlallotoc crested the stairs. "Oh good, I found you." When he saw my tears, he asked, "Are you all right?"

I wiped them away quickly. "Yes, got some smoke in my eyes, that's all." I motioned to the kettle braziers back in the temple. Clearing my throat, I asked, "What brings you here?"

"Black Otter claims we'll finally have our proof tonight, about Ozomatli."

¤

Citlallotoc didn't want me coming along with the rest of them. "It could be dangerous, My Lady," he warned when Little Reed and I met with him and his men in the palace courtyard at the midnight bell.

"I can be as well," I countered. Little Reed had also been reluctant for me to go, fearing Ozomatli might succeed in summoning Smoking Mirror this time, but when I reminded him that I'd already faced that demon once before and defeated him, he stopped pressing the issue. He implored me to be careful, and I asked the same of him, and we said no more about it.

Citlallotoc wouldn't be so easily swayed. "It's not a good idea for both of you to come. If you're both killed, who will rule until the prince comes of age?"

"You, of course, as our most trusted friend," I said. "But if you're truly concerned, it should be Topiltzin who stays behind, since I have considerable weapons that he doesn't. The more vulnerable of the two of us should be the one to remain behind."

Citlallotoc frowned, taken aback, but Little Reed laughed. "If I weren't a more confident man, I might take exception to that." He slipped an arm around my shoulder, giving me a squeeze, then told Citlallotoc, "I thank you for your concern, but let's go, before we're late." He pulled up the hood of his cloak and started out of the front gate.

At this late hour, the streets were mostly deserted, save for the occasional watch patrol, and a few stopped us, questioning why a band of cloaked figures were out so late. But with Citlallotoc speaking for us, we got back underway quickly.

Things grew livelier once we left the sanctuary of the city walls; most of the Chichimec men were up late, burning tobacco in public fire pits and chanting prayers to Tezcatlipoca over their swords and spears. Tonight was the first night of Teotleco, the Coming of the Gods, and since the Chichimecs believed this month was ruled by Smoking Mirror, his followers made offerings of smoke and prayers. The secret ceremony we hoped to interrupt would have more traditional offerings on hand.

We made our way to the edge of the fields and up the path leading into the woods. Ozomatli certainly was brazen, coming back to the same scene to commit more atrocities, almost daring us to catch him at it. We watched each step to make certain we didn't make too much noise.

When voices drifted out of the dark ahead of us, Citlallotoc signaled his men to break off into the trees and surround the clearing. "Stay close to me." Little Reed took my hand with a grip that broached no arguments. He pulled his sword and led me over to a tree trunk thick enough to shelter both of us, and there we crouched, back to back, looking around opposite sides. Citlallotoc disappeared into the dark.

Three men were in the clearing; two dressed in priest robes stood, while the third—dressed only in a loincloth—knelt on the ground, groveling. "Shut him up, before he attracts attention." Ozomatli's voice.

The second man moved to gag the kneeling man, whose groveling turned frantic. "Please! I'll give you anything you want—" but the rest of it was cut off as the other finally gagged him.

Ozomatli chuckled. "You'll indeed give me exactly what I want." He knocked the man over backwards, and told the second man, "Hold him down." As the other man clambered atop the victim, Ozomatli pulled a knife from his belt and knelt as well. Blade held aloft, he chanted, "Lord Tezcatlipoca, your day of feast is upon you! Accept this humble offering as the first of many courses tonight!"

Why isn't anyone stopping this? I started to rise, but Little Reed grabbed my arm and held me there. "Let them deal with him."

"But—"

Shouts filled the night and our men flooded the clearing. The second man leaped away, holding his hands up in the air, shouting, "He threatened to kill me if I didn't help him!" It was Black Otter.

Citlallotoc knocked him aside as he went for Ozomatli, catching the priest's arm as he swung the blade at the man on the ground. He wrestled Ozomatli back until the rest of our men swarmed over them, knocking the priest over and pinning him to the ground. The bound man rolled away and struggled to his feet to run.

But when he saw Black Otter standing off to the side, he stopped, his eyes wide. Black Otter started to speak, but the bound man went over backwards, a knife stuck in his stomach.

"Out of the way!" A hulking figure batted Black Otter aside, sending him sprawling into the bushes.

A breath later, Mextli wrenched the man up by the arm. The man gasped behind his gag when Mextli yanked up on the knife with his free hand, spilling his guts on the forest floor, then he broke into a keening cry when the giant reached up inside his open cavity and plucked his heart out as if he were picking an avocado from a tree. Mextli dropped the useless body.

"What the—" Citlallotoc called out as he turned around, but he stepped back when he saw Mextli. "You!" The other men brought their spears up, the fear in their eyes palpable even in the pale moonlight.

"Fools!" Mextli laughed, holding up the feebly beating heart. "Did you really think you could stop the Smoking Mirror's incarnation?" When Citlallotoc drew his sword, Mextli chuckled. "Admirable. Even one-armed, you don't give up, do you?"

Citlallotoc waved his sword. "I'm even better with my left."

"Then come show me, little lord."

But before Citlallotoc could rise to the bait, I jumped out from behind the tree and let loose a burst of magic, knocking the heart from Mextli's fist. He shook his hand as if burned, but when he saw me, a sly smile came to his lips.

"Ah, the Feathered Serpent's fool, come to face me again." When Little Reed stepped out from behind the tree too, sword in hand, Mextli's smile curled into a sneer. "And you're here too. That's quite a name you've given yourself: Our Prince, a prince above all other princes, just as the Feathered Serpent believes himself a god above all other gods."

"There's room for all the gods here in Tollan," Little Reed said. "We give space and honor to everyone."

"Only on terms that weaken the rest of us. Make no mistake; this treason hasn't gone unnoticed, nor will it go unchallenged."

"There is nothing to challenge, Mextli. If you and Smoking Mirror weren't so opposed to change, you'd see it doesn't weaken anyone; it's better, especially for gods such as yourself. The others see this, and so allowed Tollan's construction and the passing of the laws. Smoking Mirror is needlessly fighting the future when both of you could be at the fore of it all."

"Oh, we will be, once I'm standing over your rotting corpse." Mextli flicked the fingers of his left hand and a macuahuitl sword materialized in his fist. "Time to die, Nobody's Prince," he sneered, advancing on Little Reed.

Little Reed raised his sword—and from the corner of my eye I saw Citlallotoc leap at Mextli—but I couldn't let Mextli get anywhere near Little Reed. I let loose the magic dripping from my fingers and it crashed across the clearing, knocking everyone aside, even Mextli. When I pulled back, no one moved. The thick, acidic fruit smell of octli clung to the air. Little Reed lay unconscious next to me.

Mextli came to his feet again, his feathers standing on end. "You certainly are brazen. If it didn't tickle so, I might take exception with your defiance."

I poised myself over Little Reed. "Maybe it tickles now, but come any closer and it won't tickle anymore." I felt no need to let the desire speak for me this time; I would see Mextli in Mictlan before I'd let him hurt Little Reed.

"So eager to throw your life away."

"Everyone dies eventually."

Mextli shook his head. "You have so much to learn...and unlearn."

I laughed. "And I suppose you think yourself the one to teach me?"

"He's certainly doing you no favors." He pointed at Little Reed. "War is coming, and Quetzalcoatl will lose; it's not a question of if—for Heaven has already written the future in the stars, and the Feathered Serpent's blasphemy will end with his destruction. And that of those who helped him. That means you as well. But it's not too late yet to correct that mistake."

"And join Smoking Mirror?" I growled.

"He offers you the one thing the Feathered Serpent won't."

"And what's that?"

"The truth."

I sneered, the anger boiling over. "And here's what I think of his offer." I launched another attack, pouring twice as much magic into it as last time. How dare he think I was weak and power-hungry enough to turn against Quetzalcoatl, after all the god had given me? *I'll shut that impertinent mouth of yours.*

Mextli dropped his sword and held his hands out in front of him, as if to push back against my magic, but now his brow creased with concern. His feet slid on the ground and his arm muscles twitched, his feathers standing on end. His eyes went wide just before he suddenly burst into thousands of tiny blue hummingbirds. They flew in every direction, but then dropped from the air, pummeling the earth like hail. I shielded my head from them as they rained down on me.

Once the downpour ended, I picked one of the birds up from the ground. It twitched in my hand a moment before falling still and crumbling into glowing blue dust. As I looked around, the others did the same, covering the ground with a layer of pulsing blue that slowly dimmed. I stared a moment, taking in what I'd seen, what I'd done. "Great Feathered Serpent! I killed him! I killed a god!" And it hadn't even taken all that much out of me to do it. Magic was still pulsing in my blood, ready at a thought.

That's because we're strong, the desire purred, delighted. *Invincible!* I'd never felt so exhilarated.

But when I turned to Little Reed, he was convulsing, his eyes rolled up in his head. "Little Reed!" I rushed to kneel next to him as he twitched and flinched, a mix of spit and watery vomit leaking out of his mouth. I rolled him over onto his side and thumped his back, trying to clear his mouth and throat. *Dear gods, what have I done?* My panic grew as he went limp. *If he dies, I'll never forgive myself.*

But when he started coughing, dazed, I sat him up and hugged him. "I'm so sorry, Little Reed!" I sobbed.

He said nothing, in such a drunken haze that he had no idea where he was. When he started shivering, I draped my cloak over his shoulders and sat with him, waiting for the others to wake up.

CHAPTER TWENTY-TWO

E ven with Ozomatli in custody, we delayed the trial while Little Reed recovered. I sat at his bedside for two days, keeping watch over him, and when he asked what happened with Mextli, I was too afraid to tell him the truth. If I had indeed killed Mextli, it was amazing Little Reed was still alive, and I didn't want to admit to him that I had very nearly killed him as well.

None of the men were in good condition; Citlallotoc complained of a constant headache for days after, and Black Otter—who had been farthest from me when I'd released my magic—remembered nothing of that night. "One moment that...thing tore that man's heart out, but then I woke up as if from a long night of drinking." He'd been the first to wake from his stupor and had helped me get Little Reed back to the palace. I was glad he didn't remember me using magic, and hopefully that meant the rest of the men didn't either.

As I sat next to Little Reed's bed, I couldn't stop thinking about my conversation with Mextli, and his claims that Quetzalcoatl was keeping secrets from me. I considered going into the Divine Dream to speak with the god, to get reassurances that it was all a ploy to deceive and turn me against him, but how could I take anything that came out of Mextli's mouth seriously? I felt ashamed for even entertaining the notion.

These thoughts soured my mood for Ozomatli's trial and turned my heart to a statue. Smoking Mirror's high priest attempted to grovel his way out of his crimes, claiming to remember nothing of that night—not even going to the clearing with Black Otter and the victim. A convenient excuse. He denied any involvement in the murders, and Little Reed asked pointed questions that reduced him to tears; I could have asked questions too but I merely glared at him with a raw hatred that burned hot as the sun, especially when he tried pushing the blame onto Black Otter, claiming my cousin kept haranguing him to go back to the old ways.

"Whatever Black Otter suggested to you is irrelevant," Little Reed told him when we sat in judgment. "Ultimately, you chose to ignore the law.

While we cannot definitively prove that you killed the men pulled from the ground last month, you were seen by no less than a dozen witnesses raising a knife, poised to kill a man; and so for that reason, we find you guilty of attempted murder. As is the way here in Tollan, by royal proclamation, you are therefore forever exiled from Tolteca lands."

I'd gone along with Little Reed on the sentence when we first discussed it, but my indignation and anger boiled over as we sat for dinner in his quarters afterwards, only the two of us. "He murdered at least twelve people and nearly unleashed that demon god on us. How is only exiling him justice?" I demanded, disgust killing my appetite.

"We can't prove all those murders, and even if we could, Quetzalcoatl's way isn't one life for another," he reminded me. "Capital punishment is still murder, Papalotl. It might alleviate some of the anger in our hearts, but it doesn't heal us where we most need it."

"And neither does exiling him!" I snapped, getting to my feet to pace. I had too much furious energy that needed burning off. Ozomatli was getting away with his treachery yet again.

"We heal by learning to forgive," Little Reed said, maddeningly patient.

"And some things are unforgivable, Little Reed." When he put his arms around me, I wept into his neck. "Some things can't heal," I mumbled, holding him tight.

He held my face between his hands. "I know it seems that way, but love can heal anything. There is no magic more powerful."

I gazed into his eyes, my heart racing. He looked at me with that deep understanding I'd only ever seen in the god's eyes, that love that was the food my soul lived and died for. I wanted so badly to feel something other than this suffocating anger. "Please kiss me," I whispered, my own pleading painful in my throat.

He hesitated but did so, slow and sensual. His hands trailed down my neck, his fingertips raising my flesh so wonderfully, melting away the pain and pressure in my chest. I kissed him back, pressing up against him, the desire swelling, burning bright and delicious. My body did what came naturally; my hands parted his royal robes, exposing his firm bare chest— evidence of his daily workouts in the exercise yard with Citlallotoc. They pushed the robe back further, so it slid from his shoulders, and the knot securing his loincloth posed no challenge.

He followed my example, breaking past the ties of my own robe, fumbling with the ones at the back of my dress until it all puddled around my feet. My skin prickled with the sudden cold, but chills came when his lips left mine to work their way down my neck, my shoulders, my breasts, my belly. I clung to him, ready to float off like a cloud as he moved still lower, his tongue carving an escape path through my pain and straining faith. He knelt before me as if praying before an idol, preparing to give a bit of himself to me in sacrifice, as if I were a goddess he worshiped. Magic tingled all over me, begging for release as I ran my fingers with increasing roughness through his hair....

But memories of him convulsing on the ground...of Mextli bursting apart into thousands of tiny, dying birds, brought me to my senses. *What in Mictlan am I doing?* The desire howled but I shoved it aside. One careless moment was all it took to destroy everything I held dear. I stepped away from him, overcome with regret and shame.

He looked up, worry in his eyes, but before he could say anything, I fled the room, not bothering to grab any of my clothes. I tossed aside the door curtain, and dashed across the empty garden to my own quarters. I threw myself on my bed, huddling up, burying my face in my knees, weeping and shaking.

A moment later, Little Reed's tentative voice came from the door. "Did I do something wrong?"

I shook my head. "Forgive me, Little Reed. You did nothing wrong; it's all me. I'm so sorry. I'm so terribly unfair to you...."

He draped my robe over my naked body and sat next to me, carefully securing his own robe as he did so. "I'm more worried about you. Maybe this whole sacrifice thing...maybe you're over-thinking it, and if we just...once...so much more would make sense."

I laughed. "Nothing will ever make sense, Little Reed. I will never understand why the god chose me to be his high priestess when I'm so weak. Living this life of absolute devotion to him feels as if it's slowly killing me."

"You're not weak, Papalotl," he assured me. "You're exactly the way Heaven made you, and you mustn't be ashamed of that. The priesthood taught us to forsake our physical impulses for the spiritual and mental life, but we can't ignore our deepest needs; we might fast now and then, but it would be crazy to never eat again."

"You can't survive without eating, Little Reed, but you can survive without sex. It's not the same thing."

"No, but that doesn't make it any less important." He lay down next to me and wiped my tears away with the side of his hand. "The god doesn't want you to be miserable."

"It doesn't matter what the god wants. I didn't make my deal with him."

"I know."

Sniffling, I debated whether or not to say more, but my fear had become a rock in my chest, growing heavier the longer I held it inside. I had to tell him. "Even if not for that sacrifice, if we did...dear gods, I almost killed you, Little Reed!"

He furrowed his brow. "What do you mean?"

"That night, out in the forest. I was so angry, so out of control that I kept blasting more and more magic, and...I lied to you, about what happened to Mextli. He didn't merely go away; I threw so much magic at him that he burst into all these tiny birds and they turned to blue dust—"

Little Reed blinked, startled. "He disintegrated?"

I nodded, choking on my own tears. "I killed him, and you were so close to me when I was blasting him.... I nearly killed you too! And now, when we were back in your quarters...what is wrong with me? You give me pleasure, but all I could think about is how much I wanted to release my magic into you." I covered my face with both hands.

"But you didn't."

"No, but had we gone on.... I could have killed you!"

"I doubt it."

His casual denial stung. How could he think my magic so inconsequential, after what I'd done to Mextli? "Why not?"

Caressing my cheek, he smiled warmly. "Because I trust you with every fiber of my tonalli."

His words brought me to fresh tears and I hugged him, so grateful to have his love and trust. He pulled me to him, kissing me gently and taking no precautions to keep our bare flesh from pressing together. I expected the growling desire to jump at this second chance, but it gave me peace. His every careful touch made my stomach flutter and my head swim, and I felt as nervous as a young bride on the fourth night of her wedding, preparing to consummate for the first time—strange since I hadn't felt this vulnerable and scared when Black Otter had taken my maidenhead.

Neither was this frantic or demanding; everything moved slowly and deliberately, as it always did with the god—merely one more way to so easily mix them up in my head, confusing what I should and shouldn't do. An unspoken plea lay in his eyes; *Just once.* And if I trusted him as much as he trusted me, why not? Maybe he was right and things would finally start making sense. And maybe it was already too late; I bit my bottom lip hard, trying to suppress the moan as his gently manipulating fingers brought on the first warning waves of pleasure—

But suddenly he jumped away from me, yelping in surprise. From the edge of my bed, Yamehecatl swung his play sword at him, rage boiling on our son's face. Little Reed tried to dodge him, but Yamehecatl clipped his bare leg, sending him limping off, cursing.

"What on earth are you doing?" I yelled at Yamehecatl, scrambling for my robe as he went after Little Reed again, this time swiping his sword at his father's exposed crotch. Little Reed fended him off with both hands until I grabbed Yamehecatl from behind and disarmed him.

"You won't hurt my Nantli!" Yamehecatl shouted as I dragged him over to the bed, so Little Reed could retreat from the corner.

The guards burst into the room, spears ready. They usually stayed posted at the main entrance to our family gardens, to give us privacy, but they must have heard the commotion and come running. "Is everything all right, My Lord?"

Little Reed quickly tied his robe closed and assured them we were fine and ushered them back out onto the portico. He stood facing the closed curtain for a moment before turning his cross expression on Yamehecatl. "Why in Mictlan would you think I'd hurt your mother?"

"You were making her cry!" Yamehecatl retorted. "Lord Green Water made one of the servants cry out in the main garden the other day, and Night Wind wouldn't let me go help her, but I won't let anyone make Nantli cry. Not even you." He glared at Little Reed.

"I wasn't crying, dear," I assured him, laughing if only to not look mortified. How long had he been watching us from his nursery curtain?

"You looked as if you were crying." He still stared down Little Reed. "Citlallotoc says that men who hurt women aren't men at all."

"I wasn't hurting your mother," Little Reed assured him, irritated.

Yamehecatl looked to me and when I nodded in agreement, he pinched his mouth together, tears forming. "I'm sorry I hit you, Tatli," he muttered, his jaw quivering.

Little Reed knelt in front of him. "A good man defends those in trouble, so I applaud your desire to protect your mother...and that other woman. But for now on, it would be better for you to report things that worry you to an adult, who can better assess a situation. It's a good thing Night Wind held you back or Lord Green Water and his...friend would have been very upset with you." Under his breath he added, "Though I must talk with him about spending time with her in the gardens."

Yamehecatl nodded, sniffling. He hugged Little Reed, whispering more apologies that Little Reed accepted with gentle reassurances and chuckles. When Yamehecatl returned to me, he climbed into my lap. "Can I stay with you tonight, Nantli?"

I looked at Little Reed and he nodded, resigned but still smiling. "Very well," I told Yamehecatl, and he scrambled under my blankets, nestling in. As Little Reed turned to leave, I said, "You can stay, if you wish." The three of us hadn't shared a bed since our return trip to Culhuacan, right after Yamehecatl was born.

He thought about it but said, "We'll all be more comfortable if I'm in my own bed." He gave my hand a squeeze and left.

I stared at the curtain for a while, numb with realization. No matter how much I wanted to believe we'd built the perfect marriage and family, no matter how much I wanted to think that sex wasn't important at all—to either of us—it was in fact the invisible wedge keeping us from ever being truly happy.

And a time would come when I couldn't expect his holding out hope for something that would never happen would continue to keep him with me.

¤

With Ozomatli sentenced to exile, we needed to appoint a new high priest of the Smoking Mirror, and Little Reed had the perfect candidate.

"I know you said you had no desire to be a priest, Cousin, but I would consider it a personal favor if you took the position," he told Black Otter as we walked from our family garden towards the great hall. "You already have the appropriate training, and after helping us save Smoking Mirror's priesthood, you're the perfect man to lead the cult into the future. Your father brought Smoking Mirror's worship to the Tolteca, so it's only right that you should reform it and turn it into a strong entity that flourishes throughout the empire."

Black Otter smiled. "There was a time when I wouldn't have considered it my first choice of vocation, but the thought of turning my father's work into something positive does appeal to me."

"A noble endeavor. It's also my honor to return your noble title to you, so you might pass it and all its inherent value down to your children. And as the new high priest, we invite you to move your family into the priestly quarters of the palace, and both of your children will be guaranteed educations in the calmecac."

"That is most gracious of you, My Lord." Black Otter bowed.

"I personally want to thank you for your help with the situation with Ozomatli. You saved Tollan from possible disaster, and we shall never forget that." Little Reed embraced him.

Looking embarrassed, Black Otter embraced him back. "Thank you for your faith in me."

"There are ceremonies and fasts you must do to cleanse yourself before taking your vows as high priest, and Quetzalpetlatl will go over that with you. Now, if you'll excuse me, Lord Flame Tongue arrived last night and I'm taking him deer hunting this afternoon." He departed with a nod to each of us.

Black Otter continued walking with me. "I must thank you as well, My Lady, for this opportunity."

"It's my pleasure," I said.

"If my moving here into the palace makes you at all uncomfortable—"

"It doesn't make me uncomfortable at all, Cousin. The past is over, and you've more than proven your loyalty. If anything, I'm glad to have you back in my life, and highly pleased our sons will grow up together, the way *we* should have been allowed to. Night Wind has been a very good friend to Yamehecatl."

"You honor me, My Lady." We walked in silence a moment before he spoke again. "I never got the chance to apologize to you."

"For what?"

"For everything my father did. For all the shame he's brought upon our family."

I stopped and faced him. "And as I told your brother, you don't bear any of your father's shame, especially when...and I've debated whether or not to tell you this, but...he wasn't your father at all. Nochuatl was. And I know this because he admitted as much to me."

I expected surprise, but instead, he bowed his head and nodded. "I suspected as much, especially given how often people said I looked like our uncle, and how upset my father would get when they did. He forbade anyone from mentioning Nochuatl's name."

"You owe Ihuitimal nothing, and you bear no shame for his crimes. They are his own."

"Perhaps, but I do owe him. He knew the truth and yet...why didn't he kill me when I was a babe? Why did he instead raise me as his own son?"

I sighed. "Maybe because even the most terrible among us are capable of compassion and kindness under the right circumstances."

"Truth be told, I wanted to disbelieve my gut about him, so things would be simpler and I wouldn't feel bad about loving him."

"He was the only father you knew, so you shouldn't feel bad. He loved you, Black Otter, and Amoxtli too, and that counts for something."

"Forgive me, but I'd rather not talk about him anymore," Black Otter said, walking again. "Perhaps you could instead instruct me on what kinds of fasting and ceremonies I need to go through before taking the high priest position?"

I continued walking as well. "In most priesthoods, candidates journey to Teotihuacan to do their cleansing rituals; but as I understand it, the tradition in Smoking Mirror's order is to go into the desert. There's a camp to the north for that very purpose. You'll need to fast for a total of three days and pray for five, then return to take your vows before myself and Topiltzin. You'll leave for the camp tomorrow, so the cult is without a high priest for as few days as possible. We're sending a small regiment of soldiers north to escort Ozomatli out of Tolteca lands, so you can travel with them."

"What of my children? Night Wind is at the calmecac, of course, but Cuicatl comes home from the telpochcalli each night. I don't wish her to be alone while I'm gone."

"We'll move the two of you into the palace today and she will be looked after. And while you're gone, I'll get her properly placed in the calmecac."

"Thank you, My Lady."

We finally reached the Hall of the Gods, where we would part ways—

me to the palace steward to see to Black Otter's new quarters, and him to the temple to meet with Smoking Mirror's high priestess and other ranking priests. I'd debated all morning whether or not to tell Black Otter the other secret I had, about Ozomatli; knowing that conniving priest was walking away yet again—and this time only with a slap for his ambitions—enraged me, no matter how Little Reed spoke of the god's ways. The families of the victims deserved better. Black Otter and Amoxtli deserved better.

Black Otter started to bid me goodbye, but I cut him off. "I know you said you don't want to talk about your father anymore, but there's something you should know."

"Oh?"

"Ozomatli was poisoning his ritual mushrooms; that's why your father started looking so sickly those last few months of his life. And Amoxtli nearly died using those poisoned teonanacatl, and when he worked out Ozomatli was trying to kill your father, Ozomatli betrayed him to my brother's men, hoping Topiltzin would kill him. Luckily Topiltzin isn't that kind of man."

Black Otter stared at me with a darkness I'd never before seen in him, momentarily reminding me of Ihuitimal. "Thank you for telling me this, My Lady," he said and walked away.

No matter what conflicts Black Otter felt about Ihuitimal, the man had treated him as a son, and Black Otter would avenge him. I tried to smile, knowing justice would finally be served, but inside a part of me cringed. Was I effectively ordering Ozomatli's execution?

Part of the obligations of a ruler is making certain those who have been wronged are given justice, I reminded myself as I continued walking. But a wave of doubt and regret followed me for many days after that, for who was I to question the rightness of Quetzalcoatl's wishes?

¤

"Can I talk to you?" Malinalli lurked in the doorway of my private meditation room, looking nervous.

I set aside the copalli burner, making a place for her on the mats in front of the hearth. "Of course. What's on your mind?"

She fussed with her hands a moment, then took a deep breath. "Well, if

I can't tell you this, we must not really be best friends." She cleared her throat then said, "Remember how we talked last month, about me meeting someone?"

I nodded and before she could speak again, I said, "If it makes it easier, I already know."

She blinked at me. "How—"

"I saw the two of you in the garden, and it was quite obvious. You look at her like I look at Topiltzin."

She paused. "It doesn't make you uncomfortable?"

"I'm only embarrassed that I jumped to the wrong conclusions when we first talked about this. I'm sorry."

She let out a breath and smiled. "It's all right. That's a rather normal assumption to make, really. And I've tried to feel differently than I do; for a short while I was a nobleman's lover, while we were in Culhuacan, when Ihuitimal was still king, but that changed nothing; if anything, his taking the choice away from me solidified my predilections; no woman has ever forced me into her bed."

My stomach clenched. "Why didn't you tell me of this?" *I could have done something to stop it,* I almost added, but who was I fooling? Those were the dark days when women couldn't legally complain about such things, and they certainly couldn't demand a nobleman respect their autonomy by actually asking permission.

"You had your own burdens, and besides, it's only now that I can actually speak about it without getting upset. Mitotia has been very supportive and understanding. She's helped me move on."

I hugged her tight. "You amaze me with your strength, Malinalli. You stood up for me to Turquoise Bells when I'd behaved horrendously with Red Flint, took me in when Nimilitzli died and I thought Topiltzin was dead, saved me from Red Flint, and defended me against that horrible Captain Storm House when we were captured and taken to Culhuacan." I sighed. "What have I done to deserve such good friendship?"

Malinalli took my hand in hers. "Before you sat and talked to me on the boat ride back from Teotihuacan...I'd never had any real friends. And I've been thankful for every day since—even the bad ones." She wiped a tear away. "You won't tell Topiltzin, about me and Mitotia?"

"He wouldn't bat an eye, but no, I won't tell him."

We spent the rest of the afternoon eating lunch and reminiscing about our younger days. Oh how I wished I'd talked to her the first time I saw her at calmecac instead of waiting until that disasterous trip to Teotihuacan. So many years of friendship missed because I'd been too shy—and too hurt from life—to return her friendly smile that first time.

PART FOUR
THE YEAR TWO RABBIT

CHAPTER TWENTY-THREE

Most children don't live past the first three years of life. Many succumb to common childhood ailments or drink bad water, leaving them desiccated shells. Out in the fields, where the farmers live, more often than not wily ocelotls steal infants from their baskets in the middle of the night. And even if one survives the infancy illnesses or avoids becoming a predatory cat's dinner, childhood curiosity claims quite a few more; several children drown in the canals each year, or they slip and fall out of tall trees, or they mistake wild dogs for the tame ones the merchants raise for the dinner table.

And just as many dangers lurk in the palace: poisonous snakes and insects live in the gardens, and cruel-hearted servants take their frustrations with their masters out on the vulnerable. The most dangerous of all are the rivalries between a king or nobleman's kept women as they vie for power on behalf of their sons. Luckily neither I nor Little Reed had to worry about such nonsense in our household.

The world—and the gods—was seldom kind to children, hence the reason we Tolteca refrained from bestowing a permanent, sacred name on our children until they'd survived to the age of seven; by then, they'd learned to be careful with their lives.

Despite his fearless determination and bouts of sudden drunkenness, Yamehecatl managed what many children didn't, and he was finally going to learn his real name.

With the years, he'd developed better control of his emotions, so it was rare for him to fall over drunk anymore, but he still didn't spend his nights at the priestly dormitories with the other boys. We'd told him that if he could go six months without an incident, we'd know he was ready to go to school full-time with his friend and cousin Night Wind. The two had grown closer with the years, and Yamehecatl had made it his goal to move into the dorms by his naming day. And he'd succeeded in that too.

He was full of pride and cheer the morning of his naming day. He dressed in an eagle-feather shirt I'd made for him—identical to the one Citlallotoc wore—and I braided jade beads and feathers into his hair, so it looked as if he wore a headdress. I'd feared he'd want to wear his rabbit uniform, since he'd insisted I make him a new one when he outgrew the old, but he'd picked out the eagle shirt instead, along with a set of elbow and ankle bracelets inlaid with shell rattles. He made lots of noise when he moved, "So the gods know I'm coming to talk to them today," he told me, showing off the gap where both of his front baby teeth had fallen out last week. My little boy was growing up so fast!

We went to the Hall of the Gods to wait for Little Reed, but Yamehecatl scampered off into the courtyard when he saw Night Wind playing patolli with one of the older boys. Night Wind had sprouted up tall the last couple of years, his already serious demeanor lending him the air of a much older boy than his mere nine summers. He grinned when Yamehecatl came up and sat next to him, making my son look so little again.

"Thank you for giving him the day off from school, so he could spend it with Yamehecatl on his naming day." I turned to see Black Otter standing a bit behind me, wearing his black high priest robes, and looking tired. He always looked as much these days. He'd been scrawny and underfed when he came to Tollan two years ago and I'd expected him to fatten up once he'd moved into the palace and returned to the luxurious noble life, but he was even thinner now. Perhaps being Smoking Mirror's high priest wasn't as fulfilling as I found being Quetzalcoatl's high priestess was.

"It's my pleasure." I looked back at our boys again with a smile. Night Wind had won the game, leaving the older boy scowling as he scooped up his winnings—little clay disks the children earned in class for doing well on exams or answering difficult questions. They used them to buy extra food at meal times or tobacco from one of the high priests. "Are you coming to the feast tonight too?"

"Do you wish me to?" Black Otter asked, surprised.

I laughed. "Of course I do. Half the empire will be here, so why wouldn't I invite you? You're family."

"Thank you."

"I wish Amoxtli was here too," I added. "I've really missed him since he went back to Culhuacan." He'd taken the fire priest position there, vowing to see Quetzalcoatl's cult fully restored in his home city.

Black Otter nodded, looking sickly.

I turned to grip his arm. "Are you all right?"

"I'm fine."

"You don't look it. You're not sick, are you?"

He chuckled, looking embarrassed. "Thank you for your concern, but really, I'm not sick. It's not as easy being a high priest as I thought it would be. There's so much to do all the time. Frankly, I don't know how either you or Topiltzin do it and also rule the kingdom."

"We don't do everything ourselves. If you need to, lean on your fire priest or Yaretzi some more. The priesthood is a group effort."

"I'd rather avoid Yaretzi," he said. "She's become rather...forward in her attentions the last few months."

"Jade Flower *has* been gone almost three years now, long enough to have gone on to her eternal rest in Mictlan. Maybe it's time to start looking for someone for yourself again. Children need a mother."

"Yes, but not her," he said. "Most definitely not her."

"She's not to your tastes?"

"She's...eerie."

I knew what he spoke of, for she made me uneasy as well.

Voices from the guest wing distracted my attention. Little Reed and Citlallotoc came into the Hall of the Gods, walking with several of our allies from the valley. Flame Tongue of Xico walked at Little Reed's shoulder, speaking loudly of how prosperous Xico had become in the years since adopting Tollan's code of laws. "You wouldn't believe the sheer numbers of fish our small fleet of boats pull out of the waters these days. Xochimilco has twice as many boats, fishing the very same waters, and yet the fish practically jump into ours. Certainly a sign from the god, since Xochimilco has balked at completely abandoning human sacrifice the way we have."

Little Reed wore his smile like a mask, but I recognized it was strained. Flame Tongue had arrived last night and kept me and Little Reed up late with his incessant chatter; one would think he never got to talk at home.

Seeing me, Little Reed's smile broadened and he took the opportunity to hurry ahead and embrace me. He'd aged quite a bit in the last year; his hair had gone white, and his wrinkles were pronounced cracks. He let the stubble grow on his chin, since he found it painful to grip his obsidian shaving blade, and he would only allow me to shave him, joking that he trusted me alone with a blade to his throat. He also climbed the temple steps more slowly these days. I was dreadfully aware that there were fewer years ahead of us now than there were behind us. He kissed my cheek—leaving me hot and fidgety. "Where's Yamehecatl? Are we ready to go to the soothsayer?"

Yamehecatl tugged at Little Reed's robe. "I'm right here, Tatli!"

With a roaring laugh, he hefted Yamehecatl into his arms. "My, have you gotten heavy!" he said, putting him down slowly. "I'm afraid your tatli isn't as young as he used to be," he added, rubbing his back as he stood up again. "So, are you ready to go and find out your true name?"

"I certainly am! I hope it's something good!"

Little Reed took his hand. "All true names are good ones; even the ones that don't seem good at first, they turn out perfect in the end. The gods know us better than we know ourselves."

"I hope it's something fierce, like Bloody Rabbit or Snarling Coyote."

Little Reed laughed and ruffled his hair. "Let's get going, before we're late." He turned to the crowd stopped behind him. "I will see everyone at the ritual ball game this afternoon, but in the meantime, Lord Citlallotoc will take you on a tour of the city."

Flame Tongue and the other lords followed Citlallotoc down the stairs into the courtyard. A group of women followed behind, and when I waved to Anacoana—looking lovely and regal among her handmaidens—she hurried over to greet me. "It's so good to see you again, My Lady."

I embraced her, making her blush. "I'm so glad you could make the journey. The last time I saw you, you were still so young, but you have blossomed into a stunning woman."

Her blush deepened and she glanced at Black Otter, no recognition in her eyes; but she kept glancing back at him as we exchanged the customary pleasantries. Black Otter paid her no attention, looking out of place instead, so I reintroduced them. "My Lady, I know it's been a number of years now since you last saw him, but certainly you remember Lord Black Otter?"

Anacoana gasped. "I thought that might be you, My Lord." She gave him a courteous bow. "It's a pleasure to see you again after so long."

Black Otter gazed back at her, surprised. "Lady Anacoana? I didn't recognize you. You're so...."

"Grown up," I provided with a knowing smile.

He looked flustered, but before he could say anything, Flame Tongue called for his daughter from the courtyard. She gave me, Black Otter, and Little Reed a hurried bow then ran to catch up with the rest of the group. When she reached her father he barked at her, making her bow her head even lower than usual. He continued glaring at Black Otter as the group departed through the front gate.

"He's not at all happy to see me," Black Otter noted, a worried look on his face. He was right, and that squashed all those newborn thoughts of perhaps trying to get the two back together again now that Anacoana was a good age for marriage.

When Night Wind joined us, Little Reed asked Black Otter, "Will you take your son to the ball game today? Everyone's invited."

Black Otter shook his head, distracted. "I have things I must do this afternoon."

Yamehecatl looked crestfallen until Little Reed suggested, "In that case, if you don't mind, Night Wind can come with me and Yamehecatl and sit in the royal box. I'm certain the boys will have great fun watching the game."

Black Otter cast a questioning gaze at Night Wind, who nodded, all business. "That's most kind of you, My Lord. Thank you."

"Can Night Wind come with us when we go to the soothsayer?" Yamehecatl asked, turning pup eyes on Little Reed.

But Little Reed shook his head. "The soothsayer's house is small and cluttered, so there's barely enough room for you, me, and your mother. You can tell him all about your new name when we get back."

Yamehecatl opened his mouth to argue, but Night Wind told him, "It's all right, Cousin. I promised Blue House that I'd whip him at patolli, and I'm a man of my word."

"Let us get going, before we're truly late." Little Reed took my hand with his free one. Yamehecatl jumped up and down, excited, and ran ahead of us, his guards scurrying after him. When I looked back to wave goodbye to Black Otter, he watched us go with a sad, melancholy expression on his face.

¤

"Come on! Hurry up, Nantli! We're going to be late!" Yamehecatl tried pulling me through the sacred precinct, but when I made no move to walk faster, he let me go and ran ahead with the guards, clearing the way. I stayed back with Little Reed, holding his hand.

"In such a hurry to grow up." To Little Reed, I added, "He gets that from you, you know."

Little Reed laughed. "I remember thinking adults intentionally walked slowly just to annoy me. Now I know it's because their bones ache when they move too fast."

I squeezed his hand and smiled, determined not to show that his jest pained me.

The soothsayer's house sat at the north end of the precinct, nestled between the shadows of the temples of Xilonen and the Feathered Serpent. It was a small building made of stone, the same as the surrounding temples, but the inside more resembled a house. The single room's light came from the open door curtain and a small hearth, and there wasn't much room to move around inside; baskets overflowing with cotton cloth took up one side and stacks of maguey-fiber manuscripts filled the other. A man in a black robe sat on a reed mat in front of the smoking hearth, hunched over an open book. But when he looked up at us, he immediately came to his feet. "My Lord and Lady," he said with a flourishing bow, sweeping his fingers across the ground at our feet. "Your visit brings me much joy!"

Little Reed nudged Yamehecatl forward. "Today our son turns the seventh page of his life."

The man smiled at Yamehecatl. "Ah yes, the young prince's naming day! Are you ready to hear your destiny, My Lord?"

"Of course!" Yamehecatl answered with a bright smile. "What must I do?"

The soothsayer beckoned him over to the reed mat and Yamehecatl sat while the man ventured to one of the shelves where he kept a box of the sacred mushrooms. He chewed a small handful of them as he ran his finger over the spines of the manuscripts, counting as he went. Finding the volume he wanted, he brought it back. "Before we get to the actual naming, I shall tell you about your tonalli, so you will know who you are and what your destiny is."

"I already know I'm destined to be the King," Yamehecatl said.

"Yes, but there's more to you than that, my young lord. Reading your tonalli will help you realize your ambitions and become the best king you can be." He sat next to Yamehecatl and opened the book. "You were born on the day Nine Wind, which is the ninth day of the second week of the Tonalamatl. The god Quetzalcoatl rules your soul, for Nine Wind is one of his sacred days."

Yamehecatl looked at the book and read, "Nine Winds are compassionate people who show great sympathy for others."

"You can read the sacred script?" the soothsayer asked, startled.

"My Nantli taught me." Yamehecatl beamed at me. "She's a really good teacher."

"That's very impressive. Maybe you can read the rest to us?"

Yamehecatl dove in, reading each glyph carefully, sometimes pausing to work things out. "Nine Winds are extremely analytical and curious about the world. They want to know how the world works, and why."

"He'll do well in the priesthood," Little Reed noted, proud.

But the soothsayer shook his head. "Actually, Nine Winds tend not to be particularly religious, and they don't flourish in such environments. When it comes to spirituality, they prefer to find their own way."

Little Reed frowned, puzzled, so I offered, "But that's good too. At least he won't blindly follow doctrine. That's what we're trying to teach everyone, right?"

He nodded, conceding the point. "Does this mean we shouldn't put him in the calmecac?"

"Some elements will speak to him while others will aggravate him," the soothsayer said. "But he won't learn all that interests him by going to the telpochcalli either, where they don't teach reading or writing or mathematics."

Yamehecatl stared at us, a look of panic on his face; would we back out on our promise to let him go to school with Night Wind because of this?

Hoping to put him at ease, I suggested to Little Reed, "We can put together a special curriculum, one that brings the best of both schools to him."

Little Reed nodded. "A good idea."

The soothsayer returned the book to its stack and sat again. "I think the gods are ready to speak your name now."

Yamehecatl sat cross-legged as the soothsayer sat very still, meditating. When Yamehecatl started fidgeting, the man suddenly opened his eyes and said, "Ehecacone. That is the name the gods have chosen for you, the name you shall carry the remainder of your days."

"Son of the Wind?" Yamehecatl wrinkled his nose. "My tatli is not windy, except when he eats beans!"

The soothsayer stifled a laugh but my own came out as a bray that prompted Little Reed to blush. "That's not what is meant by the Wind," the soothsayer explained. "It refers to Lord Quetzalcoatl, Tollan's most beloved god."

"Oh." Yamehecatl tapped his chin thoughtfully, brow still creased. "But my tatli isn't Quetzalcoatl." He turned to Little Reed. "Are you?"

The soothsayer said, "Son doesn't mean actual son; we are all sons and daughters of the Feathered Serpent, for it was with his sacrifice that he gave us all life. That is all it means."

Yamehecatl glanced at Little Reed again, who gave him a smile. "Well, I suppose it will do."

I laughed and took Yamehecatl by the hand as Little Reed paid the soothsayer a bolt of fine cloth for his services. "It's a good strong name for a king," I assured him.

◻

It was still several hours until the celebratory ball game, so while Yamehecatl went to find Night Wind—to share his new name and do some roughhousing before lunch—I went to the kitchens to check on the menu for tonight's feast. The mixing aromas of roasting venison, caiman, rabbit, fish, and chiles gave the air a heavy feel, and the heat was stifling; I didn't know how the servants spent all day every day in here, preparing meal after meal for the nobles they served.

I was about to sample one of the sweet maize cakes my son loved so dearly when Yamehecatl came into the kitchen, looking cross. "No one knows where Night Wind is. We were supposed to play this morning."

"Maybe he had to help his father with something." When he peered over the edge of the large cooking stone to watch the maize cakes frying, I pushed him away. "Not so close, Yamehecatl. It's very hot."

He puckered up his face. "My name isn't Yamehecatl anymore. It's Ehecacone."

"I know. I'm sorry. To me you've always been Yamehecatl, so please forgive me if I don't immediately call you by your new name." But in my heart, he would always be my little Warm Breeze. I took his hand and led him out of the kitchen; the cooks didn't need a child underfoot.

"Do you like my name, Nantli?"

"I do."

We walked in silence for a moment before Yamehecatl asked, "Tatli isn't Quetzalcoatl, is he?"

If only he were, I thought with a chuckle. My life might have been so much simpler. "No, he's not. He's the god's son, not the god himself."

Yamehecatl nodded. Then, after a hesitation, he asked, "Is Tatli really my tatli?" He gazed up at me with pleading in his eyes.

I'd often debated telling him the truth, and I knew eventually it would come up—for Yamehecatl was intelligent and never forgot anything—but still, seeing the desperation on his face broke my heart. I had to tell him, but how to do it without hurting him?

I thought about that conversation Black Otter and I had several years ago, about his own father, and the answer came to me.

I knelt in front of Yamehecatl and took both of his hands in mine. "You know Black Otter, Night Wind's father?"

"Of course."

"Black Otter was raised by my uncle as his own son even though Ihuitimal was not really his father—someone else was—but that didn't matter because Ihuitimal treated him well and loved him the same as he would his own son; in every way that mattered, he was Black Otter's tatli."

"Then Tatli isn't my father?" he asked, near tears now. "And my name—?"

"The god might have put you in my belly, but the king is your tatli in every way that matters, and nothing can take that away from you; he will always be there for you, and he will love you no matter what."

Yamehecatl smiled, wiping his tears away. "Will you do something with me, Nantli?"

"I'd love to, but there's so much to do to prepare for tonight—"

"Please?" Fresh tears rolled down his cheeks.

I hated seeing him cry—especially when I caused it—and really, why shouldn't I give my son an hour or two? He wouldn't be a child forever and I'd regret all those missed opportunities. "Very well, my dear. What do you want to do?"

"Will you teach me how you do magic?" he asked, hopeful. "I told Night Wind that you could do magic, and he bet that I could do magic too because that kind of things gets passed down in families."

I couldn't quite keep the irritation from my voice. "You told Night Wind that I can do magic?"

"Don't worry, I told him he can't tell anyone, not even his tatli, and he promised not to. His word is good, Nantli."

"That may be, but we've discussed this before; I don't want you telling anyone about my magic. People can be uneasy about that kind of thing, and fear undermines my ability to rule."

"If I have magic, Nantli, I'm going to tell everybody because *ayya!* I hope I have it!"

I sighed. He still had so much to learn. "Tell me, do you ever get a tingling in your fingers or your hands?"

He nodded, getting excited. "When I fall asleep on my hand, or sometimes my feet start tingling when Lord Mazatzin makes me sit still for the entire lesson."

Chuckling, I said, "That's not magic. Everyone's hands and feet do that when they lay or sit on them too long. Have you ever made anything move by willing it to do so?"

"No."

"Have you ever spoken to an animal and they understood you?" He started to get excited again, until I added, "A wild animal, I mean, not the tame birds in the menagerie."

He grumbled, "No." He started to sniffle. "Night Wind was wrong."

I sighed. "Just because you don't have magic now doesn't mean you won't in the future. I didn't acquire my magic until almost eight years ago, when I became pregnant with you."

Yamehecatl eyed me, shocked. "Did you steal my magic, Nantli?"

I laughed and hugged him. "Heavens no! I'm certain yours is asleep, as mine was, and when the time's right—when you're ready—it will wake up."

He smiled, still disappointed but putting on a brave face. "Can we go to the priestly gardens and you can tell me about the flowers?"

"Anything you want, dear. It's your special day, after all."

As we passed the great hall on the way to my quarters—so we could take the secret passageway out to the priestly gardens—I spotted Citlallotoc standing with Flame Tongue, trying mightily to not look pained as the older man prattled on about the magnificence of his own great hall back in Xico. Anacoana stood off to the side, glancing clandestinely over at Citlallotoc every now and again. Citlallotoc had long ago laughed at any notion of an attraction between them, but given the flush on her cheeks when she looked at him, he'd be a fool to not notice.

I stepped into the great hall. "Lord Citlallotoc, if you wouldn't mind, I require your assistance."

Citlallotoc hastily bowed to Flame Tongue and begged his forgiveness for the interruption, then he came to me and Yamehecatl. "What is it, My Lady?"

"I'll speak with you on the way, but rest assured it is urgent," I said loudly, making certain Flame Tongue could hear me. I grabbed Citlallotoc's arm with my free hand and led both him and Yamehecatl out of the room.

Once out of earshot of the great hall, Citlallotoc asked, "What is so urgent, My Lady?"

"Getting you away from that braggart," I said with a smile. "I cannot imagine a more tedious job than entertaining Lord Flame Tongue."

He chuckled. "Was I so obvious? Thank you for the rescue."

Yamehecatl broke free of my hand and circled around to grab Citlallotoc's. "Guess what? I have a new name! Can you guess what it is?"

Citlallotoc smiled. "I wouldn't even begin to venture a guess, but judging by the looks of you, it's a good one."

"I'm now Ehecacone! I'm the son of Quetzalcoatl!"

"That is a fantastic name, very strong."

He nodded. "Nantli and I are going to the priestly gardens. Do you want to come with us?"

Glancing between me and Yamehecatl, he said, "I wouldn't want to intrude on your time with your mother—"

"We would welcome your company," I said. "Unless you'd rather go back to Flame Tongue and listen to him talk about how much better his artisans are back in Xico."

"No thank you."

I laughed and led the way.

CHAPTER TWENTY-FOUR

O nce out in the gardens, Yamehecatl ran ahead of us, swinging an invisible sword at the flowers and trees. "Don't worry, Nantli! I'll protect you!" He made his own shooting-arrow sounds and cries of invisible enemies dying.

"He certainly has war in his heart," Citlallotoc noted with a lopsided grin.

"Gods know where he gets it from," I said.

"He'll outgrow it."

"I hope so." I watched Yamehecatl barrel through the flowerbeds, leaving a swath of destruction; I always felt guilty asking the other priests and priestesses to fix the disasters he left everywhere in the garden. "Let's talk about something else," I suggested.

"Very well. What would you like to talk about?"

"Anacoana," I said with a sly smile. As his friend, I considered it not only my duty to rescue him from tedious Flame Tongue, but to also pry information out of him regarding a mutual attraction for the braggart's only unmarried daughter.

He cast me a startled glance. "What about her?"

"I bet she really enjoyed your tour of the city today." The sudden flare of color in his cheeks told me I'd hit the right spot. "I see you're not completely oblivious to that longing look she's always giving you. So, tell me, what are you going to do about it?"

He hesitated. "I'm not going to do anything about it."

"Why ever not? She's very nice and kind, and very beautiful."

He cringed when I said that. Puzzling. "She is."

"But?"

"She's too young."

I laughed. "Many would argue that at nineteen, she's too old."

"Lord Flame Tongue would never agree to a marriage between us."

"Why not?"

"Because what father would marry his only remaining daughter to someone who looks like a monster?"

I laughed again, with a touch of annoyance. "You don't look like a monster."

This time his laugh was hollow. "I know what the women say behind my back, when they think I can't hear them. 'Pity about his arm; he used to be quite handsome before that.'"

"Anyone who says that is an idiot. And we both know Anacoana is not one of them; I see the way she looks at you."

"And what way is that?" he asked, bitter.

"As if you're the moon and the stars and the gods, all wrapped up in one person. I bet even her father notices, and he's waiting for you to ask about tying your cape to her dress."

The scowl slowly vanished, this time replaced with uncertainty. "You really think so?"

"Absolutely. And he'd be a fool to turn you down; you'll make an excellent husband, and a father too—a far better one than he ever thought of being." I took hold of his arm and hugged it to me as we walked. "Don't you think it's time you settled down?"

Citlallotoc put on a distant smile. "She *is* quite stunning."

"Ask her father tonight at dinner. You will make her the happiest woman in the world."

We reached a small grove of trees and I was about to sit, but Yamehecatl came up, looking vexed. "You said you would do something with me."

"I will, when I'm ready," I scolded him. He always expected me to jump and do whatever he wanted, but the long walk left my feet aching and I wanted to rest a little while. Little Reed wasn't the only one with aches.

"We can do something while your mother takes a break," Citlallotoc suggested.

"I want to do something with Nantli!" Yamehecatl spat.

"And we will," I assured him.

He rolled his eyes. "No, you'll keep talking to Citlallotoc about that stupid woman."

I cast him a scathing frown. "That kind of rudeness is unacceptable, Yamehecatl."

One would think I'd shoved him; his eyes grew twice their normal size and he shouted, "That is not my name! Stop calling me that! That's a baby's name and I'm not a baby!"

His overreaction so startled me that I didn't say anything.

Citlallotoc didn't share my reticence; he advanced on Yamehecatl like an angry bear. "You will not speak to your mother that way, little man. You will show her respect at all times."

"I don't have to!" I caught a whiff of octli on the breeze and Yamehecatl started swaying on his feet. "Why should I, when all she wanted to do was get rid of me before I was even born?" He turned to me, anger ebbing from him. "Why did you want to kill me, Nantli? What had I done to make you hate me so?"

Yamehecatl was often nasty when the drunkenness took him, and this wasn't even the first time he'd brought up this particular thorn in my conscience, but to even suggest that I hated him stung so deeply I had no words. I wanted to hug him and apologize for something I knew I could never apologize enough for.

Citlallotoc was having none of it. "I'm putting you over my knee!" He reached out to grab Yamehecatl by the arm.

But my son darted away from him rabbit-fast, shouting all manner of profanities I didn't even know he knew. He ran fast as he could, stumbling but somehow keeping his feet. Citlallotoc moved to follow him, but I grabbed his wrist and held him back.

"Let him go," I said, my voice choked.

"You can't let him disrespect you!"

"Let him run; there's no use wearing ourselves out trying to catch him when he's in that state. He'll tire quickly"

Citlallotoc watched him bound through the tall grass near the garden's back wall. "What on earth triggered him?"

"I don't know." My choke turned to tears and I started shaking. "He doesn't know what he's saying when he gets like that."

"I'm a terrible mother," I muttered, trying not to completely lose it.

"You're a wonderful mother."

I watched Yamehecatl skipping happily, his anger now forgotten for laughter. He tripped and fell, disappearing in the grass, and when he didn't stand up again, I knew he'd finally passed out. "I so desperately want to help him, but I have no idea how."

"My mother told me once that there's no harder job than being a mother, and she always laughed when Father complained about having to sit around for a few hours listening to his war council. I think I'm inclined to believe her. Let's go and get him, and I'll carry him back to the palace for you and we can put him to bed. Maybe he'll recover in time for dinner."

I doubted that. He would probably sleep until midnight.

We walked out to where Yamehecatl fell, but he wasn't there. Great, he was hiding from us. He knew I hated that. We split up and walked through the grass, looking for him—he certainly couldn't have gone far in his condition. "Ehecacone, enough hiding. You need to go home and sleep this off." Hopefully remembering his proper name this time would help.

But he still didn't answer.

Citlallotoc wove through the grass, moving farther and farther away from me. "Enough games, little man. Show yourself."

But still nothing.

I scoured the grass around me in a wide swath with growing concern. Where was my son? I called out to him over and over again as I moved from place to place, praying he'd suddenly jump out and scare me. "Yamehecatl! Where are you?" My pulse climbed to new, painful heights.

"Come out this instant or I'll tan your backside, Ehecacone!" Citlallotoc yelled, his voice carrying over the gardens. Birds took flight from the nearby trees, but nothing more. He looked so far away now, practically at the palace gate. When we met frantic gazes, he called, "I'll fetch the guards. Keep looking for him."

I nodded and kept stumbling around, not even certain where to search anymore. I was almost to the river, where the grass gave way to bare banks, and there was no sign of footprints on either side. Would I have heard him if he fell into the river?

Suddenly, quail took flight behind me and I turned to see the grass fifty paces away moving, as if someone crawled through it. My heart skipped a beat before finally settling, my panic giving way to anger. "This is going to get you a whipping, little man," I muttered as I followed the moving grass, preparing to cut Yamehecatl off before he reached the wall.

As I got closer, he moved faster through the grass—faster than I'd ever seen him run, let alone crawl on all fours. I picked up the pace, building to a full sprint.

But just as I was about to cut him off, he stopped and I overshot him by a couple of steps. I immediately went back. "Yamehecatl?"

This time, a deep, rumbling growl answered me.

I stumbled backwards, every instinct telling me to run, but my son was somewhere in this long grass, unconscious and vulnerable. *I must protect him!* I pulled my sacrificial blade, gripping it tight in my sweaty hand, and began advancing again.

Suddenly something knocked my legs out from under me. I rolled over to see a monstrous black jaguar glaring at me with smoky obsidian mirrors for eyes. Its body glowed purple, like an apparition. It bared its fangs, drawing my attention to what it clutched in its mouth. My heart stopped.

It was Yamehecatl.

The jaguar had him by the head, a tear of blood leaking from his left eye. When I reached out, unable to breathe, the jaguar ran off into the grass again, taking my son with it.

"No!" I tried to follow but I couldn't move, as if stuck in a vat of honey. I fought it and eventually found my feet, and I dashed after the jaguar, pushing myself faster and harder. My lungs burned with the effort. *It's not too late! I can still save him!*

But the jaguar was so far ahead of me, so close to the wall, out in the open where the rabbits had chewed all the grass to the ground. It could jump the stone wall without trouble and all hope of saving my son would vanish. I had to stop it now, before it was too late.

Magic pulsing in my hands, I dropped to my knees and pushed it and all my desperation into the ground. *Please help me! Someone! Anyone!*

A strange rumbling came from the ground—not under me, but rather near the wall. As the jaguar reached the halfway point, a flood of brown and gray spilled out of the rabbit holes and crashed over it, sucking it under.

When it clawed its way to the surface again, it no longer had

Yamehecatl in its mouth. It trod the wave of rabbits, snarling and hissing, dragging the mass of gray and brown fur with it towards the wall. Soon I saw my son lying on the ground, a handful of rabbits standing guard over him as the rest of their brethren battled the demon cat.

I scrambled to my feet and sprinted to him. *Great Feathered Serpent, please let him be alive!* The rabbits backed off as I approached and I scooped my son into my arms. I clutched him to my chest, so limp, so lifeless, and when I put my hand on his head, it was misshapen and wet. I forced that to the back of my mind and stroked his face, trying to draw him awake. "Nantli's here, my dear little Warm Breeze."

He didn't respond.

I checked him for a pulse. Panic numbed me when I found none. He wasn't breathing either, so I pinched his nose and blew air into his lungs, but still he didn't move, didn't rouse. Blood flowed down his neck from puncture wounds at his temples and behind his ears, coating my hands and drying to a dark stain in the day's growing heat.

Not certain what else to do, I pushed my magic into him, focusing my thoughts on healing him, on making his heart pump and his blood flow again. But it did nothing. No matter how much magic I dumped into him, the cloying smell of death clung to him.

"No no no no no!" I whispered, crushing him against my chest in some feeble hope he'd suddenly cry out that he couldn't breathe because of it. "I'm sorry, Yamehecatl," I sobbed. "Please forgive me for failing you!"

Hissing and growling made me look up. The jaguar stood atop the stone wall, out of reach of the rabbits bouncing like fleas below it. It bared its teeth, laughing at me.

I glared right back, my fury growing with each breath, the magic burning like fire in my hands. "You will pay for this, you demon!" I screamed, and released everything I had at it.

The rabbits nearest me dropped over, convulsing, and those at the wall tried to run for cover, but they too dropped to the ground after only a few steps, their bodies shaking violently, their mouths foaming and eyes rolled up into their heads in their death throes.

But the jaguar hissed at me and disappeared over the wall.

"Come back and face me, you coward!" I screamed, letting go of everything I had left. When the roaring in my veins finally gave out, I fell over, like a slab of wet stone, my own heartbeat receding in my ears. I stared at Yamehecatl lying on the ground next to me.

The sky gradually changed colors, as if sunset was falling; the Divine Dream leaking into my consciousness. *Like the other time I died,* I thought. A jolt of fear shot through me, but when I thought about how afraid Yamehecatl must be right now, having to face the trials of the underworld by himself, I let it go. I had failed him in life, but in death, I could walk the road into Mictlan with him, holding his hand as we faced the trials together. I tried to take his hand in mine, but my body refused to move.

The sky grew a deeper orange, and soon I saw Yamehecatl standing off in the distance, resting his arm on the back of the Black Dog standing next to him. He'd been crying but now he smiled, wiping his tears away. *I'm coming, my dear Warm Breeze,* I called out to him, waiting for death to finally release me from my fleshy prison so I could hug him again.

But both Yamehecatl and the Black Dog looked off to the side. The smile melted away from my son's face.

Citlallotoc knelt next to Yamehecatl's body and felt his neck. His face paled but he immediately moved to me next, pressing his fingers hard into my neck under my jaw. My heart still soldiered on, one slow beat after another. He shouted silent orders at the guards who had come with him, and they looked shocked by whatever it was he said, but after he yelled again—brooking no further arguments—one of them pulled his own blade and cut Citlallotoc's arm at his elbow joint, opening the vein. The other man turned me onto my back and held my head while Citlallotoc let the blood dribble into my open mouth.

The first drops brought a tingling, but as he fed me more, the magic surged. The sky's orange-ness faded to blue, and the world came back one sound at a time; Citlallotoc's voice, the guards, the birds, the rustling of the leaves. My heartbeat grew stronger.

But so did my panic. *No! Yamehecatl needs me!* I tried to move, tried to fight them off, but my body refused to obey me. The blood kept coming and the hunger grew more ravenous; I longed to grab hold of Citlallotoc's wounded arm and suck every last drop of blood out of him.

Eventually I gathered enough strength to make my jaw move, but when I tried to speak, it came out as a slurring, sobbing babble. Citlallotoc finally withdrew his arm, pale from more than mere blood loss. He checked my pulse again and let out a deep breath. "One of you carry her;

I'll carry the prince."

After one of the guards had bandaged his arm, Citlallotoc gathered up Yamehecatl's body, leaning him against his shoulder as if he were asleep. The larger of the two guards cradled me in his arms and carried me away.

Yamehecatl ran after me, the Black Dog following, but when we reached the gate, he fell to his knees and reached out to me, his own voice lost to my ears. *I'm sorry, my love!* I cried, but he couldn't hear me anymore. His sobbing face was the last thing I saw as the guard closed the gate, and it followed me into the darkness once I closed my eyes.

¤

The darkness lasted forever, haunted by images of Yamehcatl crouched among the reeds around the Black Lake in Mictlan, frozen mid-sob, tears like icicles on his pale, bluish cheeks. I tried to carry him away, but when I touched him, death's cold grasp stung my skin, burrowing deep and threatening to overcome me. I could only escape it by letting him go and leaving him behind.

Eventually, the dreams faded and I swam in blackness, a welcome respite from the nightmares. Soon after that, everything became a blur of colors and shapes and incomprehensible sounds. I recognized voices though: Little Reed, Malinalli, Mazatzin, Citlallotoc, Mitotia. I tasted the tang of blood and after a while the incomprehensible sounds began making sense. But I wanted to go back to not understanding when I realized Little Reed was discussing Yamehecatl's funeral arrangements with Mazatzin and Malinalli. I wanted to fall asleep and never wake up again.

But as with most things in my life, I didn't get what I wanted.

Little Reed was the only one there when I finally woke up, feeling as if I would never sleep again. He sat in bed next to me, smoking his pipe in silence, staring into the hearth, but when I shifted my weight, he gave me a relieved smile. "Welcome back, my love." He stroked my hair.

"Water," I begged. Every muscle in my body ached.

He poured a cup and helped me sit up to drink it. I took in cup after cup until my belly ached, then I leaned back against him, exhausted again. "How long?" I asked, no will to move again.

"Four days, though for a while there, we didn't think you'd ever wake up again; we thought you'd gone too far into the afterlife."

"I wish I had," I muttered.

Little Reed kissed my temple, tension in his arms around me. "I, for one, am very glad you didn't."

I clamped my eyes shut, expecting tears, but I was dry. "He's all alone now, Little Reed."

"Not completely. Xolotl will help him."

"I should have gone with him. You should have seen him when the guards carried me away...." I opened my eyes to stare up at the ceiling. "I failed him."

"I doubt that," Little Reed whispered at my ear. "He knew how devoted you were to him."

"I never should have taken him out to the garden. I should have insisted we do something in the palace, where he would have been safe."

"The garden should have been safe. We set traps to keep the jaguars out."

"Nowhere is safe anymore," I muttered. "Mextli warned me I'd pay for helping Quetzalcoatl, and now Smoking Mirror has made good on that."

Little Reed sat up straighter. "Smoking Mirror?"

I nodded. "He sent his nahual to kill our son, and he would have dragged him over the wall and eaten him if I hadn't sent the rabbits after him." I wished I could cry to relieve the painful stinging behind my eyes. "I never should have let Yamehecatl wander off, but I thought it was better to let him calm down. He was having one of his episodes, and he said hurtful things. Citlallotoc wanted to spank him but I told him to let him be, to let him run until he passed out, so he'd be easier to deal with. I should have let Citlallotoc discipline him. He wouldn't have been alone in the long grass, where we couldn't see him...." I started choking and Little Reed poured me more water.

"You can't blame yourself, Papalotl. You did what you thought best. I might have done the same thing if I'd been out there with him. Give yourself time to heal—"

"And everything will be all right?" I jerked away from him, a deep-seated rage filling me with frightening strength. "I'm never going to be all right again!"

He frowned, the hurt plain on his face. "I know it seems so, my love, but we'll get through this, together. We've been through so much already, and while this hurts the worst of anything, we're strong, and we'll make

Smoking Mirror pay for this." A similar flame of fury burned in Little Reed's eyes.

I lay back in his arms again, relieved. He'd seemed so collected, so calm about all this, and it filled me with purpose to see he really wasn't. "What are we going to do?"

He kissed my temple. "Let's not talk about it yet. You need to rest and recoup your strength, and we must bury our son tomorrow."

I squeezed my eyes shut again, the pain and panic swelling in my chest. "Will you stay with me, so I don't have to wake up alone?"

"I will stay however long you need me to, my dearest Butterfly."

CHAPTER TWENTY-FIVE

I felt stronger by morning, though seeing Yamehecatl's body knocked that out of me again. Mazatzin and Malinalli had wrapped him in paper ribbons, according to royal tradition, and I dressed him in his favorite rabbit uniform. Maybe it would give him good luck when he faced the underworld's trials, but the sight of him in it broke my heart. There was a small tear on the right seam that he'd asked me to fix but I hadn't gotten around to it. And now he'd never again ask me to fix it, or anything else. He would never again ask me to sing him a song before bed, nor would he ever spend a single night in the dormitories at the calmecac.

Only Malinalli, Mazatzin, and Citlallotoc attended the funeral ceremony in the great hall, and I was grateful Little Reed kept it a private affair. Malinalli held my hand, her eyes red from crying as the men finished digging out the burial hole the servants had started the night before in front of the enormous hearth. I didn't cry; I'd turned into an empty cavern whose silence was broken only by a distant moaning when the pain turned physical in my chest. I was Mictlan, dark and cold, my breath tense with the misery and fear of the dead clambering down its road in search of a hard-won peace.

Once the men finished digging they washed themselves with water and crushed flowers. Mazatzin and Citlallotoc carried Yamehecatl's body to me, holding him up so I could give him one last kiss on his bandaged forehead. I made the gesture quickly, horrified by how my stomach growled at the scent of decay seeping through the bandages. They set him gently into the hole.

Little Reed carried over a small brown dog that had been tethered in the corner. It wagged its tail and shivered as he whispered soothingly to it; we'd fed it a maize cake filled with yauhtli before we'd started the ceremony, in preparation for its task. Standing in front of the pit, he prayed,

> "Lord Xolotl, we gather today to honor you,
> To beg your mercy upon our son.
> Lend him your guidance as he faces the Black River,
> The Cavern of Arrowheads,
> The Field of Fiery Flags,
> And the Mountain of Obsidian Blades.
> Nurture his courage when he reaches the plains of Mictlan,
> So he may face Lord Death's judgment with bravery
> And resolve.
> Show him the way as you showed our Lord Quetzalcoatl.
> Counsel him,
> Care for him in our absence.
> Please accept our gratitude for your work,
> For your own sacrifices in the name of humanity."

Little Reed set the little dog in the hole atop Yamehecatl's body and slit its throat. It didn't make a sound as it stumbled, oblivious, showing the yauhtli did its job. It kept its feet, bleeding profusely, but soon collapsed and laid still, the blood staining Yamehecatl's paper bandages.

Malinalli handed me a bundle of bone flowers and I tore the petals off and showered them on my son, the smell of vanilla reminding me of all the love I'd been privileged to know in my short life—my mother, my father, Nimilitzli, Little Reed, my son—all but one of them gone now. Little Reed held me close while Mazatzin recited prayers praising Quetzalcoatl.

I hadn't given the god any thought in days, but hearing Mazatzin's words filled me with questions. Why hadn't Quetzalcoatl protected our son? Certainly Yamehecatl was part of his great plan, for gods didn't make mistakes or do anything unintended. And yet he'd let Smoking Mirror kill Yamehecatl; he'd looked after Little Reed, but not our son, as if he meant nothing at all to him. Bitterness swelled inside me when I imagined the god paying no attention at all to what we did here today.

Once Mazatzin finished, Citlallotoc stepped forward and placed Yamehecatl's play sword in the hole with him. After letting his hand linger a moment, he stepped away, his face haggard.

"Are we ready to cover him?" Little Reed asked, his voice breaking as he did. When Citlallotoc answered with a silent nod, Little Reed handed out the digging sticks and the men scraped the dirt back into the hole. I couldn't breathe and had to leave the room when they reset the hearthstones.

Tradition dictated a week of feasting to honor the deceased, but I hadn't the courage to face the hundreds of nobles who'd come to celebrate my son's naming day; I didn't want them to see how raw and lost I was. Little Reed agreed I should ease myself into the public sphere, so as not to overburden myself. He walked me back to my quarters after lunch then returned to the great hall to play host to our guests while I rested.

But I did very little sleeping; I stared at the curtain over the nursery doorway, the bells tinkling softly in the breeze from my garden patio. I imagined Yamehecatl tearing aside that curtain and running to me to complain of a nightmare, confirming all this was only a terrible dream, and I finally found my tears again. When Little Reed returned later to invite me to eat with him in his quarters, I eagerly accepted. I couldn't stand being so close to the empty nursery.

"But shouldn't one of us be at the feast tonight?" I asked as the servants brought us a modest dinner.

"Citlallotoc is hosting for us," Little Reed said, filling my plate. "It's more important that we be together, only the two of us right now."

Since I'd been unable to sleep the last couple of hours, my thoughts had wandered off to the future and what Yamehecatl's death meant for our kingdom. We had no heir, and I couldn't bear any more children even if I wanted to. *You're just like your mother, and see what befell her?* Ihuitimal derided me from the grave. And Little Reed was like my father. I wasn't certain whether to laugh or cry. "What are we going to do now?"

"About what?" Little Reed asked.

"You have no heir to carry on your legacy."

He fidgeted. "I haven't really given it any thought; it seems too early."

"I know it does, but...this whole tragedy reminds me that time is short, and given how quickly you age...we both know what happened when Mixcoatl had no legitimate heir in place."

He took a bite of tamale and chewed thoughtfully a moment before saying, "I know *we* can't produce a new heir, but perhaps the god would bless you again—"

"I'm barren, Little Reed. And before you get any notions that that doesn't matter, because Mother was barren when she had you...maybe that's the reason she didn't survive. That's not a risk I'm willing to take."

"Nor would I expect you to. But how do you know you're barren?"

"I haven't bled in almost four years."

He furrowed his brows. "But you're still so young."

"I suspect my magic takes a toll on me. I'm surprised you haven't noticed how gray I've gotten the last couple of years."

"Probably because I find you as beautiful as ever," he said with a smile that should have lit up my desire, but it only irritated me. I hoped the desire never came back, so I'd finally be at peace with my lot in life.

"The point is that you can't look to me to provide our future anymore, and we must have a plan going forward."

"Of course, but must we really discuss this right now?" He looked as if I might spring at him like a jaguar at the slightest provocation. "We've only just buried Yamehecatl, and it's been a very sad day, for both of us. I agree our time is not unlimited, but we need room to grieve and heal from this tragedy; I need distance before making any kind of judgment on how to proceed."

I bowed my head, ashamed. "I'm sorry. It was selfish of me to not think about how all this was affecting you; I've been so wrapped up in my own pain, and I feel so lost...." I started sobbing when he moved over to let me lean against him. "I feel as if I'm drowning in a pit of honey, but trying to work out what to do next dulls the pain a bit, if only for a moment. It keeps me from dwelling in dark places."

He nodded. "Continuing with my daily routines has kept me from falling apart at times, so far be it from me to tell you that now isn't the time for such discussions. But may I ask one thing though? Can it wait until tomorrow? Today has been so...strenuous, and I want to eat dinner and...." He hesitated before asking, "And if it isn't too difficult for you, would you consider staying the night with me, here in my quarters? If only to have you nearby...for comfort?"

I wiped my tears away and nodded. "I'd rather not go back to my quarters. It was hard enough being alone in there today."

"Stay here with me as long as you wish." He held my dish out to me, encouraging me to eat.

After dinner, I returned to my quarters to change into my night dress. Even with the hearth filled with fire, the room felt cold and barren. I knelt before my idol of Quetzalcoatl and murmured a short prayer—which I did every night, though tonight it felt so cursory—then I hurried back to Little Reed's warm, friendly quarters.

He was already in bed, dressed in a knee-length xicolli. He held the blankets open for me. "You can have my side of the bed."

I slipped in next to him and once he'd folded the blankets over us, I nestled up against him and let out a deep breath. He hooked one arm around me but rested the other on his stomach, holding me close. I listened to his breathing and heartbeat, a lullaby that soothed my anguish like yauhtli.

I had just dozed off when someone shook the bells on the door curtain. Little Reed roused with a start and looked around blurry-eyed before calling out, "Who is it?"

"It's me, My Lord," Citlallotoc's voice answered from beyond the curtain.

Little Reed sat up slowly, yawning. "Come in."

Citlallotoc opened the curtain, but he stopped short when he saw me lying next to Little Reed. He looked away as if he'd walked in on the two of us naked. "I'm sorry. I thought you were alone."

"No need to apologize. What do you need?"

Citlallotoc cast a furtive glance back at me but approached the bed with purpose. He went to his knees, took out his sword, and set it on the ground. "I've come to surrender myself for your judgment, My Lord and Lady."

Little Reed rubbed his eyes, confused. "What are you talking about?"

"Seven years ago, you and Lady Quetzalpetlatl charged me with protecting your son, but I failed you, and the prince, costing you the heir to the throne. Therefore it is only honorable that I forfeit my life in repayment for my failures."

I snatched the sword and clutched it to my breast, my heart thudding. "You've never once failed in any of your duties to either me or Topiltzin, and most certainly not to our son," I cried. "You're not to blame for his death, and I won't listen to you beg for a punishment you don't deserve! We've already lost one loved one, so don't even think of making us suffer yet another loss. You are a dear, dear friend—practically family—and if I had another child, I wouldn't hesitate to entrust you with their care too." I wiped away angry tears.

Citlallotoc looked up at me with such anguish that I felt bad for yelling at him, even in a fit of despair. "I'm humbled by your forgiveness, My Lady," he murmured, his eyes wet.

"You don't need forgiveness, but if that's the only way to heal your heart, then fine, you have it. And my love and gratitude for everything you gave my son." I handed the sword to Little Reed then hugged Citlallotoc.

Little Reed nodded, saying nothing, but his wet eyes spoke volumes. He escorted Citlallotoc back to the door, murmuring something before handing him his sword. Citlallotoc thanked him and departed.

ㅁ

We didn't talk the next morning, for Little Reed left early to entertain our guests and let me sleep in. I finally woke up when Malinalli brought me breakfast. "Hungry?" she asked as she set a steaming tlaxcalli in front of me.

I slowly picked it apart, eating it one small bite at a time. Her expectant gaze asked how I was doing, so I answered, "I'm feeling better today."

She smiled. "I'm glad to hear it."

"What did I miss while I was unconscious?" When she hesitated, I added, "Thinking about work keeps me from dwelling."

She filled me in on the daily mundane news of our order. Classes at the calmecac had been cancelled since Yamehecatl's death, but everyone was back in school today.

"How is Night Wind?" I asked.

Malinalli shrugged. "He hasn't said much. He looks surly but goes about his duties."

"He's a strong one."

"It runs in the family. I've always admired your strength in the face of adversity."

I didn't feel strong, but her words lifted my spirits enough that I attended that night's mourning feast. I steadied my nerves in anticipation of an onslaught of concern and crushing pity, but beyond the customary murmurs of condolences, everyone was in a good mood. At first it took me aback seeing people laugh and smile, but hearing people talking about how Yamehecatl always ran around the great hall in his rabbit suit, swinging his sword and challenging them to duels, I couldn't help but smile too. And remember his smile with his unusually large front teeth, and how he'd tell me jokes that made so little sense that I couldn't help but laugh. He would never leave me—not truly—as long as I carried fragments of him in my heart, memories that could see me into the future.

With the meal finished and the men gathered near the hearth to smoke their pipes and talk, the women gathered around me for the xocolatl service. Anacoana had watched me furtively all night, so I invited her to sit with me.

"Have you enjoyed your visit?" I asked as I stirred the deep red liquid into a froth. When she bumbled over an answer, I added, "It's all right. Our days can't be all gloom and grief. That would be depressing."

Anacoana smiled. "Tollan is very beautiful, and it's so nice being away from home for a change. I just wish circumstances were better."

"As do we all." I poured her cup and handed it to her. "But life must go on eventually." I glanced over at the men, where Citlallotoc sat next to Little Reed. "You know Lord Citlallotoc?"

She flushed but nodded. "He comes to Xico to visit my father. He's a nice, honorable man."

"You like him?"

Her cheeks burned even darker. "Is this an appropriate discussion given the circumstances, My Lady?"

"What better way to honor the dead than by celebrating the joys of life? Such as love?"

She looked over at him too, and the tension left her shoulders. "I've loved him since I was sixteen, but he's not interested in me," she admitted. "Why would he be interested in someone else's scraps?"

"You're not scraps. And I know for a fact he's interested. We've talked about it."

"Really?"

"He's concerned your father will reject his proposal."

"Oh but he won't. Two years ago he was very particular about whom to marry me off to—it had to be someone who would be beneficial to Xico—but now he thinks I'm completely useless. 'All you do is eat my food and get in my way, Anacoana,' he says. A murdering bandit could indicate interest and my father would give me away to him without a second thought."

I gripped my cup tighter, magic building in my tense muscles. "He has no right to speak to you like that."

"What am I to do? He's my father."

I glared at Flame Tongue—who was also sitting next to Little Reed, cozy as a leech on a tasty host. He looked old and a bit wrinkled, but still annoyingly vital in spite of that. She couldn't rely on him dropping dead anytime soon. "I'll speak with Citlallotoc first thing tomorrow morning, and you won't have to worry any longer. He will treat you with the respect and kindness you deserve."

¤

Once the feast ended, Little Reed and I returned to his quarters and prepared ourselves for bed. "I'm glad to see you looking happier today," he noted as he turned down the blankets for us, as if we were an old peasant couple who always shared a bed.

"It felt good to be out among people again," I admitted. "I think I'll go to the temple tomorrow for a few hours, do a little work."

"If it will make you happy, then by all means." He took his new spot in bed and propped himself up on one elbow, waiting for me to join him.

"We still haven't talked," I pointed out, climbing in next to him.

"Must we?"

"I need to."

He sighed. "Then let's talk."

"We can't ignore our lack of an heir much longer, Little Reed."

"I know, and I was thinking about that today. We could designate an heir, perhaps choose one of the noble children from the calmecac—boy or girl, doesn't really matter, so long as they're wise and devoted to the god."

"Such as whom?"

"I don't know; nobody immediately comes to mind, but we could consult with Mazatzin and Malinalli, since they have more exposure to the students than we do."

I shook my head. "I'm not comfortable with that idea, Little Reed. What do we know of any of our students anyway? I know Night Wind rather well, and technically speaking he is family, but I wouldn't consider him a good candidate, given who his father is. And we know next to nothing about his upbringing before he came to Tollan. We haven't taken an active interest in the upbringing of any of the noble children, and to be honest, I think if we start making inquiries, conflicts will break out as fathers scramble to make the case that their child should be the next heir. The throne should go to someone you've raised from birth to honor Quetzalcoatl, whom you've taught to respect his ways from a very young age. The heir must be someone of your blood."

Little Reed sat up, confused. "Don't you mean 'we'?" When I shook my head, he matched me, taken aback. "I vowed to take no concubines—"

"I'm not suggesting you do."

"What *are* you suggesting?"

I swallowed the pain swelling in my chest. "You must take a new wife, Little Reed."

He climbed out of the bed to pace. "I will not set you aside, Papalotl—"

"Nor would my father set my mother aside, and we both know what that got him." I sighed, bowing my head. "We married for political considerations, and unfortunately they don't apply any—"

"I married you for love," he retorted.

"And love isn't going to produce an heir for us." I choked on the words but they needed saying. "You can't permit love to ruin everything we've worked for, Little Reed. Tollan's throne needs an heir of our blood, and unfortunately I cannot provide that any longer, so it makes practical sense that you seek a new wife who can bear your children and give everyone the future they deserve." When he didn't reply, just faced the fire, holding both sides of his head as if he might tear his own hair out, I said, "We both know this is the right thing to do."

He let his hands drop to his sides. "You ask too much of me, Papalotl."

"Far less than the god has asked of me, Little Reed," I said, holding back the indignation rising inside me.

"This means we must get a divorce, in the temple."

"I know."

"And I will have to publicly accuse you of being barren, for the official record."

"It's not an accusation, Little Reed. It's the truth."

"Still...I can't put you through that humiliation."

I hadn't thought about that. We'd intentionally made divorce easy and private in Tollan, so people could move on quickly with their lives; but as King and Queen, we weren't afforded that same luxury. Everything we did had to be out in the public eye, for reasons of legitimacy. "It will only burn for a moment," I tried to assure him.

"And then I must find a wife."

I nodded. "I can do that for you—"

"I would rather you didn't." The edge to his voice stung, but when he looked at me, no anger lurked in his eyes. "This is painful enough for both of us without me inflicting that duty on you. I will find her myself."

"I don't want to do this, Little Reed, but we have to make the hard sacrifices, for the good of everyone else."

"I know." He sniffled. "Feel free to remain here tonight, but I must go walking now." He left without another word.

CHAPTER TWENTY-SIX

I decided to stay, hoping Little Reed would come back and we could share his bed one last time, but when I woke the next morning, he still wasn't there. He came to the great hall at breakfast, looking as if he hadn't slept, and though he returned my hesitant smile when I came in, he didn't speak to me. He listened quietly while our council talked of their plans for the day.

But afterwards, he followed me out into the courtyard on my way to the sacred precinct. "I spoke with Mazatzin, about what we discussed last night," he said, keeping his voice low as we walked. "He's willing to officiate over the untying ceremony whenever you wish."

"I don't wish to do it at all," I muttered.

He took my hand and pulled me to a stop. "Then let's not. Let's find an orphan babe that we can bring home and raise as our own. Nobody needs to know the child is not ours."

"And ask Malinalli or Mitotia to lie and say they were present for a birth that never happened? And am I supposed to pose as if I'm pregnant for the next nine months, tying pillows around my waist to make it look legitimate? I don't want to live a lie, Little Reed, and if that child dies too...I can't, Little Reed. I'm sorry, but I can't go through that again. I've had to sacrifice a great deal—often more than I think is fair—but I will sacrifice no more."

He frowned, a sour look on his face. "Divorcing me is no sacrifice?"

I scowled right back at him. "Of course it's a sacrifice, and how dare you suggest otherwise? But it's the last one I'm willing to make, for the good of fulfilling the god's plans. This is the end of it for me. If the god wants something done so badly, he can come here and do it himself." I needed to get away from him, before I rattled out more things he'd misunderstand, so I wrenched my arm away and marched out of the gate, my guards following me.

¤

I found no peace at the temple. Instead I stared at Quetzalcoatl's idol with growing contempt, thinking about how little he seemed to care anymore. *At least when my mother and father died, I came to Nimilitzli and Mazatzin and Malinalli, but what good has come of Yamehecatl's death? My marriage to Little Reed is over, we're barely on speaking terms anymore, and nothing will ever be the same between us again. And yet you say nothing, you don't listen to my prayers, you don't assure me that this is all for a greater purpose and that I will be rewarded for all my suffering—*

"Forgive my disturbing you, My Lady," Black Otter spoke up behind me. He lurked in the temple entrance, wringing his bony hands, dressed in his black high priest robe.

I stood and smoothed my dress, hoping my cheeks weren't tear-stained. "No, it's quite all right. What can I do for you?"

He came inside, his gait reminding me of a timid mouse. "I wanted to say...to give you my condolences on your loss."

289

I didn't want to talk to him about Yamehecatl, but I accepted his words with the expected graciousness. "How is your own son? Is he coping all right?"

"Night Wind? Oh, he's doing well, I suppose. He's like obsidian; the more you bang away at him, the sharper he gets."

"He never did strike me as the weak kind."

Smiling, Black Otter said, "No, definitely not weak. But how are you?"

I clenched my jaw, trying to hold myself together. "Life is about as good as can be expected these days."

"I'm sorry. I've upset you."

"No, I'm fine, really."

"And what of the King? Is he handling it well?" Genuine concern on his face.

I stuttered a moment before saying, "Can we talk about something else, please?"

"Of course. Completely insensitive of me, but really, the only reason I came was to see if you were all right." He bowed again and turned to leave.

"Wait!" I called after him, feeling bad for making him slink off. When he turned back to me, I struggled to find something to say before settling on, "Thank you for your concern."

He smiled back. "If you need anything at all, even if it's merely someone to talk to, you know where to find me." He then left.

I found myself smiling in spite of how I'd felt a few moments earlier. I'd forgotten how good a friend Black Otter could be.

I went about my daily work, planning to go back to the palace and apologize to Little Reed for my harsh tongue, but as I packed up my papers in my meditation room, he came to my door, looking repentant. "I'm sorry about what I said. Of course this is a sacrifice for you, and I shouldn't have said otherwise."

"I'm sorry I made you think it was nothing."

"I know it's not nothing, to either of us. And I've been thinking all morning about this, and the more I do, the more I dread having to go through with it; it gives me the shakes thinking about it." He held his hand out to show me. "So I was thinking—and feel free to tell me if this is completely the wrong way to handle this—but I think it would be better, for both of us, if we got this over with. We ask Mazatzin to do the untying ceremony now, so we won't have time to dwell or second-guess ourselves."

I nodded, numb. "That's probably for the best. The longer we delay, the harder it will be. And our allies are only here a few days longer, and you should already be divorced before approaching any of them about their daughters."

"That too." He pulled me into a crushing hug. "I must make one thing very clear before we do this. I still love you with all my being."

"I know you do, Little Reed." I squeezed him back.

He pulled away, not meeting my gaze. "Shall we go and find Mazatzin then?"

¤

The ceremony was uneventful; we both swore on the god's name to give truthful testimony supporting our petition, and I promptly agreed to Little Reed's right to divorce me on grounds that I was barren. Mazatzin wrote the claims in the registry book where we kept record of all the marriages and divorces in Tollan, and with little else added, he declared our marriage finished. Funny how our wedding ceremony lasted four days, yet we'd ended it all before the noon-time bell.

As we returned to the palace, we didn't hold hands as we usually did. "I'd rather put off the formal announcement until tomorrow," Little Reed told me.

"I would be fine with that."

We ate a late lunch and retired to our separate quarters for a nap before the evening's feast. I missed Little Reed lying next to me—his body heat, his smell—but it was a good thing I was alone, for I dreamt of kissing him next to the temple in Xochicalco the night before he left for the army, and those sensual caresses we'd shared in the privacy of his tent; of his hand resting on my belly swollen with our child, and his torturously wonderful tongue winding its way down past my navel. I woke at dusk, the desire raging in my blood. It had never been so strong, so hungry. I feared what I might do if I went to the feast in such a condition, so I drew myself a bath, to drown the lust in cold water and shivers. By the end of it I was so numb my teeth were chattering, but at least the desire was again silenced.

We sat together at dinner as usual, and Little Reed even held my hand once or twice—to keep up appearances. But I focused mostly on

Anacoana, who watched Citlallotoc from across the room with wistful eyes. I had a promise to keep.

Once the servants cleared the dinner dishes and the men brought out their pipes, I took Citlallotoc by the arm. "Walk with me, please? I need to talk to you about something." Little Reed overheard me and gave me a questioning glance, but I promised I'd bring Citlallotoc back shortly. Little Reed nodded and returned his attention to Flame Tongue as he regaled everyone with tales of his heroic army days.

And to believe I'm going to convince Citlallotoc to marry himself into that man's family, I mused, exasperated.

Once out in the gardens, in the yellow light of the kettle braziers on the patio, Citlallotoc asked, "Is something the matter, My Lady?"

"You need to approach Flame Tongue about Anacoana tonight."

"Tonight? But certainly there's a more appropriate time for marriage proposals—"

"If you wait any longer, I think poor Anacoana will fall over dead of heartache. She told me last night that her father would be very open to a proposal; he seems to think her a burr in his sandal and he's eager for someone to take her off his hands."

He frowned. "Really?"

I nodded. "If they leave here without a marriage proposal, I wouldn't put it past him to dump her on the side of the road on the way back to Xico."

"Certainly you jest?"

Taking his hand between both of mine, I implored him, "She will make an excellent wife; she's caring and thoughtful, and I've never seen anyone who can weave more beautifully. But best of all, she's absolutely in love with you."

Citlallotoc peered back into the great hall, to where Anacoana sat with her mother. "I would be a fool not to, wouldn't I?"

"And you're no fool."

After another pause, he asked, "And you're certain the timing isn't unseemly?"

"Not at all. I welcome the distraction of planning a wedding for the two of you. So go, talk to Flame Tongue. He's harassed Topiltzin all night, so you'll be helping my brother spend a little more time with our other allies."

Citlallotoc stood straighter and raised his chin. "Very well." He marched back into the great hall, full of purpose.

I hurried back to the circle of women as Citlallotoc wove his way over to Flame Tongue. He bowed, and after an exchange of words Flame Tongue nodded and followed him back out into the garden. Flame Tongue's guards followed but lingered at the doorway to the patio.

Anacoana was watching too, so I gave her a nod and a smile. She smiled back, wringing her hands together until her mother scolded her for fidgeting.

The two men returned a moment later, Flame Tongue smiling like a pleased ocelotl, and Citlallotoc striding tall. He gave me a smile and a nod before joining the rest of the men, and this time Flame Tongue sat next to him, positively beaming.

Well, something good will come out of this after all, I thought with a smile, then turned my attention to the other women sitting around me.

□

I rose early the next morning and made certain I was first in the great hall, so I could ask Citlallotoc for confirmation of the proposal. He was always the first one to arrive in the morning, but today the rest of the council slowly filtered in, followed by guests two or three at a time. Flame Tongue and his family weren't among them, nor was Citlallotoc; they must have been waiting to arrive at the same time, so they could announce the engagement together.

A few moments after everyone else arrived, Flame Tongue and Anacoana finally walked into the great hall, but with Little Reed instead of Citlallotoc. I looked around for Citlallotoc, but still no sign of him. Anacoana wore her best dress and a brilliant smile; I'd never seen a woman look so happy about getting engaged.

Little Reed motioned Flame Tongue to take the reed mat next to his throne—where Citlallotoc usually sat—and Anacoana sat next to him, smoothing her dress and looking around, for Citlallotoc, no doubt. When Little Reed greeted me with a kiss to the cheek, I whispered, "Where's Citlallotoc?"

"He said he wasn't feeling well, so he begged off breakfast in favor of sleeping in."

That good feeling from last night vanished as I sank onto my own reed throne.

Little Reed called for silence then addressed the crowd gathered in the great hall. "Lady Quetzalpetlatl and I want to thank each and every one of you for your tremendous support during these most trying times for our family. Your strength and friendship has already set us on the road to healing, and to the future."

A somber murmur of approval passed through the crowd.

"I have two pieces of news to share; one is not so good, but the other is joyous.

"First, by mutual agreement, Lady Quetzalpetlatl and I have decided to set our marriage aside. It is not something we decided upon lightly, but circumstances dictated that we do so for the future of Tollan." When those murmurs turned to confusion, he added, "Rest assured that she remains Queen of Tollan, and shall be such till the day the Black Dog relieves her of her royal duties."

Everyone's gaze shifted to me, some filled with astonishment, others with pity, as if expecting me to break down on my throne. I trained my gaze on Little Reed so I didn't feel quite so small.

"As for the second piece of news...." Little Reed motioned to Flame Tongue.

Looking immensely pleased, Flame Tongue rose to his feet and cleared his throat. "I'm pleased to announce that my daughter Anacoana is now betrothed to Lord Topiltzin, strengthening the long-standing alliance between Tollan and Xico." He raised a cup of chocolate to Little Reed and added, "May my daughter give you many, many strong sons to carry on your legacy, My Lord."

Anacoana's nervous smile faded into panicked confusion. She plastered on a smile when Little Reed took her hand though. She darted a pleading look at me.

But I was too stunned to speak; nor would it be prudent to do so now. The betrothal was already announced in front of our allies and the council, and to raise objections now would incite an incident with Xico. As much as I disliked Flame Tongue, our alliance was too important to throw away without first finding some answers.

Breakfast dragged on forever, but eventually Little Reed and Flame Tongue went to the garden with Anacoana and her mother to discuss wedding plans and dowries. Little Reed invited me to come with them, but I begged it off, saying I had other things to do. He nodded morosely—no doubt thinking I wanted nothing to do with planning his wedding to a new woman—but he didn't object, and let me go on my way.

Citlallotoc wasn't in his quarters. After asking around with the servants, I found him in the men's exercise yard, wearing only a loincloth and beating a cotton dummy with a practice sword. When he saw me, he granted me a brief glance before pummeling the target with increased ferocity. I stood to the side, watching him until he finally backed away, chest heaving and arm muscles quivering, sweat pouring off him. "What happened?" I finally asked.

"I don't want to talk about it." He gave the dummy one last blow before retreating to the bench under the eaves. I followed him, saying nothing as he wiped himself down, but eventually he spoke on his own. "Lord Flame Tongue rejected my proposal."

"But you looked so pleased last night, after you talked to him—"

"Yes, well, that was before he found that Anacoana had better prospects." He threw the towel on the bench and glared at me. "What is this nonsense about Topiltzin divorcing you?"

I tensed. "It's not nonsense. And, not that it's your business, but we did it by mutual agreement."

"And so he cast you aside?"

"I stepped aside, for the good of the kingdom. But enough of this. What happened last night, when you talked to Flame Tongue?"

Citlallotoc shrugged. "He said my proposal was a welcome offer, and he was pleased that someone finally wanted to look after Anacoana. But this morning, before dawn, he woke me to tell me the arrangement was off."

I gasped. "He backed out on you?"

He stared at the bench as if it vexed him. "Apparently he got a better offer last night, after we talked."

I balled my fists, shaking. "Who does he think he is? You're Topiltzin's best friend—"

"I'm not going to make an issue of it. Topiltzin is the King whereas I'm merely Justice of the Peace. I'm nobody important."

I glared at him. "You're very important, and Flame Tongue will treat you with respect. You must talk to Topiltzin at once, before this dishonorable agreement goes too far."

"It's already gone too far, My Lady. What's done is done, and I don't want to talk about this anymore." He pulled his xicolli on and disappeared into the palace.

Maybe he didn't want to talk about it, but I had plenty to say to Little Reed.

CHAPTER TWENTY-SEVEN

I marched out into the garden where Little Reed and Flame Tongue were deep in discussion. Anacoana and her mother sat off to the side, saying nothing, letting the men plan Anacoana's future for her. I'd not dared speak up in front of the council and our allies lest Flame Tongue lose face—and we lose his support—but I felt no such compunction now.

Not bothering with decorum, I cut Flame Tongue off mid-sentence. "I need to say something, before you two get too far in all this wedding planning."

Flame Tongue stared at me, outraged, and even Little Reed looked taken aback. "Is something the matter?" Little Reed asked.

"Lord Flame Tongue is trying to deceive you, Brother. Anacoana was already promised to another man when he accepted your proposal."

Flame Tongue shot to his feet with surprising speed for a man of his years. "Absolutely untrue, My Lord! This is a vicious lie!"

Little Reed held up his hand for silence, and though it pained Flame Tongue to bite his words, he did so, face dark with rage. "What do you mean, Quetzalpetlatl?"

"Last night, Citlallotoc asked him for permission to marry Anacoana. Remember when the two of them went out to the garden before everyone sat down to smoke after dinner? At that time, he accepted Citlallotoc's offer—"

"He gave no dowry to legitimize his proposal," Flame Tongue shot back. "And so I had every right to reject his offer when a better prospect asked for Anacoana's hand."

"You mean the more powerful prospect," I fired right back.

Again Little Reed held up his hands, cutting off Flame Tongue before he could hurl further defenses at me. Little Reed glared at him. "This is very disappointing to hear, My Lord. I thought we had a healthy respect for each other."

Flame Tongue stood straighter. "I respect you immensely, My Lord, and because of that respect, when we spoke after last night's feast, I decided your need—and the needs of the kingdom—outweighed Lord Citlallotoc's. And I'm certain, as your honorable subject, he agrees with me."

I started to protest, but Little Reed beckoned to one of his guards. "Fetch Lord Citlallotoc immediately."

The guard bowed and disappeared inside. No one said anything as Little Reed paced, visibly upset, and Flame Tongue glared at me. I glared right back. Anacoana sat next to her mother, looking mortified.

When Citlallotoc arrived, he went straight to Little Reed and bowed in supplication. "You asked for me, My Lord?"

Little Reed motioned him to stand. "I've been told some disturbing news, my friend, and I'm hoping you can shed some light on its veracity. Did you ask Lord Flame Tongue for permission to tie your cape to Lady Anacoana's dress last night?"

Citlallotoc cast me a scathing glare before answering, "I did, My Lord."

"And he accepted your proposal?"

"He did."

Little Reed sighed and set his hands on Citlallotoc's shoulder. "I'm so sorry; if I had known you'd already asked, I would never have made my own offer. You're my best, most loyal friend, and it kills me to think I betrayed that, even unwittingly. Can you ever forgive me?"

"There is nothing to forgive, My Lord."

"On that I beg to differ. I cannot in good conscience move forward with this wedding knowing all this. Your friendship is of utmost importance to me, and I cannot bear to lose it...especially after having lost so much already."

Citlallotoc looked to Anacoana for a moment, but told Little Reed, "I vowed an oath of fealty to you long ago, to defend not only you and Lady Quetzalpetlatl, but your kingdom. Right now, Tollan's future is in jeopardy, and it would be selfish of me to put my own desires before what's best for our people. So please, go forward with this wedding without fear of losing our friendship." He looked again to Anacoana, who peered back at him with sad eyes. "I've known the Lady a number of years, and I know her to be an upstanding woman. She will be good for Tollan, and she will be a good mother to Tollan's heir." He nodded towards Flame Tongue without meeting the other man's gaze and added, "She is a testament to her father's wise parenting."

Some of Flame Tongue's surliness softened and he put on a smug smile.

Little Reed considered this, the conflict clear on his face. "Are you certain you can be at peace with this outcome?"

Citlallotoc nodded. "And you needn't fear for our friendship, My Lord; it is as secure, and strong as ever."

Clearing his throat, Flame Tongue said, "Now that we've put that silliness to rest, perhaps we can get on with putting together the details, Lord Topiltzin?"

That man irritated me to no end. Pulling Little Reed's sleeve, I drew him away from everyone else and whispered, "It's wonderful that Citlallotoc is willing to put his own happiness aside for your benefit, but has anyone thought to ask Anacoana if she's all right with all this? This treads very close to being an illegal forced marriage. She has as much right to a say in this as anyone, regardless of what her father might say."

Little Reed nodded, looking thoroughly chastened. "You're absolutely right. Let us ask her opinion."

"You must ask her alone," I added. "She won't feel safe to be truthful in front of her father."

Nodding again, he turned to Flame Tongue. "I require a private word with Lady Anacoana before we can proceed."

Stiffening, Flame Tongue said, "It would be highly improper for me to allow her to be alone with a man prior to the wedding, even if that man is her future husband."

"Lady Quetzalpetlatl will act as our chaperone, if that makes you feel better," Little Reed said, acid in his voice.

Flame Tongue's wife took her husband's hand and drew him towards the door. "Let them talk, my dear," she whispered. He reluctantly followed her into the great hall.

"I am truly sorry, My Lady," Citlallotoc told Anacoana, and he too disappeared back inside.

Little Reed watched them go, then, with a sigh, he turned to Anacoana.

"Firstly, I must apologize, My Lady, for not consulting with you before ever thinking about approaching your father about a marriage between us. I have no explanation for this failure other than my own thoughtlessness. For that I am deeply sorry, and I understand if you hold this flaw against me."

"I do not, My Lord," she answered, her head bowed.

"It is not my desire to make you miserable or keep you from what your heart wants. Tell me that you want to marry Citlallotoc, and I will gladly step aside so you two can be together."

Anacoana looked up, fear in her eyes. "Please don't do that, My Lord. I have done much to disappoint my father in my short life, but that kind of slight is one he could never forgive me for."

"I would be the one delivering the slight, not you."

But she shook her head. "I've learned that no matter who delivers it, I am the one he blames. He blamed me for having to come back home after Ihuitimal's death, and he will blame me again if this proposal falls through."

"But if you marry Citlallotoc instead—" I started, trying to calm her growing distress, but she cut me off.

"He will never let me marry him, not now. His pride is wounded, and he would rather kill me than accept dishonor. Please, if we're to not marry, I beg you; end it all for me now, quickly, for it will be far more merciful than what my father will do."

Little Reed stepped up and grasped her shoulders, the alarm clear on his face. "No one is going to hurt you, My Lady. I won't allow it. We will marry, and you needn't live in fear any longer. I promise. Go and bring your family back, and we will continue discussing plans for the wedding."

"Thank you, My Lord." She hurried into the great hall, carefully wiping tears from her cheeks with her wrist.

Letting out a breath, Little Reed murmured, "What else could I do?"

"It's the right decision," I conceded. I'd always known Flame Tongue was a harsh man but seeing her reaction.... "We're getting her away from her father and she'll be safe. That's what's important right now; the rest we can work out afterwards."

¤

A week later, Little Reed and Anacoana married in the palace's great hall; and as when I'd married Little Reed, Mazatzin officiated. This was a much more luxurious affair, with all our allies in attendance, and all of them brought lavish gifts to celebrate the occasion.

Flame Tongue strutted around the palace as if he were the one marrying the King of Tollan, not his daughter; and though Little Reed asked me to personally oversee the menus for the various feasts, Flame Tongue constantly questioned my selections and made changes behind my back. He even made jokes about me to our allies, which sometimes garnered a laugh, but were mostly met with awkward silence.

"Tragic how she's fallen barren, but the gods are less lenient when it comes to thinking one's self above their superiors," I overheard him say once. Citlallotoc heard it too, and I had to threaten him with a public lashing to keep him from confronting Flame Tongue right in front of everyone.

"Let him make his rude remarks," I said. "I'd rather he didn't think they bother me." And besides, he'd be gone in a few days and I wouldn't have to deal with him anymore.

On the afternoon of the fourth day, the bride and groom's family gathered in Anacoana's new quarters, which were next door to my own, and we watched the solemn laying of the jade stones and feathers on the marriage bed. Anacoana looked pale and nervous—anxious about the coming wedding night, no doubt—and she fumbled over the recitation of her promises of sons to fulfill Little Reed's legacy. Little Reed recited his part with what I could only describe as the bare minimum of enthusiasm required. Tonight was definitely going to be awkward for them both.

Not that the night was remotely normal for me either. I'd told myself days ago that I wouldn't get upset—had no reason to—but I lay awake late into the night anyway, staring at the ceiling and feeling as if I'd swallowed fish hooks that someone now tried to yank back out. *Little Reed's finally having that wedding night I never could give him.* I told myself it was foolish to cry, but the tears came anyway, and I gave serious consideration to seeking solace in the god's arms again. I even went so far as to prepare the teonanactl and octli concoction, but I ended up dumping it into my flowers outside my bath yard; I couldn't keep my reason for the visit secret from the god. Instead I went into the nursery and lay on Yamehecatl's bed, cradling his toys in my arms, and cried myself to sleep. The illusion that Little Reed and I could ever have been happy together in spite of all those limitations and sacrifices was finally over.

¤

The morning that Anacoana's family left, I slept late and took a leisurely bath rather than get up to see them off. I was glad Flame Tongue was finally leaving, and I doubted he cared whether I was there to bid him goodbye; if anything, he probably enjoyed not having to bow and give me compliments.

After I'd dressed, Anacoana came to my quarters, looking embarrassed. "Forgive my intrusion, My Lady, but I can't seem to find the women's hall."

"There isn't one," I informed her as I finished pinning up my hair in front of the obsidian mirror in the bath yard.

"But where do we do our weaving?"

"Wherever you want. Many of the noblewomen gather in the solarium, but I personally prefer the patio in our garden. Would you like to join me?"

Anacoana smiled. "Very much so."

I instructed my handmaiden to bring Anacoana's weaving supplies out to the patio where she'd already set up mine. "I trust you've settled well into your quarters? You're not missing any necessities, are you?" I asked Anacoana as we sat on the flagstones.

"No, I have everything I need for now, but if I do need something from the market, whom should I speak to about it?"

"Your handmaiden can send someone to buy things for you, but you're also free to visit the market yourself; you need not ask Topiltzin's permission, just always take guards with you for your protection."

She blinked, surprised. "I was never allowed out of the palace back in Xico. Except for temple services, but I had to be in my mother's company. Are there places I'm not allowed to go?"

I laughed. "Hardly. We don't believe in cloistering women behind walls here. If you wish, you may even attend the council meetings. Personally I find them boring—all talk about tribute and crop yields; I wouldn't go if I weren't the queen."

"My father never lets any woman sit in on his war council meetings."

"Yes, well, I think you'll find that Topiltzin does many things differently than everyone else."

"He certainly does," she murmured. She gasped and slapped her hand over her mouth, as if she'd spoken out of turn. When I cast her a quizzical smile, her blush deepened. "Not that there's anything wrong with doing things differently."

Now I wondered if she was talking about her first night with Little Reed, not city policy. I couldn't imagine what might have been so strange about it; granted, he and I had never gone so far as they had, but what we had shared seemed perfectly normal—no, not normal; achingly wonderful. *But you're no model of normal sexual behavior, are you?* I thought with a chuckle.

Once we both started weaving, we talked of other things; the weather, the quetzals singing in the trees, and my duties at the temple. At noon the servants brought our lunch, and while we ate, Citlallotoc came in from the main hallway, looking distracted. When Yamehecatl was younger, he'd spend his afternoons with my son, either practicing sword-play in the exercise yard, or walking through the main garden, discussing honor and fair fighting. Once Yamehecatl started school, my son often mentioned missing those afternoons with Citlallotoc, and I wondered if Citlallotoc missed them as well.

When I glanced at Anacoana, she was watching him too, a wistful look on her face. I bristled, but I caught myself. *It's not her fault; this is her father's dream, not hers.* "I'm sorry things didn't work out for you and Lord Citlallotoc."

Caught, she went back to her food. "It is all right. I've grown used to such disappointments." But when she realized what she had said, she quickly added, "Not that marrying the King is in any way a disappointment—"

"It's allright," I assured her. "I know what you mean. Sometimes it seems the gods are conspiring against us."

"I'm lucky to be here in Tollan, under Lord Topiltzin's care. I'm grateful to both of you for this."

I gave her a smile and went back to finishing my lunch, watching Citlallotoc cross the portico to his quarters next to Little Reed's. When he saw us, he promptly ducked into his room, leaving the door curtain bells tinkling in the warm afternoon air. *He's in need of a wife more than ever,* I thought, *if only to keep his lust from overpowering his honor, having to see Anacoana every day.*

But I was quite certain that any suggestion of a new prospect would be met with staunch refusal, at least for a few months anyway.

As I finished up my lunch, Little Reed came out of the hallway too. Anacoana rushed to stand and bow, but as she was halfway up, he said, "It's quite all right. You don't have to rise every time we meet; in fact, I'd prefer that you didn't."

Looking embarrassed, she lowered herself back to the flagstones.

Turning to me, he said, "If you're not too busy, there's something I'd like to talk to you about."

"Of course, My Lord." I bade Anacoana goodbye and followed him into the portico. "I thought you had temple duties this afternoon."

"I decided to work from here today." He held his door curtain open for me. "And I was hoping you might help me."

He'd set up a small working area in front of the hearth, with a slab of mahogany for a desk; stacks of papers littered the floor. "What's all this about?" I asked.

"Unfinished business." He plucked a piece of paper off one of the stacks and handed it to me. "Tell me what you think."

I read it over twice before asking, "Is this a new law?"

He nodded. "Outlawing Smoking Mirror's worship here in Tollan. It completely dissolves the cult and lays down dire fines upon anyone caught practicing any rituals or prayers related to his worship."

I said no more as I read it yet again, my insides a maelstrom of confusion and contempt. When I finally finished, I sputtered, "That demon murdered our son, Little Reed, and you think the solution is to ban his cult in one tiny corner of the empire?"

"This is what you've been asking me to do for years, isn't it?" he asked, confused. "Isn't this what you've been pushing for?"

I handed the paper back to him. "Maybe there was a time when this was enough, but now.... Little Reed, all this does is punish honest people who've followed our laws—people such as Black Otter, who have worked hard to bring the cult into alignment with our philosophies. There have been no illegal sacrifices in Tollan for two years now, but Smoking Mirror is strong as ever, and you think dissolving the cult will do anything to stop him?"

"We haven't the authority to force our allies to follow our lead," he reminded me. "But rest assured that most of them will adopt this law as well—"

"I don't want some stupid law! I want that demon dead! I want him to never be able to hurt another human being ever again!"

Little Reed blinked, startled. "Destroy him? But how?"

"My magic, of course."

Little Reed took my hand in his. "Don't be foolish, Papalotl. He's an extremely powerful god—"

"And I'm nothing?" I tore my hand away from him.

"I didn't say that."

"I destroyed Mextli—"

"And Mextli was not Smoking Mirror. Mextli was a minor deity, worshipped by one small band of Chichimecs. Smoking Mirror is far more powerful than Mextli could have ever hoped to be, and one doesn't challenge him as if he can be felled with a well-placed arrow. He has magic neither of us has seen—powerful magic—and if you try to fight him—"

"I have fought him, and I won."

"With Quetzalcoatl's help. Think about what you'd have to give to call on him again."

"I have nothing left to give," I said, tears threatening. But I wouldn't let them fall. I grabbed the paper from him and held it up. "This isn't good enough!"

He took my hands again, the paper crumpled in my fists. "I understand your anger—I feel it too—but we can't forget our own ethics. And you're right, this law isn't the right answer; we both believe one should choose Quetzalcoatl not because we've eliminated the competition, but because he deserves it. And you're right that this will hurt everyone but Smoking Mirror. We must keep doing what we've been doing; he feels threatened, but if we stay true to Quetzalcoatl's plans—keep pushing Smoking Mirror's priesthood to embrace a different kind of worship—he'll have to come around to a new way of thinking, if he wants to stay relevant. It will take time, and patience, and sacrifice, but it will all be worth it."

Smoking Mirror is incapable of change. But I held my tongue. The gulf between Little Reed and I was one we could no longer bridge because we'd cut those ties to secure the kingdom's future. He had the possibilities of a family while I had nothing. *Except revenge for Yamehecatl. Just because Little Reed's afraid doesn't mean I have to be too. Let him have his wife and new family, let him give his righteous speeches and toe the same old lines. I owe Yamehecatl justice, and letting Smoking Mirror live is not that.* I would do this without Little Reed and without the god, and I'd make the world safe from Smoking Mirror.

Little Reed anxiously awaited my answer, so I gave him the one he wanted to hear. "We'll keep the course the god laid out for us. Forgive my anger and stupidity; I have a hole in my heart that refuses to heal."

He hugged me tight. "I understand, and please don't call yourself stupid. Pain is not stupidity."

No, stupidity was continuing to do the same thing as always and expecting things to change.

CHAPTER TWENTY-EIGHT

I needed significant work with my magic before I could attempt to face Smoking Mirror again, so I began practicing right away; I had evening temple duties, but on my dinner break I went to the maguey fields in the priestly gardens and worked with my magic. I started slowly and methodically, but as the days added up to months, I found I needed to use more and more magic to keep progressing, so I decided I needed to recruit someone to provide blood, to help replenish my strength after strenuous practices.

Still, it took me a couple of days to build up the courage to approach Malinalli after classes one day. "Can we talk for a minute?"

"Of course," she said, gathering up her codices to take back to her meditation room. "What's on your mind?"

I checked the hallway, making certain we were truly alone, then I said, "I feel strange asking you this, but...I've been working with my magic, trying to teach myself to better control it—so I don't end up killing myself with it, as I nearly did a few months ago—but I can't replenish it with food. I need blood."

I expected uncertainty at this request, but instead, without hesitation, she said, "I'm happy to help!"

I breathed a sigh of relief. "Thank you. You're truly a wonderful friend, Malinalli."

"How often are you practicing?"

"Daily, but I'm planning to limit myself to one strenuous practice a week, and that would be the only time I'd need the blood. Do you think that's too often, with our daily bloodletting rituals?"

She shook her head. "Perhaps we should set up a specific day each week, so I know when to eat more?"

We settled on the middle day, and we met in the priestly gardens, tucked away by the maguey plants. She'd eat her lunch under the oak tree while I stood at a safe distance, working and pushing myself a little further each time. I'd killed all the rabbits when I'd thrown everything I had at Smoking Mirror, so I ordered the royal game keeper to set traps to capture more outside the city. I made efforts to not kill them, but I always recited offering prayers to Quetzalcoatl, in case I failed; at least that way their deaths wouldn't be a waste. When I tired of practicing, Malinalli bled her arm into a cup for me. In exchange, I scheduled her temple duties so she had more free time with Mitotia.

All progressed well, and with a few more months of work, I'd be ready to avenge my sweet Warm Breeze. Or at least die trying.

¤

One afternoon, almost exactly four months after I buried Yamehecatl, our servants came to the family garden to take our lunch orders as usual, and while I dithered over what I wanted, Anacoan knew her preference immediately. "Fried maguey worms in the spiciest chile sauce. And double the portion." She'd eaten the same thing for the last three days, and once the servants left, she confided to me, "This is so strange, because I've always hated maguey worms, no matter how much chile sauce you cook them in, but I can't get enough of them these last couple of days. What on earth is wrong with my stomach?"

I gave her a knowing smile. "You're not late by chance, are you?"

"Late?" she asked, puzzled, but then she gasped. "Well, I've never really kept track of such things, but it has been at least a couple of moons since the last time..." She paled. "Do you think I'm with child?"

"Probably." She wrung her hands together, making me wonder if she too had lost someone dear to the childbed. "You're nervous about that?" I said.

"It's so soon. I thought I'd have at least a year to acclimate to being married before become a mother as well." She wiped her cheeks, taking deep breaths.

I gave her elbow a reassuring squeeze. "I know it's scary, but I'll help you through this. And the king will be very supportive. We should go and tell him."

She looked stricken. "Right now?"

I laughed. "Don't worry, he'll be very excited."

"But shouldn't we wait until I know for certain? I don't want to disappoint him."

"I kept my own pregnancy secret early on, and I nearly lost Yamehecatl because of it. He should know that you at least suspect it, so the servants know to help you and the kitchens can serve the right food."

"I suppose you're right," Anacoana finally agreed.

¤

Little Reed was in the temple with Mazatzin, preparing for the noon-time service. Citlallotoc was there as well, lounging against one of the stone columns, and Anacoana nearly retreated when she saw him. I caught her by the elbow and she murmured, "Sorry!" before moving around to my other side, keeping as far away from Citlallotoc as she could.

Little Reed set down the basket of snakes he held. "Is something the matter, Anacoana? You look ill."

She lowered her head, cheeks bright, so I answered, "My Lady has good news to share with you, My Lord." I nudged her forward.

She looked ready to vomit, but she pulled her nerves together. "I'm with child, My Lord. Or at least I believe so."

Little Reed looked to me for confirmation so I nodded. Smiling, he closed the gap with Anacoana and I expected him to embrace her—the way he always did with me—but he only took her hand, as if he were a father learning he would be a grandfather soon. "Wonderful news indeed.

How long now?"

She looked to me this time, so I answered, "We're not exactly certain right now, but I would suppose at least two months, maybe three."

"So sometime after the rainy season," Little Reed concluded. "Right around the time we take the initiates to Teotihuacan each year."

"Looks as if I'll have to go in your place this year," I noted. A nice stroke of luck. I needed somewhere outside the city to make my challenge against Smoking Mirror, lest innocent people be injured or killed. The sacred city would be the perfect place; it was huge and empty for the most part, visited only by priests.

Mazatzin smiled and congratulated Anacoana on her news. Citlallotoc did as well, but he didn't meet her gaze. After all these months, I'd hoped that he'd moved on, but perhaps that was too much to expect.

Anacoana thanked Mazatzin but ignored Citlallotoc, an unexpected coldness to her now.

"This is such wonderful news. We should share it with our people," Little Reed suggested. "Stay for the afternoon service and I'll make a sacrifice to honor this joyous occasion."

"An excellent idea, My Lord," Anacoana agreed with a perfunctory smile.

"I must return to the palace," Citlallotoc said, wandering to the stairs. "I need to wash up before going to the courts."

"Will you join us for dinner tonight?" Little Reed asked.

"If you wish." Citlallotoc left, and Anacoana watched him, but with a scowl.

"I must go too," I said. "I have things to attend to before my temple duties tonight."

"Will you join us for dinner too?" Little Reed walked around Anacoana to take my hand—a gesture I rarely thought about but now it felt wildly inappropriate in front of his wife. "I'm certain if you asked Malinalli, she would take your shift for you."

Feeling Anacoana's gaze, I withdrew my hand carefully from his. "I wish I could, but she already has plans."

Little Reed nodded, disappointed. "I'll see you tomorrow?"

"Of course." I gave a bow to Anacoana and left too, taking to a jog once I passed out of view of the temple platform. My guards picked up their pace to keep up with me.

Citlallotoc was already at the bottom, but he walked with a heaviness about him. He flinched when I ran up next to him. "Mind if I walk back to the palace with you?" I asked, taking his arm with mine.

He smiled. "Not at all."

We walked arm in arm while my guards cut a path through the morning crowds. "Such good news for the King and Anacoana, don't you think?"

"Wonderful indeed. And Topiltzin seems very excited."

"He does."

"And you're not at all bothered by that?"

I laughed. "Why should I be?"

"Well, you two were married and had a son of your own, but now he has this new child—"

A shiver of bitter anger surged through me. "This is the life the gods handed us, so I'm happy for Topiltzin." I didn't want to talk about this so I immediately steered in a more comfortable direction. "Are you bothered by Anacoana being pregnant?"

Now he laughed. "Why would I be?"

I shrugged. "She was rather cold to you back there. You're not still pining for her, are you?"

"I never *pined* for her, My Lady. As with you and Topiltzin, those are the beans the gods rolled for us, and I'm happy for her."

"But what about you? Don't you deserve to be happy too?"

"I am."

"Really?"

He nodded. "Doing my duty to you and the king makes me happy."

"There's more to life than serving us, Citlallotoc. Just because things didn't work out with Anacoana doesn't mean they won't work out with someone else—"

He stopped and pulled his arm from mine. "You talk all the time about making everyone else happy, but what about you? How can it not burn you that Topiltzin abandoned you to take a new wife and beget a new child?"

"He did not abandon me."

"Two days after burying your son, he unties his cape from your dress and gets betrothed to a new woman. What else should I call that?"

I stared at him, a wave of dizzying fury sweeping over me. "How dare you even speak to me about such things? You know nothing about my marriage to Topiltzin, and he doesn't have to answer to you!"

"No, he doesn't, but he owed you better than that."

I walked away, but when he tried to take my hand, I ripped it away from him. The guards stopped, no doubt wondering if they should intervene, but Citlallotoc didn't try again. "Quetzalpetlatl, please—"

"Don't talk to me!" I shouted. People stopped, whispering and gawking, so I stalked up to him and said, voice low but straining, "Not that it's any of your business, but I'm the one who told Topiltzin we had to divorce, and we've worked too hard building Tollan and bringing about the god's reforms for me to throw it all away in the name of selfishness." I swallowed hard, desperate not to cry. "Sometimes love isn't enough." This time when I strode away, my guards closed ranks around me.

Citlallotoc didn't follow.

¤

For the next few days, I took extra temple duties, the better to avoid Citlallotoc in the palace hallways. It had embarrassed me to have spoken of my own inadequacies aloud, but I also didn't want his pity.

But he was determined to give it to me anyway. Malinalli told me he'd come by the temple and the calmecac several times over the last couple of days and became quite frustrated when he didn't find me. "What's going on?" she asked, as she helped me go through the robe supply in the calmecac's storage rooms. "I found him lurking outside your meditation room not more than an hour ago."

"I really don't want to talk to him."

She frowned. "What did he do?"

I sighed as I scribbled on the inventory book she held open for me. "Nothing, to be honest." I'd already talked to Malinalli about the divorce, but I didn't want to rehash it all again.

"Then why not talk to him?"

"Because I'll get upset and say things I'd rather not, again."

"What is this about?"

"I probably should have never said anything to him in the first place," I admitted. "It's...I was concerned about him. I think he's still in love with

310

Anacoana."

"It has only been four months. Lost love can take a very long time to get over."

I knew that all too well; I suspected I would never fully get over Little Reed, not even if the gods granted me an eternity to do so. On a deep level, I felt as if Heaven had made us for each other, which made our forced separation all the more difficult. "If he can't let it go, he'll ruin his friendship with Topiltzin." Though given what he'd said about Little Reed, perhaps that city had already been sacked.

"That's not exactly the kind of thing you could tell the king about, is it?" Malinalli said.

I shook my head. "He needs to meet someone new."

"That, or maybe get away from Anacoana for a while. He usually makes those trips to our allied cities at this time of year, doesn't he?"

"We canceled it, since all of our allies were here for the prince's naming day celebration," Citlallotoc suddenly spoke up from the doorway behind us. When Malinalli clutched her chest in surprise, he added, "Sorry. I didn't mean to sneak up on you two." To me, he asked, "Can I have a moment of your time, My Lady? We must speak."

It would be rude to decline in front of Malinalli, but perhaps she would help me beg off, claiming we had somewhere to be....

Malinalli, however, had no such intentions. "I have a class I must go and prepare for." She folded up the book and edged past Citlallotoc to the door. So much for best friends.

Citlallotoc stepped up and held out a small silver bracelet in the shape of a feathered serpent biting its own tail. Rubies gleamed in its eyes and leaves of gold formed the delicate neck feathers. "This is for you."

"Why?"

"An apology, for the other day." He looked chastened. "I had no right to pry into such a painful subject—and make all the wrong assumptions, especially about Topiltzin—and I'm deeply ashamed. What right do I have to call myself his friend after saying such things?"

"It undoubtedly looked that way from the outside," I admitted. "I didn't tell him anything you said."

"*I* told him; honor dictates I accept responsibility for my words and actions, and he has kindly forgiven me for my mistake. And I'm hoping you can do the same. Please?"

I sighed. "I pestered you just as hard, and I am sorry for that."

"Do you accept my apology?"

"Of course. But a gift is not necessary."

He looked at the piece of jewelry, embarrassed. "I saw it in the market the other day and it made me think of you. It was a silly sentiment."

Now how could I turn down such a thoughtful gift? Taking the bracelet, I slipped it on and smiled. "Thank you. You're such a kind man, and I hate seeing you having no one to share that with."

He chuckled. "We're all right again, then?"

"Absolutely."

◻

Matters remained tense between him and Anacoana. As the months passed, their public interactions grew increasingly chilly, with Anacoana often openly glaring at him while he cheerfully ignored her in favor of engaging me in conversation over meals or in the hallways. Whatever fear I might have had about extramarital infidelities appeared to be completely unfounded.

But I also noticed that Little Reed paid only cursory attention to his wife anymore, even as time made it clear she was carrying his child. Anytime he asked me to join him in his quarters, to talk about city business or a new law we needed to enact, she'd watch us from her doorway, staring with forlorn eyes, only to disappear behind her curtain as soon as she realized I'd seen her. I wished I could assure her that she had nothing to worry about, but I knew it wouldn't help. Little Reed had kept his promise to not stop loving me, at her expense. I hoped that when the child was born, that would bring them closer together.

As for Citlallotoc and Little Reed, they seemed closer than ever.

But then one afternoon in early summer, I passed by the great hall to hear them arguing. When I poked my head inside, Little Reed was pacing, agitated, while Citlallotoc stood by the hearth, fist clenched and eyes intense. "I did what you asked of me, Topiltzin," he said, his voice carefully modulated now. "I've always done everything you've asked of me, no questions asked, so why hold out on me on one simple request?"

"This is no simple request," Little Reed fired back.

"You act as if I ask more of you than you did of me. I risked not only

312

my own honor, but yours as well. You're my best friend, and I thought that meant something to you."

"It means everything to me, Citlallotoc!"

"Then why deny me this?"

Little Reed laughed, exasperated. "You have no idea what you're truly asking for. I won't let you fall into ruin!"

"If people find out what I've done, I'd be ruined anyway, so what does it matter?"

"It matters!"

The escalating tension scared me, so I finally stepped inside and cleared my throat. Little Reed's scowl dropped a fraction when he saw me, but he remained on edge. Citlallotoc stood straighter, looking rebuffed. "Why are you two tearing at each other?" I said.

Citlallotoc looked at Little Reed, expectant.

"It's merely a foolish disagreement, that's all." Little Reed embraced me, kissed my cheek, and smiled; quite the display to convince me. "How are plans for the pilgrimage coming along?"

"Well enough." I looked back and forth between the two; Citlallotoc looked even more vexed as he scraped his sandal over the stone floor, but he said nothing. "Is everything all right?" I asked him.

Citlallotoc gave me a false smile. "All is well, My Lady." Turning to Little Reed, he said, "Forgive my rash tongue, My Lord."

"It's all right, my friend." Little Reed patted him on the shoulder. "I do owe you a kindness and I have an idea that will meet your approval. Perhaps we could talk later?"

"I look forward to it. But if you'll excuse me, I'm late for hunting with the other noblemen." He bowed and left.

"Is everything all right between you two?" I asked Little Reed again.

"Of course," he insisted. "Just a disagreement."

"What is this favor he did for you? He said he risked his honor—"

"It's truly nothing, Papalotl," he said, his words clipped.

I'd never seen him so evasive, and that troubled me.

¤

With the pilgrimage only weeks away, I spent most of my time with temple duties and planning the trip to Teotihuacan. I especially looked forward to spending time with Mazatzin; I didn't see him for more than a few minutes each day, but the little bit we shared was always pleasant. He never stared or gawked in that blank way that other men did, and I could lower my personal shield around him. We'd once been friends in the way most brothers and sisters were—something Little Reed and I never could be—and that was precious to me. I looked forward to rediscovering that connection.

I hadn't led one of these pilgrimages since before the destruction of Xochicalco. My duties as a mother kept me from going in the years since, because Yamehecatl needed nursing for the first three years, and after that, I feared a reversion to his drunken outbursts. But it was bitter medicine knowing that the only reason I was going this year was because my son was dead, and his replacement would be born any day now.

But the thought of vengeance eased that a bit.

As the day pressed closer, my focus became exacting and my worries about being prepared and powerful enough faded away. I'd become so good with my magic that I could turn my evening cup of water into octli with only a small amount of concentration. And the octli was far more potent than anything we brewed in the priesthood. Months ago I would have balked at the idea of comparing myself to a goddess, but now I embraced it; I couldn't face a god like Smoking Mirror without a sense that I was his equal, or maybe even better. I was ready to face him.

There was only one thing left to work out; how to get Smoking Mirror to show up exactly where I wanted him when I wanted him to.

But when Black Otter came to my meditation room to deliver his cult's weekly report, the final bean fell into place on my elaborately planned patolli game.

Once we finished discussing priestly business, I asked him to stay for lunch. He sat fidgeting in front of the hearth as I split up the food between us. "You said that if there was ever anything you could do for me that I shouldn't hesitate to ask," I said.

"Do you need my help with something?"

"Something very important." Lowering my voice, I continued, "I need your help summoning Smoking Mirror."

Black Otter dropped his rolled-up tlaxcalli and spilled its turkey and squash filling all over the floor. "Why ever would you want to do that?" He avoided my gaze, focusing on picking up his dropped food.

"Because I intend to destroy him."

Black Otter stared at me, lost for words. Eventually he found his tongue again. "This is madness, My Lady. He's a god! He'd kill us both!"

"I don't need you to do the ceremony, Black Otter. It's enough that you tell me how to do it."

He frowned. "And you really think I'd let you do this alone? I'm no coward."

"And neither am I."

"If you won't allow me to be there during the summoning, then I won't tell you how to do it." He looked nervous but determined.

I sighed. "Fine. We'll do it together."

Black Otter dusted off his tlaxcalli and set it on his plate. He chewed his lip a moment before asking, "When do you mean to do this?"

"When I'm in Teotihuacan."

He nodded. "There will be fewer people around, and the ceremony is dangerous if not done properly.... It will require careful preparation, and a sacrifice."

"We haven't registered any volunteers this year for Smoking Mirror's cult."

"I can get one from one of our allied cities. The cult has a larger following in the valley than here in Tollan, and we brought last year's Toxcatl volunteer from Culhuacan. Once I secure one, I'll bring him to the palace to be registered."

"No!" When he cast me a startled look, I said, "If Topiltzin finds out about this, he'll stop us, and he'll be suspicious if we bring in a sacrifice from Culhuacan six months before the next Toxcatl. I'll question the volunteer and make certain he's willing once you bring him to Teotihuacan, all right?"

Black Otter nodded. "You're certain you want to do this?"

"Positive."

"Forgive my asking, but exactly how do you propose we kill Smoking Mirror?"

I shook my head. "It isn't we; I'll let you help me do the summoning, but once that's done, I want you out of there. This battle is between me and Smoking Mirror, and I can't have him using you against me."

Black Otter blinked. "How could he possibly do that?"

"Don't be silly. You're family, and my friend."

He smiled, grateful. "Thank you, My Lady. But you still haven't told me how you're going to destroy Smoking Mirror."

"I have my ways."

My answer visibly frustrated him, but he let me leave it at that. We ate in silence, but when he rose to leave, he paused at the door and turned back to ask, "Why do you want to destroy Smoking Mirror anyway?"

"Because first he took my uncles from me, then my parents, and now he's taken my son too." I stared into the hearth, crumbling the leftover tlaxcalli in my fist. "It's time someone did something about him."

CHAPTER TWENTY-NINE

Two days out from departure, I met with Little Reed in his quarters for breakfast, and to discuss the security arrangements for the journey. "The scouting reports haven't shown any significant hostile activity north of Culhuacan for several months now, so I think a contingent of twenty men should do the job," Little Reed told me. "I'll assign Icnoyotl to lead the detail."

"Really? Is Citlallotoc ill?" For the last seven years, he'd overseen security on the pilgrimages.

"No."

"Then why isn't he leading this?"

"Icnoyotl is a good soldier—"

"And I know nothing about him," I replied, irritated. "I'm more comfortable with Citlallotoc leading this."

Little Reed sighed. "As you wish, Papalotl." He poked at his breakfast with a curious look of dread.

"Are you two still fighting?"

"We're not fighting."

"You've been friends too long to let petty things get between you."

"Nothing is getting between us."

I still felt uneasy when I left his quarters. *You don't suppose they've been arguing about me?* I wondered, but had to laugh that egotistical thought away. Little Reed wasn't prone to jealousy, and while Citlallotoc and I were close, we were only friends; he'd never shown any interest in me as he had with Anacoana. It had to be about her.

So I watched Little Reed and Citlallotoc carefully whenever they were together, but whatever had gone between them seemed indeed fixed. On the day we left for Teotihuacan, they laughed during their goodbyes. Anacoana ignored them with her usual coldness, and gave me a tired farewell. She was very large now, a good sign for the baby she carried, but all this drama and resentment wasn't good for either of them.

When Little Reed bade me goodbye, I warned him, "Take good care of your wife while I'm gone. Spend some time with her; rub her sore back and give her warm baths. The last month is the most tedious, and she will be grateful for your attention."

"I'll keep that in mind." But already I knew he wouldn't do any of it; I could tell by how long and tight he hugged me. I didn't understand it at all. He couldn't keep his hands off me, yet he balked at simply holding Anacoana's hand even for public appearances. How on earth had they managed to conceive at all? I felt as if I was reliving that moment before Black Otter left to negotiate for Amoxtli, where he'd kissed me as if we were on our way to bed rather than saying goodbye in front of half of the palace. And, just as back then, Anacoana watched us, but without the blindfold of youthful inexperience protecting her.

Yet I might never see Little Reed again, I thought. If the battle with Smoking Mirror went badly, this was the last time I'd ever see him, and I wanted to kiss him more passionately than I ever had before, so I'd have no regrets on the road into Mictlan.

But I couldn't be that cruel to Anacoana. I stole a sisterly kiss to his cheek and whispered, "I love you, Little Reed," and turned away quickly, accepting Citlallotoc's help up into the royal litter. Once behind the safety of the curtains, I peeked back out to find Little Reed looking back at me with a wistful, distant look on his face. I watched him the whole way out of the courtyard, until I couldn't see him—or Anacoana—anymore.

¤

When we reached Teotihuacan, we camped in the same courtyard as we had for that first pilgrimage eighteen years ago. The hole in the courtyard wall—which we women had crawled through to escape hostile Chichimecs—had grown larger with the years, and the wall in the adjacent courtyard, the one Nimilitzli had fallen from and broken her hip, had completely tumbled down. It was an acute reminder of how all things changed and crumbled away with time.

And I noticed, for the first time, that Mazatzin's hair had silvered at his temples, and he'd developed a slight hump on his back. He was older than his father had been when I'd first come to Xochicalco, but whereas Cuitlapanton had fathered over twenty children by then, Mazatzin—his only remaining heir—was unmarried, childless, and devoted to the god. When Mazatzin died, Xochicalco's royal bloodline would end. Just as my father's royal bloodline would die with me, thanks to Yamehecatl's death.

In the morning we gathered on the summit of the Temple of the Sun to meditate, but I watched over the city with a wary eye, for signs of enemies; a habit I'd developed after that first pilgrimage. Even though it had been a long time since I'd last been to Teotihuacan, it was one I couldn't shake. But unlike then, the morning was bright and warm, and the Black Dog wasn't prowling the streets, slathering victims with his deadly tongue.

At least not yet, I thought. During my vigil, I noticed a small field of maguey plants growing just northwest of the city, bordered by a meandering brook. It was too far away to see clearly, but there appeared to be a colony of rabbits there too; many small dark blotches moved among the maguey and the scrub brush. The perfect confluence of everything I needed to make the best possible strike against Smoking Mirror. *A good omen.*

And when I took the young women to the Feathered Serpent's pyramid for an augury demonstration, the entrails reinforced my confidence. The guts showed signs of yet another year of abundant rainfall and plentiful crops: more prosperity for Tollan. A positive sign that I would defeat Smoking Mirror and eliminate the one remaining imperfection in the god's utopia.

Yet, in the corner, some of the entrails pooled into a second omen: self-discovery. It wasn't bad, but it gave me pause. It sat completely apart from everything else, unconnected to the prosperity the rest of the omens promised, and I was the only one to see it.

While my novice women cooked dinner, I wandered down to the men's camp, searching for Black Otter. I found him talking with Mazatzin, but he quickly split off to see me.

"You brought what we need?" I asked, keeping my voice low.

Black Otter motioned to a man standing with the other male servants we'd brought with us. He hurried over and Black Otter took all three of us out into the crumbling corridor, leading us towards the women's camp. "This is Falling Eagle."

Falling Eagle bowed his head and I returned the gesture, as was customary when addressing someone who'd offered themselves as a sacrifice. "You're aware of why you're here before me?" I asked.

He nodded. "I am to honor the Smoking Mirror with my blood and breath."

"You enter into this sacred ritual of your own free will? No one has coerced or tricked you into forfeiting your life on the eagle stone?"

"It is a great honor to give my life to the Smoking Mirror, and I give it without regret or reservation."

I couldn't imagine why anyone would willingly give their life to a demon god, but who was I to tell this man whom he should and shouldn't give it to? As required by the law, I kissed the man's cheeks, placing the royal blessing on his new status as a sacrifice. "I hereby note and permit your final offering in the name of Tezcatlipoca the Smoking Mirror."

Falling Eagle nodded, grim, then returned to the camp.

"When do you want to do this?" Black Otter asked as we continued walking.

"Tomorrow night. Is that enough time for us to prepare?"

"We can do it anytime you want. Do you know where?"

"There's a field off that way, outside the city." I pointed to the northwest.

"The one with all the maguey plants?" When I nodded, he said, "I suppose they'll make good cover in a fight."

I'm not going to use them for cover, I almost said, but the less I had to admit, the better. As we approached the entrance to the women's camp, I said, "Let's meet at midnight tomorrow, behind the Pyramid of the Moon, and you bring everything we need." I bade him goodnight and retired to the courtyard, where the smell of fresh tlaxcallis and stewed beans had my stomach rumbling.

¤

The day dragged by like a snail crossing the northern desert, but eventually the sun set on what could be my last day on earth. All the waiting allowed the doubt to build up, but as the camp wound down and the girls went to their tents one by one, my moment of reckoning was close at hand.

I went to my tent too, but didn't sleep. I thought about praying to Quetzalcoatl for strength and giving him an offering of blood, to ask him to watch over me, but I decided I couldn't afford to go into this battle even remotely depleted. I stared at the ceiling, listening to the night until only the mutterings of the guards disturbed the silence.

Using the pretext of visiting the water yard down the passageway, I left the women's camp, but once alone in the yard, I climbed the back wall and stole into the night, toward the Pyramid of the Moon. Jitters turned my steps light and quick. *Finally I can avenge Yamehecatl and rid this world of an evil monster—or die trying.* I let the magic build in my hands, igniting my confidence and easing my nerves.

Black Otter waited for me behind the pyramid, pacing until he saw me approach. Falling Eagle stood nearby, looking as nervous as my cousin.

"We're ready?" I asked.

Black Otter bowed, but glared at the other man when he didn't follow suit. "Show proper reverence, man. You're standing in the presence of the Empress of the Tolteca."

Few people ever addressed me as the Empress, so hearing Black Otter honor me so made made the desire glow inside. *After all of this is done, he deserves some extra recognition, a position on the council perhaps,* I thought, granting him a smile. *And maybe a position in our bed as well.* Normally I would scold the desire for its depravity, but I would need it tonight against Smoking Mirror.

Falling Eagle moved to prostrate himself, but I wanted to hurry. "You two follow me." I led us out into the field.

Walking through the maguey was like walking through a forest, for they towered on every side, their fully-bloomed stalks standing sentry against the full moon. And rabbit holes littered the ground all over. I couldn't have asked for a better location.

When we came to a small clearing with the brook a handful of paces away, I stopped and looked around. "Let's do it here."

Falling Eagle looked around, visibly sweating now. "But where's the eagle stone, My Lady?" His voice shook.

Before I could say anything, Black Otter grabbed Falling Eagle from behind and plunged a blade into his back.

As one of the highest priests of Tollan, it was my duty to oversee every human sacrifice performed, to make certain that anyone who wanted to back out at the last moment could do so. It wasn't unusual for a man's survival instincts to take over and fight back once the sacrifice started, but when Fallen Eagle rounded on Black Otter, he fought back with the ferocity of a man who truly didn't want to die. He grabbed Black Otter by the throat and started throttling him, but Black Otter reached around and twisted the knife, making him roar in agony. Black Otter finally ripped the blade out and tackled him to the ground, dodging Falling Eagle's pummeling fists. "Quick! Pin his arms down!" he called to me.

But I stood frozen, my mind reeling.

"Get over here and help me!" Black Otter panted. "It takes two priests to hold down a sacrifice!"

"But he's not willing!" I cried.

"Too late! Hurry or he'll bleed to death and all this will matter for nothing!"

I hesitated while Black Otter's words sunk in; Falling Eagle was going to die—there was no preventing it now—so there was no use wasting his death. I finally shook off the paralysis and rushed over, pressing my knees against Falling Eagle's arms. I started murmuring a prayer to Quetzalcoatl—begging his forgiveness for what we were about to do—but Black Otter snapped, "Don't do that! You'll give the sacrifice to Quetzalcoatl and we'll have nothing to summon Smoking Mirror!"

He was right, but I still felt as if I were abandoning my scruples when I pressed down harder as Falling Eagle made one last effort to buck both of us off. Black Otter sat on his chest until he laid still, struggling to breathe; but when Black Otter made the incision under his ribcage, Falling Eagle screamed, "Gods save me!"

I clamped a hand over his mouth, stifling his cries. He thrashed, nearly tossing Black Otter off, so I flopped my whole body over his shoulders and head, smothering him under me. I clenched my eyes shut, trying to reassure myself that we weren't committing murder.

When Black Otter thrust the man's feebly-beating heart into my hands,

I thought I would vomit—I was seven again, standing in my father's room, my entire world ending. I nearly dropped it, but Black Otter clasped his hands—hot and sticky—around mine. "Repeat everything I say," he panted. I nodded, numb, but did as he said.

"Tezcatlipoca,
Lord of Darkness and Deceit,
I call you forth from the veil.
Come forward and answer for your crimes,
Face me,
Face your reckoning!"

I repeated the invocation over and over, each time with growing conviction and anger until I shouted the challenge. Power vibrated in my limbs as the heart shook, but I didn't even flinch when it burst into purple flame in my hands. When it disappeared—leaving me unscathed—I hurried to my feet, magic throbbing in my hands.

But nobody came.

I turned in a circle, sure he was trying to sneak up on me. "What are you afraid of?" I shouted into the night. "Is the so-called great and powerful Smoking Mirror too afraid to come out and face me?" When no one answered, I unleashed a gush of magic at the nearest maguey plant, letting my frustration and anger flow out with it.

As the plant thrashed in the night air, Black Otter backed away from me, his eyes wide. "How—?"

"You summoned me?" a familiar child's voice suddenly asked, and I whirled to see Night Wind standing with Mextli—*Mextli!*—in the bright moonlight.

I stared at Mextli, dumbstruck. "How...you're still alive? But I destroyed you!"

Mextli laughed. "You think you can destroy me with a smattering of octli magic? My, you're an egotistical one!"

"You...faked all that?"

"I couldn't just leave and let you think I run from fights. It was already embarrassing enough that I had to regroup after our first battle."

I turned my disbelieving gaze to Night Wind. "So you took the boy prisoner?"

"Hardly," Night Wind answered. "You summoned me, and I came."

His response confused me at first, but then the truth struck me like an arrow. "You're Smoking Mirror!"

Night Wind nodded, a broad grin on his young face.

"Cowardly dog! You took over an innocent boy so I'd have to slaughter him to actually face you!"

He shook his head and wagged his finger. "While it's true that my bond with him can only be broken with his death, someone else made that decision years ago. The boy you know as Night Wind has been gone a very long time now."

"But Ozomatli never completed the summoning ceremony—"

"Even years before that."

I couldn't wrap my brain around this. "You...you were in Night Wind all along, and you've been living in my palace, playing with my son...? Dear gods, you were Yamehecatl's best friend; he looked up to you!" My skin crawled.

"Why so shocked? Someone needed to encourage him to find his true nature rather than languish in that weak human form he was born to. Mictlan knows his father has no interest in such things. And why shouldn't I take an interest in my nephew? We're all family."

"And that's why you killed him? Because he's family? Because as Quetzalcoatl's son, he must be some kind of threat to you?" Hot tears spilled down my cheeks.

Smoking Mirror glared back at me. "I am many terrible things—things I take great glee in being—but I didn't kill my nephew. I liked him; sharp and prone to bouts of temper that could put even me to shame. He would have made an excellent ally for my cause when he was older."

"He would never join you! You're evil!"

"You say that as if it's a bad thing. Without death, there is no life, without night there is no day, and without evil, there is no good. Everything exists in a balance, and to rid the world of one throws everything into chaos. Is that what you were intending to do tonight? Throw the world into chaos?"

"You killed my son," I repeated through gritted teeth.

"I didn't do it."

"Liar! You ambushed him in the grass in the garden, and when I sent a horde of rabbits after you, you dropped him and fled over the wall like a coward!"

"Yes, but did I say anything witty to insult you?"

His inane question took me aback. "No, but you already know that."

"Of course I know, because my nahual doesn't speak when I'm not in its head, you silly little girl, and had I been there, I would have taunted you, because that's the kind of god I am. You might not believe it, but I would never hurt Ehecacone. But not all of us share that sentiment, do we, Black Otter?" He glared past me.

When I whirled around, Black Otter shrank away, opening a giant chasm in my heart. "You killed Yamehecatl?" Desperation choked me to a whisper. *Please don't let it be so!*

Looking exceptionally pale in the moonlight, Black Otter pressed closer, filled with resolve. "We are meant to be together, Quetzalpetlatl. The first time we made love...my soul opened up and I heard the gods themselves! But you ran off and married Topiltzin and had his son, and I knew so long as that child tied you to him, you wouldn't come back to me. I did what I had to do."

"You're a monster." I didn't shout or scream, merely stated fact, too numb to feel anything.

He glared at me, his posture tensing. "I made sacrifices for you; I gave my soul to the river goddess for a chance to come back to you; I poisoned Jade Flower so she couldn't stand in our way once I came back to Tollan. I gave Smoking Mirror my son's body so he could walk the earth, and I gave him countless more tonallis in the years since, to ensure our future together—"

"You've been killing people, in Tollan?"

"The god requires constant feeding to keep his essence settled in his host. I've just gotten better about hiding the bodies since you and Topiltzin found the grave."

Dear gods, Ozomatli was innocent! I choked on my own guilt as I sputtered, "And what about Ozomatli? Did you kill him too?"

"What do you care? He was far from inculpable; he was poisoning my father, and he tried to have Amoxtli killed. Granted, he did all that under my orders, to help me secure Culhuacan's throne and eliminate my rivals, but he was an easily manipulated coward too afraid to stand up for himself, even when I was his subordinate. His end wasn't anything he didn't deserve."

I was such a fool; I didn't know Black Otter at all. And neither had his father, or his brother. "But...why summon Smoking Mirror? Why is he here?"

"Because I must eliminate Topiltzin; he's the last thing standing between us, and only a fool would challenge him without divine help on their side." He looked at Smoking Mirror, his brow furrowed. "But I grow impatient with your stalling, and your excuses. Tonight you will finally put an end to him."

Mextli stepped forward, his feathers standing on end. "How dare you order around the Lord of Sorcerers—"

But Smoking Mirror grabbed his hand, stopping him.

Black Otter chuckled. "That's right, Lord Nobody. You can't hurt me; I made certain your slippery friend couldn't turn on me, or set his allies on me either. My father taught me enough to know that one doesn't make deals with the gods—especially the Smoking Mirror—without covering all contigencies. You harm me, and he ends up in Mictlan for breaking a solemn vow before Heaven—and are you prepared to pay a hefty price to Mictlantecuhtli to get him back?"

Mextli balled his fists, but Smoking Mirror chided him, "Patience, Mextli."

"Enough stalling!" Black Otter barked. "You will bring Topiltzin here, right now, so I can watch you destroy him!"

I'd felt as if my mind was slowly floating away, but the mention of Little Reed brought it crashing back in a fury. The magic poured out of my hands, down my legs and into the ground. *Make him pay!* the desire hissed with glee.

Black Otter didn't notice the maguey moving behind him, nor the roots slowly snaking out of the ground beneath him. Only when they crept up his legs, twisting and winding did he suddenly break off ranting at Smoking Mirror. "What—what are you doing, Quetzalpetlatl? You can't—Smoking Mirror! What is the meaning of this?"

Smoking Mirror grinned. "She's not my ally."

Black Otter tried backing away from the twining roots, but they shot up around him, lashing over his shoulders and pulling him to his knees. "Don't you understand that I love you, Quetzalpetlatl?" he cried, struggling. "I did everything for you!"

But when I knelt in front of him—my body no longer under my own control—he stared back in awe, and terror, the way Ahexotl had looked at me before he died; the way my uncle had as well. "Heaven save me," he murmured. "Your radiance...your beauty...so sweet an agony, My Lady. My soul, my very life I shall give to no one but you. Forgive me for not seeing the real you until now...for not seeing the truth, for not worshiping you properly!" He froze when I leaned forward and kissed him.

No demanding arousal accompanied the gesture, not even when he returned the kiss with ferocity, trying to wrestle my tongue into submission. The desire was in complete control, calculating and unmoved by any of it, and when I pulled away, he gave me a drunken smile.

"You should have stayed drowned, Black Otter." I looked past him, to the brook a handful of paces away. "Time to correct that mistake."

He watched me with that drunken smile, oblivious as the roots pulled him away from me, but when the water lapped over his feet, he started fighting again. "No! Please! Don't let her have me! Please, My Lady! I love you! I will give my life for you! I'll give it *to* you!"

I said nothing, just basked in the heat of justice flowing over me as the maguey roots wrestled him into the brook, holding his head under the water. He struggled mightily, but only for a moment. I felt his slowing heartbeat through the roots, and as the life seeped from his body, the energy flowed back through them, into my limbs, and my body drank it up with a savor unlike anything I'd ever experienced. The sky took on the vibrant purple of the Divine Dream and I could see Omeyocan high among the clouds.

But when I looked at my own hands, I finally saw what Ahexotl, Ihuitimal, and now Black Otter had seen. A cloud of pale orange light surrounded me, mist-like, licking the air in silent, vibrating wisps. I turned to Smoking Mirror and Mextli, and they too glowed: Mextli with turquoise and Smoking Mirror a bright violet, as with his nahual.... I gasped. "I'm a goddess?"

Mextli chuckled. "I told you she'd work it out."

"And she convinced someone to sacrifice himself to her before even knowing who she truly was. Impressive indeed!" Smoking Mirror conceded. "But it's still disappointing that it took her thirty-five years to see the obvious."

"Obvious? How could I have possibly known—"

But when I really thought about it, the signs had always been there: my perfect memory, my magic, my bizarre cravings for the rotting smell of the temple, and my strange aura that made men—and some women—completely lose focus. Red Flint's obsession I could dismiss as unfortunate, but Black Otter too?

But which goddess was I?

I was about to ask, but those clues were there too: my ability to control maguey plants and my octli magic—all things associated with the fertility goddess Mayahuel. "But she's dead," I whispered, my heart pounding drunkenly in my chest. "The Earth Monster destroyed her."

"Did you learn nothing in that quaint little priestly school of yours?" Smoking Mirror shook his head. "Gods don't die; they just sleep until they rise again."

"But why didn't I know? And why can't I remember anything even now?"

"Because the mists around the Black Lake feed on memories," Mextli provided. "The longer you sit waiting to be resurrected, the more you lose, and the longer it takes to regain those memories. Give yourself time and you will remember again."

"Why didn't you tell me all this to begin with?"

I turned to Black Otter lying face-down in the brook. Might it have spared my friend the madness I'd inflicted on him?

Smoking Mirror and Mextli exchanged glances, as if conversing silently, but then Smoking Mirror laughed. "Why ever would I? It amused me, watching you go around oblivious, unintentionally harming your friends and loved ones." He giggled and shivered as if remembering something hilarious. "And besides, if not for Mextli, I would have let you languish and die a mortal, which is the only way you can truly destroy a god, my dear. Your weak love and octli magic isn't up to the challenge of turning me mortal."

"I have no words for how...disgusting you are," I snarled.

"I tell you the truth about yourself and I'm the disgusting one? What about your precious Feathered Serpent? He kept you blind and deceived you far longer than I did."

His words punched my chest. *Quetzalcoatl knew?* "You're lying...trying to turn me against—"

"Who do you think brought you back from the dead?"

I snapped my mouth shut, unable to breathe now.

"Of course he knew! And long before me or Mextli worked it out. And yet he chose not to tell you the truth. I wonder why? If you'd died a mortal, you could never come back, and yet he chose to keep you ignorant. Why would the god who claims to love you—to love humanity—why would he condemn you to eternal oblivion by keeping your true identity secret from you?"

My stomach rebelled. Smoking Mirror couldn't be right, but...in those countless hours we spent intimately wrapped up in each other in the Divine Dream, why didn't Quetzalcoatl tell me any of this? How many times had I nearly died over these thirty-five years? *Nearly? You actually did die, and it was Little Reed who saved you from oblivion, not Quetzalcoatl. Black Otter's betrayal is unforgivable; but if not for that, would you have ever found out the truth?*

My voice broke when I finally spoke again. "Why does any of this matter to you anyway? You didn't care until Mextli said you should."

"Because war between the gods is coming," Mextli answered. "And the time for picking sides will end soon, and those who choose wrong will pay the ultimate price. Quetzalcoatl's conduct is shameful; you deserve to know the truth of your divinity, and to realize your full potential. You belong in Omeyocan with your own kind, adding your voice to the discussions of the future—not trapped here as a mortal, ignorant of the anger and discontent your actions send through Heaven. You deserve to make an informed choice about which side you truly want to be on once the war begins."

I laughed bitterly. "It's certainly not your side."

Mextli sneered. "So you would continue fighting for the god who lied to you for the last thirty-five years, who would have seen you disappear forever, completely forgotten a hundred years from now?"

The truth stung so badly. My beloved god *had* betrayed me, and I'd be a fool to continue following him, and yet...I'd always seen such love and devotion in his eyes when we were together. How could I reconcile all of this?

"I don't want anything to do with either side."

"Whether you like it or not, you're already involved, Mayahuel," Smoking Mirror said. "More than a few gods already speak your name as if it is a curse. Join me and Mextli against Quetzalcoatl, and we will protect you from them."

I shook my head, my mind reeling. I needed time to think, to digest this new reality and what it meant for my future. "Go away and leave me alone!" I cried.

Smoking Mirror sighed. "Very well, but having eternal life again doesn't mean you have eternity to make up your mind." To Mextli, he said, "Let's go now. This infernal human host requires rest and its complaining muscles and fuzzy brain annoy me."

As Smoking Mirror turned to leave, Mextli stepped up, towering over me. I shied away.

"I understand this is a lot to take in, and after being fooled by one god it's difficult to trust any other. But when you're ready to embrace who you are and what it means, know you could have an ally in that journey, if you so choose." He gave me a pointed look, then turned and strode back to Smoking Mirror—who shook his head and laughed as they walked away together into the night.

I watched them until they disappeared, then my gaze settled on Falling Eagle, lying on the ground. I clasped my hand over my mouth, stifling the sob in my throat as I crumbled to my knees. What had I done? *I've committed murder, which means exile from everything I know, everyone I love—*

Black Otter murdered him, not you, the growling voice of my desire said. *He pulled the fool's heart out.*

But I told him to!

He didn't have to. He chose to.

I should have listened to Little Reed.

And still not know the truth? That man's death wasn't pointless; it brought you back to immortality.

"Wonderful. Now I have an eternity to feel guilty about it," I muttered.

The maguey roots snaked over Falling Eagle's body and pulled it under the upturned soil. I scrambled to my feet, repulsed as the ground writhed like a nest of feasting maggots. "What in Mictlan—?"

His life was nothing before he met you; now it has meaning. It nourishes the earth, it grows the maguey, and it fills the sap that makes the octli. It feeds the goddess, and she is grateful for his sacrifice.

"And it conveniently hides the body," I noted dryly.

You have so much to relearn, Mayahuel.

I walked over to Black Otter, lying face down in the brook. I tried to conjure some guilt for him, but I couldn't let go of all he'd done. The friend I'd loved had died long before that day on Lake Metzliapan, and what came back in his place was someone I didn't know at all.

What will I tell Cuicatl? I wondered, numbness settling over me. *In one day she loses both her brother and her father—*

Black Otter started to groan.

I yelped and jumped away, my heart racing. He rose to his knees, the front of his priestly robe stained with mud and moss; but when he tried to speak, it came out as a shrieking cry.

To my horror, his body transformed right before me. His hands gnarled into claws and glossy hair sprouted from his arms and legs. He tried to stand but only managed to hunch over, his feet contorting and stretching. His face became elongated, more hair growing from his cheeks and jowls while whiskers sprouted from his snout; dagger-like fangs pushed out his human teeth. His whole body stretched, becoming longer and his robe slid off his narrowing shoulders. A tail with a ghastly hand at the end lashed out like a scorpion's stinger.

The dreams! I realized, backing away slowly. It had been years since I'd last dreamt of him rising from the lake as a monster with a grasping hand on its tail—this very monster—screaming, "Mine! Mine! Mine!"

And he shrieked those very words as he lumbered at me.

I stumbled away, summoning magic to my hands, but he suddenly stopped, hissing and pawing at the ground. "Mine!"

I stared, confused, but then noticed the tail's hand clung to the edge of the brook, keeping him from going any further. *Can he not leave the water?* To test my theory, I moved away a couple more steps and called, "Yes, I'm yours, so come and get me!"

He scowled and bared his fangs. There was nothing human in those ink-black eyes, only a single-minded purpose: possessing me. This must have been his payment to the river goddess Jade Skirt for saving him. He beat his paws on the ground, shrieking, and pity and shame filled me. I was as responsible for him becoming this monster as she was.

"I'm sorry I did this to you, Black Otter," I said, unleashing my magic on him. The least I could do was end this terrible existence.

The magic blasted him backwards, across the brook, but again the hand held him to the bank. He squealed in frustration and scrambled to his feet again, none the worse for my attack. I blasted him again, and this time, he retreated down the brook, hissing and howling at me over his shoulder as he went. I chased him, shooting magic, growing more and more furious that it did nothing but drive him on. But eventually he outran me and disappeared, only his calls of "Mine! Mine! Mine!" giving evidence of his existence, but those too soon faded into the night.

Chapter Thirty

I intended to go back to camp, but by the time I reached the Pyramid of the Moon, I found it impossible to continue walking, so I sat on the steps, my chest aching under the crush of everything. Where did I go from here? So much fear, confusion, guilt and resistance raced through my mind, tearing me in so many different directions at once, but one thing was clear: I had a lot to answer for.

Gods don't answer to anyone for anything. They aren't held to weak human morality.

It was my own morality I didn't live up to, I retorted.

"Quetzalpetlatl?" Citlallotoc jogged across the precinct to me, worry painting his face. "What are you doing out here alone? Everyone's been looking for you."

I laid my head in my hands, the tears arriving in a flood.

"Your guards woke me when they couldn't find you in the water yard," he went on. "Then we heard screaming, and no one can find Black Otter—"

"Black Otter's dead."

"Dear gods, what happened?"

The pain rose fresh and sharp in my chest. "He killed my son...he set Smoking Mirror's nahual on him...he couldn't let me go.... And I did such terrible things...."

Citlallotoc sat and wrapped his arm around me. "It's all right," he whispered. "We'll work it out. You're safe, and that's what's important."

But rather than calming me, his closeness and warmth ignited the desire festering inside me. I gripped him tighter, trying to force it back, but my resolve crumbled when all the other things I'd learned and done swirled through my mind. I needed a reprieve from the suffocating panic and chaos; I needed to meditate, or sleep it off until I could think more clearly.

But instead I kissed him.

He didn't react at first, stunned perhaps, but soon he returned the gesture with a forcefulness that spoke of hidden longing. The desire took command with silent ease, and I let it; pleasure was as good a liniment as anything—

But what about my sacrifice? I reminded myself, yet still reluctant to resist.

You pledged it for the rest of your mortal life; now, you're immortal, and you're free to do as you want.

I had said *for the remainder of my mortal days.* I was indeed free of that sacrifice. Which meant I was finally free to have the relationship I'd always wanted with Little Reed....

So what was I doing here with Citlallotoc?

You think too much, the desire growled. *You always did.*

To my surprise, Citlallotoc pulled away, panting and bewildered. "We can't do this," he muttered, and started to stand.

But I grabbed his xicolli and held him down. "Why not?" the desire purred, pressing my body closer to his.

He gazed at me with a blankness I knew too well, but he shook it off and looked away, fidgeting. After contemplating the precinct in silence, he muttered, "I still can't believe Topiltzin divorced you. If I were married to you, nothing would convince me to let you go."

I laughed. "You want to marry me?"

He shrugged in lieu of an answer.

My arm hooked itself with his and I leaned in and whispered, "How long have you felt this way?"

"Far longer than an honorable man should."

"What has honor to do with anything?"

"You were my best friend's wife."

"But not anymore, so why the dilemma?" I slid my hand across his thigh, and his leg muscle twitched under my splayed fingers.

He cleared his throat before speaking again. "Because I promised Topiltzin I wouldn't pursue you."

"Topiltzin doesn't own me; even when we were married, I wasn't his property, and now I'm free to share my bed with whomever I wish." He tensed when I straddled him, but he couldn't hide his arousal once I settled onto his lap. "And I want to share it with you," I whispered and moved in to kiss him again.

But he blocked me with a firm hand against my sternum. "I think he still loves you, Quetzalpetlatl."

The desire growled jaguar-like in my head but kept my voice sweet when it asked, "Why would you think that?"

He hesitated a moment, debating something before blurting, "I'm the father of Anacoana's child."

I drew back, startled, but also amused. "You cuckolded the King?"

"I didn't do anything he didn't ask me to," he insisted. "He refused to bed her, and he needed an heir, so he begged a favor of me. And being his best friend...I did it."

So this was the mysterious favor that could cost both of them their reputations and honor. A smug satisfaction nestled in my belly; Little Reed did still love me, and so much so he couldn't bear to bed another woman. "What has this to do with us, right now?" the desire asked, impatient. "Did you ask him for permission to court me after the divorce?" When he looked away, embarrassed, I stifled a laugh. "And he denied you? You speak of precious friendship, but what kind of friend denies you happiness for his own selfishness?"

Citlallotoc started to speak, but stopped.

"That's what I thought." I leaned in again, our touching noses sending a shiver through him. "You want me, and I want you, so let's stop playing games and see where this goes." I leaned in all the way and kissed him again.

Again he silently wrestled with his honor, but only for a breath. He kissed me back, gently at first then with growing ferocity, as if an animal had awoken inside him. The desire relished it, kissing him back harder, encouraging him. His initial fumbling with my robe ties turned to pawing and yanking—a task made all the more difficult by his lack of a second hand, and I had to pull away to help him. He watched me with the look of a drunk as I abandoned my clothes and relieved him of his loincloth, and when I eased myself back down on his lap, enveloping him, he fell back against the stone steps as if it were too much to take. "Not so fast!"

he moaned, making me laugh, for within a few moves it changed to desperate pleas of "Faster! Faster!"

Even after seven years of celibacy, my body hadn't forgotten anything; every move was perfectly timed and measured, as if I instinctively knew exactly what Citlallotoc liked, and how much. As I'd known with Black Otter, too. Only with Quetzalcoatl had it been a mystery in need of solving. *But then he had been my very first lover....*

And with that one thought, the stone walls imprisoning all my lost memories crumbled down, as did the world around me.

I was back in the garden in Omeyocan. The Earth Monster, with her caiman-head and bat wings—Tzitzimitl, my grandmother, whom I took after in every way but my heart—slept in her cave. I lazed among the flowers, staring up into the blue sky overhead, dreaming of how the world looked beyond the monumental stone walls surrounding me. Were there others like us? How did the clouds move overhead while everything inside the garden stood still, never changing, never growing....

I was watching bees visiting the flowers next to the wall when I first heard the mysterious whisper. *Climb the wall, little goddess. Let me show you all the beauty of the world! You deserve to know more than centuries trapped behind these walls. You deserve companionship and freedom, the same as the rest of us.*

The words—they were a man's—excited a strange buzzing in my chest and belly, and with each passing day, my heart grew braver and stronger. I had no idea how he looked—or even what his name was—but already I ached for him so badly that, by the third day, I couldn't contain it anymore. I had to climb that wall; I had to see him.

And so I climbed and climbed and climbed. The magic imbued in the walls tried to frustrate me and turn me back, as it had so many times before, but this time I refused. I would see what lay beyond these walls, and who lived there. Or else I would spend eternity trying.

When I finally reached the top, he was waiting for me, all shimmering feathers and sharp fangs and fathomless eyes. I'd never seen a snake or a bird, and so had no vocabulary to describe him except a single word my heart provided, with no definition and no reference: Love. And when we flew together to earth, he showed me everything and gave it all names; the mountains, the oceans, the valleys where the deer roamed. He even gave me a name of my own, one so soft and yet so filled with yearning that when he spoke it, my heart cried for joy. He showed me all the gifts the gods had granted the world, every one of them precious and beautiful.

Every god gives at least one gift to the world, he told me. *Isn't it time you shared yours?*

But how do I do that? I asked.

He whispered, *Close your eyes and I'll show you.*

After that everything was softness: his feathers on my scaly skin as he twined around me; the stretching and melting into each other as he taught me the secrets of creation one slow, sensual movement at a time; the years spent knowing only the throb of his magic, the sound of his thoughts swimming with mine, when the physical acts fed the emotional ache in an endless cycle, and sex became more than mere pleasure—it became lovemaking, it became new life, it became the future. We became the tree that bloomed Love from its branches and shed its gift upon the world.

The memory brought on the familiar rush of pleasure, filling me from toes to fingertips. My limbs throbbed with magic, and my head buzzed. I followed my old habit of staring up at the sky and watching the Divine Dream leak into my consciousness like water breaking free of a dam. I was flying again, the wind whipping through my hair—

Suddenly I stood on the platform outside the Temple of Quetzalcoatl in Tollan. The face on the sun blazing overhead blinked down at me, its tongue jutting out in a perpetual smirk, but as always, it said nothing. Around me the city was empty.

But inside the temple, a man knelt in the middle of the floor, meditating. As I pressed closer, my stomach knotted: he had the god's green quetzal feathers in his hair. It had been years since I'd last seen Quetzalcoatl.

With Smoking Mirror's accusations plaguing me, my first impulse was to run away, but I stopped. *There has to be a reason he didn't tell me the truth.*

A cry rose outside the temple, as if a monstrous beast had woken to a terrible wound. The sky blackened as something blotted out the sun. *Who has stolen my granddaughter?* a chillingly familiar voice rang. I went to the edge of the platform and looked up to see Tzitzimitl plunging from Omeyocan like an arrow, focused on the tree in Tamoanchan where Quetzalcoatl and I had bound our bodies in love....

I'd felt no fear when I'd heard her coming, for I was with Quetzalcoatl

335

and our love would protect us. Except that as her shadow descended over us, I felt the bonds between us loosen and snap. Suddenly I was alone and vulnerable.

She tore me apart like starving wild dogs; even now I felt her claws ripping into me, her teeth tearing my flesh into chunks, my life leaking away like an offering from a blood bowl.

Eventually Quetzalcoatl did come back, and he showed the humans how to bury my scattered parts so something new and useful would grow. *Your real gift to humanity is not Love, but your death,* he'd whispered over my grave. *For when the people drink your tears, they will know how to serve their gods.* And he'd laughed. And laughed. And laughed.

I turned to see Quetzalcoatl still kneeling, oblivious to everything. I'd misread everything about him, from the moment I first saw him atop the wall in Omeyocan to the last time we'd made love in the Divine Dream. Everything he did was a manipulation, a lie.

He stood up and turned to leave, but started when he saw me. *Papalotl!* His face lit with joy and he reached to embrace me.

I stepped away, shaking with fury and magic. He stopped mid-step. A piece of my heart crumbled at the confusion and fear in his eyes. *What if I'm misremembering?* Unlikely given my divine origins, but still…. Should I give him a chance to explain himself?

Give him the perfect opportunity to tell you the truth and see what he does.

"My Lord," I replied with a careful bow. I didn't return his smile.

After an awkward pause, he said, *I'm glad to see you again. It's been a while now.*

"I had some…issues I needed to work out."

Then you have done so? he asked, hopeful.

I shook my head. "I'm more hopelessly confused than ever. But I thought perhaps coming here and speaking with you…maybe you will give me some answers."

He folded his arms behind him. *I will give you whatever answers I can.*

I paced the floor between the stone columns; I didn't have to fake wringing my hands, for the fear coursed hard through me. "My entire life is falling apart. Nothing makes sense anymore, and I think there's something…different about me."

Tell me.

I laid it out piece by piece for him: my magic, my perfect memory, and the strange, unsettling affect I had on people. He listened but said nothing, making me angrier by the breath. "And there's you!"

Me?

I nodded. "Here I am, a supposedly normal human being and yet I spent years in a relationship—a sexual relationship—with you. Why would you even be interested in me? It's not as if I'm a goddess or something!" I couldn't possibly give him a better reason to tell me the truth right there.

Yet Quetzalcoatl sat there, a contemplative look on his face, as if weighing something.

Stamping my foot, I yelled, "For Heaven's sake! Tell me what I need to know! Why am I like this? Why do you even care?"

He looked at me, sadness in his eyes. *I wish I could help you—you have no idea how badly I want to—but some things are not mine to tell. Some things one...must discover for oneself. And I care because I love you, Papalotl.*

I stared at him as if he'd shot me with a poison-tipped arrow. "You love me, but the truth isn't something you can help me with? I have to find it out on my own? Is that all you have to say for yourself? Or maybe you want to lecture me about how my real gift to the world isn't love, but my death?"

He dropped his arms to his sides, alarm on his face. *You know?*

"Who I really am? Yes, but no thanks to you. I had to find out from Smoking Mirror, of all people!"

He furrowed his brow. *Smoking Mirror told you?*

"Do you know how awful it is to know that the god who killed my parents is more forthcoming with the truth than the one who supposedly loves me?"

Papalotl—

"No! You don't get to call me that anymore! You've lost the right!" I strode out of the temple, my anger shaking the ground under me with each step.

Quetzalcoatl suddenly materialized in front of me in a swirl of white smoke, blocking my way down the stairs. *It's not what you think—*

"I was foolish enough to believe your lies once; the second time I was ignorant of how you really are, but I remember now, and I won't be fooled again."

But please, I must explain—

"I don't need more of your lies; in fact, if I never saw you ever again, that would be the first good thing to happen to me in this life!"

His jaw quivered. *I never meant to hurt you, Mayahuel. I love you.*

"And I loathe you."

I didn't want to be there anymore, didn't want to look on his face lest his betrayal transfer to Little Reed. I closed my eyes and willed myself to leave the Divine Dream; but when I felt the hold loosening, I took one last furious stab at him. "Your son would be a far better god than you could ever be."

When I opened my eyes, I was back on the stairs of the pyramid, Citlallotoc still between my legs, fast asleep. I peered up at the sky once more but then climbed aside and sat with my knees jammed to my chest, tears of disappointment and heartache muddying my vision. I doubted Citlallotoc could hear me cry, for he didn't stir when I moved off him. I'd done this hoping to feel better but instead I'd only made myself feel worse.

I couldn't sit naked out here all night, so I dried my eyes and put my clothes back on. Picking up Citlallotoc's loincloth, I went to wake him.

It had always been challenging waking Black Otter after sex, so Citlallotoc's unresponsiveness didn't surprise me. I shook his shoulder, starting gently and working up to full intensity, until his head flopped to and fro. When he didn't rouse, I gave his cheek a small smack, gritting my teeth as I did it, but still, no response.

Leaning closer, I noticed he was barely breathing. I peeled back one of his eyelids to find his eyes unmoving and his pupils dilated. A quick check of his pulse found it as weak as his breathing. "Citlallotoc?" I slapped his cheeks again, rougher this time, but still nothing.

My own heart racing, I wrestled him off the steps and laid him on the ground on his back, trying various techniques Nimilitzli had taught me long ago to revive someone who had passed out or stopped breathing. But all I could think about was how nothing had saved Yamehecatl, and the rising panic soon paralyzed me. I screamed for help as loud as I could.

¤

Within moments, several guards arrived, and when they saw Citlallotoc's condition, one ran back to camp to fetch the surgeon while the others tried to revive him. I stayed out of the way, huddled up like a terrified child. *What did I do to him?* My brain barely registered it when one of the guards announced that Citlallotoc was finally awake; but when they helped him sit up, I burst into tears.

The surgeon arrived a few moments later and checked Citlallotoc over, making him drink some water from a skin and swallow some medicine. He instructed the men to help Citlallotoc back to camp. "And one of you remain with him until I get there." He then came to me. "What happened?"

I fumbled for an answer, my cheeks ablaze, but now wasn't the time to hold back the truth because it embarrassed me. Citlalltoc's life might depend on it. "We were...we had sex, and I thought he'd fallen asleep, but I couldn't wake him."

If the surgeon was scandalized by my confession, he did a fantastic job of hiding it. "Then he was awake when he finished?" he asked, his tone completely professional.

I shook my head, trying to swallow the panic. "I don't know." I'd been swept up in the flood of memories and the Divine Dream; I might as well have not even been there. "Is he going to be all right?"

"He's severely dehydrated, but he should be fine with some rest and plenty of water."

"Thank the gods," I whispered. When I realized what I'd said, I almost started chuckling at the absurdity of praising the likes of Quetzalcoatl and Smoking Mirror—and myself—for this mercy.

The women's camp was alive with activity when I returned, and many of the novices cast me curious looks as I hurried to my tent, desperate to be away from their prying gazes. *I never should have listened to the desire,* I thought, crawling into my bed. *Bad things always happen when I listen to the desire.*

You are so whiny, the desire growled. *How are you going to feed if you continue to cling to those weak human morals?*

I hadn't noticed until now how full and glutted I felt, as if I'd finished a celebratory feast. "I feed through sex?" I whispered, repulsed, but I couldn't deny it. My hunger and desire always went hand-in-hand, and Black Otter had become weaker and sicker the more we were intimate. I had been devouring him one night at a time.

And I'd fed on Citlallotoc and nearly killed him in the process. If I bedded Little Reed...?

A guard came to my tent flap. "Lord Citlallotoc asked for you."

The stares were worse in the men's camp. Had rumor already spread about what Citlallotoc and I had been doing out on the sacred precinct? I held my head high, determined not to blush or crumble under their gazes, but relief washed over me when I finally ducked into Citlallotoc's tent.

As a high-ranking nobleman, Citlallotoc could have used one of the large, multi-room tents that Little Reed and I used when traveling, but he always opted for a small, one-person tent, the same one he'd used back in his army days; he wasn't the kind of man to indulge in luxury for luxury's sake. The surgeon had to leave to make room for me, but not without first imploring Citlallotoc to keep resting; the man gave me a pointed look on his way out. I couldn't stop the burning blush.

Citlallotoc looked tired but he still smiled, taking my hand with his. "I'm sorry about what happened out there, on the precinct. Did I scare you?"

"You...definitely worried me," I admitted, not meeting his gaze.

His cheeks flared. "That's never happened to me before; at least not while doing...that. It must mean it was really good."

Or really, really bad for you, I thought, but bit my tongue.

He rolled on his side so he could lie closer to me. The look of adoration and happiness on his face made my chest hurt. "When we get back to Tollan, if we both go to Topiltzin and tell him how we feel about each other, he can't go on telling us no, right? He'll see we're in love, and he'll have to bend."

All this talk of love turned my mouth dry. "Citlallotoc, about tonight...it was a mistake, and we can't let it happen again."

His grip tightened on my hand, tense and possessive. "What do you mean?"

"Let go of my hand, Citlallotoc," I said, trying to keep my voice even and non-threatening. I'd seen that same look in Black Otter's eyes more than once.

And for a moment I thought I would have to call my guards to make him, but he finally let me go, looking as if I'd stuck him in the back with my sacrificial blade. "You don't love me?"

"I do; you're one of my dearest friends, but it's not like that—"

"You mean not like you feel for Topiltzin," he interjected.

I bit my lip.

Growing agitated, he said, "But you kissed me. If you didn't feel that way about me, why did you do that? Why did you let it go as far as it did?"

I shook my head. "I'm sorry. I was upset—"

"Oh dear gods!" He sat up, bewildered. "How am I ever going to face Topiltzin again when I took advantage of his sister?"

"You didn't take advantage of me—"

"If you hadn't been upset, would we still have done what we did?"

After a guilty pause, I admitted, "Probably not."

"What will Topiltzin say when he hears of this?"

"He doesn't have to know. I can tell the surgeon—"

"Of course he has to know! I can't lie to my best friend!"

I pushed him back down on his bed, fearing his rising agitation would worsen his illness. He set his hand over mine again, that possessiveness back. "I'd still make a good husband, Quetzalpetlatl. I will devote my life to you, to making you happy; I will give you my heart, with no conditions attached—"

"Citlallotoc—"

"We can take care of each other when we're old. I owe you that much at least."

"You don't owe me anything," I protested.

But he shook his head, tears in his eyes. "I cost you your son—"

"No, you didn't."

"I didn't protect him well enough." He let go of my hand and looked away as the tears broke free. "So why should you expect me to be able to protect you, to care for you either? So of course Topiltzin wouldn't let me marry you. He would want someone worthy and strong marrying you."

"Please stop this," I choked, my own tears running sudden and thick. "You are strong, and worthy, and any woman would be lucky to have you."

"But you don't want me."

I don't want to hurt you the way I hurt Black Otter, I almost said, but the cotton in my throat blocked it. The desperation in his voice was impossible to miss. Within a few months I would strip him of everything he was, everything he cared about in this world, except me; he wouldn't care about honor or duty, or Little Reed.

But Citlallotoc wasn't the only one displaying alarming behavior. Little Reed and I had never consummated and yet he'd refused to bed Anacoana, and used his friendship with Citlallotoc to keep him from pursuing me. He was as singularly focused on me as anyone, and if Citlallotoc became real competition, might he resort to murder as Black Otter had? I didn't want to think Little Reed capable of such things, but I never would have thought Black Otter was either.

And what if I rejected Citlallotoc for Little Reed? What would Citlallotoc do?

You can't ever go back to Tollan, I realized. *If you do, eventually, you'll destroy them both.*

Citlallotoc pulled my hand to his lips and gave it a gentle kiss. "But maybe, with time, you could learn to love me?"

I pulled my hand slowly away from him, every fiber of my being yelling at me to run. "I think you should rest, and we can talk about this later. We've been through a lot tonight."

"We should sleep on it," he agreed, a hopeful smile on his face.

"Exactly."

"If you want, you can sleep here tonight." He pulled open his blanket, showing that he was naked—and ready—under his waist-length xicolli.

I averted my gaze, the desire growling. I hated that voice so much. "You heard the surgeon," I scolded him with a smile as I went to the tent flap, itching to leave. "I'll talk to you tomorrow."

"I'm looking forward to it."

And finally I escaped out into the night air, my heart hammering painfully against my ribs.

Mazatzin came over from his tent, looking weary but concerned. "Is he going to be all right?"

"He'll be fine," I assured him. *Especially once I'm gone from his life. And from Little Reed's.* I glared when my personal guards pressed close to me, determined not to let me out of their sight again. I wouldn't get far with them following me everywhere.

To Mazatzin, I said, "Would you mind escorting me to the Temple of the Feathered Serpent? I feel the need to make prayers for Citlallotoc's recovery."

Mazatzin nodded, and after fetching his robe, we went to the sacred precinct, the guards following at a discreet distance. We walked in silence most of the way before Mazatzin asked, "Something is weighing on you, and I wish you'd talk to me about it."

Laughing, I said, "I'm surprised you don't already know."

"About you and Citlallotoc? That's not what I'm talking about. Something else is bothering you; you've been secretive since we left Tollan, and you sneaked away in the middle of the night and ended up at the Temple of the Moon with Citlallotoc. And now you're asking me to go and pray with you—"

"It's not what you think," I assured him, holding my hands up.

"And I'm not thinking you're going to seduce me, if that's what you're worried about," he replied. "I don't see you that way, and I trust you to respect that."

Maybe you shouldn't, I thought. If he'd been the one to find me instead of Citlallotoc, might things have still gone as they had? And if he'd resisted more vehemently than Citlallotoc had, what might the desire have done? I shivered to even consider that I might have something in common with Ahexotl. "I wish I could tell you, Mazatzin."

"Why can't you?"

"Because it would change everything between us, and I'm dealing with too much of that already with too many other people. I need the stability of our friendship, just as it is."

He nodded. "I'm honored to be a rock for you to cling to in your time of need."

We reached the Pyramid of the Feathered Serpent with its many statues of Quetzalcoatl and Tlaloc the rain god. As Mazatzin started up the stairs, he asked, "Have you given any thought to which story you want to tell at the vision ceremony tonight?" He stopped when I didn't follow him.

"I won't be here for the vision ceremony."

"Are you not feeling well?"

I shook my head. "I'm not going back to Tollan either."

He came back down the stairs, his expression confused. "What do you mean?

"Everything I touch...I destroy it."

"How can you say such a thing?"

"Because it's true. I can't be around other people."

He stammered a moment before asking, "But where would you go?"

A good question. And I knew the answer: if I couldn't be around humans without hurting them, I needed to be around other gods instead. I knew so little about how to be a goddess, how to do any of the things gods did—for Tzitzimitl and Quetzalcoatl had kept me ignorant of these things—and I needed guidance. But could I really trust Mextli? I stared at the grinning feathered serpent heads decorating the temple's walls in rows, interspersed with heads of the goggle-wearing Tlaloc. *I certainly can't trust you.*

When I looked at the embroidered feathered serpents on the front of my robe, my anger boiled over. I stripped the robe off and threw it at the temple. "You can keep your damn priesthood and pick someone else to be your foolish high priestess, because I'm done!" I shouted.

Mazatzin stared at me, agape. "Why would you...what has happened, Quetzalpetlatl?"

Tears leaked down my cheeks. "I've finally seen the truth: Quetzalcoatl is a liar who paints beautiful pictures of the future but doesn't warn you of the price it demands until it's too late. He doesn't tell you that your parents will die, and that you won't know any happiness for it; he'll make you believe he loves you when in fact he's waiting for the next opportunity to unleash the Earth Monster on you!"

I tore the sacrificial blade from my belt and started to throw it too, but when I saw the stag horn handle in the shape of the Feathered Serpent, I paused, my gut clenching. This wasn't my mother's sacrificial blade, for I'd lost that for good long ago, but I'd paid someone to make one exactly like it in shape and design, and I'd spent days adding the wear marks and dents myself, all from my last memory of holding it. While this wasn't my mother's blade, it was the closest thing I had to having anything of hers, of the woman who had loved and cared for me with no expectation or judgment, and I couldn't bring myself to throw it away.

I returned the blade to my belt and held the handle tight, taking deep, calming breaths before continuing, "All I can say is that everything has changed, and I can't be Quetzalcoatl's high priestess anymore; nor can I go back to Tollan where I'm surrounded by reminders of the god."

"But what about Topiltzin?" Mazatzin asked. "How will he go on without you?"

"He has a new wife and child, and he deserves the happiness that brings. If I'm there, he'll never find that. Promise me that if he talks of coming to find me, you will talk him out of it. Promise!"

He hesitated, then nodded. "I won't pretend to understand all this, but I will do as you ask."

"And you must tell Malinalli goodbye for me. Please tell her I'm sorry I didn't come to say it myself, but that I know she will do well as the new high priestess. But warn her to beware of gods making outrageous promises."

"I will tell her." He frowned deeply. "Will I ever see you again?"

I took his hand between mine and tried to smile, but instead it came out as a frown. "As much as I'd like that, my friend, it would be better if you didn't." My jaw quivering, I turned and walked off past the pyramid, into the open field beyond it, into the rising sun.

My guards shouted for me to wait for them, but when I looked back, Mazatzin held them back. He still stood next to the temple, a slump to his shoulders, but he was letting me go, and I silently thanked him for that.

Once away, I didn't look back again. The past held only pain and disappointment, and I couldn't afford to live there anymore. I knew my real name now, but I still needed to find myself, and find my future. And if I'd been able to come back from the dead—twice now—maybe I could bring my son back too. The thought gave me the first joy I'd felt in months.

And hopefully Mextli could help me on that journey.

If I could find him; if I could trust him.

◻   ◻   ◻

AUTHOR'S NOTE

The goddess Mayahuel's origin story appeared in *Histoyre du Mechique*, a French translation of a much older, incomplete Spanish missionary text detailing the exploits of the god Quetzalcoatl, both on earth and in the heavens. The story is detailed as such:

With the rebirth of humanity in the wake of the end of the Fourth Sun, the gods wish to give their creations something to provide them with pleasure and happiness. It is Quetzalcoatl, in the guise of Ehecatl, who thinks of the virgin goddess Mayahuel, who is kept prisoner by her fierce grandmother, the goddess Tzitzimitl. He abducts her while her grandmother sleeps, and he takes her to earth, carrying her upon his shoulders, and once there, they come together to form a tree.

But when Tzitzimitl wakes to find her granddaughter gone, she enlists the help of the tzitzimime—star demons—to hunt her down. They search all over the earth for her, but they are only able to find her when the tree's two branches inexplicably split away from each other, making Mayahuel recognizable. The star demons descend on her and devour her, leaving only her bones behind.

Meanwhile, Ehecatl has survived the attack unscathed and he gathers Mayahuel's bones and buries them. From that sacred ground, the metl tree—the maguey or the agave—grows, and from its milky-white sap, humans learn to ferment the sacred wine called octli—or now commonly known as pulque.

As many Central American gods are want to do, Mayahuel doesn't stay dead forever. She becomes the wife of the medicine god Patecatl and gives birth to the Centzontotochtin—the Four Hundred Rabbits; the god Tepoztecatl—otherwise known as Ehecacone (Son of the Wind)—being among them. She becomes a symbol of fecundity and fertility, and she's often portrayed as suckling a baby at one of her four-hundred breasts.

While the mythology doesn't support a conflation of the goddess with the mysterious mythical figure of Quetzalpetlatl, there are enough interesting details to form a tangible "what if" story. After all, both Mayahuel and Quetzalpetlatl are little more than pawns in the machinations of the gods—Quetzalpetlatl is used by Tezcatlipoca to religiously—and sexually—discredit Topiltzin, and Ehecatl exploits Mayahuel's innocence to lure her to her death, all to give humanity the gift of octli. Both women's stories are incomplete and dissatisfying on their own, but together, they make for something interesting, not just for themselves, but for those around them as well.

LIST OF CHARACTERS

Ahexotl – (deceased) former high priest of Quetzalcoatl in Xochicalco

Amoxtli – son of Ihuitimal, brother to Black Otter, cousin to Quetzalpetlatl and Topiltzin

Anacoana – daughter of King Flame Tongue of Xico, former concubine of Black Otter, Topiltzin's second wife

Black Otter – son of Ihuitimal, former husband of Quetzalpetlatl, high priest of Smoking Mirror, father of Cuicatl and Night Wind

Bitter Rabbit – Ten Spine's wife, mother of Mitotia

Blood Wolf – member of Culhuacan's war council

Chalchiuhtlicue (Jade Skirt) – goddess of rivers, streams, and seas

Chimalma – (deceased) wife of Mixcoatl, mother of Quetzalpetlatl and Topiltzin

Citlallotoc – Topiltzin's best friend and Justice of the Peace

Corn Flower – daughter of King Toztli of Chimalhuacan, former concubine of Black Otter

Cuicatl – daughter of Black Otter and Jade Flower

Cuitlapanton – (deceased) king of Xochicalco

Ehecacone (Yamehecatl) – son of Quetzalcoatl and Quetzalpetlatl, heir to Tollan's throne

Flame Tongue – king of Xico, father of Anacoana

Growling Monkey – king of Xochimilco

Huemac – younger brother to Citlallotoc, king of Acolman

Ihuitimal – (deceased) brother of Mixcoatl, former king of Culhuacan, father of Black Otter and Amoxtli

Ixchell – priestess of Quetzalcoatl

Ixtlilxochitl – governor of Culhuacan

Jade Flower – Quetzalpetlatl's half-sister, concubine of Black Otter, mother of Cuicatl and Night Wind

Malinalli – fire priestess of Quetzalcoatl, Quetzalpetlatl's best friend

Mayahuel – goddess of the maguey plant

Matlacxochitl – member of Culhuacan's war council, younger brother of Blood Wolf

Mazatzin – fire priest of Quetzalcoatl, brother of Red Flint

Meconetzin – king of Chalco

Mextli (Huitzilopochtli) – god of war, leader of the Mexica

Mitotia – daughter of Ten Spines and Bitter Rabbit, priestess of
  Quetzalcoatl

Mixcoatl – (Deceased) former king of Culhuacan, father of
  Quetzalpetlatl

Mixcoatl (the Cloud Serpent) – god of the hunt

Mothotli – (deceased) former fire priestess of Quetzalcoatl in
  Xochicalco

Nahuacatl – King Toztli's son, heir of Chimalhuacan

Night Wind – son of Black Otter and Jade Flower

Nimilitzli – (deceased) foster mother to Quetzalpetlatl and Topiltzin,
  former high priestess of Quetzalcoatl in Xochicalco

Nochuatl – (deceased) brother of Ihuitimal and Mixcoatl

Ozomatli – high priest of the Smoking Mirror

Papantzin – former concubine of Black Otter

Quetzalcoatl (the Feathered Serpent) – god of civilization, father of
  mankind. Also known as Ehecatl, god of the wind.

Quetzalpetlatl (Papalotl) – sister/wife of Topiltzin, mother of
  Ehecacone, high priestess of Quetzalcoatl, Empress of the Tolteca

Red Flint – (deceased) Cuitlapanton's legitimate son, heir to
  Xochicalco

Ueman – shaman of the god Mixcoatl

Ten Spines – chieftain of the Tollan Chichimecs

Tezcatlipoca (the Smoking Mirror) – Chichimec god of war and
  sorcerers, god of the night

Tlaloc – god of rain

Tlanextli – priest of Tlaloc, husband of Ixchell

Topiltzin (Little Reed) – son of Quetzalcoatl, brother/husband of
  Quetzalpetlatl, Emperor of the Tolteca

Toztli – king of Chimalhuacan

Tzitzimitl (the Earth Monster) – grandmother to Mayahuel

Xolotl (the Black Dog) – servant god to Mictlantecuhtli and the
  guide of the dead

Yaretzi – high priestess of the Smoking Mirror

FURTHER READING

Richard Blanton, Stephen A. Kowalewski, Gary Feinman, and Jill Appel, *Ancient Mesoamerica: A Comparison of Change in Three Regions*, Cambridge University Press, 1981.

Burr Cartwright Brundage, *The Phoenix of the Western World: Quetzalcoatl and the Sky Religion*, University of Oklahoma Press, 1981.

David Carrasco, *Quetzalcoatl and the Irony of Empire: Myths and Prophecies in the Aztec Tradition*, University Press of Colorado, 2001.

Sophie Coe, *America's First Cuisines*, University of Texas Press, 1994.

Nigel Davies, *The Toltecs Until the Fall of Tula*, University of Oklahoma Press, 1977.

Richard A. Diehl, *Tula: The Toltec Capital of Ancient Mexico*, Thames and Hudson, 1983.

William Gates, *An Aztec Herbal: The Classic Codex of 1552*, Dover Publications, Inc, 2000.

Rich Holmer, *The Aztec Book of Destiny*, BookSurge, LLC, 2005.

Miguel León-Portilla, *Aztec Thought and Culture*, University of Oklahoma Press, 1963.

Roberta H. Markman and Peter T Markman, *The Flayed God: The Mythology of Mesoamerica*, Harper San Francisco, 1992.

Mary Miller and Karl Taube, *An Illustrated Dictionary of the Gods and Symbols of Ancient Mexico and the Maya*, Thames and Hudson, 1993.

H. B. Nicholson, *Topiltzin Quetzalcoatl: The Once and Future Lord of the Toltecs*, University Press of Colorado, 2001.

Guilhem Olivier, *Mockeries and Metamorphoses of an Aztec God: Tezcatlipoca, "Lord of the Smoking Mirror"*, University Press of Colorado, 2003.

John M. D. Pohl, *Aztec, Mixtec and Zapotec Armies*, Osprey Publishing,

1991.

John Pohl, PhD and Adam Hook, *Aztec Warrior, A.D. 1325-1521*, Osprey Military, 2001.

Fray Bernardino de Sahagún, *The Florentine Codex: The General History of the Things of New Spain*, translated by Arthur J. O. Anderson and Charles E. Dibble, The School of American Research and The University of Utah, 1975.

Jacques Soustelle, *Daily Life of the Aztecs*, Dover Publications, Inc., 2002.

ACKNOWLEDGMENTS

The bulk of my thanks must go to my critique group *Written in Blood*: Genevieve Williams, Keyan Bowes, Janice Hardy, Juliette Wade, Doug Sharp, Douglas Cohen, and Christopher Cevasco. Some of them even read this beast twice, once when I had no idea what I was doing and a second time when I'd finally figured it all out.

A special thank you goes to Samuel Tecpaocelotl Castillo and the many people at the Mexica History Facebook page, where they discuss and challenge the accepted knowledge about the history and mythology. I'm constantly learning and re-evaluating thanks to them.

An extra big thank you to Dario Ciriello, my editor, without whom this whole series probably would have remained hidden on my hard drive, unpublished.

And as always, my friend Aliette de Bodard is an inspiration and challenges me to take my stories to the next level.

Thank you Jeff, for supporting my decision to make the move to self-publishing so the rest of this series could see print.

And finally a heartfelt thank you to all the readers who came back to continue sharing Quetzalpetlatl's journey. You're the ones I do all this for.

ABOUT THE AUTHOR

T. L. Morganfield lives in Colorado with her husband and children. She's an alumna of the Clarion West Workshop and she graduated from Metropolitan State University with dual degrees in English and History. She reads and writes way too much about Aztec history and mythology, but it keeps her muse happy, which makes for a happy writer, so she has no plans of changing her ways.

You can join her mailing list at www.tlmorganfield.com to receive updates on her latest work.